After Light

After Light

Catherine Hunter

Signature
EDITIONS

Cover design by Doowah Design.
Photo of Author by Leif Norman.

Acknowledgements

This book was printed on Ancient Forest Friendly paper.
Printed and bound in Canada by Marquis Book Printing Inc.

We acknowledge the support of the Canada Council for the Arts and the Manitoba Arts Council for our publishing program.

Library and Archives Canada Cataloguing in Publication

Hunter, Catherine, 1957–, author
        After light / Catherine Hunter.

Issued in print and electronic formats.
ISBN 978-1-927426-73-9 (paperback).--ISBN 978-1-927426-74-6 (epub)

        I. Title.

PS8565.U5783A64 2015   C813'.54   C2015-905903-8
                                            C2015-905998-4

Signature Editions
P.O. Box 206, RPO Corydon, Winnipeg, Manitoba, R3M 3S7
www.signature-editions.com

This book is for Kevin and for Rocky
and in memory of Gayle

Contents

BOOK I

Deirdre

1

The River

1.1

CANADA, 1999

BUILT OF DISCARDED DOORS AND MISMATCHED WINDOW FRAMES, the old greenhouse is impractical. It's weathered and leaky and generates more work than profit. But Von Garrison still breeds long-stemmed roses here. This morning she's harvesting roses for a bridal bouquet, carrying her shears and a bucket of water among the raised beds of bristling green leaves and many-coloured petals — buttery and fiery and ivory and golden orange. In the warm, enclosed air, their delicate scents blend into the kind of heady, layered fragrance she's been breathing all her life. She chooses Sweet Vermilions and Hearts of Ice, varieties she developed herself, and inspects each bloom for blemishes before she cuts its stem, cleanly, close to the bush. When a thorn catches the skin of her thumb, she stops to blot a tiny bead of blood with her handkerchief, then uses the handkerchief to wipe sweat from her forehead. Heat soaks into her skin. She's thirsty. She looks up through the freshly washed panes of the ceiling. It's early June, a clear day, the clouds mere wisps in a blue sky. Light everywhere.

In the yard, Von's greenhouse manager, Jeanne Lajoie, is loading flowers into the back of the van, which is nearly full — wedding season has begun. Jeanne takes the red and white roses from the bucket and wraps them for transport. "That's the lot," she says, as she checks the invoices. "Once I deliver these, we're done for the day."

"Why don't you come for dinner later?" Von asks her. "I could bake a pie."

"Thanks. But I'm visiting my parents tonight," says Jeanne.

"Give them my love, then."

"I will!" Jeanne jumps into the driver's seat and waves good-bye. She drives across the field and disappears into the trees, and Von's alone again.

She's lived alone here since her father died. Her mother died years before, and her sister, Rosheen, lives in New York. Von never married. If anyone asks why, she says she's unlucky in love, making it sound like a joke. There are few people around here now, besides Jeanne and Jeanne's parents, who remember Bobby. Driving with one elbow out the window. Trying not to smile but smiling anyway. Blond hair and freckles so light they seemed to lie beneath the surface of his skin. His sure hands. Von never thinks about him.

During the week, Jeanne and the two other workers Von employs are always on the grounds. But today is Saturday. Jeanne only came in to help with the wedding rush. Tomorrow she won't come at all. It'll just be Von and the plants. Every weekend, Von and the plants. Well, somebody has to be here to keep them all alive.

Behind her house, a row of poly-covered domes stretches to the windbreak of American elms at the edge of the property, and unlike the old wooden greenhouse, the domes are efficient, money-making nurseries, where Von and her staff grow seasonal crops like poinsettias and Easter lilies. Right now the domes are full of bedding plants — herbs and flowers for suburban gardens — and the sidelot is full of decorative shrubs. Von plans to spend the afternoon potting the Parkland bushes. They're big enough now to be purchased — or adopted, as Jeanne would say — by local gardeners. After that she'll start the watering.

First she walks back through the greenhouse, which is attached to the house, and enters the kitchen for a glass of iced tea. But before she can open the fridge, the phone begins to ring.

It's a stranger, calling from New York to tell her that Rosheen has died.

Rosheen was four and a half years younger than Von. When they were little girls, they were close. But when they grew up, their lives diverged in ways they never could have imagined. Rosheen moved to New York to live with their grandmother, Deirdre, while Von stayed home. In the past nineteen years, Von and Rosheen have visited each other only three times. When their grandmother died seven years ago, Von went to New York, and when their father died four years later, Rosheen came home for a while. Then six months ago, when Rosheen asked Von to come for Christmas, Von spent three days with her in New York. It wasn't easy. Rosheen, as always, was asking too much. Wanting Von to come to Ireland to help her with some family research for an art project.

Vonnie, I need you for this project. Von can hear those words right now, as clearly as if Rosheen were standing here in front of her.

She realizes suddenly that she's climbing the stairs of her house, but she can't remember why. Was she coming upstairs to get something? Since she hung up the phone, she's been wandering from room to room, unable to sit still. The stranger who called, a doctor from a Brooklyn hospital, said Rosheen's heart had stopped in the night. She died in her sleep. No suffering. Von keeps climbing past the second floor and the third floor, up to the attic, where she kneels and leans her forehead against the window. Her mouth is dry. She can't catch her breath. In the distance, the rusty St Boniface water tower, long defunct, rises high on the horizon. She looks down at the greenhouse and the gravel road that crosses the green field and zigzags its way through the orchard and the thin strip of forest to the highway. Grief, she remembers, feels a lot like fear.

Von slept late the day after Christmas, her last morning at Rosheen's Brooklyn apartment. The last day she ever saw her sister. When Von woke, Rosheen was sitting cross-legged on the bed, hugging a green notebook. Rosheen was thirty-eight and still slender, almost childlike. But not pretty. She was recovering from another round of plastic surgery. The skin over her right cheekbone looked raw and painfully tight. Her hair was a mess of orange tangles. She handed Von a cup of coffee and began to spread documents across the bed. Maps. Letters. A scrapbook of clippings.

"We can go to Holland first," she said. "Tour the battle sites."

"I'm not going," Von said. She'd been saying this for two days. She sat up and sipped her coffee. She hated the idea of digging into the family history, and she wasn't ready to pretend she and Rosheen were a normal family, planning a trip together. She thought she had forgiven her sister for the mistakes she'd made in her youth. But when Rosheen acted as if nothing had ever happened, Von felt the turmoil of her old anger still boiling in her stomach.

"Don't you want to see where Dad was, during the war?"

"No," said Von. She got out of bed.

"But you'll come to Ireland, won't you? To help with Deirdre's story? Our grandmother is practically a legend in the west of Ireland, according to my sources. I want this to be—" She swiped her hand through the air above her head, as if reading a marquee. "*Two Granddaughters Tracing the Truth about the Past.* We'll film it!"

"I don't think so, Rosh. I've got a business to look after." When Rosheen didn't respond, Von added, "The family business? The one that pays your bills? Maybe you've forgotten—"

"But that's the whole point. This is a *family* project."

Von pressed the heels of her palms to her forehead, closed her eyes.

Later, after Rosheen had showered and dressed and brushed her wild hair into glossy curls, she stood in the hallway to say good-bye, one denim hip leaning on the doorframe. She was too thin. "Vonnie," she said, "I need you for this project. Say you'll do it? Promise?"

Von looked at the red scar that crossed the right side of Rosheen's face from temple to cheekbone and ran down like a slash through her mouth, as if to delete anything she might say, to silence her. "All right," she said. "All right. All right. I promise."

There is no way, now, to take that promise back.

———

Rosheen's closest friend was Alex Hart, who runs the Northside Gallery in her Williamsburg neighbourhood in Brooklyn. Von knows

Alex only slightly, but she trusts him. He was always good to Rosheen. Now, over the phone, his voice breaks as he tells Von some recent history that she didn't know. A few weeks ago, in Amsterdam, Rosheen suffered a flare-up of the hepatitis that had plagued her on and off for years. Then she developed a bronchial infection, and a serious case of pneumonia. The Dutch doctor suggested she go home to recover, before continuing her travels. So Rosheen flew back. Alex met her at JFK and took her home. But the next day, when he went to pick her up for a doctor's appointment, she didn't answer the door.

"She never told me she was sick," says Von.

"She was afraid you'd use it as an argument against the trip to Ireland," he says.

Rosheen's will is still with her lawyer. But she left a letter, which Alex reads over the phone. It's dated the day before she died, so she must have sensed she was dying, though she didn't call anyone for help. In her letter, Rosheen requests cremation, her ashes to be scattered over Ireland. Her way of making sure Von keeps her promise. The letter, Alex says, was clipped to the green notebook. Rosheen asks that Von complete her research project, film the interviews, piece together the clues to Deirdre's past, discover the true story.

"Then there's all the work Rosheen has left behind in Amsterdam," says Alex.

"One thing at a time," says Von.

"Of course." Alex's voice wavers. He's trying not to cry. "But she always wanted you — she always wanted this project to be a collaboration. That was important to her."

"I know." Von's voice is steady. She's learned how to lock the pain deep inside the body. It's a difficult art to master, but she's had more practice at it than Alex has.

———

Jeanne, who is not only Von's greenhouse manager but her closest friend, her only close friend, has offered to house-sit and run the business while Von's away. It will be a long journey. First, Von will go to Brooklyn and arrange the cremation. From there, she'll fly to Ireland to finish Rosheen's research. Jeanne says this will be good for her. Then Von will return to Brooklyn to clear out the apartment, which has been in her family since 1920, and put it up for sale.

The day she leaves, Von washes her hair and scrubs her fingernails, ridding herself of the greenhouse dirt. She packs a brand new journal, with a red cardboard cover, for taking notes on Deirdre's story. It's been over twenty years since she bought herself a journal. She wonders if she'll remember how to write. She packs sandals and two summer dresses, and chooses a white cotton blouse and comfortable jeans to wear on the flight. These are the only good clothes she owns. Finding an old lipstick in the bathroom, she applies it sparingly, then brushes her hair. She stands before the mirror, inspecting her public self, a self she seldom sees. She expects to see a woman worn at the edges, forty-four and plain. But her skin is flawless, her grey eyes clear. The beauty is still with her. She wipes off the lipstick. Pulls her hair into a ponytail and ties it tight.

As she carries her suitcase down to the porch, she hesitates, thinking of the journey ahead. But she must do this for her sister. Jeanne says it will bring her closure. She walks down the hall and into the greenhouse to say good-bye to Jeanne.

"All ready to go?" Jeanne is misting a flat of seedlings. Her eyes are red from crying. Jeanne's parents worked for the Garrisons, and she's known the family since she was a little girl. She used to idolize Rosheen.

"Make sure to pot the Parkland bushes," says Von.

"Von, I'll manage. Don't worry. You have more important things to think about."

"I don't know if I can do this," Von says.

"You can do it," says Jeanne. "And when you come home, you can tell me the legend of Deirdre Quinn."

1.2

IRELAND, 1916

THEY SAY IT WAS A ROGUE NORTH WIND THAT BLEW DEIRDRE Quinn downriver the day before her wedding. A sudden blast that swept in from the North Atlantic, stripping leaves from the trees and feathers from the wings of birds. A weird twist of fate. Some say Deirdre braved that wind because she was an arrogant, headstrong girl, without a lick of sense. And some say she did it for love.

There was no sign of a storm when Deirdre woke in her Aunt Grace's house that morning in Galway. She tiptoed past her sleeping cousins and climbed the ladder to the roof to look at the sky. Her heels were sore. The day before she'd walked five miles in her bare feet, coming with her parents from their home in the country. They were staying with Grace, her father's sister, to be near the church where Deirdre was to be married. The palms of Deirdre's hands were sore, too, for she'd pushed a barrow of peat the whole long way so her parents could sell it at the farmer's market for her dowry. Everyone knew that her husband-to-be did not need the money, but he had accepted it nevertheless. It was tradition.

Deirdre stood at the northern edge of the roof, surveying the town of Galway. She had come here many times since she'd been old enough to make the long walk with her father or mother, and she knew her way around the streets better than they could have guessed. This morning, with no hint of fog or cloud, she could see the stone roof of Lynch's Castle and the clock tower of St Nicholas's Church. She could see the river and part of the bridge and closer still she could see the fish market, empty at this early hour, and the Spanish Arch where she would hurry later in the day.

She could hear her parents quarrelling down below.

"There's no need for new clothes," her father was saying.

That was no surprise. Deirdre never dreamed he'd buy her any new clothes. He had many times sold her coat and her boots, and she'd often stayed home from school for want of a dress.

"Shoes and stockings at least," insisted her mother.

"Let her husband buy her shoes," said her father. "It's his lookout now."

To the west, she could see the cold blue water of Galway Bay, like glass at full tide now, barely shimmering in the morning light. The hookers anchored in the harbour and even the smaller boats moored to the docks at the river's mouth were still. Across the harbour, she could see the banks of the Claddagh, where the peasant fishermen lived, a place she had been taught to avoid. She squinted and searched until she caught sight of a tiny crimson patch on one of the roofs, like a wee spot of blood. A red scrap of sail, woven into the thatch. This was the home of Daniel Mac Michael, the boy she was trusting to rescue her.

Deirdre had stopped going to school altogether once she was twelve and could read and write and do any sums a girl might need to do. Her brothers stayed in school a little longer. Her father wanted them only in summer, when he took those who were strong enough to the bog and set them to cutting turf. Then he'd send his sons home while he trudged off with the wages earned, and nobody knew when he might return or what state he'd be in, or whether he'd bring home anything to eat. But Deirdre's mother needed her all year round.

Mornings, it was washing and mending and cooking, and afternoons it was feeding chickens and gathering eggs, and cooking again. There wasn't much to cook, the garden no more than a patch of limestone and a scatter of soil. Vegetables thin and sickly as her little sisters and brothers, who crowded her, begging for their tea. She lived for the days she could take the eggs to market or slip away to the sheltered cove where she gathered seaweed for the garden.

It was at this cove she had first seen Daniel Mac Michael. He was standing naked under the waterfall that rushed over the cliff edge into the creek that ran down the beach to the sea. She hid in a rocky fold of the cliff and watched him washing himself and singing. His wet skin gleamed as he scrubbed, as though he were polishing himself. She had never seen a boy stop work in the middle of the day to wash. She wondered whether he might be a fairy man, but then she saw his currach beached among the reeds and knew he must have rowed in from the sea.

He stepped out of the waterfall and shook his head, flinging drops of water from his black hair, and walked into the sunshine. From the creek, he pulled a wet shirt and a pair of trousers, which he wrung out and draped across a large rock in the sun. He put on a dry set of clothes and lay on his back, with his arms crossed under his head, and closed his eyes.

When Deirdre thought for sure he was asleep, she ventured down to the water. The tide was ebbing, laying bare a ribbon of seaweed on the sand. She walked slowly, filling her basket with bladderwrack and kelp, until she came within a few feet of him. His skin was browned by the sun. She studied the shape of his forehead and his eyelids and his mouth. The sun was so warm and the lapping of the sea so quiet, she felt perfectly calm. She wasn't afraid when he opened his eyes and looked up at her. He was unsurprised, and she realized he'd been aware of her all along. She watched his eyes lighten as his pupils contracted in the sun. He smiled. Deirdre was fourteen years old. She did not yet know anything about men. She smiled back at him.

On Sundays, Daniel and his father did not fish, so Deirdre met him at the cove. Or, if she couldn't get away, he would come walking and look at her house from the road. If she saw him from the window, she'd run out to fetch water from the river, just to exchange a few words with him. Her father didn't approve of the Claddagh men, saying they were savages, but Deirdre knew he was mistaken. Of all the men she'd met in her short life, Daniel was the kindest. His English was limited and slow, so at first they spoke of little beyond the weather and their families. But he let her know with his gentle ways that he loved her. His eyes were blue, green, blue, and he brought her cupped yellow flowers from the roadside and seashells he found on his travels to the islands. She had never known anyone who cared so much for the beauty of things.

Once she'd known Daniel a year, Deirdre let him kiss her and hold her hand. Whenever she went to market in Galway and stayed the night with her Aunt Grace, Deirdre slipped from the house after supper and met with Daniel down at the quay. He introduced her to his brother and sister, and once even took her to his home to meet his father, and all of them were friendly. Not at all like her own family. It was a pleasure to sit with Daniel and his sister on the shore of the bay. He carved little fish and birds and animals out of driftwood with his knife, figures so cunning Deirdre could scarcely believe them possible. He carved a fat harbour seal, swimming, its tail flipped up. So lifelike it was a sort of miracle, but so small she could conceal it in her palm. He gave it to her for a keepsake, and she kept it hidden, for if her mother saw it she would ask where it had come from, and Deirdre could not lie.

When she was fifteen, and her next youngest sister had learned to cook, Deirdre's parents sent her out to work for Galen O'Nolan, a pig farmer down the road, whose second wife and newborn son were ill. With the war on, and the price of food nearly doubled, O'Nolan's farm was prospering, while Deirdre's family, and most of the neighbours too, often went hungry. So O'Nolan gave her parents a few pennies each week, and plenty of pork, for Deirdre to walk the two miles to his farm every day, to feed his children and clean the kitchen and bake the bread.

These were not easy tasks. Deirdre could never manage to shush all the children at once. Someone was always crying, and no matter how she scrubbed she could not rid the O'Nolan house of its dark stink of fever and blood and the reek of smoke on Galen O'Nolan's clothes and the pig excrement ground into the soles of his boots. When he came to the table for his supper, she lowered her eyes so she wouldn't see him looking at her while she served the meal. From a chair by the fire all winter his second wife had watched them both, a wild glint in her eyes, clutching her firstborn to her breast as if Deirdre were going to steal it away. Galen had to pry the baby from its mother's arms so Deirdre could bathe it, and at those times the second Mrs O'Nolan stared with a fierce, delirious hatred that made Deirdre's fingers shake as she worked.

The baby survived. But the second wife succumbed to the fever and was now buried under a wooden cross beside the first wife. Deirdre's mother had taken the baby in and nursed it at her own breast. But there were also the six children of the first wife to be fed. The eldest, Nora, was only seven. Clearly, said the neighbours, O'Nolan needed a third wife. And clearly, said Deirdre's parents, who daily remarked how big she had grown, how much she was eating, Deirdre needed a husband.

One day Deirdre's father went to the King's Head in Galway to down a few pints with Galen O'Nolan, and when he came home, he announced he had sealed the match. Under his armpit he carted a hefty shoulder of pork, wrapped in a cheesecloth.

"Father Barry will do it in June, at St Augustine's in Galway," he said. He handed the pork to his wife and told her to make it up into sausages. Smoked, he said. With cracked pepper.

Deirdre waited until he left the house. Then she said to her mother, "I'm only fifteen."

"You'll be sixteen by the wedding day," said her mother. "There's lots of girls wed at sixteen."

"But he must be forty year old!"

"He's a hard-working farmer," said her mother. "He has a fine barn and a cart and a donkey."

Deirdre began to cry.

"He has a bicycle," said her mother. "There's not many about has a bicycle."

And that was the end of it.

Since she'd been sent out to work for O'Nolan, Deirdre's Sundays at home were filled with chores, and often she could only glimpse Daniel from the window. After her marriage was arranged, ten days went by before she was able to tell him about it. Daniel promised right away that he would marry her himself. They had never spoken of marriage, being so young, but now he clasped her hand tightly against his heart and swore in his ragged English to be her man and take care of her forever. He would ask her father for her hand that very day. She warned him it would do no good, but he was determined.

Daniel came to call and tried to reason with her father, but her father ran him off with his sleán. When Galen O'Nolan found out, he threatened to kill Daniel. He said he would hang Daniel by the neck from a tree in the woods, and Deirdre believed him. So she and Daniel made plans to elope.

Daniel's mother had come from the Aran Islands. She was dead now, but her people still lived there, a long sail off the coast, a good place to hide. The obstacle was that Deirdre could not get away from home. If she tried to walk, she knew her father would catch her up or Galen O'Nolan would come after her himself on his bicycle. She could not outrun the bicycle. So they decided to wait until the day before the wedding, when Deirdre and her parents came to town to prepare. Daniel would meet her at the Spanish Arch at two o'clock and they'd sail across to his cousin's home on Inis Mór. They would be married there by the visiting priest. The plan was for Daniel to leave his father and fish with his cousin, and Deirdre would keep house for them both, until her transgression was forgotten. She hoped someday to see her mother again.

Deirdre tried to comfort herself with thoughts of this coming rescue. But every night she dreamed of O'Nolan's sausage fingers and tobacco-stained teeth and his two dead wives with their glittering dead eyes, and every morning she woke with dread like a bag of stones sunk in her chest.

Cut through the stone of the ancient city wall, the Spanish Arch was deep and wide. Four or five people could walk abreast as they passed under it. As Deirdre waited there for Daniel on the day before the wedding, she couldn't be seen, not even from the roof of her aunt's house.

The fish market was laid out in the square beside the arch. Daniel's ten-year-old sister, Mab, was there, with a basket of clams nearly as tall as she was. Mab could barely manage to hold the basket upright, let alone swat away the gulls that surrounded her, swooping down and pecking at her wares. Whenever a seabird managed to steal a clam, it carried the prize in its beak to the top of the wall and dropped it to the rocks below to crack it open. But Deirdre only watched from inside the arch and did not help. She could not let herself be seen. As the clock in St Nick's tower struck three, a tremor rippled through her body. Daniel was an hour late.

By half four, Mab had sold all her clams and gone home, dragging the empty basket behind her. The square was soon deserted. By six, Deirdre could wait no longer. She covered her head with her shawl as she crossed the bridge over the Corrib estuary and entered the Claddagh.

Two old women mending nets on the quay spoke to each other in Irish as she passed. Were they speaking of her? She could not tell. She turned into the first crooked street of the village. When she came to the cottage with the red rag in its thatch, she was relieved to see Mab, who spoke better English than the others, shaking a rug out in the yard.

"Where is Daniel?" Deirdre blurted, forgetting her manners.

"Gone with our da to Lough Corrib," Mab told her. "They're after catching some trout."

"Not today!" Deirdre cried. "They didn't go today!"

"They went yesterday," Mab said. "Sure I thought they'd be home this morning. But the trout must be running thick. Or maybe they plan to wait out the storm." She looked up at the sky, which to Deirdre looked perfectly calm.

Deirdre's hands began to shake inside the shawl. She took a few steps backwards.

"Don't worry," said Mab. "There's an old stone hut up there they use for shelter."

Deirdre turned and ran back the way she had come. But when she reached the bridge, she stopped dead. She could not return to her aunt's house. She walked to the beach, where she sat down heavily on a driftwood tree trunk and stared out to sea. Why had he not come for her? He knew full well that today was their only chance, that by tomorrow it would be too late. She could only think that his father must have discovered their plan and forbidden it.

She knew of the stone hut Mab had mentioned. It was four miles north, where the lake flowed into the Corrib River. Her eyes fell upon a row of beached currachs, the light craft used by the Claddagh fishermen. If she followed the river upstream, she could find him. Maybe he was this very minute coming down the river with his father, their boat full of silvery trout, and she would meet them on their way. She would plead with Daniel's father to let Daniel take her away to be married. This very night. He seemed such a kind man. Surely she could make him relent.

The smallest currach, the one with the leather painter, had belonged to Daniel's grandfather, who had made it himself on Inis Mór with the help of his own father, years ago. It was a one-man currach, seldom used. The family kept it to honour the old man's memory, Daniel had told her. To honour the old ways.

The water was choppy. She was rowing against the current, and against the north wind, and one of the oarlocks was cracked. But she was a strong girl and she soon gained control. By the mills, she saw her aunt's friend Mary Lynch gathering kindling on the riverbank.

Mary waved and called out, "Where are you off to?"

Deirdre bowed her head as though she had not heard. She pushed on with long, even strokes, keeping her eyes straight ahead until she rounded the bend. She didn't glance toward shore again until she had passed through town. The sun was still bright. By the ruins of Terryland Castle, a flock of wild white swans floated on the water and their white reflections floated in the reflection of the sky.

A sudden chill breeze came up as she reached the rapids, where the lake poured into the river. But she steered against it, into the shallows, then took off her shoes and waded, dragging the boat up the grassy beach. As she was tying the bowline to a willow branch, a gust of wind lifted the shawl from her shoulders and sent it scudding across the marsh grasses into the river. She splashed in to retrieve it, soaking the hem of her dress and her petticoat to her knees.

She hiked uphill. From the top of the rise, she saw heavy rainclouds gathering over the lake. She saw the stone hut and several miles of lakeshore to the east and to the west. No boats were out on the water. She called Daniel's name, but no one answered. She clutched the edges of the shawl to her throat, her knuckles cold against her collar bone. She was alone. The wind exhaled upon her the frigid air of glaciers and ice floes from the north. A storm was rising. Perhaps Daniel and his father had taken shelter in one of the inlets on the lake. She ran back down the hill, determined to row along the lakeshore and find them. She sloshed through the shallows and lifted herself into the currach again. Her arms were stiff now, and a thin pain ran like a sewing needle up and down the back of her neck whenever she turned her head.

Twilight approached. Dark clouds flew toward her. By now her parents would know she had run off. Mary Lynch would say she had seen her going north on the Corrib in a currach and people would be filled with wonder, but her father would know the reason, and if he ever saw her again she feared he would kill her. The rapids were rougher now, the rolling waves high and heaving beneath her. She pulled on the oars but could make no headway against the current. A heavy rain began, and in less than a minute, her clothes were soaked through. Rain lashed her eyes. She fought hard to row toward shore, but the wind was too strong. It swept the currach back into the river, hurtling Deirdre south toward town.

She wielded one oar like a weapon, fending off the rocks that threatened to tear a hole in the boat. Within minutes she was passing Terryland again. The flock of swans had fled the river and taken shelter in the castle ruins. She caught quick flashes of their white bodies through the holes in the walls. As she blew through town, she could barely see for rain. The wind ripped branches from the trees and sent them flying. A squawking chicken, tangled in a fish net, and a flat board — she thought it was a pub sign — whipped past her head. A clothesline, shedding shirts and stockings, sailed above her like a kite. The currach itself, tossed high by the waves, seemed ready to take flight. Then it plunged violently downward, nearly bouncing her overboard.

When she passed the fishery tower near the river's mouth, she heard a great crack as a boulder split the stern. The current carried her under the bridge and soon it would carry her into the wild Atlantic if she did not fight. She gathered her resolve as she entered the salt water of Galway Bay. Through the mist and dusk, she saw the white tower and beam of the lighthouse on Mutton Island, not far off shore. Then a surge of the tide pulled her past the wooden docks along the quay, and she knew she must grab onto one before she was swept to sea. She lifted the oar and wedged it between the planks of the last dock. She held fast, trying to steady herself. Perhaps she could steer a course toward Mutton Island. If the waves didn't crush her against the rocks, she could land there. She pictured herself sleeping on the little island under the stars, cold but safe. They would think her drowned. In the morning she could fix the boat. Stuff the crack with her woollen shawl and escape to the Aran Islands. It was a mad plan, but before she could think of another, a new wave, the highest one yet, came bubbling toward the currach and burst across the gunwale, tearing her loose from the dock. She was swamped, the whole stern heavy with water now, the vessel sinking. The wind rose high, so fast it might have been angry with her. Night fell. Mutton Island was a fool's goal. Impossible. She had two choices: death or Galway.

All she could see of the town were a few wavering lights, and she steered toward them. The wind pushed and the tide pulled her out to sea, but she fought on, with fingers frozen nearly to stone, paddling with all her strength, and finally she felt the currach shudder as she hit a rock. She was close to shore. She lowered her body over the gunwale and held on to the currach with both numb hands, kicking toward shore until she reached water shallow enough to wade in. The rocks near shore, uneven and slimy with weeds, provided hazardous footing. She tried to walk upright, dragging the bowline behind her, but the wind thrashed her hair and her clothes, and twice she slipped, scraping her legs and cutting the palm of one hand on a rough cluster of barnacles. At last she had to let the currach go. She felt the tide pull it out of her hands and take it away, out to sea, where it would surely be dashed to pieces. Daniel's grandfather's boat, the boat he'd built with his own two hands.

Her dress had torn down one side, and she lifted the sodden remnants and tied them into a knot at her waist, exposing her mud-streaked legs. On her hands and knees, she dragged herself up the bank and lay soaked and shaking on the stony ground. Perhaps even now Daniel was waiting for her at the Spanish Arch. Perhaps he'd only been late. She never should have left their meeting place, never should have doubted him. She rose and limped as fast as she could toward the shelter of the Spanish Arch. Daniel was not there.

No one was there. And no one was out on the quay. The lanterns were dark. She pictured her parents and Grace huddled around the kitchen fire, speaking of her. Her mother and aunt would be worried, but her father would know she had tried to run away and he would be cursing her. Wondering, if she was dead in the storm, would he get the dowry back. Deirdre lay down in the stony lane beneath the Spanish Arch and wrapped herself in her wet shawl. It did not warm her.

Near dawn, she woke with sore muscles. All was calm. Her first thought was to seek out Daniel. Shakily, she got to her feet and took a few steps toward the sea, then a few steps toward the river. From the direction of the town, she heard somebody call her name.

"Deirdre Quinn!" The voice of Galen O'Nolan.

She turned. At the far end of the lane, his hunched bulk wobbled toward her on the bicycle. He gripped the handlebars tightly as the tires juddered over the cobblestones. Deirdre's body sagged against the stone wall as she understood, at last, what her life was to be. Sinking to the ground, she closed her eyes and waited for it to begin.

1.3

EIGHTY-THREE YEARS LATER, THE MUDDY LANE BENEATH THE Spanish Arch has been paved over. The field of rock and weeds has vanished, and a cut green lawn stretches the length of the quay. This evening, like most summer evenings, a slow throng of people makes its way down to the estuary, tourists and locals arriving from town in twos and threes, carrying paper bags of hamburgers or boxes of fried fish and bottles of wine. They gather on the low benches and spread blankets on the grass. One man carries a Guinness in its pint glass down from the pub. In the shade of an ancient plane tree, an

Italian family gathers for a picnic. The grandfather rips up long loaves of bread, and slices a wheel of cheese. A young American leans against the Spanish Arch, tuning an old guitar. He strums "Oh Susanna," while beside him two teenage girls in white cotton dresses pour cheap cava into plastic cups. The seagulls circle. Laughter and music and the smell of the sea drift up through the low slanted rays of sunlight. The girls in the cotton dresses break into giggles and raise their foaming glasses to each other. *Don't you cry for me.* Soon they are dancing, their white skirts whirling, bare feet sliding through the grass. They're kids. No younger than Deirdre was on her wedding day.

Galen O'Nolan's farmhouse is no more. In its place squats an over-priced tourist motel. The owner says he can't compete with the nearby seaside resorts, but he does all right. He points out a crumbling medieval tower, visible from the motel windows, a romantic touch that no doubt allows him to charge his outrageous rates. He's surprised to hear that Von's more interested in the old farm. He tells her the dip in the middle of the field marks the location of the old root cellar.

Von signs the guest register, using her whole name, Siobhán Saoirse Garrison. She hasn't thought of herself as Siobhán for many years. She and her sister, baptized Róisín Dubh, both changed their names when they were young, becoming Von and Rosheen — modern, anglicized girls. But since Von arrived in Ireland last month, it seems her birth name has reclaimed her. At the airport, the bank, and the car rental agency, people look at her passport unsurprised and pronounce her name perfectly, dislodging memories. It's as if she's returned to her girl self, surrounded once again by her family. Siobhán Garrison. A known person, one who belongs.

"You can go and take a look, Siobhán," says the landlord. "You can see the caved-in walls of the root cellar, if you wade into those tall weeds."

So she wades in. She kneels and explores the remains of the old foundation. Digging among the stones, she finds half of a stoneware pitcher. It's too sharp and heavy to take back to New York, but she gets out the video camera and films it, showing where it lay among the stones. Then she stands and turns in a circle, capturing the view from every angle of Deirdre's former home. The tower ruins and wild flowers, a stand of beech trees at the end of the field. She films until the light fades, then walks back across the field, feeling the grasses and leaves of the wild plants sweep against her bare ankles and calves — thistles, angelica, loosestrife, valerian. The scent of wild roses lingers on the air, though all the petals are closed against the dark. Dark roses. Róisín Dubh.

Deirdre always said it was a shame her granddaughters didn't care for their Irish ancestry, their beautiful Irish names. Remembering this, Von is visited by images of her sister at the age of eight, her little face a maze of stitches, her thin freckled arm bruised where the intravenous needle entered her vein. Her hoarse voice: *Look, Siobhán, I'm floating. I'm way up in the air.* A dazed, self-absorbed look in her eyes, pupils contracted to pinholes, as if trying to squeeze out the light. Von strides hard across the darkening field, shaking off the memory.

She returns to her motel room and consults the green notebook before packing it away. She needs to secure it with two thick rubber bands, because Rosheen crammed it so full of research notes and addresses and pasted-in maps that it won't stay closed. Von washes her face and changes into her nightgown, settles into bed with a book of Edna O'Brien stories. But she's too keyed up to read. Tomorrow, she will follow her grandmother's story south. Deirdre never said anything about her youth, except that she grew up in county Galway where the landscape was pretty and jobs were scarce. At the age of nineteen, she said, she answered a personal ad placed by Tomas Garrison of Brooklyn and sent him her photograph. He replied with a proposal and paid her passage to New York. Though she lived to be ninety-two, Deirdre never said anything more than that about her life in Ireland.

But Rosheen, who lived many years with Deirdre, was convinced she had a secret in her past. Rosheen had found strange letters and keepsakes hidden in Deirdre's Brooklyn apartment, and Deirdre, in her old age, called out names Rosheen had never heard before. *Fiona. Brendan. Daniel.* Deirdre sometimes looked right at Rosheen and called her *Daniel.* So Rosheen had decided to seek out the truth.

Rosheen had expected to uncover here a windswept Irish romance. And it's true there seems to be plenty of wind in the story. But now that Von has followed up on Rosheen's leads, and interviewed members of the Quinn and O'Nolan families — some willing to be filmed and some not — she isn't convinced this story is a romance.

The Quinns and O'Nolans possess long memories. Over the past few weeks they've recounted for Von the tales their parents told them, the gossip that raged through the countryside in Deirdre's wake — and every teller has a slightly different version. That's the nature of the truth, Von supposes. Or the nature of the Irish.

She turns out the light. Tomorrow she'll drive south to Cobh. In a few days she'll fly back to New York to finalize her sister's affairs — she hopes to be done with that in a week — and then she'll have closure. She'll be free to go home to Canada, to resume her life. To run her business and tend her roses.

Sensitive and temperamental, the roses are familiar with Von's touch, and she rarely leaves them even for a day. When she phoned home this afternoon, Jeanne assured her they were fine. She closes her eyes and imagines them, tender and safe beneath their glass.

Róisín Dubh was a delicate baby, too small and thin. Her skin was too white. A mere wisp of pale orange hair, like fairy dust, sprang from her tiny head. Siobhán wanted to brush that wisp of hair, but her mother said not to. Babies' heads are fragile.

Róisín was born too early and needed to be held at all times or she would cry.

"Not like you," Siobhán's mother said. "You were a sturdy baby." She was carrying Róisín in one arm while she stirred the oatmeal.

"Didn't I cry?" asked Siobhán.

"Ah, no. You're the independent type. You don't need your mother all the time."

Yes, I do, Siobhán wanted to say. She wished she had known, when she was little, to cry more. She held the broomstick with two hands, down near the straw part, and swept away the potting soil that had spilled out of the burlap bags propped up against the kitchen wall. She carried a stack of clay pots one by one into the greenhouse. It was only a few steps away, but seemed a different world entirely, warm and moist and smelling of earth and leaves, and when the roses were blooming, the air was heavy with the mingled scents of the different breeds.

Siobhán's mother was busy with the new baby. Siobhán was five and could do a lot of things to help. She folded towels and dusted the baseboards. She ran and fetched anything her mother wanted, if she could reach it. When she couldn't reach, she stood on a chair. She was especially good at finding lost things. One morning she found Daddy's cufflink under the dresser when he was late for work and the taxi driver was waiting and the baby was crying and Mama was just about to cry too because the house was so topsy-turvy and Daddy was shouting.

"Siobhán, you have absolutely saved the day," her mother said, when the cufflink was finally fastened to Daddy's sleeve and he had left the house. Siobhán liked to repeat that sentence to herself. It seemed a beautiful, shiny thing to do, to save a whole day. Absolutely.

The Garrisons were often disorganized. Three days a week Daddy needed a white shirt and shined shoes and his briefcase, and Mama got flustered with all the things to do and the baby's crying. But the days when he stayed home to work in the greenhouse were just as anxious. Mama walked up and down in the kitchen jiggling the baby and speaking to her in a sing-song voice, in between telling Siobhán what to do.

"Measure the coffee, honey. Four tablespoons. No, the big spoon. That's it."

Daddy, if he had slept, would be up and dressed. He poured juice and sometimes he helped by making pancakes. Other days he had a headache and stayed in bed or listened to the radio in the living room. Then they would never know when he might want his breakfast. Or when he might come in to interrupt.

"Mama," Siobhán asked, "can I light the stove?"

"No, honey. You let Mama do that. Can you fetch me a match?"

Siobhán put the coffee pot on the stove and climbed on a chair to reach the matches. Mama put Róisín in her bassinet and placed it on the kitchen table.

Daddy came in while Mama was lighting the stove. "What is this?" he asked. He was holding a toy house in his hands. Part of a building block set.

"That's Siobhán's."

"Then *what* is it *doing* on the *stairs*?"

"Why, Frank. What's the matter?"

"I nearly broke my neck!" Bang. He hurled the toy house down onto the table, beside the bassinet.

"Frank!" she cried. "The baby!"

"Oh, simmer down," he said. "I'm not going to hurt the baby."

One Sunday morning when Mr and Mrs Ross from the church came to pick up Mama, Mrs Ross happened to say that she was glad Róisín was to be baptized, and Siobhán's father had asked, roughly, "What do you mean?"

Siobhán knew what it meant. She had seen babies baptized at church before. The priest sprinkled them with water, and they cried.

But Mama didn't want to talk about baptism. She said, "We're late for church. Good-bye, Frank." She already had on her coat, and she was holding Róisín in her arms. She took Siobhán's hand and led her out to the car, leaving Mrs Ross in the hallway with Daddy. Mr Ross was out in the driveway, beside his car. "Good morning!" he said. He opened the car's back door and Mama got into the back seat with the baby. Siobhán climbed in beside her. The little Ross boy was standing in the front seat. He turned around and grinned at Siobhán and stuck out his tongue. He was three years old and didn't talk much, but he liked to play.

"Hi, Raymond," Siobhán said.

Raymond covered his face with his hands.

"Where did Raymond go?" asked Siobhán.

Raymond giggled. He peeked out over the tops of his fingers with his big brown eyes. He had long, dark eyelashes, like a girl's, and dark curly hair.

"There's Raymond!" said Siobhán. Raymond giggled so much he dissolved in a heap in the front seat.

"Settle down, son," said Mr Ross. From the back seat, Siobhán could only see Mr Ross's shoulder and one side of his face as he looked down at his son. But she could tell he was patting Raymond's head and ruffling his hair. Gently. In a happy way. Then he looked back at the house and asked, "What's taking Mary so long?"

"Oh, she's just talking to Frank," said Mama.

"What about?"

"Theological matters, no doubt," said Mama. She was very cross.

After church, Mama said that if Siobhán would get the baby carriage out and change her shoes, they could go for a walk by the river and look for pussy willows and rabbits. Siobhán took the carriage out of the garage and pushed it over the grass to the front driveway and went into the house. The baby was sleeping in her bassinet on the floor in the front hall and her parents were in the kitchen, arguing. Siobhán was still wearing her Sunday best — a yellow dress of dotted Swiss and a scrunchy crinoline. But Mama had not said to change her dress, just her shoes. So she went to the hall closet and took out her rubber boots. She sat down on the bottom step and began to unbuckle one shoe.

They were arguing about baptizing Róisín. The priest had done it this morning at Mass, and Daddy was upset. There were two things Siobhán heard that day that she never forgot. Mama saying, "I promised my mother," and Daddy saying, "Your mother is dead."

Later, Siobhán ran that conversation over in her mind, recalling the two shocks, one after the other. Mama had a mother. This was an idea so novel it had stopped her cold, one shoe on and the other dangling from her hand by its patent leather strap. If her mother had a mother, then where — ? But then immediately her father's words had cut through to a deeper level of shock. Dead? A dead mother? She thought of the dead birds she had seen, dead flowers and frogs, and then strangely she was aware that she had always known that mothers could die. Mothers and fathers and sisters and her own self someday could die. Would die. She knew. She had always known. At night, when her father's shouts or the crashing of the furniture woke her, this was the dread that rushed through her ears with a sound like boiling water.

But right now, waiting in the hall, she needed to listen for what might come next. Would Mama say anything more to annoy him? If she did, would he come out through the swinging door from the kitchen into the hall? If he did, would the bassinet be in his path? If it was, could Siobhán drag it out of the way in time? She struggled with the buckle of her second shoe, her ears on alert for any noise from the kitchen.

"For crying out loud!" her father said. His footsteps came toward the swinging door. Siobhán ran to the bassinet and tugged with both her hands on one of its handles. She towed the bassinet, and the baby inside, across the floorboards of the hallway. The kitchen door swung open. With one yank, she pulled the bassinet into the living room and sat down hard on the carpet, just as her father strode past, one hand stretched out, seeking the banister. When he touched it, he stamped upstairs, holding his head high.

Mama took a long time to come out of the kitchen. When she did, Siobhán could tell she was sad, even though she was smiling. Mama put the baby in the carriage, and she and Siobhán walked down to the river, where they saw some turtles. It wasn't as fun as Siobhán had hoped. It couldn't be fun with Mama unhappy. Siobhán walked beside the carriage and didn't talk.

At bedtime, when Siobhán couldn't find her pyjamas, her mother discovered they were still on the line outside, chilly and damp. She had forgotten to bring them inside. "Never mind," she said. "I'll hang them by the wood stove while we read some stories, and you can have a bubble bath. By then, the pyjamas will be nice and toasty, and I'll tuck you in."

Siobhán went downstairs to choose some books from the shelf in the living room. Her father was sitting alone in his chair, with his elbow on his knee and his chin resting on his fist. She didn't want to talk to him, but she had to. That was the rule.

"Hi, Daddy."

"Where's your mother?" he asked. "When you go up to see her you tell her I'm sorry, will you? Tell her I didn't mean to yell."

"Yes, Daddy."

"Tell her I'm hungry."

"I can get you a snack," said Siobhán. In the kitchen she got a plate and some crackers from a box and an apple. She poured a glass of milk and called her father to come.

"Sit with me," he said, and she sat beside him while he ate. "Tell me about your day." So Siobhán told about the turtles. That was the only part of the day she wanted to tell. While she talked, she watched his face to see if he liked the story. But she couldn't be sure. She could never be sure what he was thinking. His eyes never looked into her, and she knew they were made of glass. After she told the story, she washed the plate and cup and threw away the apple core.

When she finally crept upstairs, her mother was asleep in her chair, and Róisín was asleep in her crib. Mama had forgotten about Siobhán's bath and the toasty pyjamas. Siobhán stood a long while, waiting. She wanted her mother to wake up, but she knew better than to say anything. Daddy had many times explained that Mama had a tired heart and needed her rest.

After a while Siobhán went into her room and got into bed, still wearing her church clothes. When she crawled under the covers, the scratchy crinoline bunched up around her tummy. She turned off her lamp, but it wasn't dark yet. She could still see everything in her room.

She covered her head and closed her eyes tight. "You have saved the day," she whispered. "Absolutely saved the day for everyone."

1.4

DEIRDRE HATED THE DARKNESS OF THE ROOT CELLAR. SHE ONCE saw the shade of the second Mrs O'Nolan down there, darker than the dark, stooped and muttering among the potatoes, searching for the baby she had left behind. The sight made Deirdre scream and drop a clay jug on the stone floor. The jug broke in two, and she kicked the pieces into the darkest corner so Galen wouldn't find them. After that, she took to sending the oldest girl, Nora, to fetch the vegetables. Still, she sometimes saw Mrs O'Nolan's ghostly figure crossing the fields at night, heard her long skirts rustle and her fingernails scratch at the shutters. Coming to reclaim her son.

Deirdre expected the baby to waste away under this unwholesome watch. But the baby thrived. Within a year of the wedding, he had grown into a plump, creamy little boy named Brendan, who believed that Deirdre was his mother. He toddled after her as she tried to slop the pigs, grabbing her legs with his grubby fingers. Kevin and Owen, the twins whose births had killed the first Mrs O'Nolan, were three. Next oldest was Margaret, four, and Faye, five, a pale little thing, unlikely to grow up. And then Fiona. Fiona was six now, with wide blue eyes and a freckled nose, and something about her — Deirdre couldn't say what — that was fresh and clean. When Fiona was happy she laughed and when she was sad she cried, and sometimes she threw her arms around Deirdre's waist and hugged her. She was frank and open and somehow uncontaminated by the pig farm. But Nora, at eight, was sullen and kept to herself.

There were seven children altogether, and Deirdre had to feed them constantly. No end to it. She was glad she had no baby of her own and did not want one. At night Galen rolled on top of her and tried to make her pregnant, though she couldn't imagine why he would want more children. In any case, he could not do it easily. His big stomach hindered him. He had to bunch it up with one hand and then fumble below with the other hand to position himself properly, all the while trying to hold her still and keep her from covering herself up with the bedclothes. By the time he had done all of that, he could usually go no further. Soon she learned that the more he drank the less capable he was, so she poured beer into his soup and whisky into his stew, to supplement the copious amounts he poured for himself, and usually he was snoring before he could take off his clothes.

She could no longer slip away to the cove. He would not let her. He would not let her go anywhere, not even to her parents' house. Deirdre's mother rarely had time to walk the two miles to visit her daughter. If she did, Galen let her in and gave her some pork chops to take home. But if anyone else came calling, he spoke to them in the doorway, blocking Deirdre's view with his broad back, so that she could not even have the pleasure of seeing another face.

One day a Mr O'Malley had come to call with a man from Dublin, asking would Mr O'Nolan consider selling the north field with the old cottage and the tower ruins on it. Galen had let them come in for a drink of whisky, only because they were well-dressed businessmen. He'd been surprised that a city man would want a country house. It was a concept he couldn't quite puzzle out. But seeing as money was involved, he shrewdly stayed quiet and heard the man's offer. He would think about it, he said. After that he began to ask around about the price of land, trying to figure out the best way to profit. But there was no manner in which he could sell his land and keep it too, so it seemed a question without any answer.

As the second summer of the marriage came to a close, Galen began to take Deirdre with him when he took the cart to town. They would leave Nora, now nine, in charge of the house. At first, Galen kept Deirdre close beside him on these trips, even making her stand in the wet street outside the pub where he could see her from the window as he drank his pint and conducted his business with the men of the town. But as the months went by and she showed no signs of running off, he grew confident. He let her do the shopping on her own and even allowed her to visit her aunt and her cousins from time to time.

She was on her way to visit her Aunt Grace one spring day, when she saw Daniel's sister Mab at the Galway fish market, with a basket of trout.

"Oh, Missus," Mab called. "Do you not remember me?" Mab was taller now, but still scrawny and ragged. Her face was dirty. "I'm Daniel's sister, remember?"

Deirdre had been married two years now. Out of habit, she looked round to make sure Galen was not watching. Then she stepped forward. Part of her wanted to believe that Mab had lied to her that day of the storm, but part of her wanted to know the truth, whatever it was. And she was eager for news of Daniel, any news. To hear he was dead, or even to hear he was married, would be better than not knowing.

Mab stuttered a bit before she could get the words out. "Daniel said if I ever saw you in town to say he is sorry and could you send word —"

"He says he is *sorry?*" Deirdre shifted her weight, moving her legs further apart. She was sore where Galen had battered her last night during a bout of sex she'd been unable to prevent.

"Yes, he's sorry," continued Mab, "and he asks could you send word to him how you are faring and whether you might be able to come to him sometime?"

Deirdre looked past Mab to the Spanish Arch where she'd waited the long afternoon and then lain the long night shivering, until Galen had come to claim her. "No," she said.

She continued to her aunt's house, determined to learn anything she could about Daniel. Normally her aunt and mother told her to shush if ever she mentioned his name. But this day Deirdre persisted in begging for news of him, until her aunt gave in.

"The day before your wedding," Aunt Grace said, "four soldiers from Dublin came to town, searching for a pair of rebels said to be hiding up at the lakeshore. They took their truck up there to look and found nought but Daniel Mac Michael and his father at the stone hut, and they beat them something terrible. Broke Daniel's legs, I heard, and kicked his father so hard he coughed blood every day for the rest of his life."

"His father's dead, then?"

"Aye. Dead this past Christmas, and some say the beating was the cause of it."

"And Daniel?"

Grace shrugged. "He's fishing again, so I suppose he's recovered himself."

Deirdre softened a little then. If only she'd gone upriver sooner, she might have arrived in time to vouch for him, to tell the soldiers he was innocent.

Still, he should have sent word to her. Let her know what had happened.

A year later, Aunt Grace's son Jimmy, a sailor in the British navy, came home on leave and put a new twist on the story. The three of them were having their buttered bread and tea, when Deirdre asked Grace to tell again what had happened, and Grace repeated her story.

"Now, Mother, you know that's half the truth," said Jimmy. He turned to Deirdre, his blue eyes clear and steady. "You might as well know, people are saying your husband was behind it."

"Sure that's a pack of lies," said Grace.

"Sure it's the truth," Jimmy said to his mother. "O'Nolan knew about Deirdre and Daniel, and he was afraid they'd run off as soon as she came into town. So he sent those soldiers after Daniel. It happens the Cleary brothers were up at the King's Head and saw O'Nolan come in, face red as a beetroot, and call the soldiers into the street."

Deirdre's mouth went dry. She could only whisper. "Not truly?"

"Truly," Jimmy told her. "They say O'Nolan paid them each half a crown to keep Mac Michael away from you."

"Jimmy," said Grace. "You don't know what it is you're saying!"

"I do, Mother. They kicked the father black and blue and beat poor Daniel Mac Michael near to death and that's a fact. Tom Cleary found them after. He took them in their own boat to Nun's Island. Daniel couldn't walk for months on end. Even now he limps like an old man."

It was all Deirdre could do to remain upright in her chair.

"I'm sure Galen didn't want the boy hurt," said Grace. "Now you mustn't fuss, Deirdre. It's for the best. You've a good home now, and a good husband. Just look at the pork chops he sent over this morning for me and the children."

"Where is Daniel now?" Deirdre managed to ask.

"Nowhere near," said Grace hastily. "He's not been seen since his father's funeral."

"I hear he lives on Inis Mór," said Jimmy. "They say it's too dangerous for him in Galway. When he comes to town, he stays in the Claddagh, and his sister sells his fish for him. Once it's sold, he leaves straight away. He steers clear of your part of the world, Deirdre, for if he came round, your husband would have him murdered, and everyone knows it."

"Can you not… Did no one tell the police?" asked Deirdre.

Jimmy shook his head. "With the war on, and all the troubles here at home? You don't understand the politics of it, Deirdre. The police are too busy suppressing rebellion, and anyway, they're not likely to favour a Claddagh boy over a well-established farmer."

"You're Galen's wife now," Grace added. "That's all there is to it."

She was Galen's wife. She clothed his children and bathed them and slapped them and cooked their meals and mopped the floors and tended the garden in summer and carried the firewood in the winter time. But someone had loved her once. She knew that now. She was grateful to Jimmy and sorry for Daniel, and whenever she went into town, she visited the church of St Nicholas and lit a candle for all men in peril at sea.

When Deirdre had been married nearly four years, Galen became embroiled in a bitter disagreement with his donkey. On several occasions, when the cart was loaded with pork and Galen was ready to take it to market, the beast refused to pull. One morning in March, the donkey drove Galen nearly into an apoplexy. He chased the animal around the barnyard, cursing so fiercely the children hid under the covers in their beds. Finally he cornered the poor thing and began to flail at it with a switch. The donkey twisted and bucked, dodging the blows. So Galen circled around behind it, trying to catch it unawares. Deirdre could see the donkey's bared teeth, and knew this was a bad idea, but she did not call out a warning. She was not on Galen's side in this dispute. Let him get himself in trouble. And he did. He brought the switch down hard across the donkey's hind quarters, and the animal raised both hind legs and kicked him square in the chest. Galen's mouth opened in astonishment. He walked into the house and sat down on a chair.

"Galen?" she said. "Are you all right?"

He seemed to be listening to some faraway sound and did not answer.

Deirdre hurried out to see to the donkey. It shied away, but she grabbed hold of its bridle and tied it up in the barn. Ten minutes later, when she looked in on Galen again, he was stone dead. This was the story she told the constable, who wrote it down in his ink-spattered book.

The story of the donkey's kick spread through the nearby farms and some of the farmers arrived to help. The men gathered in the yard to build the coffin, and the women came into the house, bringing soup and pies. They fed the children and sent them back to bed.

Deirdre did not speak to anyone, except to thank them. She rode off on the blue bicycle down the road toward Galway. She was going for the priest, said some of the neighbour women. She was after buying new clothes for the children, said others, so they'd look respectable-like at the graveyard. They set to washing the body and preparing it for burial, and when Deirdre got home that night, Galen was snug in the coffin. Deirdre sat in a chair against the wall with her eyes wide open, apparently seeing nothing. The neighbours stayed up all night with the body, and some of the men got drunk on Galen's whisky, but it was a quiet wake, a sombre affair, given the young wife and the seven children left behind and the fact that nobody, not a single person any of them could think of, had liked Galen O'Nolan or would miss him.

She had the children's faces washed and their hair combed for the funeral service at the gravesite next morning. But the neighbours remarked there were no new clothes to be seen. The prayers were said. Deirdre tossed a handful of dirt onto her husband's coffin and stood quietly by for the burial. Then she took the children home.

The day before, when she'd gone to town, she had not been buying clothes. She'd been at the office of George O'Malley, lawyer and real estate agent, who represented the Dublin man wanting to purchase the north field. Galen had refused that offer, but now, Deirdre told George, the entire estate was for sale. Not only the cottage and tower ruins but the house and fields. The barn, the chicken coops and chickens, the pigpens and the very pigs themselves.

As it turned out, the Dublin businessman didn't want the animals, so Deirdre drove the pigs to the farmer's market near Oranmore. She piled the cart high with Galen's clothing and household items, a crate of chickens and the bicycle. She hitched the donkey to the cart, taking care to treat him kindly, and walked beside him, heading east, herding the pigs with a stick. Other women were walking to market, too, with smaller loads, a basket of eggs or a single sheep. But Deirdre did not want to be talking to anyone.

At the market, she sold the pigs and chickens for a good price and then she went into the shops of the town. She sold Galen's pocket watch and his tools and his shoes and pants and even his hat and his handkerchiefs. She sold the butter churn and the pitchfork and the kitchen crockery. Finally she sold the donkey and cart to a carter from up near Sligo. By the time she pedalled the bicycle home in the dark, the moon was rising and her apron pockets were heavy with coins.

The following day she was seen on the road, the seven wee ones trailing after her. She marched them past the graveyard, heading east, and that was the last anyone in Galway ever saw of her.

————

Little Faye had been sick for days, growing thin and coughing, and she could not walk. So Deirdre set Faye on the seat of the bicycle and walked along beside it, holding the girl upright. She told Nora to carry Brendan, who was five and fat, and Nora staggered under his weight.

"Where are we going?" Nora asked, and Deirdre would only tell her they were going to the main road where they might find a ride. She wheeled the bicycle forward and called to them all to hurry or be left behind. The children tripped and fell and cried and rubbed at their faces with their dirty fingers. From time to time Nora's arms sagged and she let Brendan's heels drag on the ground as she lugged him along. The smallest stragglers got farther and farther behind until Deirdre could no longer see them, and she had to wait for them to catch her up. After half a mile the twins, who were six, sat down in the dirt. Deirdre lowered Faye to the ground and set her in the grass beside the bicycle. She pulled one twin up by his arms. Then she pulled up the other. But as soon as the second was standing, the first sat down again. Then Margaret began to wail. Nora put Brendan down hard and he wailed too. Deirdre smacked him, but it didn't stop his noise. It never did. And if a man with a cart and two horses had not come along right then and offered to let them all ride, she didn't know what she might have done next. The man was a horse trader, he told them, on his way to Athlone. He hopped down and helped them all in, Deirdre and the seven children, and the bicycle. When they reached the turn off to Ballinasloe, Deirdre asked to be let out and the horse trader obliged. He tipped his hat and said good day, and Deirdre wheeled Faye on the bicycle into the town, with the others trailing after her.

"Where are we going?" Nora asked again. Deirdre said they would stop with the nuns a while and take their tea. When they reached the convent gate, she pulled a bell rope, and a young novice came and admitted them to the yard. Deirdre asked for some bread and water for the children, and the novice hurried away, asking her to wait. Deirdre laid the bicycle down and told the children to come through the gate and march up to the front door. But they had all flopped down in the grass. Brendan had already fallen asleep. Deirdre grasped one of his hands and wrenched him to his feet. The twins, not wanting similar treatment, helped each other up, and Margaret helped Faye. Faye was dreadfully pale, now that Deirdre took a closer look. She leaned on Margaret as they walked to the convent door. Fiona came last. Deirdre had washed Fiona's fair, wispy hair that morning but now it was coarse with grit from the road and tangled by the wind. She reached down to sweep a lock off the girl's forehead. Fiona raised her wide blue eyes. She was tired and sore. Too much walking and too many parents lost in her short existence. Too much change.

Six children obediently crowded onto the stone landing outside the convent. Behind them, Nora, eleven and suspicious, still stood outside the gate, her arms crossed over her chest and her sly, narrow eyes fixed steadily on Deirdre.

Deirdre walked toward Nora, looking straight into her eyes. Nora did not waver until Deirdre was right in front of her. Then she flinched. Her hands came up before her face.

But Deirdre did not strike her. "I'll just be putting the bicycle away," she said. She walked past Nora and mounted the bicycle and pushed off with her left foot and began to pedal down the road. She wanted to turn around and take another look at Fiona, but she was afraid that Nora would see her face and know the truth. Nora would cry out and the nuns would come.

Who would sing to Fiona now, when she wept at night? Who would wash her hair? Don't think of it, she said to herself. You are only going for a ride to take some fresh air. You are off to market to fetch a few potatoes for their tea. And by telling herself this story, she resisted taking that one last look. She pedalled all the way to the curve in the road and disappeared from view.

———

The children were eventually discovered. The horse trader told the story to his wife and his wife told her friends and the story got back to

Deirdre's parents. Deirdre's father went to Ballinasloe to look for the children, and through his inquiries he learned that his daughter had delivered them up to the nuns. The nuns told him she knocked on the convent door and begged for some bread and water and then, when the sisters weren't looking, she jumped on the bicycle and pedalled away like the wind. The nuns ran an orphanage, as Deirdre must have known, and they said they would keep the O'Nolan children with the other orphans while they waited for Deirdre to return. But before anyone could discover all this — indeed, before Galen's soul could even begin its descent — Deirdre herself had boarded a train and was well on her way to Queenstown.

1.5

QUEENSTOWN HAS LONG BEEN CALLED COBH, FOR IN THE 1920S, the towns of the southern counties cast off their colonial names and were reborn in Irish. Cobh is pronounced "Cove," and that's where it is, on the southern shore of an island in a deep cove off the southern coast of the country, in Cork Harbour where the big ships dock. The Americans call it "Cawb," and the Irish laugh at them.

"So he asked me where was 'Cawb,'" says a young man at the next table. "And I says, 'Cawb? Never heard of it!'" His friends laugh. It's lunchtime and the Cobh pub is crowded with fishermen and tourists watching football. Von is drinking tea, waiting for the rain to stop. She's haunted by the image of those seven orphans, suddenly homeless and bewildered. When she interviewed Nora's grandson in Galway, he said Nora described the scene many times, the bell rope, the iron gate, the bicycle. Nora lived to be eighty-eight, never forgetting a detail and never forgiving Deirdre.

Von has just come from Mass at St Coleman's Cathedral, an elaborate neo-Gothic structure that looms above the citizens of Cobh from the high cliff that overlooks the lower town and harbour. It's the same cathedral where Deirdre must have attended mass, though surely she couldn't have gone to confession. She couldn't have spoken her sin out loud. Any priest would have sent her back home at once. As for Von, she wouldn't know where to begin to confess her own sins, and if she began she wouldn't know where to end. She simply listened to the music and admired the architecture. Afterwards, she bought a postcard of St Coleman's to send to Alex in New York. According to the postcard, the cathedral took nearly fifty years to build. The finishing touches, the spire and the carillon that sounds through town every quarter hour, were completed in 1916. So Deirdre would have heard the bronze bells chime the angelus and seen the spire in its grim glory everywhere she went. For you soon discover, as you wander the town, there's not a single spot from where that spire can't be seen. Just so you never forget who's in charge. Von can see it right now through the rain-streaked window of the pub. Through the other window, she can see the cove. Gulls wheel below the storm clouds, and fishing boats roll on the waves. The rain has dissolved the horizon, leaving no seam between the grey sea and the grey sky.

She opens Rosheen's notebook and removes the envelope tucked in the cover flap. Reads again the only legible words of the address: c/o Doyle House, Queenstown. The letter, which Rosheen found hidden in Deirdre's linen closet, is brittle and yellow. It rips slightly when Von unfolds it. She should have made a photocopy and left the original back in New York.

Dear Deirdre It is hard for Dan now his leg is bust from the train blast. it will be a time before he can travel. Dan asks can you come to him now as he is hurt bad. You can sell the tikets for fare and give Mrs Doyle her do for room and bord. Mab.

No mention of the O'Nolan children.

Rosheen had been excited when she showed this letter to Von. "See?" she said. "Dan! Daniel! Maybe in Cobh we can find out who he was, who Mab and Mrs Doyle were."

Von had merely glanced at her watch, saying, "I have a flight to catch." The memory of that gesture chills her now. The door opens, and a wet wind enters the pub, seems to blow right through her, like a little ghost.

———————

Róisín was only five when her parents sent her all by herself to stay with Grandma Deirdre.

"I can look after her here, at home," Siobhán insisted.

Her parents said no. Siobhán must go to school, and Dad must go to work. Yvette and Manuel had to keep the greenhouse running.

Grandma Deirdre had to stay in New York and supervise her sewing girls. But she would love to have Róisín come to visit.

Their mother was to have an operation to repair a heart valve, but Siobhán only learned this when she was much older. Her parents never explained the gory details to the children. Mama's heart was tuckered out, they said, and the doctor would make it stronger. Then Mama would need to rest in the hospital for a few weeks. How did her heart get so tired? She wouldn't say, but Siobhán knew it was from looking after the greenhouse and looking after her father and her sister and herself, without enough help. Siobhán wanted to help. But sometimes she hid in the attic or greenhouse and got lost in *Heidi* or *Alice*, and if the vacuum roared or the doorbell rang or her mother's footsteps ran frantically back and forth, she pretended she didn't hear. So she knew she was to blame.

Siobhán couldn't go to New York, because her parents needed her. Her mother marked pages in the cookbooks, showing her Dad's favourite recipes. She showed her how to iron Dad's shirts. Sprinkle them with water. Do the collar first. Then the cuffs. Place the tip of the iron under the buttons. Could she manage that? Yes, she could. She was ten years old.

But Róisín must be sent away. Just until Christmas. Their mother opened the atlas and put her little finger on Winnipeg. That was home. She touched New York with her thumb. "See? Not very far." Róisín seemed to accept this. The whole family had taken several trips to New York, the last only two years before. Maybe Róisín couldn't remember how very long it took, but Siobhán did.

It was a cold November morning when Róisín left. She kissed her mother good-bye at home, and then Von and her father took her in a taxi to the Winnipeg airport. A stewardess met them there and gave them candy. She said Róisín was the cutest little thing and promised to stay with her all the way to the airport in Toronto. Grandma Deirdre would meet them there and take Róisín on another plane to New York.

"Don't worry," said the stewardess. "I won't let your sister out of my sight. I can tell she's very special." She stuck a lollipop in Róisín's mouth and took her away. Róisín didn't cry. But when she turned to look back, Siohbán saw her face. Betrayed. She had obviously never understood they were really going to leave her there, alone.

Siohbán led her father outside to the taxi stand. He gripped her arm with one hand and kept his cane folded in his pocket. He didn't need his cane when he had his daughter.

"What if Grandma forgets?" Siohbán asked. The wind ripped across the open prairie outside the airport, and she had to shout to be heard.

"Don't be silly," said her father.

"What if Grandma gets lost in the airport in Toronto? What if she can't find Róisín?"

"Watch for a taxi, will you?"

Róisín was supposed to be home for Christmas, but Mama wasn't well enough to send for her until spring. At Easter, when Deirdre finally brought her home, Róisín clung to her mother all day, and if her mother was busy, she clung to Siobhán. Deirdre stayed a few days, to visit. Róisín was a quiet thing, she said. Siobhán and her mother exchanged a look of mock surprise. Quiet? Róisín? She had missed her mother terribly, said Deirdre. She'd be happy now that she was home. But a few days later, when Deirdre flew back to New York alone, Róisín was inconsolable. She had two mothers now, two homes, so she was always homesick.

Is that the word to describe Róisín, *homesick?* Von remembers her at eight, her bruised arm tethered to the morphine bag, longing to come home. At sixteen, her eyes blue with codeine and gin, afraid to come inside. At nineteen, with her infant in her arms. *Vonnie, please.* Standing in the rain beneath the white lilac, the intermittent scent of petals on the wind. *Please let me stay.* Von's throat aches. She sips her tea, forces the images from her mind.

The Irish rain thins to a fine drizzle and stops. By the time Von steps outside, the clouds have shifted from charcoal to silver, thinning in places to a gunmetal brilliance that makes her squint, and the few pockets between the clouds are lined with deep blue layers of sky. The sun flashes white as pearl on the wings of the birds. A good afternoon for filming. She walks through the lower town with the video camera, recording the main street, lined with shops and pubs and old hotels. In 1920, Deirdre would have found ticket agents on this street too, selling passage on the Cunard and the White Star Line. Von films the monuments to emigration, the statues and plaques and the long splintered wreck of a dock, pierced with rusted nails, they call Heartbreak Pier.

She imagines twenty-year-old Deirdre standing on this boardwalk, touching this same metal rail, it's old enough, watching the ships come in. Like Von, she would have watched alone. For Deirdre, in the spring of 1920, must have been despised by all decent Irish people who had heard of her. Exiled from everything she'd ever known — home and family, church and town and fields and every friend. The sea, perhaps, was the one familiar element. Listening to the waves and the gulls, Von conjures the loneliness easily, feels it in her own empty belly. It was a cold act, deceiving seven children, stealing their inheritance, leaving them among strangers. An act that must have severed Deirdre clean and forever from her past.

Deirdre had found lodging in Doyle House, an establishment that teeters still on the edge of the steep rock bluff. Von is boarding at Doyle House too. She scales the steep stone stairs that lead up the cliff, and when she reaches the top, she turns to look back at the town. The long row houses with laundry hanging on the lines. The mighty freighters coming in to port. Imagine, leaving your entire life behind you. Beginning again. A terrifying prospect. Yet Deirdre must have been glad to be cut loose. After all, wasn't that why she had done it? To move about with no siblings or stepchildren clamouring after her, no father to sell her for a packet of pork chops, no husband to police her every movement. Here in Cobh, she could have walked the streets without being watched, listened to her own thoughts, breathed free for the first time in her life.

———

Tammy Doyle is a stout, busy woman of sixty, who took over the running of this house from her mother-in-law, who took it over from *her* mother-in-law, who was Georgiana Doyle, Deirdre's landlady in the spring of 1920. The Doyles have always kept a guest register, and ever since the sinking of *Titanic*, they have held on to every volume. Cobh was the last port of call for *Titanic* in 1912, and the Doyle House books hold the signatures of some who went down on that ship, as well as hundreds of others over the years, including many Irish men and women who later became famous in America. Over the winter,

Rosheen had sussed this out and written to Tammy, who promised to let her look through the books when she came to Ireland.

"You're doing the right thing, coming here," says Tammy now. "You want the family history for passing along to the children and the grandchildren. So they know who they are."

"Yes," says Von. She doesn't have any children, and Rosheen lost her only child a long time ago. But she can't say this to Tammy.

Tammy clucks approvingly. She shines a flashlight across a row of dusty ledgers and announces calmly, "Here we are. Nineteen twenty to twenty-five. If you carry it down, I can let you take a look in your room, private-like."

"Thank you," Von says, a bit unnerved by such casual handling of history.

She begins her search in March of 1920, the month of Galen's death. The late Mrs Georgiana Doyle, landlady and amateur historian, had made notes in the margin about her guests, their occupations and ages, the towns they came from, and — when they checked out — their destinations and sometimes the ships they sailed on. Encouraged, Von runs her finger down columns of names, but there are very few women alone, and there is no Deirdre Quinn or Deirdre O'Nolan.

In the morning, she returns the book to Tammy, who is mystified. "If she was here, her name should be in the book," she says. "Maybe she boarded somewhere else in town?"

"Maybe." Von takes her tea out to the porch and inhales the sea air. She has already stayed longer than she planned, and yet she decides to extend her airline ticket one more time. There's one more lead she wants to follow up. She knows she's no longer pursuing this story just for her sister's project, but for herself. She has never felt as close to her grandmother as she does now. *Dan asks can you come to him now as he is hurt bad.* Did Deirdre go to him?

Daniel Mac Michael and his sister Mab are both long dead. But many of Mab's children are still alive, including Patrick O'Neill of Cork City, a few minutes' drive from Cobh. Patrick's number is in Rosheen's notebook, along with a note that he's a retired history professor. Rosheen has underlined this note twice. When Von phones him, he's intrigued. He's writing his own family history now, he says. They must get together and compare notes.

"Can you come to Doyle House?" Von asks.

"Certainly," he says. "You're Deirdre's granddaughter? I've always wanted to know what became of Deirdre."

"I'd like to know what became of Daniel," says Von. "I've only just found out he existed."

"My son will drive me in," he says.

———

"My Uncle Daniel lived alone," Patrick begins, over tea in Mrs Doyle's parlour. Patrick is a handsome man of seventy, with a keen memory for the details of his childhood. On the couch beside him, Von takes notes in her new black notebook — she's used up the red one. Patrick's son, Sean, and a curious Mrs Doyle are listening just as intently. But Patrick is distracted. He's pulling papers from a briefcase balanced on his lap and piling them on the coffee table next to the Doyle House guest ledger. "I have a photograph in here somewhere."

His son, Sean, a jovial middle-aged fellow, relieves him of the briefcase. "Let me have a look, Dad," he says. "You go on with your tale."

"Uncle Dan fished all his life with his cousins off the west coast," Patrick continues. "Shifted for himself in a leaky stone hut on that godforsaken rock they call Inis Mór. Whittling odd little figures from driftwood. Not even a goat for company. When I was a boy, my parents used to take us across to see him. It was like travelling back a hundred years. We sat on the bare cliff, throwing stones in the tide pool all day, while our mother mended his few clothes.

"We asked her why he didn't have a wife and all she ever told us was he'd had a romance in his youth. The girl married someone else and it broke his heart, she said. That was the version suitable for children, anyway. It wasn't until I was grown she told me the whole story."

"Here's Uncle Daniel," says Sean, pulling a photo from the briefcase.

Daniel looks about forty. With the aid of a staff, he balances on a rocky shore, lifting a peaked cap from his head and looking at the sky. The wind has made a black blur of his hair. For a split second, the tilt of his head and his hard, upright posture seem familiar.

"Do you have a photo of Deirdre?" Patrick asks.

"No. I'll have to send you one when I get back home," Von says. "I have a letter, though, from your mother, Mab, to Deirdre." She pulls it out of the notebook. "I wonder if you can tell me anything about it."

Patrick leans forward and takes the letter. He unfolds it, but at first, instead of reading, he runs his fingertips lightly over the surface of the page, touching his mother's words. Von is glad she brought the original after all.

Sean peers over his father's shoulder and reads aloud: "*his leg is bust from the train blast.*" He places a hand on his father's arm. "So," he says. "So Deirdre knew?"

"It seems she did," says Patrick.

"What happened?" asks Von.

"It was 1920," Patrick says. "The war was escalating."

"But the war was over," Von says.

"Other war," Sean explains. "The Irish War of Independence."

"Deirdre sent Daniel a letter immediately after O'Nolan died," says Patrick. "She wrote to say O'Nolan was dead and his children gone to live with relatives — a lie as it later turned out. And to ask Dan did he want to go to America with her."

"And did he?"

"He wanted to," said Patrick, "and if he'd packed his things and said his good-byes to his family as soon as he got the letter, the story would have a very different ending. But the trouble was that Daniel couldn't read. Deirdre sent the letter to Inis Mór, where Dan was living with his cousin. But neither of them knew how to read. By the time Dan took the letter to the Claddagh and had Mab read it to him, Deirdre was nowhere to be found. He got on a train straight away and went down to Queenstown to look for her."

"And was hurt on his way down?" Von asks.

"No," says Patrick. "He got down to Queenstown all right, and managed to find her, and they made plans to emigrate. They even purchased the tickets. But before their ship sailed, Dan wanted to go home to the Claddagh, to settle his affairs and say good-bye to his family. He'd left in such a hurry, you see. So he took care of all that, and he was on his way *back* to Deirdre..." He looks again at the letter Von gave him. "My mother always assumed that Deirdre never received this letter, that she never knew what happened to him."

"There was a blast? Some kind of explosion?"

"Local Volunteers tossed a grenade through the window of his train. Likely they thought some Black and Tans were in that car, but my mother said they were dead wrong. Anyway, the blast tore my uncle's knee to shreds. He was that close to death. They sent him back to Galway, where the doctors tried to save his leg, but finally they had to amputate."

Mrs Doyle crosses herself.

"He never could work like he was used," says Patrick. "A man needs both his legs in a boat."

"So, what happened? She left without him?" Von asks. "I understand she had to leave the country, after what she'd done. But why didn't she wait for him in New York?" She thinks of Deirdre, on the brink of freedom, a brand new life. "Oh, no. She didn't want a disabled husband, did she? She called it off, decided not to marry him?"

"Oh, but they *were* married," says Patrick. "They married before he went back home."

"No," says Von. "That's impossible."

"I've seen the marriage register with my own eyes," says Patrick. "Daniel and Deirdre were married in the chapel of the Queenstown Cathedral in June of 1920." He opens a folder and shuffles paper. "June 28." He hands her a photocopy.

"This can't be," Von says, though the document she's holding says it can. "Deirdre was married that same summer to my grandfather, Tomas Garrison, in New York."

Sean looks at his father. Patrick looks away, busies himself by rooting in a tobacco pouch and filling his pipe. Mrs Doyle, scandalized, is thoroughly enjoying herself.

"I don't suppose they ... divorced?" Von asks.

Patrick and Sean and Mrs Doyle all shake their heads, their eyes downcast. "Of course not," Patrick says.

"But my dad was born in 1921," says Von. "In March."

Patrick lifts his head. "March of 1921?"

Mrs Doyle is counting on her fingers.

Patrick says, "Daniel and Deirdre were married in June of 1920. It was September when he was injured in the train blast. That's when my mother sent this letter. So Deirdre must have still been here, in this very house, in September, or later, of 1920."

"She's not in the guest book," says Von.

"Did you look for a Deirdre Mac Michael?" asks Mrs Doyle. She picks up the book from the coffee table and opens it. "If Deirdre stayed somewhere else when she first arrived in town, and moved in here after her wedding…" She busies herself, searching, and soon says, "Look."

She lays down the ledger, open to a page recording that Mr and Mrs Daniel Mac Michael moved into the third-floor suite on June 28, 1920. Deirdre's handwriting then was stronger and more sure than it was in her old age, but Von recognizes that sloping *D*, with its superfluous loops at head and tail. So it was true. Deirdre had married Daniel at last. But then what happened?

"When did she check out?" Von asks.

Mrs Doyle takes the book back and continues turning pages. Everyone is quiet, waiting. Sean searches the folders for photographs. Patrick steps outside to smoke. Von is remembering Deirdre's voice, her Galway accent. She was a woman who spoke only necessary words. Except for the lullabies she sometimes sang to Rosheen, she was strictly practical, passing along advice, instructions, admonitions, recipes. She gave her granddaughters tips for baking, cleaning, sewing, behaving when company came to call. But she never spoke of her own life. And Von never asked.

Just as Patrick wanders back inside, Mrs Doyle says, "Here she is. At the very bottom of this page."

Von takes the ledger and reads the last line. A Mrs Deirdre Mac Michael checked out in the spring of 1921. The scribble in the margin says, "Booked on the Celtic to NYC, May 19." A whole year later than she always claimed she made the crossing. Why? Then Von sees the word "and" at the end of the line after Deirdre's name. She turns the page and there, on the top line of the very next page is the name of the person checking out with her. A person named Frank Mac Michael, an infant of two months of age.

She has found her own father.

Before she leaves the country, Von accepts an invitation to visit Patrick and Sean in Cork. They have gathered their wives and Sean's siblings and in-laws and a band of children for an outdoor barbecue and a chance to meet this long-lost relative from across the ocean.

"Great to have relatives in New York," says Sean's wife. "Sean will be there on business this fall, and If I can talk him into taking me along, I'll see you there." She laughs. "We'll shop!"

"I'm only there briefly, to wrap up my sister's affairs," Von explains. "I live in Canada."

Sean pours her a glass of whisky and makes a toast. "Welcome to the family, cuz."

"Second cousin," says Patrick's wife, Kate. "If Siobhán's dad is Daniel's son, you two are second cousins." She has copied two more photos of Daniel for Von to keep. "What do you think? Can you see a resemblance?"

"I can," she says. The shape of the head, the high angle of the chin, and the long legs are unmistakable. Both men were exceedingly tall, for Irishmen, and shared the same posture. Ready to meet the world and take whatever it might dish out. And give it back double. "I'm sure my dad never knew who his father really was," Von says. She tells some stories of her father's childhood in Brooklyn, the mischief he got into. There's nothing she wants to tell about his adult life.

After dinner, she asks if they'd mind talking on camera, for Rosheen's art project. Patrick and Kate, and Sean and his wife, are willing. The others drift away to get up some games with the children. "It seems many people have heard about Daniel and Deirdre," Von says, to get them started. "In Galway they say that Nora O'Nolan remembered my grandmother to the end."

"Brendan remembered her too," says Patrick. "O'Nolan's youngest. When he grew up, you know, he went to New York City to look for her."

"No!"

"That's what Grace Quinn told my mother," Patrick says. "When Brendan grew big enough he worked in the Cork distillery to earn his passage to New York, where he searched for her in every Irish pub and meeting hall and church. The last his family ever heard from him he said he thought he'd found her address in Brooklyn. But when he went there and knocked, a woman slammed the door in his face. Nearly caught his nose in the jamb."

Well, Von wants to say, *that sounds like Deirdre Quinn O'Nolan Mac Michael Garrison for you.* But she doesn't speak. She keeps the camera trained on Patrick and his family.

Then Sean's wife says, "Heartless."

"But Deirdre wasn't really Brendan's mother," Sean counters.

"She was the only mother he had," his wife replies. Then, perhaps recalling that Von is the heartless woman's granddaughter, she rises from her chair and says she'll see to the dishes.

"Deirdre never asked for O'Nolan's children," says Kate. "She never wanted O'Nolan. She wanted to elope with Daniel."

"She would have, too," says Patrick.

"Only for the wind," murmurs Kate.

"It was a rogue wind," says Patrick.

"That's what they say," adds Kate. "Like a hurricane it was."

"Blew her right back into Galway," Patrick concludes. He lights his pipe once more and puffs until its fire goes out.

Only for the wind. It's a story Rosheen would have liked and wanted to believe. Only for the wind and the soldiers who broke Daniel's bones and Galen O'Nolan who paid them to do it and Aunt Grace who kept the secret and Daniel Mac Michael who never learned to read and Deirdre who committed a crime so wicked she could never go home again and the rebels who bombed the train and baby Frank who somehow got himself conceived in the midst of it all and Deirdre who would not wait but bought a steamship ticket and sailed for America with her baby as soon as she possibly could. Only for that.

The day before her flight home, Von wakes to an overcast Galway sky. A steady drizzle smudges the world beyond the windowpane. Good weather for taking Rosheen's remains to sea.

She buys a ticket for the ferry to Inis Mór, because that's where Daniel and Deirdre wanted to live together, and Rosheen was like them both. Ill-starred. Unable to live the life she dreamed for herself, though she was a powerful dreamer.

By the time the ferry docks at Kilronan, the clouds have dispersed. The day turns cool and sunny. Above the fishing boats in harbour, the town appears as a single row of painted shops, white and yellow, and blue, with grey-tiled roofs. Bright signs advertise ice cream and sweaters for sale and bicycles for hire. Von rents a brand new three-speed, and consults the map Patrick drew, showing where Daniel lived his life of solitude. It's a hard, uphill ride past small farms and beaches and seals sunning themselves on the high rocks offshore. Everything's stone here, from the dry stone fences to the stone church. Too much sacrifice, said Yeats, can turn the heart to stone. She parks the bike on a cliff above a small bay and descends the steps carved into the rocky slope to the sea. She enters the water in her running shoes, wades in up to her thighs. Then she opens the cardboard urn she brought with her from New York.

When she was a child she imagined someone watched over her, making sure she did what she was told, even when she was alone. He wasn't a guardian angel, like other children had, but a lesser angel, the sort assigned to kids with godless fathers. She wishes he would return to her today, for she needs his sense of duty and of ceremony, to perform this final service for her sister.

A breeze ruffles the water as she tips the urn upside down. The coarse powder rushes out, plunges heavily into the salt water, turning it murky. Briefly, a skein of dust and cinders floats upon the surface. Before it's submerged, a north wind rises, lifts it like a veil into the cold blue air, and blows it back toward Galway.

The City

2.1

THEY SAID THAT IRELAND WAS A COUNTRY OF FAMINE AND WAR, but New York, too, was hungry and perilous. When Deirdre crossed Metropolitan Avenue on Saturday afternoon, she saw two gangs of boys facing off in a vacant lot, gripping sticks and broken bottles in their fists. She turned, pushing the baby carriage, and ran as quickly as she could back the way she had come, going three blocks out of her way in the pounding heat to avoid the donnybrook.

When she reached North First Street, she saw Mrs Heintz hanging her sheets to dry in front of her building.

"Vat's your hurry, dear?" called Mrs Heintz.

Deirdre waved and kept running. She had no time for Mrs Heintz. If she told her about the gang of boys, Mrs Heintz would only ask were they Irish boys, and Deirdre would have to say yes.

The bumpy ride made the baby cry, and when she got home, he was still crying. "Hush," she said. "Be quiet now, and we'll go upstairs and I'll give you a nice biscuit." But he would not stop, so she left him in his carriage outside the front door, where Mrs Heintz could see him, and climbed the stairs to put her groceries in the icebox. She fetched the straw broom from the fire escape and poked at the mouse trap behind the stove. Nothing caught and squirming there today. She began to sweep the floor, which was black with ash that had fallen from the pot-bellied stove this morning, but the broom only ground the ash deeper into the grain of the boards. She knew she should get on her knees and scrub, but she did not want to heat water today. The apartment was an oven. Already the end of September but still so hot she could barely move without sweating. She would gladly do without a cup of tea, but she knew she must cook the meat and potatoes. She laid a fire but did not light it, then sliced the potatoes and plunked them in a pot of cold water. She stood on a kitchen chair and opened the skylight. If she could only get some fresh air she thought her headache might go away.

But today, like most days, there was little fresh air to be had. The fumes from Schaefer Brewery blew straight into the apartment whenever the wind came up from the south, and some mornings she woke thirsty and sick from sleeping all night with the gummy taste of beer, weak prohibition beer, in her mouth. Domino Sugar, where Tomas worked, was even closer. The sugar refinery, a complex of tall brick buildings and funnels and smokestacks and silos, ruled the waterfront in Williamsburg. It loomed over the neighbourhood where its workers lived, and its sickly caramel scent followed them home at night, snaking down the streets and slinking through their open windows. From her kitchen, Deirdre could see the chimneys churning out black clouds of smoke. The noise and dirt and smells of the factories never let up except for Sundays, and even on Sundays, when Deirdre walked out of Our Lady of Consolation after Mass, she saw the tips of those smokestacks marking the way home.

Both the brewery and the sugar factory backed onto the East River that was no river at all but a sea, jammed like a New York street with ferries and freighters and steamers delivering supplies, and barges piled high with lumber, coal, sugar, clothing dye, flour, and barrels of oil and crates of tools and machinery. She thought with sorrow of the river Corrib, its cool breezes and clear water sparkling with salmon. She thought of the simple Irish people she used to see at church or at the shops in town, how they smiled and waved and said God bless you, child, and how is your mother? In Williamsburg you never knew who you might meet in the street, with Italians and Jews living but a few blocks east and Protestants going to school with Catholic children and coloured children going to school with the whites. On the *Celtic*, coming over, Deirdre met a man who told her that white and black did not mix in America. He read to her from a book in the library about separate drinking fountains and parks and separate establishments of all kinds for white and black. But in Williamsburg, it seemed, no one had read that book.

She tried not to think of the time the Corrib River turned against her, or the times Daniel Mac Michael abandoned her (not once but twice, twice!), or the night his son came searing out of her body, nearly splitting her in two, in that little attic bedroom above Queenstown harbour with no one there to help her but a grim paid nurse whose name she never knew. She stowed those things away and tried to forget them.

In a very small spot in her mind, up near the top where she thought about Jesus and Mary, Deirdre kept a round, lighted window, like a small picture of the sun, and on rare occasions like this afternoon, when she was all alone and the wash was done and the housework not too pressing, she allowed herself to open that window and wander there, to scenes she remembered from the days before she came to America. The delicate wildflowers and the tall grass of the fields and the taste of bread with Irish butter. Or the light, fresh scent of wee Fiona O'Nolan. Once, when Deirdre was washing mud from Fiona's arm, a strange tenderness had taken her over and she'd kissed the crook of the girl's arm and then laid kisses all the way up to her shoulder, while Fiona giggled. Deirdre remembered exactly the sound of that giggle, the shape of the arm, the freckled face, the puzzled blue eyes.

She remembered the afternoons she walked the roads with Daniel and he offered her gifts of yellow flowers and the little animals he carved. She had kept the wee harbour seal, sewn into the pocket of a dress, so Galen and the children would never find it, and now she kept it on the dresser by her bed.

Deirdre's wedding day in Queenstown was tucked in the memory window too. The young priest ushered her into the vestry where two women from the congregation covered her head with a white lace scarf and gave her a sprig of white daisies to hold when she stood beside Daniel in the chapel. How kind they were, seeing she had no family. Her family was dead, she told them. The women gave her a new Bible, with her wedding day inscribed inside, and later Deirdre pressed the

white petals between its pages for a keepsake. She and Daniel lived
in an attic room high above the harbour, all through July and August,
and she was happy. But that was back when she was a foolish child and
believed in Daniel Mac Michael the way Mrs Heintz's stupid children
believed in St Nicholas.

There. She had spoiled it again. The scenes all vanished. She could
enjoy them only so long as she could forget what happened after. That
Daniel insisted on going home to see his people one more time, though
she begged him not to, saying she feared he would miss the sailing they
had booked. She could not tell him her true fear, that he would learn
what she had done. Anxiously, she waited for his return, praying his
innocent faith in her would not be broken by some loose remark he
overheard in town. Then came the horrid news of the explosion and
Mab's letter, telling of Daniel's injured leg, asking Deirdre to come for
him. But Deirdre dared not answer the letter. Instead, she waited for
him to recover and return to her. She waited while their ship sailed
without them, and his child began to move inside her. But he did not
come. One day she saw a couple from Galway coming down the street,
and she turned away quickly before they could recognize her. After
that she began to wear her shawl loosely over her head, hoping to
conceal her face, as she ran her errands. Oh, and when Mab wrote once
again, begging Deirdre to come home to Galway, saying that Daniel
would never be whole again, that his leg had been severed from his
body! Deirdre had wept for days. Whatever had Daniel done for God
to punish him like that? Deirdre did not know, but it must have been
very terrible. She had placed her hands on her belly and thought of
the future. If she stayed too long in Queenstown, she felt sure she'd be
caught and returned to Galway, and most likely thrown into prison.
And the child deserved a whole father, a strong, healthy father. A man
who could work.

That winter, she answered an ad placed in the *Irish Times* by Tomas
Garrison of New York: "Wanted to meet: Irish girl for housekeeping
or matrimony," and received his reply. In spring, baby Frank was born
and baptized, and Deirdre boarded the *Celtic* with him, leaving behind
the Bible, with its flattened petals, at Doyle House. She showed Tomas
Garrison her marriage papers, to prove the baby was not a bastard, and
he agreed to accept the boy as his own. Her only lie was that Daniel Mac
Michael was dead. He might as well be, though, for all the good he had

ever done her. She had given him a drowning death, lost at sea, and who knew but that might be true by now, and she had put into the story that Daniel was only just come from church when he drowned, very sudden-like, after doing penance, so that he had gone straight to heaven.

Soon after Deirdre and baby Frank passed the health inspections at Ellis Island, Tomas Garrison arrived to escort them to the third-floor walk-up where his sister lived in Williamsburg. Every immigrant woman needed an escort from Ellis Island before she was let go, and some had to make do with a nun or a social worker from the Benevolent Society, but Deirdre was proud to have handsome Tomas Garrison come for her in a clean white shirt with an umbrella to protect her face from the sun and a pink corsage for her to pin on her dress. Tomas's sister, Lucy Keogh, was Deirdre's age, twenty-one, and already the mother of two sons, with a third child very soon on the way. Her husband, John Keogh, was at a sanatorium for tuberculosis, so Lucy, lonely and in need of help, was happy to welcome Deirdre into her crowded apartment and eager to show her the ways of the modern world. Lucy took her to a seamstress to have her hems raised and to a beauty shop to have her hair bobbed, and four weeks later, Lucy held the baby while Deirdre married Tomas at Sacred Heart of Jesus in Manhattan. They had the baby baptized in the same church. Deirdre was the only one who knew he was already baptized. She didn't mention it, not even to the priest, because she wanted the American certificate — and surely it couldn't hurt a child to be doubly baptized, why, it was probably good luck. Then Deirdre and Tomas moved into this fourth-floor suite, upstairs from Lucy, with its nesting mice and peeling walls and splintery kitchen floor, and the sickly smells of beer and sugar and the neighbours.

Williamsburg was nearly as crowded as Ellis Island, all sorts of immigrants shoved in together with their funny clothes and strange foods. How shameless they were, speaking their languages openly in the streets. Over at St Mary's Queen of Angels on Roebling, they even confessed and said their prayers in Polish. Jesus Christ Himself didn't know what they were saying. And then there were the Jews. Deirdre had never met a Jew before. Tomas said the Jews were learned people and he wouldn't hear any talk against them in his house. He said New York was a place where everyone should be equal and get along, and Deirdre supposed that was true. But her new sister-in-law, Lucy, warned her to watch out when she went shopping because the Jews would overcharge her, they would lean on the scale when they weighed the meat and keep back the choicest cuts for their own people. Mrs Heintz down the street said the Jews made the best bread and the best pickles and their smoked meat was the best as well, and people should show them more respect, but Mrs Heintz was German. Deirdre could barely understand what she was saying, through all the spit and gargle, and she did not trust her. You never heard that kind of talk in Ireland. To be sure, the learned priests spoke Latin, but everyone else spoke the normal English language. Except some backward folks, like Daniel Mac Michael's family, who still had the Irish.

Deirdre reminded herself to look out the window over the front sidewalk where she had left Daniel Mac Michael's son in his pram. She leaned out over the sill and looked down and listened. She heard no crying. He must be sleeping. She was glad the sun had dropped in the sky and the pram was now in the shadow of the building. Perhaps he would sleep until Tomas came home. She went to the icebox and looked at the quarter pound of beef the Jewish butcher cut for her yesterday morning. Was it truly a quarter pound? At least the soup bone was decent, with a fatty bit of meat on it. He had not cheated her on that.

Deirdre settled herself into a chair before the window in her favourite spot in the apartment, a small alcove off the parlour, where she liked to sit after dark. The alcove looked out on the tenement next door, and she liked to watch the lighted windows and the people moving within the frames. The alcove felt separate from the rest of the suite, and sometimes she imagined she was living there all alone. That the alcove belonged only to her.

Deirdre knew only one woman who lived alone, the seamstress she'd met when Lucy first took her shopping. The seamstress was a single woman who made a living very nicely out of her own home, a small first-floor apartment on Vernon Street, with a card propped up in the window, advertising "Alterations and Dress-making." Deirdre returned several times to visit this woman, for buttons and trimmings, and the two struck up a friendship. When Deirdre asked about the sewing machine, the seamstress let her sit down and sew a seam across a scrap of cambric. If Deirdre was serious, she said, she'd teach her to sew. Deirdre readily agreed to pay a small fee, and for weeks now she'd been taking the baby there and practising her sewing.

She wanted a sewing machine of her own. She had money left from the sale of Galen's farm, which she had changed, little by little, into American dollars that she now kept hidden in a tin of soap flakes in the nursery closet. Enough to purchase a fleet of sewing machines and pay for delivery. But of course she could never explain to Tomas where she had gotten the money. Instead, she planned to take in piecework and save the earnings. Once Frank started school, she could buy a machine and start her own business.

Where was the baby? Someone had knocked on the door and made Deirdre jump to her feet. She had fallen asleep in her chair, despite the heat, and woke disoriented. Where was Frank? For a long, confused minute, she could not think, and then she remembered he was out in front of the building in his carriage. She rose and walked through the apartment toward the door, but before she could reach it, Tomas's sister, Lucy Keogh, came inside and sank into a chair.

Lucy's face was more flushed, if possible, than yesterday. Her legs and ankles more swollen. Her boys, who had trailed in behind her, tried to crawl into her lap, but she had no lap. They hugged her knees. Davey was two and Paul was almost two, and they both looked scared.

"Are you all right?" Deirdre asked.

"I have to sit," panted Lucy. She had lately been too short of breath to lift the washtub or mop the floor, so Deirdre often ran errands for her and saw to her chores.

"Come here, boys," said Deirdre. "Let your mother alone, now." Lucy's boys were used to obeying Deirdre. When Lucy was tired, Tomas often brought them upstairs when he came home from work. Then he would fall asleep in his chair, leaving all three children for Deirdre to mind.

"You rest," Deirdre told Lucy. "I'll run down and get Frank. I put him to sleep in the shade, it was so hot up here."

Lucy only groaned.

Deirdre ran down the stairs as fast as she could, calculating. If Lucy was not able to get her own dinner tonight, Deirdre would have to make do with the quarter pound of beef to feed them all. Perhaps she could cut it into small pieces and make a hash. She would add more potatoes and find an onion somewhere, such a nuisance.

Frank was awake in his carriage, lying on his back with his toes in his fists, gazing at the sky and cooing to himself. When he saw her, his face crinkled into a big smile. He chuckled and held up his arms to be lifted. He was so sweet and helpless he filled her with terror. Since she'd been forced to leave Daniel, she knew how hard it hurt to lose someone she loved. She never wanted to feel that way again. She picked Frank up. He was easy now, but in a few months he would be crawling and then pulling himself up to walk and run and then there would be no respite from worry.

Tomas wanted another baby. Although they were raising Frank as Tomas's natural son, and only a handful of people knew otherwise, Tomas still wanted a son of his own. Deirdre would not mind so much if she could have a girl. A girl might be nice. But there was no way to be sure what you might get, so she paid attention to her body and gave herself up to Tomas only when she knew it would do no harm. She wanted no more children.

By the time Deirdre hauled the carriage inside the building and carried Frank upstairs, Lucy was on the floor. She lay on her side, in agony, arms wrapped around her distended belly. Tears rolled down her face, and her boys were crying in fear. As soon as Frank heard them, he began to cry too. Deirdre put him on the sofa and then, afraid he'd roll off, placed him in his basket on the floor. She dropped to her knees beside Lucy. "Is it the baby? Is the baby coming?"

"I don't know," Lucy cried. "I don't know-oh-oh."

Deirdre placed her hand on Lucy's hot forehead and said, "I'm going to fetch a doctor for you or a nurse." Lucy's face stretched in a long grimace. Her dress was rutched up and her apron askew, and her naked belly burst out, roiling like a storm at sea. Deirdre remembered a terrible case Mrs Heintz once described, a breech birth with the stuck baby suffocating inside. Mrs Heintz! Yes! Mrs Heintz had worked for a midwife in Germany. Promising Lucy she'd return right away, Deirdre put on her hat.

"Watch the baby," she said sternly to Lucy's two-year-old.

She hurried across the street to Mrs Heintz's house, praying that she was still at home, and indeed, where else would she be, just before the dinner hour, with five children of her own?

Mrs Heintz came to the door drying her hands on her apron and asked Deirdre, "Vat is the trouble, my girl?" When Deirdre explained,

Mrs Heintz became efficient. She asked her husband to fetch her bag and set off straight away, after Deirdre.

Somehow, Mrs Heintz undressed Lucy and moved her onto Tomas and Deirdre's bed, while Deirdre bundled the children into the nursery, jamming the door closed with a chair. She could hear them all crying in there, as she went into the kitchen. Mrs Heintz had told her to boil water, so she could wash her instruments, but before Deirdre could even light the stove, Mrs Heintz was calling her back into the bedroom. Deirdre arrived to see the baby's head surge forth from between Lucy's thighs. Then the whole red body, as though propelled from within, slithered out at once and Mrs Heintz caught it with her bare hands. It was a boy.

Deirdre stood with her back against the bedroom wall and stared at the child who'd emerged from the gap in Lucy's body. Though she'd given birth herself, she had known only the great waves of pain, had never imagined such a sight. Never before had she witnessed anything so frightening. She did not know a word for it. It made her think of Lucy as an animal, and her own body — she screwed her eyes closed to rid her mind of it.

While Mrs Heintz bathed Lucy, Deirdre wrapped up the new baby and walked up and down the apartment with him. She was high with relief. She had done the right thing. Lucy was alive and the baby was alive. Davey and Paul and Frank, who had been quiet a while, began to cry again, louder and louder, so she knew they were all right, too. They must be very hungry.

She tiptoed into the bedroom, where Mrs Heintz was washing her hands in a basin of water. Lucy was snoring softly.

"How is he?" asked Mrs Heintz.

"He seems just fine," said Deirdre. She felt a rush of warmth for Mrs Heintz, though she'd never liked the woman before. "Thank you ever so much."

Mrs Heintz twisted her lips in a peculiar way. "You should have told me."

"What do you mean?"

Mrs Heintz jerked her head toward the pillow case beside Lucy's head, and Deirdre saw blood there, blood and spittle. Streaks of blood in the drool escaping Lucy's open mouth.

"What is it?" Deirdre asked.

"It's the T.B., girl," said Mrs Heintz. "If you're going to ask people into a house with the T.B., you should let them know."

"But I didn't —"

Her voice was drowned out as the howls of the hungry children rose in volume. The new baby joined in, and four little boys, all wailing, outnumbered the women in the apartment.

2.2

AS HER PLANE DESCENDS TOWARD THE GOLD AND SILVER TOWERS of New York, Von sees a flock of coloured kites above Battery Park, and the white tourist ferries sailing between Ellis Island and the Statue of Liberty. Deirdre used to take the girls for outings on those ferries. You couldn't visit Ellis Island back then. Ellis Island was a deserted wreck. But you could go to the statue and take the elevator inside her and look out over the city and the harbour. The summer she was twelve, Von decided to climb the 354 stairs all by herself. Halfway up, dizzy and tired, she regretted her own ambition, but she refused to give up. She made it to the top. Deirdre remarked she was certainly determined, just like her father, and it hadn't sounded like a compliment.

It's late afternoon by the time Von clears customs and immigration, collects her bags, and takes a cab to Williamsburg. In front of Rosheen's building, the peonies that were budding when Von left for Ireland have bloomed and are already shedding their petals. In the lobby, the bare bulb in the ceiling has burned out. But Von can see the papers bulging through the vents of Rosheen's mailbox. Mail that Von will need to deal with soon. She hauls her suitcase up half a flight and pauses as two tattooed teenage boys come barrelling down, all long legs and elbows, each scrambling to be first. One knocks her sideways into the wall as he leaps over the last few steps to the floor.

"Watch it!" she yells. "You nearly —" The front door bangs and they're gone. She waits, in case someone's chasing after them. But all she hears is a crying baby and a television laugh-track. As she climbs she hears rock music too. The Stones. "Paint It Black." Louder and louder until she reaches the fourth floor and puts her palm flat against Rosheen's door. She can feel the vibrations. Yes, the music is blaring from within. Who? She slips in her key and enters, reaches into the closet, and grabs the baseball bat kept leaning in the corner. Garrison-style security system. She sneaks down the hall.

Adrenalin surges through her when she sees a person standing at the desk by the window. Two drawers pulled out and empty. Papers strewn across the desktop and onto the rug.

"Hey!" She stands in the doorway, gripping the bat with both hands.

He looks up. He's young, twenty at most. A tall, skinny white kid with shaggy hair. Faded jeans and threadbare high-tops. An army-green backpack slung across one shoulder like a purse. Caught, he stares at Von with his mouth open. The song comes to an end, and for five long seconds the record continues to circle, the scratch of the needle amplified though the apartment. Von takes one step forward, brandishing the ball bat. The kid backs away. She raises the bat above her head, and he runs — through the kitchen and onto the fire escape. She follows and watches him clatter down the metal ladder. He's slow, his worn sneakers slippery on the rungs. She could probably run down the stairs inside the building and catch him out on the street, but then what would she do with him? He hangs by his hands from the last metal rung, twelve feet above the ground. Swings back and forth to gain momentum, thrusts his bony body forward and lets go. Lands on his feet. Looks up once and sees her and tears off down the sidewalk.

No point calling the cops. He hasn't stolen anything of value. Nothing of value to steal. She lifts the needle from the record. Inhales the silence and tries to quiet her accelerated heart.

Later, she inspects the apartment. She knows the desk held no credit cards or cash, just some of Rosheen's letters, now dumped on the floor. Nothing else has been disturbed. The back bedroom's a mess, but it's always been a mess. The kid had nothing to do with that. She examines the kitchen door and finds a small pane of glass missing, above the deadbolt. So, he came in from the fire escape. Must be more athletic than he looks, to have reached the ladder, so high off the ground. Or he lives in the building and got onto the fire escape from his own suite. She'll keep her eyes open for him. Maybe he knew Rosheen. One of her neighbours, looting the place for any drugs she might have left behind. Sorry, buddy. She ate them all. She drank and smoked and sucked them into the vacuum of her little body until they ripped her apart, blasted her to ash.

She tacks a piece of cardboard across the broken window. But all evening, she's haunted by the feeling she's missed something important. Or maybe it's jet lag. She sleeps for a couple of hours, then wakes suddenly from a dream of lightning and glass. Bobby's hands reaching for her. Rain beating on the greenhouse. Fragments that recede, disintegrate. She's sitting up, eyes open in the darkness. Sirens in the street below. In the heavy, humid air of the apartment she can't get back to sleep. She rises and carries her notebook to the kitchen table. A thin breeze, laced with the tang of the East River, twists in through the open window.

From here, she can see the roof of the school her father attended. She can see the sugar factory, its brick walls bleached in the glow of security floodlights. Tomas Garrison spent most of his life there, refining the raw sugar that came in barrels on the long boats from the south. Never knowing his wife was still married to another man. Von sits down and writes, filling the last few pages of the notebook with the facts she learned in Cobh. When she reaches the end, the story feels unfinished, and she realizes what is missing: someone to tell. She's recording all this history for no reason, for nobody.

In the morning, she stands in the doorway to the back bedroom, staring in. This is the worst room, the one she should tackle first. The wall-to-ceiling shelves Rosheen installed are laden with her craft supplies and hoard of family relics, keepsakes from every decade of the century spilling out of tins and boxes, waiting to be sorted. Von longs to be back in Canada, among the roses in their orderly, fragrant rows. But she can't go home until she cleans out this apartment and puts it up for sale.

When their father died, Von and Rosheen had tacitly agreed to a truce. Frank, for once in his life, had made things easy for his daughters. His will forbade them to hold a funeral service. He donated his body to the medical school. He left a generous, well-deserved gift of cash to Manuel and Yvette Lajoie, his loyal, long-term employees, and he left the St Boniface property and greenhouse business to Von and Rosheen, in equal shares. Then, as now, Von lived in the house and ran the business. She had always sent Rosheen an allowance, even when she wasn't speaking to her, but now the arrangement was more formal. They were co-owners. Together, they calculated a fair salary for Von and agreed to split the remaining profits half and half. Then they went through the things that their father, and their mother before him, had left behind. Von wanted to throw away everything that wasn't strictly useful, while Rosheen didn't want to throw away anything at all. They argued, and in the end Von told Rosheen to keep whatever the hell she wanted, as long as she took it back to New York. So Von was spared the sight of it all.

Until now.

So far, she's looked into one shoebox. Lying inside, like a doll in a crib, is a foot-long Jesus, nailed to the cross and bleeding. Von recognizes this monstrosity. It used to hang on Deirdre's wall. Rosheen must have taken it down, and no wonder, after Deirdre passed away. The box also holds a thimble, a Braille wristwatch, and a plastic cup. The cup is pink with two handles, made for a toddler. The two dancing bunnies on the side have faded to a brown smudge, but Von remembers them. She remembers filling the cup with water in the evening and leaving it on her sister's bedside table, so she wouldn't have to walk through the house at night to get a drink. The house at night. The crash of overturned furniture or breaking glass. Noises that could stop your heart. She replaces the lid of the shoebox and returns to the kitchen where she makes a cup of tea and forgets to drink it. How long will it take to sort through so much stuff? This is the punishment reserved for those who survive: the stuff.

She forces herself to begin with the stack of scrapbooks on the back bedroom floor. Rosheen had kept scrapbooks since she was big enough to glue two things together. Not the kind of scrapbooks kept by neat and tidy girls. No pink lace or cute captions. Just a mishmash of drawings, photographs, and clippings. The first few books are full of fashion models torn from Eaton's catalogues. Von chucks these in a box she labels "garbage." But the next scrapbook gives her pause. Each page is an odd collage of characters cut out of different comic books and mixed together. Cute cartoon animals cavort among slimy monsters and teary-eyed romance heroines. Superman flies through a jungle with Hamlet tucked under his arm. Von wants to laugh. Then she remembers it was Bobby who supplied most of the comic books.

Siobhán didn't know Bobby's name back then. He was only the paperboy, coming to collect on their overdue bill. It was late May. Siobhán was almost twelve. She was reading in the old greenhouse and didn't see him when he first arrived. She lay on a tarp under a long table of seedlings, engrossed in *Jane Eyre*. Hiding from her parents.

The jingle of the bicycle bell made her look out and see him. Blond and sturdy. Her own age, but very tall. Riding a red racer, with a wooden crate tied to the rat-trap over the rear wheel. He propped up the bike with the kickstand and ran to the porch, where he spoke to Mrs Garrison through the screen. While he waited for her to locate her purse, Róisín came out and began to poke around in the crate on his bike.

"Róisín!" called Siobhán. "Leave that alone." She stepped out of the greenhouse.

"He said I could look," said Róisín. "See? Comics!" She plunked a bundle onto the lawn.

Siobhán tried to gather them up, but they slipped out of her hands. She was crouched in the grass when the boy came back to help her. "Sorry," she said. "My sister." She looked up. Saw the afternoon sun intense behind his head. She raised a hand to her forehead to shield her eyes.

"It's all right. I told her to take a look. I'm finished with them." He had a broad smile and an open, friendly face. "Hey, you go to Provencher School."

"Yes." She watched him as he put his collection book away. He had slate-blue eyes and tanned skin. A band of paler skin ran above his collar and below his short sleeves, as if he were rapidly growing out of his shirt. His blond hair was wavy and too long. She liked it.

"I've seen you in the yard. You always take a book and sit in the sugar shack by the rink and read at lunchtime. I'm Bobby Sullivan," he said. "You're Suh-von."

"Shu-von," she said. "You could just call me Von. This is Róisín."

"She's like you," said Bobby. Róisín was lying on her tummy in the grass, looking at *The Fantastic Four*. "She likes to read."

"She can't read yet," Siobhán said. "She's seven, but she still can't read or write. She likes to cut out the pictures. She loves pictures. She draws her own pictures everywhere." Ruefully, she showed him the flyleaf of *Jane Eyre*, decorated with Róisín's planets and rocket ships.

"Well, she can take whatever she likes. I was only going to give these away to the hospital book sale." He took the rest of the comics out and set them before Róisín. "Are you going to the fireworks this weekend?" he asked Siobhán. "There's going to be a rock band."

Siobhán shook her head. "I have to help my mum." It was Victoria Day weekend, when most homeowners planted their gardens. The Garrisons would be working long hours.

"I could bring some more comics for your sister," Bobby said. "Next week?"

"No, that's all right. She'll just scribble all over them and chop them to pieces."

"I could bring her some paper to draw on. There's lots of leftover newsprint at the press."

Siobhán studied his face. He maintained a serious expression, but she saw his lips twitch. "Maybe you should," she said. "Wednesday after school?" Her father would be at work.

"Wednesday," he said. He grinned outright and rode away. Róisín was engrossed in the comic books, but Siobhán watched Bobby until he vanished into the orchard.

———

By noon, Von has filled four "garbage" boxes with old scrapbooks and things too worn or broken to be any use. She has filled two "charity" boxes with things to give away, and she's placed a very few items in a box marked "to keep." She can't give away her father's silver cigarette case, engraved with the inscription *Baker Hall* (he never smoked, but used to keep his cufflinks in it). Or his *Collected Poems of WB Yeats*. How many times did she read to him from this? *I have met them at close of day…* This job is going to take longer than she expected.

Late in the afternoon, she phones Alex Hart at the gallery. He sounds stronger now. He's energetic, wants Von to come over right away. He received her postcards from Ireland and says he's dying to hear about her trip. Alex, she remembers, had helped Rosheen with this project. He'd been more involved, and more encouraging, than Von ever was.

Alex had always been kind to Rosheen. Years ago, when she needed a lawyer, he set her up with his cousin Carol. When she needed a job, he let her work at his gallery. When she wanted a darkroom, he lent her the use of his own. He even included her in his social life. Von's not sure why a circle of hip New York artists had befriended Rosheen. Maybe artists accepted difference more readily than most. Maybe her disfigured face didn't shock them as it shocked conventional people.

———

When Von arrives at the Northside Gallery, a stranger is standing in the doorway, blocking the entrance. He's talking to someone inside while he leans against the door, his hand on the push bar, preparing to leave. All she can see is the hand and the wide shoulders under a white shirt, and the back of his blond head, golden blond, like Bobby's hair. But she doesn't want to notice that. She raps on the glass and he turns. His eyes light up, as if he recognizes her, and he steps back, opens the door wide.

"Welcome," he says. "Come on in." He gives her a smile she hasn't seen for a while, open male appreciation for her presence. She looks away. Where is Alex?

"Von! Come in!" Alex strides toward her, dark and intense. He kisses her on both cheeks and starts in right away with questions. Von is aware of a lot of young people working at the back of the gallery. They seem to be speaking a foreign language. Swedish? They're moving furniture and hammering. But Alex demands her full attention. "So?" He holds out his hand. "Photographs?"

Von gives him the still shots she's had printed. She tells him she's glad she went to Ireland, that she learned a lot. As she tells the story of Deirdre's youth, Alex listens with great interest, laying the photographs out on his desk — the rushing Corrib River, the Spanish Arch, Heartbreak Pier.

One by one, the young people at the back stop their work and gather around, listening. The blond man at the door, who had seemed to be leaving, hasn't left. He listens too, and when Von concludes the tale, he speaks.

"Alex," he says. "Who's your friend?"

"Ah, sorry," says Alex. "Von, I want you to meet Leif Jonasson, painter. Leif, Von Garrison."

"Pleased to meet you," says Leif. He has a slight accent and spirited blue eyes. He offers her his right hand, and to be polite she shakes it. As soon as she feels the strong current that flows from his hand to hers, she looks up. Their eyes meet, and she's flooded with warmth. She can't look at him. Can't. She looks at his clothing. A clean white T-shirt and jeans, spattered with blue and white paint. Leather sandals. Long fingers. No rings. Clean hands except for something white — paint? — lodged in the cuticle of the thumb.

"Leif's here with the Icelandic kids," Alex says. He gestures toward the young workers. "They're art history students here on exchange from — where?"

"Reykjavik," says Leif.

"They're helping me set up for the party tomorrow," Alex says. "It's the gallery's twentieth anniversary." He hands Von an invitation, then turns his attention back to her photographs. "This is a great shot." He holds up a view of St Coleman's Cathedral. "We can use this."

Just then a woman enters the gallery, and the students call out, "Hi, Ingrid!"

Ingrid is wearing white overalls. Her white hair curls almost to her waist. She's lugging a tall coffee percolator, and one of the students rushes to carry it for her.

"Von, this is Professor Ingrid Silver," says Alex. "Ingrid, this is Von Garrison —"

"Rosheen's sister!" Ingrid moves forward and sends Von off balance with an unexpected hug. "Oh, my dear, your sister was one of my all-time favourite people!"

"You were…friends?"

"I first met her when I saw her show here, five years ago. I was blown away by her collage technique, so I asked Alex to introduce us. Now I teach her work in my Contemporary Art course. These kids are taking it." She nods toward the Icelandic exchange students. "It would be great if you could talk to them about Rosheen. Give them some context."

Von looks at the students, who are conferring with Leif about where to set up the bar for tomorrow night. They're studying Rosheen's collages? Was that a joke?

"I miss Rosheen," Ingrid continues. "Not just for her creative work, but for her gorgeous smile. Her fabulous dinners. Her spaghetti Genovese!"

"Rosheen *cooked* for you?" asks Von. But the students have summoned Ingrid to ask her advice, and then Leif comes over to say he must leave now but hopes to see Von tomorrow.

"It'll be a great party." He has to duck slightly to catch her eye. "You should come."

He smiles broadly, and she can't help smiling back. For weeks, grief has numbed her. Now she feels warmth welling in her chest, a thin spurt of light.

Before she leaves the gallery, Alex speaks to her at length about his plans for exhibiting Rosheen's project. But Von doesn't see the point.

"It's been good of you to give your time for this project," she says, "and extremely generous to offer to display her work, but why? I mean, why do it now, without her?"

Alex stops talking and studies Von's face. "Look, this isn't some favour I was doing for your sister. This is a real show. A four-week, one-woman show, already advertised and funded." He hands her a card from a stack on his desk.

Róisín Dubh: The Afterlight
Northside Gallery, October 1–28, 1999

She backs away from Alex. "But Rosheen never finished the project."

"That's why we're turning the focus onto her process. Didn't you read the notes I sent?"

Von's head begins to ache. "I haven't checked the mail."

"Ingrid and I are rewriting the catalogue copy. We're adding Rosheen's drafts and raw materials, trying to give a sense of how she worked. We'll need her scrapbooks, too, from the apartment. Have you found her war book?"

"War book?" The headache branches out, sends tendrils winding down her spine.

"Yellow scrapbook. Spiral binding." With his hands, he frames a large square. We need the pieces she was working on in Amsterdam, too. As soon as possible."

"Listen, Alex." Von slings her purse over her shoulder. "This project of Rosheen's was a family thing. Private. Not public. In Holland, she was looking into what happened to our father over there. I mean, it's all very personal."

"Great!" he says. "That part should be at the very centre of the show."

The following evening, when Von arrives late for Northside Gallery's anniversary celebration, the party is still going strong. Bodies are packed closely into the small space around the makeshift bar. Laughter, argument, and exclamations bounce off the ceiling.

Ingrid spots her instantly. "Come, come! My students want to meet you." She leads Von past the bar, scooping up two glasses of white wine. She presses one into Von's hand and steers her toward a crowd of young people. "Everyone," she says, "this is Von Garrison."

"Rosheen's sister!" cries a petite young woman in a silver dress.

A bearded young man steps forward. "You're the writer!"

"I'm not a writer," says Von. "I run a greenhouse. In Canada."

Ingrid frowns. "But Rosheen said her sister was always writing stories."

"Oh," says Von. "When I was a kid."

"How great to meet you," says the woman in the silver dress. "Rosheen is, like, a hero to me." She's holding hands with an even tinier woman, in a coppery dress. They both wear metallic necklaces, earrings, and bracelets.

"I'm writing a paper about her work," says the tinier woman. "The theme of self-image."

Von sips the wine. Cheap and warm, medicinal.

The two metallic students have brought their own bottle of wine, which they're passing back and forth, too quickly, between them.

Von scans the room. Once. Twice. Then she sees him. Leif, the Icelander. He is standing at the edge of the crowd, listening. Alex is listening too.

"If there's anything you want to ask," Ingrid tells the students, "this is your chance."

The students crowd closer. The one in the copper dress has a lot of theoretical questions. She describes a collage Rosheen made of her own self-portraits, torn and glued crookedly back together, and asks Von if she thinks it's a feminist statement on beauty, or a sign of the disintegrating personality in the modern world. Von says she hasn't seen that piece. The student reads out loud from her notes, a paragragh dense with jargon, and gets weepy. Her girlfriend puts her arms around her. They find Rosheen romantic. Tragic damage.

The other students seem fascinated too, though more sober. They ask about her early years. Where did she grow up? Von describes the tall white house in St Boniface, the greenhouse. The attic where Rosheen spread rolls of newsprint on the floor for her endless drawings. Did she make pictures when she was a kid? Yes. With what? Scissors, of course. Also crayons and coloured pencils, and later watercolours. What college did she attend? She didn't.

"How did she — what happened to her face?" asks one of the boys.

"A childhood accident," says Von. The memory is swift and vivid. A soft thud. A whisper, like a broom sweeping the floor. The blood.

"Excuse me." She slips into the washroom and splashes water on her face. She looks in the mirror at her own grey eyes, her smooth skin, the fine shape of her lips. Not a mark on her.

––––––––

When she emerges from the washroom, she runs straight into Alex, who pulls her aside.

"I want to show you some of your sister's recent work," he says. "The more you know, the better you'll understand. Come into the storage room —"

"Not now, Alex." She peers over his shoulder, trying to see where Leif went.

"Take this at least." He presses a magazine on her, pointing out an article he's bookmarked: "Róisín Dubh: Translucent Memory."

Von steps aside. "Excuse me. I just — " She holds up her empty wine glass. Stuffing the magazine in her purse, she heads toward the bar. She can't stand, really can't stand, to think about Rosheen any more today. She waits in line, letting the chattering voices blend into incomprehensible sound waves. When it's her turn she plunks her glass down in front of the bartender. "White, please."

While he pours, she hears one distinct voice behind her. "Hello again." She turns to see Leif waiting in line.

"Oh, hi. I just — I came to get a drink," she says.

"A mystical coincidence," he says. "That's the very same reason I'm standing here."

"Amazing."

He orders Scotch, and when they both have their drinks in hand, he points toward the front of the gallery. "Not too crowded over there."

She follows him, and they stand together, looking out at the neon signs of Driggs Avenue and the people passing on the sidewalk. She catches Leif's eye, blinks, and looks away.

"I didn't know your sister," Leif says.

Von glances at him, then lowers her eyes. "That could be a point in your favour."

"I was hoping it might be."

They both face the window. They're silent, watching each other's reflections.

The door opens and a gang of students streams in, speaking Icelandic. They wave at Leif and hurry away to join the party.

"Ingrid sent three students from New York to Reykjavik in June," Leif says. "This is the thanks she gets. Seventeen Icelanders invading New York."

"And you're supervising them?"

He smiles. "When they let me."

"For how long?"

"Six weeks. Only two weeks left," he says. "The time's gone fast."

Von drinks. It feels good to drink, good to let go. Only two weeks? He really is astonishingly handsome. Makes her feel young again.

One of the girls comes running toward the door, breathless. "Leif! We're driving back to the hotel for the last set. Are you coming?"

"Ten minutes." To Von, he says, "There's a jazz band they want to hear at the hotel bar. They're tireless. Last night I took them to a Cuban club down the street. The night before it was R & B at the BAM, and now jazz."

"I like jazz," says Von.

"You do?" He smiles again. One of those slow male smiles she likes.

"I do."

"Do you want to come with us and hear some?"

"I do." Her cheeks ache from smiling. This is the first fun she's had in a very long time. She expected it would hurt, and it does.

The hotel where the Icelanders are staying is an old building, elegant, despite its shabby carpet. The lounge is quiet and dim. Low-wattage bulbs in the stand-up lamps. Fringed lampshades with fabric baubles at the ends of the fringes. A waiter moves silently among the scattered customers, dropping brandy and sherry glasses on the tables. Everyone seems drowsy, as if the hotel guests have all just gotten out of bed and come down for a midnight snack.

The band is playing old-fashioned jazz, the kind she used to listen to in the Assiniboine Hotel back home, the kind her parents listened to. The eight art students who have come are fading fast. The boys each have a beer, and the girls order desserts and coffee. Then they fold, one by one, say good night, and head up to their hotel rooms.

The band plays "Bye Bye Blackbird," and Leif asks her to dance. His moves are smooth and American. He holds her firmly, swings her around as if he's in a Hollywood movie, and it's fun. The other customers watch, sleepy-eyed and smiling. She forgets how many years it's been since she enjoyed dancing. Bobby's hands always so loose and light on her body, trusting her to follow. The band plays "Skylark" and "Unforgettable." Von leans her forehead against Leif's shoulder, closes her eyes. Lets herself be ever so slightly off balance and needing him. Then the band plays "Haunted Heart," and it's over. They're packing up their instruments.

At the table, Von fans herself with a coaster and says, "Time to go home."

"Where's home?"

"I can take a cab." She smiles to let him know she doesn't mean it.

"Seriously, where do you live?"

"North First. It's only ten blocks."

"I'll walk you," he says.

He walks quickly, and she likes that. She's a walker, comes from a family of walkers. She asks him about Iceland, and he tells her stories about his childhood, his pet dog, his mother's cooking, his love of playing ice hockey. He tells her nothing of his present life.

When they reach her apartment block, he climbs to the fourth floor with her. "Good night, then." He takes her hands in his. He bends and kisses her lightly on the forehead and then on the lips. Then he releases her and takes two steps backward.

"Can I see you again?" he asks.

"Of course."

She slips into the apartment and keeps smiling at him as she closes the door. It's been ages since she's been so powerfully drawn to a man. She's had a few brief affairs over the years, usually while out of town at business conventions. But not with anyone as attractive as Leif.

In the kitchen, she pours a glass of water and opens the window, leans out to watch him exit the building. But when he comes out he doesn't head back the way they came, toward the hotel. Instead he crosses North First and walks toward Driggs and the gallery, as if he thinks the party is still going on. Maybe it is. But Von is tired. She's had enough. She knows if she went with him…actually, he didn't ask her to go with him. But she likes that he's still going strong, after she's played out. She brushes her teeth and takes off her clothes, climbs under the covers of the bed and falls asleep, the songs of the night still playing in her dreams.

2.3

TOMAS'S SISTER, LUCY, DID HAVE TUBERCULOSIS, JUST AS MRS Heintz suspected. After her third son was born, she spent most of every day sleeping. Her husband, Johnny, was still in the sanatorium, and until he recovered, Johnny's brother, Mark, was paying her rent. Tomas and Deirdre helped with her other expenses. Deirdre took in piecework from a garment factory, earning a few cents per basket for hand-stitching pockets onto vests and cuffs onto sleeves, but with four small boys to mind, she didn't accomplish much. She planned to set up shop in the alcove as soon as Johnny came home to look after his family.

But Johnny never came home. He died when his youngest, John Junior, was only three. The church service was a quick, bleak affair, with Tomas and Mark doing arithmetic on the back of the funeral bulletin, calculating the life insurance and subtracting the debts.

Rain fell all through the prayers at the cemetery, and after the body was laid in the ground, the mourners came to Deirdre's apartment in their wet clothing to eat her apple cake and drink her coffee. Tomas and Mark stood in the hallway, sharing a tin flask of whisky. They greeted each visitor, tipping their hats to the ladies and offering the gentlemen a slug. The men all swallowed and grimaced and said "Poor Johnny." Then Mark and Tomas paced the hall, hands in their pockets and bowed heads close together, talking.

After the guests went home, Tomas and Mark looked over the figures, while Lucy lay on the parlour sofa, crying. The doctor had said she was not ill enough to need the sanatorium. "But as you can see," said Mark, "she's too weak to work." He said he could no longer pay her rent, now that Johnny was gone. He could not pay her rent for the rest of her life.

Deirdre, washing the teacups, listened to the men discuss Lucy's future. In dull disbelief, she heard Tomas agree that Lucy must move in with him and Deirdre. The alcove off the parlour would be given to Lucy and John Junior. Tomas and Mark would carry Lucy's bed and her things upstairs at the end of the month. Her other boys, Davey and Paul, would move into the nursery with Frank. Tomas almost seemed pleased with these outrageous plans.

That evening, Deirdre could not bring herself to speak to her husband. There was little chance for him to notice this, however, with the two older boys getting into the coal bin and the two younger ones crying for more milk. Later, when Tomas sat in the kitchen reading the newspaper, Deirdre carried a chair into the alcove and sat by herself, looking out the window at the building across the street, where a foolish neighbour had hung up her wash that morning, heedless of the clouds. Rain had been falling steadily all afternoon, and the sodden work clothes hung so low the pant cuffs and shirttails trailed in the dirt.

Now there would be no sewing room. No sewing machine and no time to sew. Lucy's bed would fill the alcove and her children would fill the apartment, and there would be nowhere, nowhere at all, for Deirdre to be alone.

Tomas called her name very sweetly and asked her would she make a pot of tea. She thought perhaps he had noticed her mood and was trying to say he was sorry. This did not move her. She stood at the stove with her back to him, watching the kettle. He turned the pages of his paper, making small murmurs of surprise, intended to catch her attention, but she was silent. When the water boiled, and she passed behind him to fetch the teacups, she could feel, coiled tightly inside her muscles, the urge to dash the entire shelf of china to pieces on the floor.

If the boys were not chasing each other, one of them was upsetting the mop bucket or falling into the mop bucket or trying to eat a shoe button. Lucy slept late most days, until Deirdre scolded her to get up. Then Lucy shuffled into the kitchen and drank tea until the afternoon, when she had "a little lie-down" until Tomas came home. Tomas gave Deirdre six dollars every Saturday for the week's groceries. But no matter how thin she stretched the porridge or the strained apples, the children would eat it all and ask for more. They tore their clothes and spilled their soup. They peed their pants and peed their beds. They broke the kitchen clock and the mirror and John Junior's collarbone. And every so often, when Tomas was home in the evenings, and the boys were asleep, he would say wistfully that his only wish was to have a son of his own.

Once Lucy's older boys were both in school, the days were quieter. Still, Deirdre was busy with Frank and John Junior to watch, and Lucy to worry over. Sometimes she thought she'd go mad, stuck in the stuffy apartment. When she had errands to run, she took Frank with her, to give him some fresh air. Frank, at five, was a monkey. Some days he was calm and held her hand and chattered away to her. It was only boyish nonsense about candy or clouds shaped like sailing ships, but she enjoyed it. Other days, the devil got into him, and he would climb a construction scaffold or run into traffic to chase a fire engine, with no thought to what might happen. At those times Deirdre crossed herself and tried to deliver a spanking he would remember.

One afternoon, as they passed by a vacant lot, Deirdre saw two stray dogs locked in heat. Immediately, she turned her back on Frank and spread her coat open, to shield him from the evil sight. It took him less than a minute to disappear.

"Frank!" She turned in a circle, but could not see him.

"Mama!" His voice came from a place so high she thought she was imagining it. Shading her eyes from the sun, she raised her head higher and higher until she saw, at the top of a telephone pole, nearly touching the power lines, her only child. She nearly fainted.

"Frank Garrison, you get down from there, you hear me?"

"I'm in the sky!" he cried.

"Get down here this minute, you hear?"

He slid down a few feet, and Deirdre's stomach dropped. She could not look. She turned and pretended she was going to walk away, toward the store.

"Mama, wait!"

Hail Mary, full of grace. Do not let him fall.

"Mama, wait for me!"

His voice was closer now. She dared to look. He had descended to a foothold just above her head and was looking out over the field of weeds. His eyes were blue. She was startled to see his eyes so clear and blue. She realized she rarely saw him outside the dim apartment. In full sunlight, his eyes were lively as two blue flames.

He looked down at her and laughed, and she saw the irises of his eyes spark green. His father's eyes exactly. Daniel Mac Michael was inside of Frank, looking out at her.

"I was up in the sky," he told her.

"Come here," she said. She must stop him from taking these terrible risks.

When he jumped to the ground, she took hold of him and hugged him tightly so he could not get away while she spanked him as hard as she could.

———

John Keogh's insurance company paid out a small pension to his wife and three sons until the stock market crash and then promptly went out of business.

It was hard to manage without the insurance money. By this time, Lucy's boys were eating a great deal. Davey was twelve now, and Paul was eleven. Frank, at nine, was tall and broad-shouldered, and constantly asking for more to eat. John Junior was nearly nine, but small and sickly and always in need of medicine. As the years went by, the family sank deeper into poverty. Household items broke down and got lost. Things wore out. Deirdre gave Davey's clothes to Paul and Paul's clothes to Frank and Frank's, if their seams still held, to John Junior. In winter she stuffed the window cracks with cardboard, and when there was no coal she burned the cardboard and stuffed the cracks with rags. She still took in as much piecework as she could

61

handle, but the rates had dropped. She was earning less and often had to dip into her secret savings. Now that the boys were older, she had moved the money to a tobacco tin she hid under a loose board beneath her bed, and it was distressing how many times she found herself flat on her belly, wriggling through the dust toward that floor board, to take out another dollar. But the doctor kept prescribing new medicines for Junior, along with new diagnoses. Junior was said to have a cold, the grippe, the influenza, a lung infection, and the chronic bronchitis. Finally, the doctor arranged for Lucy to receive some financial relief from the government. This was a help, but now that Lucy was on relief, a government social worker came to visit once a month.

Lucy's social worker, a Mrs Gray, was nothing but a paid busybody, said Lucy. Imagine giving other women advice, when the only husband she could get for herself was a cripple.

"What's a cripple?" asked Frank. He was under the table, playing with a piece of coal. "Put that back in the coal bin!" said Deirdre. "A cripple is a person with broken legs."

"That's how God punishes bad people," said Lucy.

"Dirty little boys who don't do what their mother says," warned Deirdre.

Frank crawled out and put the coal in the bin. "Why?" he asked.

"Dirty little boys who ask too many questions," said Lucy.

"Wash your hands and face," said Deirdre. "You're filthy."

Mrs Gray was not a good mother either, Lucy said, as Frank splashed in the basin. She went out to work and left her only child, a girl named Nancy, with her husband. Nancy had been seen out in the rain, in a pair of trousers, her hair all knots and tangles. It was a scandal.

Mrs Gray herself wore a hat and matching gloves, which she never took off. She spoke with her lips pursed and never opened her mouth to smile. She liked to run a gloved finger across your furniture and then thrust her finger in your face to show you how dirty it was. She was hated by all the wives and mothers she visited. But the problem was that Mrs Gray had power. Everyone knew she'd sent Mrs Burke's son to the reform school and lost Mrs Leavey her widow's pension by reporting she'd never been legally married. It wasn't smart to cross Mrs Gray.

On her first visit, Mrs Gray called Frank to stand before her and examined his head for lice. She prodded his ribs and told Deirdre her son needed more nutrition. Then she gave Deirdre a long lecture. Deirdre must boil Lucy's bedding and pillow slips once a week. She must set aside special cutlery and a special plate and cup that were to belong only to Lucy. These items were to be placed on the sideboard ("we have no *sideboard*," said Deirdre, and Mrs Gray said, "the windowsill then"). They were to be properly covered with a clean tea towel and were not to be used by any other member of the family. Deirdre must toss the lot into a pan of boiling water, towel and all, every evening without fail. As if Deirdre had nothing else to do but wait on Lucy.

Mrs Gray told Deirdre how to make soup from a bone and how to darn socks. When she sensed Deirdre's impatience, she said, "I'm only giving you the benefit of my experience, dear. You are so very young."

Deirdre couldn't say Mrs Gray's soup tasted like dishwater and her notions of special spoons were nonsense. And she most certainly couldn't say she had taken care of seven children and a husband perfectly well at the age of sixteen without Mrs Gray's help. So she stayed quiet and endured the loss of her pride for the sake of the few dollars worth of relief every month.

Mornings, Deirdre fed her husband as much porridge as he could eat, and at noon she sent Frank to the factory with a hot pail of stew or baked beans for him. Frank always wanted to eat his own lunch before he went, but Deirdre explained that his father worked hard and deserved to eat first. He had to be kept strong. Sometimes, Frank got down on his knees and pleaded for a biscuit or a spoonful of honey before he left, but Deirdre forced herself to push him away. "Only tramps beg," she reminded him. "Have you no pride?"

She was afraid for Frank. He was headstrong and impulsive. He played hooky whenever he could. He chose poor companions, and it was up to Deirdre to correct him, explaining who he could and could not play with. The boy didn't understand how important it was, when you lived in a slum like this, to keep up your place, not to slip down any lower than you already were.

He had to repeat the third grade, and at the end of his second time around, the teacher suggested his parents take him out of school to learn a trade. But Tomas would not hear of it. Tomas himself had stayed in school through tenth grade. He knew geography and could make up a budget. When his neighbours had trouble with landlords or banks, he was proud to help, composing letters in his tidy writing. He kept a poetry book from his schooldays and sometimes read aloud to the family. Frank liked to hear the poems, but could not read them for himself.

Tomas believed the school's methods were to blame. The teachers were old-fashioned. "They should give the boy something that interests him," he said. "If it's something he wants to read, he will learn." He brought home a penny scribbler. After dinner, he opened the poetry book to Frank's favourite poem, "Sea Fever," and made him copy out the letters of the poem. The method was a success. While Deirdre scrubbed the pots and pans, and Tomas read his newspaper, Frank sat quietly at the kitchen table, applying his pencil, his tongue between his teeth as he laboured for an hour. Tomas caught Deirdre's eye and winked, and she smiled. Neither of them had ever seen the boy sit still so long. Tomas decided to reward him with a glass of milk. He placed the glass down beside his son and peered at the pages in the scribbler.

"What's this, then?"

"It's a tall ship," said Frank, "and a star." He turned the page back. "And this is the sea and the whale in it, and —"

"Frank, you are a naughty boy," said Deirdre, when she saw what he had done. The pages were covered in pictures, not letters. The first page bore the poem's title in ragged capitals, but underneath there was only a drawing — a rather good drawing — of a sailboat on a stormy sea. She flipped through, finding page after page of fanciful pictures. He had used up half the scribbler.

Tomas reminded Frank sternly the scribbler was for learning to write, and sent him to bed without the milk. After that, Tomas sat right beside Frank every evening and watched him copy verses from the book, correcting him when he made mistakes.

To prevent Frank from playing hooky, Tomas devised a system of giving Martha Waters a nickel every week to walk him to school and wait until she saw him go inside. Martha Waters was an oversized girl of fifteen who helped many of the mothers on the street. She came every weekday morning, pushing a carriage with two or three babies in it, to escort Frank to school. But it didn't improve his grades. Tomas said it was because he did not pay attention, and the teacher said it was likely due to the time he fell off the schoolyard flagpole onto his head. Secretly, Deirdre worried it was down to some flaw in the blood of Daniel Mac Michael. But whatever the cause, Frank was slow to learn to read.

Yet he was quick with his hands. He helped Mr Edison, the carpenter who lived across the hall, on jobs around town, and Mr Edison said he'd make a good carpenter someday. When he was only nine, Frank made Deirdre a little box out of wood he found at a work site and hardware he cadged, along with advice, from Mr Edison. He painted it white, and with a thin brush from the hardware store he made a design of blue flowers on the lid. Everyone said how lifelike the flowers were, and how beautiful. So Deirdre did not think he could really be stupid.

And she had to admit that the pictures in the scribbler were very pretty. Her favourite was a page with great floating clouds stacked high in an imaginary sky full of birds and kites and even an airplane. Part of her had wanted to cut it out and put it up on the wall, as a kind of decoration. But she was afraid that would only encourage him.

When she grew anxious about Frank's future, Deirdre often thought of Daniel Mac Michael. She reminded herself that Daniel must never find out about Frank or Tomas, and that they must never find out about him. When she thought back to the summer of 1920, in Queenstown, when she very nearly got exactly what she wanted, it seemed like a dream. The white daisies and the bed where Daniel Mac Michael touched her with his clean, sun-browned hands, her husband. What did God make of it all, she wondered. Did He consider Daniel to be her true husband, since he was Frank's father after all, and her life with Tomas a crime? Or did He consider Tomas her husband and her love of Daniel Mac Michael, seeing it was him she wanted, him who had given her pleasure, to be her sin? But most of the time her mind was occupied with boiled turnips and the price of shoes.

One spring morning Mrs Gray arrived with a clay pot of dirt under her arm. A limp stem and a cluster of wrinkled leaves stuck out of the top of it.

Deirdre was sewing, and would never have known the social worker was coming if Frank hadn't sounded the alarm. He was hanging out the window, trying to untangle a kite string that had snagged on the clothesline, when he saw her.

"Ma!" called Frank. His voice sounded distant and hollow from outside the building.

"What is it?" Deirdre called. "Junior, pull him in."

"I can't," said Junior. Frank was much bigger than Junior. Frank was even taller, now, than his older cousins, and the system of hand-me-down clothing was all mixed up.

"You kids." Deirdre got up and yanked her son by the hips.

He toppled in, landing on his back on the floor. "Mrs Gray," he said. "She's coming up."

"Hurry, then," Deirdre said. "Frank, you sweep the floor. Junior, fetch me a tea towel there from the stove." Quickly, she gathered a plate, cup, and spoon from the cupboard. She set them on the windowsill and tossed the towel over them.

Frank glanced at the covered dishes. Deirdre gave him a sharp look. He was eleven years old now, and she sometimes saw a grave expression in his eyes, almost as if he were judging her. "You'll keep quiet," she said, "if you know what's good for you."

Footsteps sounded in the hallway, then a brisk rap, and she entered. She never waited for Deirdre to answer the door. Today she was wearing a crisp yellow seersucker dress, with a yellow straw bag on her arm and a new yellow hat perched on her head, the colour of an Easter lily, and yellow gloves. She extended the pot of dirt toward Deirdre.

"It's a geranium," she said, in her peculiar, tight-lipped way. "When it blooms you'll have a lovely bouquet of red flowers to gladden your front room and give it a welcoming touch."

"Thank you," said Deirdre, accepting the pot of dirt. "May I offer you some tea?"

"Goodness," said Mrs Gray. "In this warm weather? No thank you." Then she smiled at the boys. "How is little Johnny today?"

John Junior stared at her, with his finger in his nose.

"Junior!" said Deirdre.

Junior removed his finger from his nose and put it into his mouth.

"He's getting better," said Deirdre. "He should be back to school in a few days."

Junior coughed, deep in his chest.

"Really? And how is Frankie?"

Frank looked up at Mrs Gray. In his hands he held a torn kite tail and the wad of tangled string. His shirt was dirty from where he'd lain across the windowsill.

"Be careful with that kite, Frankie," said Mrs Gray. "Last week a boy was playing on his roof with a kite and he ran right off the edge and fell four storeys into the street."

Frank's eyes lit up. "He was flying it from the roof?" Deirde saw that he had never thought of flying a kite from the roof. Mrs Gray had given him the idea.

But Junior was solemn, asking, "Did he die?"

"Indeed he did," said Mrs Gray. She walked to the windowsill, where Frank had been dangling a minute before, and lifted a corner of the tea towel. "I see you are remembering to keep the patient's dishes separate. That's very important."

Frank looked at his mother. "Ma, why did you cover the dishes?"

"Never mind," said Deirdre. "It's something we do for your Aunt Lucy. You run off to school, now." She set the clay pot on the stove and wiped his shirt with her handkerchief.

"Martha isn't here yet," said Frank. "Why did you —"

"Here," said Deirdre. She reached to the back of the stove, where she was keeping two biscuits and a boiled egg for Tomas. She plunked them into a bag and held the bag out for Frank.

Frank stood still, his mouth open, and did not take it.

"Go on," said Deirdre. "Take this for your lunch and you can stay and play ball with the other boys at noon." She smiled gamely at Mrs Gray. "He loves to play ball."

Frank reached out cautiously, and took the bag. Then his eyes lit on the basket of plums Mrs Heintz had brought for Deirdre to make into jam. "Can I have a plum?"

Deirdre glared at him. He'd been asking for a plum all morning, and she'd told him no. She plucked a small one from the basket and offered it to him. "Now get along to school."

Frank, taking no chances, seized the plum and ran out the door.

"He loves to play ball," Deirdre said to Mrs Gray.

Junior began to cough again.

Mrs Gray picked up the potted geranium. "This is no place for a plant," she declared. She placed it on the windowsill, beside the covered dishes, saying, "A plant needs light."

And so the geranium became another one of the social work clients on North First. On every visit, Mrs Gray examined its leaves and poked its dirt, declaring that Deirdre must water it more. But as the seasons went by, the geranium remained as pale and listless as Lucy and John Junior. Not once did it send forth a bloom, and Mrs Gray had plenty of opportunities to imply that Deirdre couldn't help anything to thrive. At such times, Deirdre would close her eyes and beat back the impulse to knock Mrs Gray's head off her shoulders with the cookstove poker.

2.4

THE LAW OFFICES OF HART AND DAUGHTERS TAKE UP THE MAIN floor of a brownstone in Brooklyn Heights. The waiting room is small and decorated like a cozy home, with fresh flowers, chintz curtains swaying in an open window, and comfortable chairs. Above an empty fireplace hangs an oil portrait of Lena Hart, Carol's mother and the firm's founding partner, in her judicial robes. On the opposite wall are five smaller works of art in simple frames. Scenes of nature. Among them, a watercolour sketch in a style Von recognizes. One of Rosheen's birds. A nuthatch, lonely on a bare twig. Payment for legal services, no doubt.

"Your sister's will is simple," Carol Hart says. She pulls a file from a stack on her desk and opens it. "You have inherited the Williamsburg apartment."

Von nods. She was expecting that. She's relaxed. Carol's assistant has made her welcome, carried in a tray of cookies and poured two steaming cups of black tea. Carol's is on the desk. Von is holding hers in its saucer. She blows gently on the surface to cool it.

"And there are two, um, requests." Carol peers at her client over the top of her glasses. "First, Rosheen has asked you to serve as her artistic executor. This means you take responsibility for preserving

her artworks. Let's see, she lists sketchbooks, scrapbooks, collages and
'other works on paper.' Do you know the location of these items?"

"Yes." Von lets out a mock sigh. "They're all over the apartment.
But they're not valuable. That was just Rosheen's thing, pasting paper
together. Ever since she was a kid."

"She asks that you keep them or try to place them in galleries or
in private collections."

"Surely not the scrapbooks."

"It's pretty clear here that she's including them."

"But they're scrapbooks," says Von. "They're full of *scraps*."

"Alex can help you decide about that," Carol concludes.

"Yes, of course," says Von. She remembers that Alex is interested
in *process*. She sighs, for real this time, and decides not to mention the
scrapbooks she's already thrown away. "Sorry. And the other request?"

"Rosheen has left her share of Garrison's Greenhouse to Kyle
Garrison, and she's requested that you —"

Von nearly spills the hot tea in her lap. "Let me see that." She
sets the cup and saucer on the tray and reaches across the desk. Carol
passes her the will. Von reads in dismay, so surprised she can't speak.

Von should have inherited everything. She'd certainly assumed
she would. Rosheen never married. She had no close friends. No
parents, no other siblings. As for the one child Rosheen had borne,
a child she never mentioned — a child *nobody* had mentioned for
years — Von had not expected his name to come up. But here it is,
neatly typed: *To my biological son, Kyle Robert Garrison, I leave my
full share of the business Garrison's Greenhouse. Kyle can be reached c/o
Ruth and Larry Penner of Minnedosa, Manitoba.* And above the line,
in Rosheen's shaky blue ballpoint cursive: *Von, I want you to drive up
there and introduce yourself to him. I want you to explain what happened.*

Von begins to protest, but Carol stops her. "The share belonged
to Rosheen," Carol says. "She had the right to choose who she left it to."

"I know," says Von. "I know. And I don't mind parting with half
the profits — half always went to Rosheen anyway. It's only fair to let
him — let Kyle — have that now. But to drive up to meet him? To
explain? That's asking too much."

Carol nods. "I understand. Don't worry." She explains that
her law firm has already contacted the Penners. The firm can move
forward and take care of all the financial arrangements, if Von wishes.

They can set up automatic quarterly payments, neat and tidy. As for Rosheen's other request, it's not legally binding. Von doesn't have to drive anywhere or talk to anyone, Carol assures her, until she's ready.

Von is relieved. She can't imagine ever being ready to talk to Rosheen's son. She doesn't even like knowing, as she does now, that he's been living in Manitoba — three or four hours from her own home.

"Here's the Penners' phone number," Carol says. She writes it on a piece of paper and slides it across the desk.

Von stares at it. "Don't they seal these records in an adoption?"

"There was no adoption," Carol says. "Not legally. Your sister never signed the papers. The Penners were his foster parents."

Von thanks Carol and stands to leave.

"Don't you want the phone number, at least?"

Von bites her lip. The last time she saw Kyle, he was sleepy. So sleepy he rubbed his curly head against her shoulder, as she carried him downstairs. He called her "Bon." The memory brings a sudden rush of longing. To see him again — to see him now.

"You should call," Carol urges. "Even if you don't tell him the whole…the whole story."

Von can never tell him the story. No child — no person — should have to live with that knowledge. Von herself can barely live with it. She leaves the phone number on the desk.

"Suit yourself," says Carol, coldly. She doesn't understand.

Von won't take the number because she's afraid that some day, in a weak moment, she might try to contact Kyle. And she would only hurt him. Lie to him or hurt him. Those are her only choices. He's better off without her.

———

The day Von finds the photo albums, she stops working for an hour, just to look at them. One album holds her mother's family photos, her mother's handsome brother and smiling parents, all gone now. Another, very thin, holds four portraits of her father's family, taken on formal occasions. Her father's family never owned a camera. The third is from her own childhood. Plenty of baby pictures. Fewer as the girls got older. There's Siobhán at eight, with four-year-old Róisín in a wading pool. Róisín, at five or six, in her little snowsuit, feeding chickadees, flinging birdseed from her mittened hands into the snow.

Róisín at seven, as a flower girl, with the whole family dressed up for the wedding of their greenhouse workers, Yvette and Manuel. Róisín wears a lacy dress and carries a basket of flower petals. She's holding Siobhán's hand, but her head is turned, her big solemn eyes on her parents. Watchful. Róisín at her eighth birthday party, giggling with a dozen other little girls in party dresses. So many friends. There are no more photographs of the girls after that. Last is the baby album, a blue giraffe and the name *Kyle* embroidered on the cover. Von sets it, unopened, in the box with the others. She'll look at it some other day, when she's stronger.

She still hasn't found the war scrapbook, the one Alex wants, though she remembers it. She saw it just last Christmas. Its first section is dedicated to the fiftieth anniversary of the liberation of the Netherlands. Pictures of old men in Bergen-op-Zoom, their shirt fronts sagging with medals. That ceremony had been a sore point between the sisters.

Leif Jonasson phones every day and one morning persuades Von to take a whole day off. They go into Manhattan for a fancy lunch on Park Avenue, then spend the afternoon in the Museum of Natural History. He's comfortable in the city, in the world. He steers her through the exhibits, explaining them as if he's been here hundreds of times. He doesn't talk about himself, except to answer her questions. He's a portrait painter, he says, and an art teacher. He loves his work. She senses that things have come easily to him, good health, talent, knowledge.

Afterwards, they enter Central Park. In the late afternoon, sun slants through the green leaves and glances off the pond. He takes a picture of her.

"You're beautiful," he says. "I'd love to paint you." He smiles and holds her hand as they walk across the park. He accepts Von's beauty, the light of day, this freedom, as his due.

Von needs a taxi to take all of Rosheen's "works on paper" to Alex for evaluation. He says he'll have to keep them in storage until he has time to look at them. She's relieved he has the room.

"We need to bring her work from Amsterdam here, too," he reminds her.

"I don't think I can do anything about that, Alex. Can't you get it shipped?"

"It's a delicate task," he says. "It needs to be done in person, by someone who cares about the show. Someone who cares about Rosheen. I thought, as part of your collaboration —"

"Alex, I have a business to run, back home."

"The greenhouse. Yes. Rosh told me how much work the greenhouse is. She —"

"She talked about it? Oh, come on, Alex. The greenhouse never crossed her mind."

Alex stands quietly, watching her, curious. She regrets the bitter note she let slip in that last sentence. Regrets letting him hear it.

"That's not true," he says. "Come with me." He takes her hand and pulls her into the storage space. He guides her along a row of crates and canvasses draped in cloth, until he stops and unveils a glass box, about four feet square. On its pedestal, it's a few inches taller than Von.

"This one is called *The Winter Garden*," he says. "She completed it last year."

Inside, suspended from the ceiling of the box by wires, hangs an unframed photograph, the tinted silhouette of a building on the prairie. Alex flicks a switch and the photo lights up. It's the old greenhouse in winter, transferred onto a sheet of glass. Von can see right through it into a labyrinth of smaller glass panels that hang at different heights and angles, revealing and concealing each other. She circles the case slowly, watching the scenes appear and disappear. She's never seen these pictures before. Yet she recognizes every image. A winter-blue sky, visible through the ceiling glass. Paper birds, cut out of newsprint, taped to the upper panes. The crop of miniature Cinderellas that would not bloom, six flats of blind shoots reaching toward the light but never budding. Close-ups of grafting operations, sharp knives and cut stems bound to the thorny stock with strips of nylon cut from Mum's old stockings. The outdoor bed, dark rosehips dangling from frost-riven stems. The dozen Gypsy roses Bobby sent to Von one Valentine's Day, the ones she pitched into a bank of snow. Rosheen must have photographed that bouquet daily, for here it is in every stage of its disintegration, from the first morning when the flowers were fresh and red, their pink ribbons clean and fluttering in the wind, until they faded and darkened and froze to death, their crumbling petals black as soot against the snow. The whole case is a magic forest under glass, a labyrinth of overlapping roses. The evidence on view, disguised in nothing but its beauty. Rosheen must have been documenting the greenhouse for years, hoarding these images of childhood like a secret archive. How long had she been plotting to reveal them in this public display?

Von thanks Alex and excuses herself. She needs some privacy to absorb what she's been learning about her sister. She walks back to the apartment slowly, choosing a route that takes her through Grand Ferry Park, where two men with shiny new rods and reels are casting lines from the riverbank. What kinds of creatures might swim in this contaminated waterway she can't imagine, but the men seem hopeful. They lean forward, raised slightly on their toes, peering into the murk, as if expecting a fat, shimmering jewel of a fish to surface any moment.

Every image in *The Winter Garden* rouses memory. Von realizes that of course those images can't really be photos taken in the greenhouse years and years ago. They must be recreations, staged by Rosheen. From memory. Rosheen was only eight when she made those paper birds and asked Manuel, the greenhouse worker, to tape them to the high glass ceiling. And she was eighteen when Bobby sent those roses. Rosheen, it seems, remembered everything.

She enters Rosheen's bedroom. Here are the everyday things. On the dresser, a jumble of earrings, a little carving of a seal, loose buttons. A steel comb Rosheen bought as a teenager, joking, *It'll last me the rest of my life.* Only Von knows how many combs had lost their teeth or snapped in two on Rosheen's tangles. Only Von knows the meaning of the memories in the glass collage. But she understands now that she's not the sole owner of the art Rosheen has made of those memories. The art must be shared.

First, Von calls home. Jeanne says all is well. The plants are healthy. Summer business is brisk. When Von asks if Jeanne can stay there into October, Jeanne hesitates. But Von offers a large bonus, and after Jeanne thinks about it for a couple of hours, she calls back, saying yes.

Next Von calls the studio in Amsterdam. It's an international artists' co-operative, and the co-ordinator was obviously a friend of

Rosheen's. He offers his condolences. "I've been waiting to hear from her family," he says. He explains that Rosheen's work is still in the studio, but he can't keep it much longer. Other artists need the space. Von promises to come as soon as she can.

Then she calls a travel agent and books a flight to Amsterdam that leaves at the end of the month.

———

On Friday, she'll be going out with Leif again. To the hotel where they first went dancing. It's the last night for the old-fashioned band. This time, when he walks her home, she'll invite him in. She daydreams of cooking a meal with him, setting the table together here in the apartment. On impulse, she calls and asks him to join her in hosting a dinner party Saturday evening. Sure, he says. So she invites Alex, Carol, Ingrid, and — why not? — Ingrid's two sentimental students, and they all accept. She takes Deirdre's good china off the shelf and washes it.

At an expensive hair salon on Metropolitan, she gets her hair cut, and on the way home buys a new blue summer dress. Back at the apartment she washes a load of linens, changes the bed sheets. She closes the door on the two piles in the back room: artifacts and trash. Throughout the history of the human race, certain people have been chosen to determine which is which, and few have been as unqualified as she is. But she's willing to try.

———

That night the band is sweeter than the first night, the cocktails more delicious. Leif and Von dance and then drink for a while and talk about what it might be like to spend a winter together in Greece, or maybe the south of France, and then they dance some more. At midnight, high on gin and jazz music and kissing, they fall into the apartment when Von unlocks the door. They dance down the hallway while Leif tries to sing the few words he can remember of the band's final song. Von takes his hand and leads him into the bedroom where they collapse, laughing, onto the bed with the newly laundered sheets. Leif lies on his back and pulls her on top of him. He runs his hands under her dress and pulls it over her hips and unbuttons the buttons down the back. She unbuckles his belt and slowly, clumsily, they undress each other until they are both almost naked, and then they fall unconscious in each other's arms and sleep until dawn.

2·5

Mrs Gray visited the Garrisons' apartment every month for years. But all her fussing and tea towels made no difference in the end. Lucy died in November of 1933. By then she'd been so ill for so long that even twelve-year-old John Junior was resigned to it. Lucy's older boys, Paul and Davey, were thirteen and fourteen, but they wept like girls. They were orphans now.

Lucy's brother-in-law Mark hosted the wake, and Deirdre was shocked to see that he and his wife had plenty of room in their house. Surely they could have taken in Lucy and her boys with very little trouble. Tomas didn't notice this. He was devastated to lose his sister. He wasn't normally a drinker, but in his distraught state, he started in heavily on Mark's whisky. He spoke to everyone of Lucy, such an angel she was as a girl, in her dear communion dress with the white sash embroidered all over with doves. Mama had sewn that herself. Ah, poor Mama, and so on.

When Deirdre mentioned to Mark what a fine big house he had, Mark only said that he and his wife would be glad to let Davey and Paul move in, once they were working and able to pay their room and board. But Tomas insisted his nephews must finish high school. He delivered a speech on the importance of education and then fell flat on his back in the middle of the parlour. Mikey Finnegan, the boxer, stepped on Tomas's hand without even noticing, as he helped himself to a piece of treacle cake, and Tomas's hand was never the same again. Sometimes Deirdre felt that God had sent men into the world to try her. But she had sympathy for Tomas. She knew how it felt to have someone you loved ripped out of your life.

Deirdre often recalled the day she'd waited at the Spanish Arch for Daniel, and he never came. How hard she'd struggled in the currach up that river. How she'd hoped and hoped, while all the while Daniel was lying helpless, both legs broken by the British soldiers. She'd vowed that never again would she want anything so badly. But four years later, she had waited at the station for his train from Galway. She recalled the agitated people on the platform, and the murmurs, the awful rumours passing through the crowd about a bombing. The people sick with fear. Then, finally, learning of the horror. No, never again. Better to want nothing.

She tried to resist these memories, but they pressed themselves upon her if ever Frank was late coming home. She could not bear the agony of waiting. A mad streak in her brain, like the beam of light at the Paramount movie house, projected picture after picture on a screen behind her eyes. First, the ugly disasters that had befallen Daniel in the past, and then the future disasters she imagined befalling her son. The other boys were usually reliable, and her husband, Tomas, always sent word if he was to be late. But Frank worried her nearly to death.

On a Friday in mid-June, when he was thirteen, Frank left the apartment early, claiming he didn't have time to wait for Martha Waters to escort him to school. His friends were getting up a ball game in the schoolyard early today, before the bell.

"Don't forget to come straight home," Deirdre called to him out the window. Frank waved, so she knew he'd heard her. She had told him several times she needed him today. Davey and Paul were to go to their Uncle Mark's at noon. They were to spend the whole weekend there, to help him with painting his house. So there would be no one but Frank to take Tomas his dinner at midday. Deirdre would be trapped inside, looking after Mrs Heintz's little grandchildren, so Mrs Heintz could stay with her daughter, who had been in labour all night. Deirdre had to look after John Junior, too. He'd been sick for weeks with a terrible cough. Yesterday his fever rose so high that she'd run out to the drugstore and bought the syrup the doctor had recommended, though it cost half the grocery money. But it had helped him sleep. The whole family had slept better last night, without his coughing.

Tomas ate quickly and left for work. Davey and Paul left soon after. Deirdre had twenty minutes to herself, which she spent on emptying the mousetraps and setting new ones, before Mrs Heintz brought her grandchildren by at nine. Deirdre laid a blanket on the parlour floor and set the children side by side with the toy dolls Mrs Heintz had brought. They were one and two years old, red-faced, with chubby cheeks and the wispy golden hair of little angels. But Deirdre knew better. She had looked after them before. The creeper and the crier, she called them. Never mind. She owed Mrs Heintz many favours, and she did not begrudge her this one.

At eleven, Junior woke up, groggy and talking nonsense. He staggered and nearly keeled over when he tried to walk. He muttered something about going sledding, so Deirdre set him in a chair by the window to show him it was summertime. He touched the cracked window pane and said, "broken ice." Deirdre hoped it was only the fever making him talk like this. She did not want a crazy person in the family. That would be the limit. She went to the linen closet and rummaged for a cloth, and when she came back he was trying to climb out of the window.

"Junior! No!" She hauled him back in and pulled down the sash, though she dearly needed the air. She dipped the cloth in cold water and wrapped it around his head to cool him down. Then she put on a pot of water to make a soup with the last of the carrots and potatoes. She had a few leaves of cabbage left as well, and she sliced them in. She wished for a bit of meat, but she didn't dare leave the babies or Junior alone in the apartment.

She fed a bowl of soup to the Heintz children and put the rest in a small, covered pot, ready for Tomas. She realized she was hungry and looked at the clock. Ten minutes past noon. Frank was late. He knew she was stuck inside, and yet he was late. She went to the window to watch for him, but he didn't come. When she saw Martha Waters come past with her baby carriage, Deirdre called down and asked Martha to deliver the pot of soup to the factory for Tomas. "Since you didn't have to walk Frank to school today," Deirdre said, in case Martha was expecting a penny.

By twelve thirty, a sick, desperate bubble was forming in Deirdre's stomach. Frank must have had an accident of some kind. She repeated to herself the sentence Tomas had so often used to calm her down: "If Frank got hurt, the school would send word." Was it true? She tried to be reasonable. That's what Tomas called it, being reasonable. But she knew that when Frank skipped school altogether, the teacher often did not even notice. With so many children crammed in the one classroom, who could keep track of them all?

At one o'clock, she tried to imagine the boys had got up another ball game, and Frank was spending the lunch hour playing. This made her angry enough to distract her from worrying. She would have to wait, now, until he got out of school at four.

At three, when a loud boom sounded through the neighbourhood, Deirdre could not suppress the scream that tore out of her mouth. She hurried to the window, scooping up the babies and holding one on each hip as she peered out the window. Did the boom come from the factory, where her husband was working? Black smoke billowed from the chimney stacks at Domino's Sugar, but black smoke always billowed out, so this signified nothing. In a minute, alarm bells rang, and a siren came whining through the streets. She could not see the source of the siren. Was it a fire truck? Sugar was combustible. If a man got careless with a lamp, or a machine overheated, a spark could ignite the particles of sugar, causing a fire or explosion. Men had been injured that way. Was it an ambulance siren? It sounded close, though she could not see it. She pictured the narrow catwalks high above the vats of boiling sugar. The whirling steel machinery she'd glimpsed through the door. Blades that could take a man apart. She thought of the butcher, bringing his cleaver down upon a shank of beef.

And where was Frank? She thought of all the dead children she'd heard of lately, the boy who tumbled off a rooftop chasing his kite, the girl who was trampled by a horse in Classon Street, and the Persian immigrant boy who drowned when the raft he made broke to pieces in the river. Where was her son?

By ten after four, she was alert to every sound. Twice she mistook the banging of the janitor for the sound of her son coming home. At four thirty, she heard footsteps on the stairs, too heavy to be her son or husband. The knock, when it came, gave her such a shock she screamed again. Was it a policeman? Come to say her husband had been chopped in two, or burned to death? Come to say her only son was dead?

She made a quick bargain with God: *if you must take one of them, please, take my husband.* She crossed herself and opened the door.

The man in the hallway wore no uniform. He was tall and blond, with a peaked cap on his head. He was thick, with a broad face and freckles and a ridge of a forehead under which two pale blue eyes looked out from narrow slits. Bearer of bad news.

"What is it?" she asked, thinking death, dismemberment, grief. But no. This was a disaster of a different kind.

"It's me," he said. Sour beer on his breath. "Do you not know me?"

"I do not." She looked him up and down and was quite sure she had never seen him before, though his voice was familiar, the voice of the west of Ireland.

"How can you not know me?" he asked. "I'm Brendan, your son."

She shut the door. She felt her heartbeat, hard and unsteady in her breast. Thank God that Tomas and Frank were not at home. Thank God. But what if he came back later? Best to get rid of him now, for good, while she was alone. She opened the door a crack and said, "I've no son Brendan."

"How can you say that?" he demanded. "I'm Brendan O'Nolan, your youngest. I've been looking for you these past twelve months, and here I am. Are you not going to let me in?"

"I'm not your mother," said Deirdre. She heard footsteps coming up. Peering around the bulk of Brendan O'Nolan, she saw her neighbour, Mr Edison, arrive at the top of the stairs.

"Hello, Mrs Garrison." Mr Edison tipped his hat. "I've just seen your man down at Reilly's, and he's —"

"Mr Edison," she called. "Could you please help me?"

"Why? What's the trouble?"

"No trouble," said Brendan. His voice was rough with menace. He pulled himself up to his full height and lurched toward Mr Edison.

Mr Edison was not as tall or heavy as Brendan, but he put his hand on the hammer he carried in his carpenter's belt. It was enough to make Brendan retreat.

"This young man is lost," said Deirdre. "He's been drinking, and he's up here pounding on doors, looking for someone. He's got the wrong building."

"Better move along, fella," said Mr Edison. He lifted the hammer from his belt and hefted it, shifting it back and forth in his hand.

Brendan backed up to the top of the stairs. "I've got business with her," he said.

"I don't know him," said Deirdre. To Brendan she said, "I've no business with you."

"We'll see about that," said Brendan. He turned and grasped the railing and stumbled down to the street.

By five, Deirdre was frantic. What if Brendan went down to Reilly's? Mr Edison had said the name Garrison and the name of the pub. Brendan could find Tomas easily now. Or perhaps that fateful meeting had already occurred, and this was why Tomas had not come home. Perhaps even now, in that dark little hole in the wall where the men of the neighbourhood sipped their beer, Brendan was leaning toward Tomas, telling tales of the O'Nolan farm in Ireland and the pigs and the chickens she had sold. The bicycle she'd stolen. The convent. For a moment she wondered what it was like in the convent orphanage. Were the sisters kind? But she must never, never ask Brendan that question. She must make him believe he was mistaken.

If Tomas discovered her lies, what would he do? He could not abide a lie. And he would like the truth even less. She feared he would throw her out, the way that man she'd heard about, in Queen's, had thrown out his wife when he discovered she'd once been a working girl. Deirdre could lose her home, her good name, and her son as well, for Tomas was not likely to give up Frank. And where was Frank? Why was he so late?

It was near six when she saw the gang of kids turn the corner at the far end of the street. Although she was four storeys up, she recognized her son among them. A flood of relief washed over her, weakened her, nearly knocked her to the ground. Then immediately, a fierce anger overtook her. She saw Frank break away from the gang and start down the street toward home. He wasn't even hurrying. He tossed a baseball back toward the other kids and called good-bye to them. A red-headed boy, one of those Higgins brats, and some bare-headed Protestant girl tagged along behind him. Frank stopped and waited for the girl to catch him up. His mother and his mother's needs were the last thing on his mind. He didn't care how she suffered, how her heart nearly burst from worry over him. He had forgotten her. She heard the kids laughing as if life were one big joke. As they came closer, the girl began to look familiar. Surely it wasn't — yes, it was. Nancy Gray, the social worker's daughter. Deirdre had forbidden Frank to speak to her. Her hands tightened around the geranium pot on the windowsill. As he reached the pavement in front of the building, he looked up at the sky, and Deirdre caught a good glimpse of how happy he was. Before she knew what her hands were doing, she lifted the flowerpot and hurled it out the window, letting it fly straight at his head.

2.6

WHEN SUNLIGHT SEEPS IN BETWEEN THE CURTAINS, VON WAKES, feels Leif's body solid and warm beside her under the sheet. She opens her eyes and immediately pulls the sheet up over her head. She hears Leif groan. Too many drinks last night. She laughs, and he curves his body around hers and they laugh together.

"It was fun, though," says Leif. He gets out of bed and she hears his bare feet go down the hall, the floorboards creaking. He returns with a glass of tap water and a bottle of pain killers from the medicine cabinet. He closes the curtains more tightly, blocking out the morning glare. They both drink water and swallow tablets, and he falls asleep first, touching her only with one arm flung across her back. She hears his breathing slow and deepen, feels the warmth radiating from his body. It's been years since she shared a bed with a man. She closes her eyes but lies awake, listening to him breathe. Maybe she should get out of bed now. If she stays here, he might make a move on her when he wakes up. She smiles. He will make a move on her, and she knows it. He's only sleeping now to prepare himself to do it well. She's still smiling as she drifts back to sleep. At noon, he wakes her again and they make love.

"It's too bad you'll be going home so soon," she says. She leans into him, revelling in his warmth, the scent of his body, and he wraps his arms around her.

"I don't have to go home yet," he says. "I can stay for coffee." His grin is catching. She can't look at him without smiling. She feels again the ache in her jaw from laughing last night.

"No, I mean *home* home," she says. "To Iceland."

"I'm not going to Iceland."

"But you're an Icelander," she teases. "You have to go back to Iceland."

"Not me," he says.

"In a week." She counts again. "Six days, now."

"Not me. I live right here in Brooklyn."

Von pulls away. "Alex said you were with the group — from Reykjavik —"

He laughs. "Yeah, but no. I'm just the chaperone. Showing the kids around. I'm a New Yorker." He looks at her. "What? I am. I live two blocks from here. I teach at Hunter College every winter." He winks. "I'm more American than you are."

Von sits up, covers herself with the sheet. "I don't believe you. You sound —"

"I moved here twelve years ago," he says. "Still got a bit of an accent, I guess. But I'm an American citizen."

Von is pulling on a bathrobe. "I don't believe this!"

He laughs. "Do you want to see my papers, officer?"

She opens the closet, gathers clean clothes for the day and takes them into the bathroom, where she locks the door. He lives in Brooklyn?

She manages an hour of light banter over coffee and a breakfast of sliced oranges and yogurt. Then Leif kisses her good-bye. He's entirely too happy. She hears him singing as he runs down the staircase. Sounds like John Lennon's "Imagine."

When she thinks about tonight's dinner party, she feels trapped. But she can't cancel it now. Alex and Carol are coming, Ingrid and her two students. She had envisioned the next few days filled with one long leisurely good-bye. Lots of intense, sorrowful sex. Expressions of regret. Shared dreams of future flights to Iceland for romantic weekends, none of which would ever come true. She had been looking forward to all that.

She plans a simple meal. Pasta and salad. She'll pick up a cake at the bakery later this afternoon. Nothing special. The fun of preparations has gone flat.

At the market she buys romaine lettuce, mushrooms, spinach, red and yellow peppers, tomatoes, garlic, and a loaf of crusty bread. Two bottles of white wine. Maybe a red. No, she'd better get two reds. The clerk wraps each bottle in paper and stows the four bottles in one paper sack. She carries the vegetables and bread in a string bag slung from her shoulder and hugs the sack of wine to her chest, interlocking her fingers to hold it in place. Only five blocks to walk.

She enters the street beneath the bridge and sees in the crisscross shadows of the girders a loose gang of teenagers smoking and watching her. Idle and hungry. She is walking straight toward them. Ah well, she thinks, better to be facing them than to have them behind her. She looks up and catches the eye of the nearest boy. "Hi," she says quietly. He nods, lets her pass. This neighbourhood is no worse, she thinks, than when she was a girl. In fact it's gentler, at least on the surface. There are no signs of gang fights, stray dogs, obscene graffiti, or the hippies who once made Deirdre so nervous. There is nothing to fear anymore. Except for fake Icelanders, masquerading as one-night stands. Ha. A woman passes on high heels, toting a little grey poodle in her purse. Even the Williamsburg dogs are harmless these days.

She spots him as soon as she turns the corner onto North First. He's leaning against the fence in the shadow of her building, cleaning his fingernails with a pocketknife. Same army-green backpack slung over one shoulder. Same threadbare sneakers. He senses her staring and looks up. Bolder this time. Not at all reluctant to be seen. She realizes he must have been standing here a long while. Waiting for her. What does he want? He meets her gaze and holds it. Blue eyes. Bluer than Rosheen's. Her heart contracts. The paper sack of wine is heavy, heavier than she realized. She wants to open her clasped hands and let it drop. The boy steps forward. Asks one question.

"Do you know who I am?"

He emerges from the shade. As the sun shines in his eyes, she sees the green light flicker in the depth of the blue irises, and yes, she knows who he is. But she does not say so. Not yet. If she tries to speak right now she will break into tears.

BOOK II

Frank

The Sky

3.1

FRANK LAY FLAT ON HIS BACK, HIS SPINE A SIZZLING WIRE FUSED to the spinning ground. Noise like a choir of demons mumbling Latin. The smell of burnt sugar. Taste on his tongue like the time he had the fever. His head rang like a struck bell.

White clouds revolved in the blue sky. His mother's face shimmered in the window as he sank deeper into the ground or maybe the building was rising. His mother's face became a pinprick of light and she was gone. He was travelling away from her, being born.

"You're bleeding," said Nancy.

Her voice reached him through viscous waves, the voice of a girl underwater.

"Frank!" That was Corky. Scent of tobacco and mint leaves.

All at once a dozen sounds rushed in — wagon wheels, dogs barking, two dragonflies buzzing in the grass. His eyes were open, they'd been open all along. He lifted his head and a great weight like a bucket full of broken glass shifted inside his skull. He saw on the pavement jagged shards of crockery and a spindly plant, its roots sprawling out of a ball of dirt. Two legs he did not know at all, though they wore his pants. Was he inside someone else's body? He held a hand before his face, looked at the dirty palm. Nothing was familiar, except the dull ache in the belly. Hunger.

Nancy kneeled beside him, gazing with big eyes up at the window where, mere minutes ago, the geranium plant had lived quietly in its pot. "Come, Frank, get up. We can't stay here." She tugged at his arm, and Corky tugged at his other arm. They pulled him to his feet. Nausea rose within him like a bird taking flight.

The street and buildings whirled before his eyes. He tried to focus on Nancy. She was pale with fear. Her copper freckles seemed to float in the air before her face.

"Don't be afraid," he told her.

The three kids staggered arm in arm down the sidewalk toward the river. Nancy looked back over her shoulder every few seconds until they were well out of sight of Frank's building. Children played in the street while women ran their last errands before supper. Men who had spent the day looking for work or drinking beer at Schneider's or Reilly's now sat, smoking or dozing, on kitchen chairs dragged onto the stoops of their apartment houses.

At the end of the street, Kevin Higgins stood with his arms crossed, talking to Mrs Casey in front of her house. Kevin delivered charcoal in his horse-drawn cart, and now the horse stood with bowed head, waiting to go home, and the cart was empty. Kevin must have finished his rounds for the day and dropped off the leftover charcoal for Mrs Casey, whose husband was killed in the iron works the month before.

"Hey, Uncle Kev," called Corky. "Give us a ride to the piers."

"Go on home," Kevin called back. "Go home and help yer ma!"

Corky used an empty crate as a step-stool and helped Frank into the back of the cart. Corky and Nancy climbed up after. In a few minutes, Corky's uncle stepped up into his seat without looking at them. He tapped the flank of the nag with a stick and she began to move.

This end of Kent Street was rough with mud and broken cobblestones, and Frank's sore head jounced against the wooden floor of the cart. Nancy sat down in the coal dust with her legs straight out before her and lifted his head onto the soft flesh above her knees. She pulled a handkerchief from her dress pocket and dabbed at Frank's hair above his right temple. When he saw the handkerchief come away soaked with fresh blood, he lifted his hand to his head. His hair was matted and sticky, and when he touched the wound, a fresh stream of blood flowed over his temple and into his ear. Nancy staunched it before it stained her dress.

Frank wanted to close his eyes but when he did his head whirled and his empty stomach lurched, so he kept them open. To the left, he saw the tall windows in the brick walls of the sugar factory that ran the length of the street, and to the right, the eaves and roofs of the buildings where the people lived. As the cart moved out of the shadow of the factory, the sunlight hurt his eyes. The day's heat lay on him, heavy as a blanket. Yet far above, fast winds cooled the air and tore apart the high white clouds and stretched their edges ragged across the sky.

He thought of the hundreds of bits of paper that had drifted to earth like snow this afternoon, after he blew the school's trash barrel to pieces with a stick of dynamite he'd found at a construction site. What a noise when it blew. He and Corky had jumped right out of their hiding place in the ditch. And what silence afterwards — for a few precious minutes the silence seemed to stretch for miles across the city. But then someone sounded the alarm, and the boys ran as far and fast as they could. Two blocks over, they joined a pick-up game of baseball, and when the coppers came past, asking questions, they were waiting their turns at bat, not knowing nothing about no dynamite. Frank was glad they hadn't been caught. His father would have been disappointed in him. His mother was always angry at him. There was nothing he could do about that. But he dreaded his father's disappointment. Worse than any flowerpot to the head.

Corky and his brothers and sisters and mother lived with his Uncle Kevin's family in a crowded apartment on a dark block of Wythe Street under the rise of the Williamsburg Bridge. The horse soon plodded to a stop in front of their building and Kevin jumped out. As the children climbed down from the wagon, Corky's oldest brother, Simon, came toward them, carrying his gym bag. Simon was a boxer who had won the Golden Gloves tournament last year and was a hero to the boys. He had given them many lessons on how to defend themselves.

"What's happened to you?" he asked Frank.

"It was an accident," said Frank. He was trusting Corky and Nancy to keep quiet about his mother's temper. Corky's family would laugh at him, and Nancy's mother would speak to Frank's mother about it, and then there'd be hell to pay.

"Bad luck!" said Simon. "Better put some ice on that!" He went into the apartment block, and a minute later Corky's sister came out on the stoop, a wooden spoon in her hand.

"Can we get some supper?" Corky asked his sister. "We ain't had nothing to eat all day."

"Send your friends home," said his sister. "We got no extra for giving away."

"Aw, please," Corky started. But his sister pushed him inside.

Frank turned to Nancy. "Let's go down to the piers."

"My mother's expecting me home," said Nancy. She held out her bloody handkerchief.

Frank understood. She could not bring it home like that. He put it into his pocket.

"Good-bye, Frank!" She turned away, and he was alone.

The street had emptied out. Everyone was inside, eating with their families. Frank's head ached. He walked into the cool shade under the bridge and sat in a patch of weeds and wished for a drink of water. He had nowhere to go.

He knew his mother was angry because he had skipped school that day and come home late and because she saw him playing with Corky Higgins, who she said was filthy, and Nancy Gray, who she said was wild. But it seemed she never wanted him to have any friends. He remembered the day she had caught him playing with Henry Taylor, when he was ten years old. She had whipped him so hard he couldn't sit down and had to stand beside his desk at school the next day. She said white and coloured people should not mix. The memory made him sad.

By now he was starving. He thought of the carrots and potatoes he'd earned by helping the Greens in their grocery store the other day. He imagined Deirdre cooking them into a stew, with onions and a beef bone, and serving it with hot biscuits and a pat of butter. The grocery store should still be open! If he hurried, he could get there before they locked the doors and went home. He could help Mrs Green sweep the floor, and she would offer him something. Peanuts, or maybe an apple. He began to run.

But when he got there the store was locked and the awnings pulled down. He continued south toward the piers. He and Corky liked to come here on hot days and loaf in the sun until they were about to catch fire and then run like sixty down the piers and cannonball into the swift, sour water of the East River.

They were not allowed here. The wharf guards threw stones at them and threatened to arrest them. But the boys could not be caught. Sometimes the head guard chased them, but he was easy to dodge. The boys slipped through the narrow gaps between the stacked shipping containers, where the guard could not fit. They called out, "Fat, Fat, the Water Rat!" and watched him turn red. They darted around the great coils of rope and metal cleats to evade him. Or they ran up a gangplank to the deck of a ship and across it to the vessel docked beside it, leaping from boat to boat. If in danger of getting caught, they dived into the water.

Now, Frank took a seldom-used path down to the river, well out of sight of the guardhouse. He turned onto the maze of narrow slips laid out for the smaller boats, and stopped at the farthest pier, where a red and black tugboat hid him from view. Lying down on the rough planks, he dangled Nancy's handkerchief in the water, washing away the blood, and laid it flat to dry, weighed down with a stone. The odour of rotting meat and ashes floated to shore as a passing barge hauled waste from the city dump. The gulls that followed it screeched and squabbled, and for a short half hour, until the barge passed under the Brooklyn Bridge, its stink overpowered the sticky-sweet smell of the sugar refinery.

Frank turned onto his side and rested his head on one outstretched arm. It was high summer. The sun still hovered above the Manhattan skyline. Resting only inches from the surface of the river, he felt the wake of the big ships passing. Again he thought about stew and biscuits. But it was too risky to go home. Tomas would have finished his supper by now and gone out to Reilly's for a glass of beer. Frank was safer here. He closed his eyes and listened to the slap of waves against the floats and the hulls of the boats. His body rose and fell with the motion of the river as he let himself slide into the only sure defence he knew against the pains of hunger, sleep.

All week his mother would not speak to him. Whether from shame for nearly killing her only son or rage at him for surviving, he did not know.

The cut on his head healed slowly. When his father first saw it, the morning after, and asked how it had happened, Frank's mother was standing right beside him, with a hot kettle in her hand.

She said, "Frank had an accident. That flowerpot fell off the windowsill when he was playing out on the stoop."

Frank's father washed and bandaged his head. "Does it hurt?" he asked.

"It hurts when I touch it," said Frank.

"Don't touch it then," said his mother. She was feeding him even less than usual, slopping small spoons of porridge onto a plate in the morning and shoving a meagre lunch at him — a heel of bread or a cold potato. At supper time she was forced to relent, since Tomas was at the table, ladling soup and asking Frank what he learned in school that day. In the evenings, Frank ate until his stomach ached or the soup pot was empty. But still he woke early every morning with hunger raking the inside of his belly, like a small animal scratching to get out.

On the third day of hunger, he walked to school as usual, letting Martha Waters follow him up to the gates. He knew she was watching him as he passed through the tall arch of the entry. He walked slowly down the crowded corridor, so as not to draw attention to himself, past the classrooms of grades four and five and then past his own grade six classroom — at thirteen, he should be through with grade six anyway — and then he slipped out the back door through the play yard and climbed the fence and hurried down the lane until he came to Green's grocery and drugstore and asked Mr Green for a job. Mr Green was glad to hire him.

Every morning that week Frank managed the same getaway. Martha didn't see him, and his teachers didn't miss him. It was almost the end of June, and if he could avoid being caught until then, he'd be free for the whole long summer. What might happen next September did not concern him. He had never in his short life thought that far ahead.

Frank's job was to load up the customers' orders into the baskets on Mr Green's big bicycle, and ride through the neighbourhood, getting each order to its right address. He was fast and accurate, and he felt himself growing stronger every day. With the money he earned delivering groceries, he bought apples and walnuts and raisins and frankfurters and once in a while a ripe tomato, which he ate whole, leaning over so he wouldn't drip juice down his shirt. He had to take care to keep his clothes clean and not to get any rips in them, because Mr Green said he was representing the store and people wanted the store where they bought their food to be clean and neat. Mr Green sounded proud of his store and he made Frank feel glad to work there, made him want to do a good job.

When Mr Green's brother, the dentist, visited the store, Mr Green introduced Frank as his best employee. Someone you could count on. Dr Green said he needed a reliable boy. Could Frank come to Manhattan on Saturdays? Frank said yes, and soon he was delivering dental supplies and prescriptions every weekend. Dr Green said he was a fine boy and he could come by the office any time if he needed a tooth fixed, even if he didn't have the money up front. Frank recognized this as an honour that raised him above the other people on his street, even his own father.

When school let out, Frank's parents let him work for their neighbour Mr Edison, the carpenter. Mr Edison taught him how to install a window so it wouldn't rattle and how to hang a door so it wouldn't stick. When they built a new shed in the lot by McAdam's garage, Frank did most of the work himself.

"Best helper I ever took on," Mr Edison told McAdam.

Frank learned more on his jobs than he'd ever learned in a classroom. When he handed his earnings to Deirdre, he felt proud to be helping the family. He decided he was never going back to school.

Frank still worked for Mr Green when Mr Edison didn't need him, and one summer evening as he left the store, he saw Annie Taylor, Henry's sister, run past him on the street, probably late home for her supper. Annie would be fourteen now. He called a greeting to her, but she ignored him. He had always liked Annie, but since his mother had whipped him for playing with Henry, she kept her distance. He watched her tear around the corner at the end of the street, as if Frank didn't exist.

When he reached McAdam's garage, Frank heard a shrill sound. A scream? He took a shortcut through McAdam's lot, moving toward the sound he'd heard. But he stopped short when he heard a harsh, familiar laugh. His old enemy, Don Cuthbert. Don was thirteen, the same age as Frank, but heavier and six times meaner. He had beaten Frank up regularly, until last year, when Frank tried some of his boxing moves on Don and beat him square. But Simon Higgins, who had taught Frank and Corky how to box, said they should use those lessons only in the ring. When it came to the street, he said, it was better to prevent a fight than to win one. So Frank always tried to avoid Don. His impulse now was to turn around and take another route. But who had screamed?

He peered over McAdam's fence. In the alley he saw Don Cuthbert and the broad back of Don's older brother Malcolm. They were closing in on someone. He knew it was a girl, a Negro girl, because he could see her braids and her brown bare arms. The recent rain had turned the packed earth of the alleyway into gravelly mud, and she was slipping and sliding as she tried to evade Don's approach. Then he saw her pink dress and he knew it was Annie Taylor, who had run past him ten minutes ago. He'd thought she was hurrying home, but she must have been running away from the Cuthberts. Why hadn't she called Frank for help? In his heart, he felt a hot rush of anger at his mother.

Don was swinging a dirty cloth bag in a circle above his head, saying, "This bag's full of rocks. I killed a cat with a bag of rocks like this."

Malcolm picked up a sharp stick and came toward Annie from behind, using words Frank had never heard at home and some he'd never even heard in the street. Words of hate. Malcolm poked Annie's leg and lifted the hem of her skirt with the stick. She began to shake, as if she were freezing cold.

Frank stepped out from behind the garage. "Leave her alone."

Don and Malcolm, startled, looked up in fear, then scanned the alleyway in four directions, and when they saw nobody there except Frank, they began to smirk.

"Is this your sweetheart?" Malcolm asked. He poked Annie's thigh with his stick.

"Leave her be." Frank moved forward. Why hadn't he thought to pick something out of the junk in McAdam's lot, an old pipe or a gas can? Both boys had turned away from Annie and were coming for Frank, Malcolm wielding the sharp stick and Don his bag of stones.

"Annie," said Frank. "Run now. Run home, quick."

Annie didn't hesitate. She ran down the alley and darted around the corner.

Don started after her, but Malcolm called him back. He advanced on Frank and jabbed at him with the sharp stick. Frank jumped out of the way.

"Aw never mind," said Don. "Leave the retard alone."

"Leave him alone?" cried Malcolm. "When he's asking for it, like this? Rushing in and playing the big hero?" He looked at Frank. "You're that Garrison kid, right?"

Frank didn't let the question distract him. He was concentrating. Watching the way Malcolm moved. Keeping track of where Don was.

"Frank Garrison," said Don. "His dad's down at the sugar plant."

"That so?" said Malcolm. "Down at the sugar plant, lar dee dar, when our old man can't get a job nowhere." He grabbed Frank's arm and held him so he couldn't run. "Get him, Donny!"

Don hauled back with the bag of stones and brought it down hard, aiming for Frank's head. But Frank ducked and the blow caught him on the shoulder. Malcolm was behind him now. He had dropped the stick and was using both his hands to hold Frank's arms behind his back. Don raised the bag again and tried to drive it deep into Frank's face, but his aim fell short. The bag glanced off Frank's chest, landing in the mud. Frank staggered backwards onto Malcolm. Malcolm lost his footing and lost his grip. In the next moment, the three boys stood in a tight triangle, facing each other, none of them armed. The balance of power had shifted.

Frank hit Don first, because he hated him the most. He remembered everything Simon had taught him about posture and poise and footwork, as he laid a beautiful right hook into Don's jaw that sent him sprawling to the ground. Then he pivoted on his toes and delivered the same to Malcolm. Malcolm didn't go down as easily, so Frank followed up with a left hook to the ribs, and in a moment both boys were sprawled in the dirt. One, two, three, it was that easy, and they didn't look like they were getting up any time soon.

"Keep away from her, or I'll know about it," he said. He decided to walk away now, while they were both immobile. He strode down the alley without looking back, and the only thing he feared was that his elation was going to lift him right up off the ground and send him soaring to the sky.

———

Frank's first delivery one hot morning in August was to the Grays' house on Clinton Street. Nancy was away on a church retreat, but he knew Mrs Gray, since for years she had come to inspect his home. Frank admired Mrs Gray, though he knew Deirdre despised her. Mrs Gray always wore pretty clothes and a pretty hat and smiled at him as if she liked him. She led him to the kitchen, where he set down the groceries.

"Look at these rosy apples," she said. "I love this time of year for the apples." She leaned into the bag and inhaled the smell. "I believe I'll make pie today. Do you like apple pie, Frank?"

"Yes, Ma'am."

She smiled at him. "You come by the house at two o'clock. Come and keep my husband company while I go to a meeting." Frank had never met Mr Gray, a World War One veteran in a wheelchair, though he had once or twice seen Mrs Gray pushing him through the park. "I'll have pie for you and a cup of coffee. Do you drink coffee?"

"Yes, Ma'am," said Frank.

The thought of a slice of fresh-baked pie drove his work all morning. He managed his route so he stopped at her house at two. When she let him in, he removed his cap, and she led him into the dining room, where the uncut pie sat on a glass dish on the table.

"Have a seat," she said.

Frank sat down, keeping his hands clear of the thick linen tablecloth.

Mrs Gray set a fork and a serviette and a white plate before him. She cut into the pie with a silver knife and lifted out a slice on a silver triangle and placed it on his plate.

"Just make yourself at home." She returned to the kitchen, leaving him alone.

Frank cut into the crust with the fork and shovelled a piece into his mouth. The flakes of fresh pastry melted on his tongue, and the apples were still warm and sprinkled with cinnamon. When the plate was empty, he scraped up the crumbs with his fingers, and as he was licking them, Mrs Gray returned. She was holding a cup of coffee in her hand.

"My goodness!" she said. "Are you that hungry?"

Frank's face burned. He saw his reflection in the sideboard mirror. Crumbs on his chin and collar. He brushed them off. His skin was too dark, his face looked dirty. His hair was black as boot polish and too long, and his blue eyes, under their dark brows, too bright. The expression on his face was so pitiful he would have laughed if he hadn't known it was himself.

"It's all right," said Mrs Gray. "A boy can be hungry." She set his coffee down and cut him another piece of pie.

After he had eaten, Mrs Gray brought him into the living room and introduced him to her husband. "I'm off to the Red Cross," she said. "I'll only be an hour."

Mr Gray nodded and gestured for Frank to sit down. His attention was absorbed by the work on the easel before him, a pencil sketch he was filling in with ink. Frank sat on a hassock beside Mr Gray's wheelchair and watched him work.

Mr Gray was drawing the statue of George Washington in the square near the bridge. Washington was on horseback, and the horse had its head bowed low to its chest. Frank knew the statue well. The scene had been drawn on a sunny day. The artist's eye had been low, his focus slanting across the plaza and up the shallow steps of the base and the pedestal, up the muscled chest and head of the horse, resting finally on the pensive rider. Frank saw exactly where Mr Gray had been when he made the sketch. Under the chestnut tree in the corner of the square. Frank had looked at many pictures before, he liked to look at pictures, but he'd never before thought about *where* the artist was when he made it.

Dipping his pen into the ink bottle, Mr Gray drew with quick strokes a series of thin, vertical lines across the ground below the statue. Then he dipped the pen in the ink again and drew, at an angle, a series of horizontal lines across the vertical ones, making a kind of grid that spread over the sidewalk in a shape that mirrored the shape of the statue, but stretched long, and then Frank saw it was the shadow of the statue — late in the afternoon. He drew in his breath.

Mr Gray smiled at him. "Cross-hatching."

"Cross-hatching," Frank repeated. He liked the word.

"Gives things a little substance," said Mr Gray.

That made sense. Frank could see, now, the cross-hatching that indicated the rise of the steps, the folds on Washington's cloak. An ink mesh, a net to catch the shadows. It gave shape to the tree trunk and the lady's open parasol. Nothing remained flat. Each object took on weight, as the page grew dark with ink. The remaining white paper glowed, became the light of day.

"What do you think?" the artist asked.

"It's good. Gosh, Mr Gray, it's good enough to be in a magazine."

"Well, I hope so," said Mr Gray. "Since that's where it's going to go."

"They give you money for that?" Imagine, being paid to draw pictures!

"Some," said Mr Gray. "These are hard times, boy. Hard times. Not like the old days."

Frank had heard this refrain a hundred times and had no answer for it. He continued to watch in silence until Mrs Gray came in at the door.

On the way home, he barely felt the burden of the heat. He was thinking of his own drawings, how childish they seemed, mere outlines of trees and buildings, nothing but lines on paper. Flat squares and sticks that floated in air with no, what was the word, *substance*. No connection to the rest of the world. He wondered what would happen if he tried to add shadows, as Mr Gray had done. If he tried to draw exactly what he saw, from exactly where he was. ·

3.2

VON FACES HER NEPHEW KYLE IN THE LIVING ROOM ON NORTH First Street. She's sitting on the overstuffed chair that once was Deirdre's favourite, and he's on the couch. Between them, an untouched pot of tea and plate of oatmeal cookies wait on a low coffee table. This is the same room where they met last week, when Von threatened him with a baseball bat and chased him out the door. Now, though she tries not to stare openly, she can't stop looking at him. Half circles like pale bruises under the narrow blue-green eyes, sharp cheekbones, wrists that have grown past the cuffs of his shirt. Shaggy hair, dirty blond with a tinge of orange. A light dusting of freckles, like spilled nutmeg, over the blue-veined skin. Looks like he's never seen the sun. So vulnerable she aches for him.

"Why did you come here?" she asks gently.

"Because of my birth mum, my mother," he says. "Her lawyer called my folks, my foster parents, and told them she died and she left me some money. But I wanted…" He lowers his head. He needs a haircut. And a pair of socks. His blue jeans are too short. They have ridden up, exposing thin bare ankles, none too clean. He needs a bath and a whole new set of clothes. How did he manage to get all the way here on his own?

"My folks told me lots about my dad," he says. "They gave me pictures of him and some of his things. But they never said hardly anything about my mother." His lower lip is trembling.

Who are these Penners, she wonders, who brought him up with no defences?

Finally he pulls himself together and blurts: "I didn't mean to steal nothing. Honest. I only wanted to look around. I just wanted to see…"

"It's all right. What did you take?"

He hesitates, then reaches for the bag in his lap. Undoes one buckle and lifts the flap to show her a spiral-bound edge of yellow cardboard. The war scrapbook she's been looking for.

"What did you want with that?"

"I was just looking around to see if there was any pictures of her, and if there was anything here that was, you know, about me." He runs his fingers through his hair. Bites at a thumbnail. "When you came in, I was holding it in my hand. I just shoved it in my bag and ran."

"It's okay, really. How did you get this address? From the lawyer?"

"No. From my mum. She wrote to me. She sent me a birthday card a couple years ago, when I turned eighteen. It had her address on it, and I kept it. I thought I might come here someday. To meet her. My folks said to be sure I was ready before I decided." He gives her a wry smile, suddenly seems much older. "I thought I had lots of time to get to know her."

A soft ache spreads through Von's chest. She wants to say, "Me too." But it's not right to lay her burdens on this boy. She's the adult. She says, "It sounds as if your foster parents meant well."

"They do mean well. But they don't understand how important it is to know your real mum."

"Still, they sound like good people. You're happy with them, aren't you?"

He frowns. "I told you, I turned eighteen two years ago."

"What do you mean?"

"Once you age out, you can't be a foster kid," he says, as if that's obvious, everybody knows that. "I was lucky they kept me as long as they did."

"So, where…?"

"I found a rooming house in Winnipeg."

She feels stricken when she hears the phrase "rooming house," and Kyle must see the concern on her face, because he hurries to reassure her.

"It's okay. I mean, it was hard at first, but the people are good. They're all young like me. Most of them. We try to cook together. We got a communal garden out back. And ever since Meredith moved in — that's my girlfriend, Meredith — things have been good." The thought of Meredith seems to warm him.

"That's where you met her? In a rooming house?"

"Meredith and me are gonna get our own place."

"Didn't you ever think to call me?"

Kyle blinks. "Call you? I didn't know where you were."

"The Penners didn't tell you about me?"

Kyle looks embarrassed. "Look," he says. "I don't think the Penners know anything about you. My birth mum, she mentioned in her letter that she had a sister. But she never said where."

Von stands and begins to pace the floor. "Where are you staying in New York?"

"I was at the Y at first. But now I'm in a sort of a hostel." He names an intersection some twenty blocks south. "I wanted to stay in New York until you got back. The lawyer said you might not see me, but I wanted to, you know, I wanted to meet you." He looks up at her through the lock of hair that's fallen in his eyes. "You're sort of like my aunt."

"I am your aunt."

A little twitch at the corner of his mouth, like a smile.

Once Kyle relaxes, he eats four cookies and answers Von's questions. She wants to know about his plans for the future. He graduated from an adult ed program, only recently — "scraped by," he says. He has — he corrects himself, he *had* — a job with a landscaping firm, before he took off for New York. Lawn care and pruning. "Totally organic." He doesn't think he'll get that job back. He and Meredith will get married, he says, as soon as she's finished grade twelve. Then they'll get jobs, maybe start their own business, buy a house. It's clear he's a dreamer, with only a dim concept of what the world is and how to live in it. Von feels she should suggest some more realistic plan. Something specific. But before she gets a chance, her telephone rings.

"It's me," says Carol Hart. The lawyer. "What can I bring?"

"Oh, God," says Von. "I forgot."

"You forgot?"

"I have a visitor," she tells Carol. "Unexpected. It's, um, Rosheen's son, from Canada."

"He's here? Wow. Can you talk?"

"Not now."

"All right. Wow. I'll come as soon as I can. What should I bring, though, for the dinner?"

"I've got everything under control."

"Right," says Carol. "Wine it is." She hangs up.

"Listen," Von says to Kyle. "I'm having some people for dinner. They'll be arriving soon. Do you want to stay?"

"These people, did they know my mother?"

"Most of them did, yes."

"Then, yeah," he says. "I'll stay. Can I help with the cooking?"

"Sure. Let's set the table first."

He helps her spread the tablecloth. Can he really be twenty? He takes the cups and saucers down from the upper shelf, and his height makes the long years seem real. As she watches him move around the table, from place to place, setting Deirdre's forks and knives upon the napkins, she remembers the first day she ever saw him.

Von was mowing the lawn in front of the greenhouse when a bright red pickup truck with a defective muffler came rumbling up and parked in the driveway. A tall man in cowboy boots got out the driver's side. He was dressed in an undershirt and a pair of jeans. It was Jean-Claude Allard, the son of the woman who managed the Nicolette Hotel. He walked around the front of the truck and opened the passenger door. Rosheen got out, holding her baby, wrapped in a flannel sheet. Von held her breath. Since Rosheen left home last fall, Von hadn't seen or spoken to her. She'd heard about the baby from Yvette, but he hadn't seemed real until this minute. Jean-Claude draped his arm loosely over Rosheen's shoulder, and together they walked toward Von.

Not wanting to look at Rosheen, Von looked at Jean-Claude instead. He had a stubble beard and leathery, creased skin, like a man who'd been drinking for twenty years, though surely he was no older than twenty-two.

"What are you doing here?" Von demanded.

"She needs some of her things," said Jean-Claude. "She needs clothes."

"Hurry up and get them then," said Von. Rosheen was looking at her, expectantly. But Von only said, "Try not to wake up Dad."

She wanted to see more of the baby, to touch him. She wanted to hold him while Rosheen went inside. But she would not give Rosheen that satisfaction. She turned away, knowing it wasn't right to feel so bitter in the presence of the baby. But she couldn't help it.

Rosheen carried the baby into the house.

Rain clouds drifted in from the west, so Von pushed the mower across the lawn and put it into the garage. When she came back, Jean-Claude was leaning against the truck, by the open driver's door, arms folded across his chest. He jerked his head, to let Von know he wanted her to come closer. He had something to say. She walked over to the truck.

"What?"

"I'm sorry," he said. "I didn't know where else to take her."

"What do you mean?"

He swung himself easily into the driver's seat. "Look. She's in no shape to be taking care of a kid," he said. "And I can't be, you know, involved. If something goes wrong. I don't need no trouble."

"You weasel," said Von.

He shrugged. "Ain't my kid."

"Get out of here," said Von. The rain began to fall.

Jean-Claude handed down a large diaper bag. "Formula and stuff." He shut the door.

When he started the motor, Rosheen came running out of the house. But she was too late to stop him. As he drove across the field, she began to sob.

The white lilacs were blooming, their scent wavering on the breeze. Rosheen held the baby in her arms. In the rain. How old was he? Three months? God, she couldn't stay straight and sober three months?

Von walked toward her sister, saw the dark circles under her eyes, deep hollows under her cheekbones. Rosheen's skin was washed-out, almost grey. She looked close to death. Only the scar burned with a vital intensity, as if it had sucked all the energy from her body and grown brighter.

Rosheen held the baby out, offering him up. "Vonnie, please!"

She took the baby from Rosheen's arms. He was light. Warm. Beautiful. Rosheen was a mess, mascara and snot running down her face. Von wanted to tell her to leave. Go home. But the baby was too small. Von didn't know how to look after him by herself.

"Get inside," she said.

She made coffee and sandwiches and persuaded Rosheen to eat. They gave the baby a bottle and fixed a bed for him in a dresser drawer. Some of Rosheen's old dresses, the ones she wore before she got pregnant, were still hanging in her closet, and they fit her. She took a bath and came downstairs in a green dress and bare legs, thinner than ever, looking like a high-school girl with a case of the flu.

By the time Frank woke up, his two daughters were relatively peaceful, working together on making a cake for the tenth birthday of Manuel and Yvette's daughter, Jeanne.

"Rosheen is here, Dad," Von told him. She did not elaborate.

Frank lowered himself into a kitchen chair and placed his elbows on the table. His recent small stroke had left him confused. "Rosheen?" he asked. "Did Rosheen come home last night?"

"Yes, Dad," said Rosheen. "I'm right here." She reached over and touched his arm.

He moved swiftly, found her hand and captured it with his own. It seemed his body remembered her, had missed her sorely, though his mind was drifting elsewhere.

When Manuel and Yvette arrived with Jeanne, it seemed like a family reunion. Ten-year-old Jeanne, ecstatic to see Rosheen come home for the first time in months, rushed into her arms. Yvette patted Von's shoulder, whispering, "You've done the right thing."

Thus began a brave attempt at reconciliation. Von tolerated Rosheen by treating her as if she were a child again. She insisted that Rosheen must not go out, but stay at home with her and Frank, at least until she gained some weight. She made an appointment for Rosheen to see a doctor and a counsellor. She rocked Kyle and sang to him every evening, so Rosheen could get some sleep. She bought a stack of books on baby care and read—out loud, so Rosheen would hear—about the proper way to raise a healthy child.

———

Carol Hart arrives early to the dinner party, just as Kyle and Von begin chopping vegetables. She asks if she can have a few minutes alone with him, so Von leaves them in the living room while she finishes with dinner. She can't hear what they're saying, only the rhythms of their voices, Carol's calm, professional tone interrupted by Kyle's rapid questions. Alex arrives soon after, eager to meet Rosheen's son, to tell him about his mother and her work. How good her show will be. The show, Von thinks. Will Kyle want to see the show? What does Kyle want?

Leif, the fake Icelander, arrives with a chocolate cheesecake, which is a good thing because she's forgotten all about going to the bakery. He give her a quick kiss on the lips, which makes Alex smile, but no one else seems to notice, or care.

Dinner is noisy and the guests are excited to meet Rosheen's son. He's a bit of a celebrity. Carol and Alex try to draw him out, get him to talk about himself. What's his favourite kind of music? Favourite band? Sport? TV show? He appears to like everything. Ingrid's two students, only a few years older than Kyle, charm and bewilder him with their talk of New York bars and clubs he absolutely has to see. Then for fifteen minutes, Ingrid stuns them all into silence with a lecture on the theoretical implications of Rosheen's collage techniques.

"Von, have you booked a flight yet?" Alex asks.

"Leaving the end of the month." She's cutting a piece of cake for Kyle.

"Where are you going?" Kyle asks.

"The Netherlands," says Alex, "to gather Rosheen's final works for the exhibit." The phrase "final works" hits the dinner guests hard. They all lean back from the table, as if receiving a blow. Alex rephrases: "The project she was working on in Amsterdam."

"The packing and shipping will be difficult," Ingrid cautions. "You'll need help."

"Maybe I could help you," Kyle says to Von. No one else hears him.

"I can handle it." She smiles at him. "Do you want coffee?"

"I should go with you," says Kyle. "It will be my mum's stuff, her paintings and that, right? I should help."

"You don't want to do that," she says. "Believe me, it'll be a lot of work." To Ingrid she says, "Don't worry. I'll get expert advice on the packing."

"Kyle," says Alex, "I have some of Rosheen's work at the gallery. You should come by."

"Oh, yes, you have to come by the gallery," say the girls.

After dessert, Ingrid and the students leave first, then Alex and Carol.

Privately, Von asks Leif to go home, too. "I need to talk to Kyle," she says. "He's staying at a hostel way south of the bridge. I don't want him walking all that way this late at night."

She names the street, and Leif says, "God, no."

"I want to ask him to spend the night here, and it'd be better if, you know..."

"I understand," says Leif. Von walks him out. When they're alone in the hall, he holds her tight and gives her a long, lingering kiss that would have absolutely thrilled her, yesterday.

———

It was easy to convince Kyle to stay the night, since his hostel is so far away. At noon the next day, he showers and eats a huge granola and pancake brunch with blueberries and half a cantaloupe. He likes food, and he's very much in need of it. It's a pleasure to feed him. Von is embarrassed that she can't stop looking at him, but he doesn't seem to mind.

She gives him the photo albums she found in the back bedroom, and he's fascinated to find pictures of himself as a baby. He's never seen a baby picture of himself, he says.

"Your great-grandmother Deirdre made you that blanket," Von says. "That ball was your favourite toy." Every page of the album holds a picture. Though Rosheen was disorganized in those days, or to be honest, she was a wreck, she managed to document Kyle's early life quite thoroughly.

He looks through the whole album twice, then sits holding it on his knees, smiling. "She kept this," he says. "She kept it a long time, eh?"

"Yes."

"But she's not in any of the pictures."

"I guess she was always the one taking the pictures," says Von. She shows him the other albums, pointing out who everyone is. He loves the photos of his mother as a child, but he asks to see more recent pictures of her, as an adult.

Von makes a loose gesture with both arms, indicating the vast amount of material in the apartment, its unruly state, the futility of guessing what might lie hidden there.

Kyle seems to disapprove. "Don't *you* have photos of her?"

"Oh, back in Canada."

He spends the afternoon looking at Rosheen's sketchbooks, her everyday pencil exercises. He drinks them in, though they're nothing special. Dandelions in a jar. A glass bowl of eggs. A ripe peach, sliced in half and darkening. "She was *good*," he says.

In the evening, Von takes him to the Polish café for perogies, and then for a walk through the neighbourhood. She shows him the Northside Gallery, closed for the night. Along the way she points out Deirdre's church, Frank's school, the pub where Rosheen spent so many hours.

"Did she drink a lot?"

"That's partly what ruined her health." If he's going to hang around the gallery and talk to her friends, he'll find out soon enough. She might as well prepare him.

"What was the other part?"

"Cigarettes, marijuana, morphine. Any kind of opiates." She takes a deep breath. "Heroin."

He turns and stares at her.

She tries to soften the blow by adding, "Near the end she went for prescription drugs when she could afford them. She tried not to score on the street."

He absorbs this information stoically. Asks nothing more.

Von walks along beside him, worrying. What other facts might surface, with Rosheen's show coming up? Even Von, who lived through it all, can't bear to remember it. She can't inflict it on Kyle. And wasn't that exactly why she resolved not to seek Kyle out, not to get to know him? Why has she let her guard down? Why is she letting him stay?

Pure selfishness on her part. She doesn't want to let him go.

Back at the apartment, Kyle phones his girlfriend, and Von can hear the excitement in his voice. She can tell the girlfriend makes him happy, and she's glad. She decides to let him stay a few more days. Let him visit Rosheen's friends and look at some of her art. Then she'll send him home. Maybe this winter, when she's back in Canada, she'll take him out for dinner at a restaurant or something. Maybe even make that a regular thing. Encourage him to go to college.

At eight o'clock he's hungry again, so she makes him macaroni and cheese and a green salad, and sits with him at the dining room table, drinking tea. Once again he raises the idea that he could travel to Holland with her. He seems to have made up his mind to go.

"It's Europe," Von says. "You can't just take off and go to Europe on a whim. You need time to prepare. You need a passport."

"I have a passport," he says. "I got one to go to Germany last year with the Penners." He goes to the couch where he slept the night and returns with his pack. Digging through the pockets, he pulls out a plastic sandwich bag with a blue Canadian passport inside. "See? I'm good to go."

"It's an expensive trip," says Von.

This deflates him. He sits down at the table, the pack at his feet, and tucks the passport back inside. He eats the rest of his macaroni slowly, in silence.

"Carol says..." He stops. He picks at the crumbs left on the plate.

"Do you want some dessert? Strawberries?"

"Carol says the first two payments from the greenhouse are already due to me. Spring and summer. I could use that money for the trip. It's enough for Meredith to come, too. She's already got a passport. She'll be finished summer school next Friday, so —"

"Meredith?"

"She wants to come." His voice speeds up, rises in pitch. "As soon as I told her about Holland she wanted to come. We could both help you with my mum's stuff, and then me and Meredith could go to France. She speaks French. A little. She's always wanted to go to France."

"Do you think that's wise?" Von asks him. "To make such a sudden decision? Don't you think you should save this money? Use it for practical purposes, for college, or for —"

"This is practical," he says. "It's practically exactly what I want. It's what we both want."

"I don't know, Kyle. Here you are with no job and no education, living in a rooming house…" She hesitates to hurt him, but it's necessary. "And the first few thousand dollars you get you're going to blow on a trip to Europe?"

"Well, yeah," he says. "Sure."

But he's slowing down. He's rethinking it.

She gathers the dishes and takes them to the kitchen. When she returns, the dining room is empty. She finds Kyle kneeling in the front hall pulling on his sneakers.

"Are you going out?"

His laces are too long. He makes extra large loops and ties a double bow to keep them from dragging on the floor. When he's finished, he stands and faces her.

"I get it," he says. "You don't want me around."

Von lets his words hang in the air. She looks at the floor. She wants to argue with him, let him know he's wanted. At the same time, she wants to protect him, let him go.

He's still, listening to the silence. Then he nods — not to her but to himself, as if confirming some long-held suspicion. He slings his pack over his shoulder. Stands there a moment as if he's going to say something. Then turns and walks out the door.

Von fastens the deadbolt behind him. A flash of regret, but it's best to let him go.

She looks out the window and watches him walk east until he turns south, out of view.

Too late, she remembers he still has the yellow scrapbook.

3.3

BRENDAN O'NOLAN DIDN'T STAY AWAY FOR LONG. THREE DAYS after Mr Edison scared him off, Deirdre opened her kitchen curtains early in the morning to see him sitting on the low stone wall that skirted the tenement directly opposite. The wall was too low to sit on, and his legs were spread wide and sprawled out over the sidewalk in front of him. He had a dirty face, or maybe a black eye, and his clothes seemed wrinkled and stained. He looked up at her window, and she ducked. When Tomas and Frank left together in the morning, she watched from behind the curtain, so tense her shoulders ached. But she was relieved to see that Brendan barely glanced at them on the street. He did not know who they were. How long could she keep him from finding out?

Brendan stayed out in the street, until Mrs Heintz came by and gave him a scolding and threatened to call a policeman. That got him moving. He lurched to his feet and lumbered off, clutching his belt buckle to keep the waistband of his pants from sliding down the slope of his belly. Was this really the little boy she remembered? How hard it had once been to make him stay put. She had many times needed to splash a little whisky into his milk to slow him down. Once she gave him too much and when Nora was bathing him he fell into the dishpan and nearly drowned. Deirdre had pounded his back until he spit up the water he'd swallowed. She could hold him under one arm then. Now here he was, on the other side of the world, bloated and slow, an utterly different creature. She had to devise some method to get rid of him.

Brendan soon attracted notice in the neighbourhood. He was seen in the pubs, where he drank too much and was said to mutter to himself or badger strangers with long, nonsensical ramblings. He became known among the men as "that pale-faced Irish lout." Even Tomas brought home a tale about the new immigrant down at Reilly's who couldn't handle his liquor.

Twice, Brendan approached Deirdre in the street, trying to speak with her, but she brushed him off, maintaining she did not know him. She couldn't tell if he believed her or not. She could only hope, uneasily, that he would give up, since he had no proof. She heard he'd taken a room above a tavern on South Fourth and worked as a janitor in the building. She avoided that street and any place associated with him.

But his absence frightened her as much as his presence did. After nine days without seeing him, she feared he had sailed back to Ireland, where he would tell everyone where she was. Perhaps Nora O'Nolan would show up to scratch out her eyes, or Daniel Mac Michael would come on his one leg to claim her. She dreamed of the first and second Mrs O'Nolans as gaunt fairy women riding the night air, red eyes glowing, bony fingers reaching for her neck.

In July, she finally ventured onto South Fourth Street. She faced straight ahead, glancing left and right under lowered eyelids, and when she reached the end of the block, she turned and walked back the other way. As she passed his building the second time, she dared to slow down. The tavern door was closed, and the curtains in the small window were drawn. Beside the tavern, a rickety addition housed the staircase to the apartments above. The door to this addition stood open, and just as Deirdre peered into its murky depth, Brendan came out to the sidewalk and grasped her by the arm. She didn't resist. Though she wasn't sure why, she understood that she had wanted him to find her.

He pulled her inside. The hallway was dark, and she tripped up against a metal wash bucket and slipped on the wet floor. Only his tight grip on her arm kept her from falling. He shoved her against the wall and placed his hands on her shoulders. He was a head taller than she was. His narrow eyes were more open and more clear than she'd seen them before. He was sober and smelled of raw onions. She turned her face to the side.

"Why did you never send for us?" he hissed. "Your father and mother came. They couldn't take us home because they had their own children to care for and no room for us." He leaned hard against her. "They said you sold our house. They said you were after emigrating, to get us a better life. They said once you got to America you would send for us."

"You've got the wrong person," Deirdre whispered.

"I know you, Ma. I know your voice."

Surely it was impossible he could remember her voice after so many years. But she thought it best to say nothing more.

"Did you think the nuns would want us?" He pressed harder, and she heard her shoulder blades crunch against the wall. "I'll tell you they didn't. They had too many brats to feed already. A wretched lot, full of lice they were, and fever. The sisters hated them and hated us too."

Deirdre did not want to hear what might be coming. She made a mighty effort to wrench away, but he held her fast.

"You might think nuns are all good women but they're not, I tell you. When the children got sick with the nervous fever they put them in quarantine. All alone in a back room, cold and full of spiders. Left them alone to die. One by one. My own brothers and sisters." He lowered his head. She saw his shoulders quiver, though he still held her fast with his hands. "It is a horrid disease. Faye lay bleeding from her mouth and from her nose, and Owen went mad, crawling on the floor like an animal. Poor Nora —"

"And Fiona?" asked Deirdre.

Brendan dropped his hands. A moan escaped his mouth and he fell silent.

"Fiona?"

"Fiona too," said Brendan. "She was calling and calling for you. Nora held her and told her you were on your way back, that you'd come tomorrow. Fiona lived on for two days, and Nora kept stretching the lie, until finally Fiona passed." He wiped his eyes with the back of his hand. "Where *were* you?"

Deirdre began to weep freely. She wept for Fiona, her sweet freckled face and the clean tones of her childish laugh, and because she knew, as soon as she'd spoken Fiona's name, she had closed the trap on herself. She couldn't deny any longer who she was.

While they stood there, both of them weeping, a man came out of the tavern and entered the hallway. "What is this?" he demanded. He was short and squat, and his English was tinged with a Polish accent. He gave Brendan a cuff. "I hire you to mop, you mop!"

Deirdre took this chance to slip out the front and hurry along the street toward home, hiding her face with her handkerchief. When she passed Our Lady of Consolation, she stopped at the wrought iron fence, fighting against the part of herself that wanted to rush inside and confess her sins to Father Madden. For she knew she must maintain her position in the church, as wife of Tomas Garrison and mother of Frank. Brendan must be made to understand that he couldn't tell a word of his story to anyone else. How could she convince him? What would he want in return?

When she reached the apartment, Frank was at the kitchen table, drawing on the back of an old calendar Tomas had given him. A picture of a big ship in harbour. It reminded Deirdre of the hope she once had of setting off for a new life in America. She told Frank she had a headache and needed to lie down. She asked him not to disturb her. Frank looked up at her in surprise, and she remembered she had not spoken a civil word to him in weeks. His blue eyes, so guileless and curious, made her reach over and place her hand on his head. "Let me rest a bit and I'll make you a pudding for your dinner," she said.

His eyes widened. For a second he seemed about to speak, but thought better of it.

She closed the bedroom door. Then lowered herself and crawled under the bed, pried up the floorboard with a shoehorn and took out the tobacco tin. She sat on the bed to count the bills and the coins. How much would he want? Fifty American dollars? A hundred? That was a fraction of what she had got for the farm. Was it enough to keep him quiet? She thought of the crumbling building where he lived, the menial work he did, his love for liquor.

She did not sleep that night. She lay beside Tomas until he began to snore, and then she went to the kitchen and drank tea. As the sun began to rise, she decided. She wrapped a hundred dollars in a clean paper bag and put it in her pocket. If Tomas woke before she returned, she'd say she'd been at church, lighting a candle for something. For Lucy. That would please him. She slipped out and walked down to the third floor. Then she turned and came back upstairs. Perhaps she would need only half. She scrounged among the shelves for another bag and found one, stained with tea, but it would do. She divided the money in half and placed one bag in each of her coat pockets and went out again.

A card tacked in the entryway listed the tenants, most with unpronounceable Polish names. B. O'Nolan was in 2B. She crept upstairs, hoping everyone was still asleep. It wouldn't do to be seen here at this time of day. When she tapped on his door, he was not surprised to see her.

She sat on the one chair, and he sat on the bed. The only other furniture was a narrow chest of drawers, its top crowded with a washbasin, a whisky bottle, and a dusty candlestick.

"I wanted to send for you," she said. "I wanted to send for all of you, but my husband…" She was not sure how far she should go.

"We had nothing," Brendan said. "Nora and Margaret and Kevin and me, those of us that lived, we had to go out on our own, with no family to speak of. English people living in our own father's house. All his hard work gone to nothing. Nora and Margaret went into service over in London. Kevin and me got jobs in Cork. But there was never enough work. Kev lives in a slum there now, his wife and children dressed in rags."

"We're not much better off here," Deirdre said. "We —"

"I've no time for your troubles," he said. "It's because of you my life is a misery and my family destroyed." He folded his thick arms and stared down at the floor. Waiting.

Deirdre sat in silence, calculating. Her gaze rested on the frayed hem of his pant leg. On both of his shoes, the upper part had separated from the sole. A dirty sock showed through the crack of one shoe and a row of bare toes peeked out of the other.

"If I had some decent clothes," he said. "I could find work."

Deirdre pulled one paper bag from her pocket and held it on her lap. "I've only a little saved. If you need, if you need a few things." She reached in and pulled out a handful of bills. Keeping her face turned toward the floor, she stretched out her arm, and let him take them.

He shuffled them in his hands, counting, and when he had finished, he snorted. "Twenty-one dollars," he said. "For a man's home and family."

"It's all I —"

"Some say you married that Claddagh fisherman —"

She thrust the whole bag at him, and he snatched it. He spilled the paper and coins on the bed and began to count.

"But you must say nothing. My husband would be very angry."

Brendan looked up sharply. "Is he a violent man?"

"He's — yes. Yes, he is." Deirdre saw Brendan's face tighten. This frightened him. "Why he once threw a flowerpot at my son's head and nearly killed him," she said. "I don't know what he'd do if he found out I've given you so much. He might — you mustn't say a word to anyone."

Brendan sat on the edge of the bed, sorting and counting. He had fifty dollars now. "I can be quiet," he said. "I didn't come to cause any trouble. I only wanted…a little help."

Their eyes met for the first time, each admitting they recognized the nature of the bargain.

"I'd best be off then," said Deirdre. "I've work to attend to."

She stepped into the hallway. Though the light was dim, she recognized the Polish man she'd seen there before, home from an early errand. He wore a felt hat and carried a newspaper under one arm. He was unbuttoning his coat, but when he saw Deirdre emerge from Brendan's room, his fingers stopped moving. He looked past her at Brendan, who stood in the doorway.

"You filthy Irish," he said. "I'll throw you out on the street." He strode toward them.

"I washed all the floors last night, Mr Wolnski," said Brendan. "It's all done —"

Wolnski reached over Deirdre and slapped Brendan's left ear with the folded paper. "Bringing a woman into my house!" Then the right ear. "Do you think this is a brothel that you can bring some —"

"Mr Wolnski. It's not — no! It's — this is my mother."

"Your mother?"

Deirdre could hardly deny it. She attempted a smile. "Pleased to meet you."

He looked her up and down and must have decided she was respectable enough, for he took off his hat. "Good morning, Ma'am."

Deirdre hurried home. By the time Tomas got up, she was cooking porridge as usual, so she did not need to lie. She felt relieved, though it was only a mild sensation, since she knew it was temporary. Lying was inevitable now. She must memorize what to say on every occasion, the way she memorized recipes. There had once been a time in her life when a lie was a sin to be scrupulously avoided. But those days were so long ago she could barely remember them.

———

At first, it seemed that Brendan O'Nolan would honour his unspoken promise to leave Deirdre alone. On the few occasions she saw him in public, he gave no sign that he recognized her, and she was grateful. He was wearing good clothes and new shoes, and it seemed he'd given up his heavy drinking and his role as public nuisance. Still, she did not trust him. When she heard no more gossip about him, she took to walking down his street from time to time. She stopped to chat with Mr Wolnski, who seemed to think more kindly of Brendan than before, and learned that Brendan had taken a second job. He was caretaker of the Polish church on Havermeyer. So it seemed he had reformed. But in her hardened heart she wondered if it would last.

Sure enough, before the leaves fell from the trees, he accosted her at the Bedford Station as she returned with a basket of piecework from the glove factory. He followed her closely, telling a long tale of woe — he had lost his place at the church, he had been robbed by a pick-pocket — until she promised him twenty dollars, getting rid of him only minutes before Frank arrived to walk her home. She met with Brendan four more times after that, paying him something each time.

She dreamed of him as an oversized baby she was trying to hide. He was chubby and white, in swaddling clothes but big as a four-year-old. She shoved him into laundry baskets or steamer trunks and in one gruesome nightmare hid him in the cook stove and watched in horror, unable to speak, as Tomas lit the fire.

This went on until Thanksgiving, when, in a desperate bid for freedom, she let him have fifty dollars to go up to New Rochelle, where he said he had work as a servant in a rectory. If she would only let him have fifty, he promised, he would never ask for more.

———

Father Madden had taken an interest in Frank recently. He went to the gym to watch Frank sparring, and one day after Mass, he asked Deirdre and Tomas if Frank could represent the parish in a boxing tournament against Father Duffy's parish in the Bronx. Tomas hesitated. Frank was in grade seven now, he explained, and the schoolwork was difficult for him. He should spend more time with his studies. But it was hard to say no to a priest. Father Madden stressed that the boxing winnings went to the poor and sick in the parish, and finally Tomas relented. Father Madden purchased a new pair of gloves and paid coaching fees to Simon Higgins, so Frank could train in earnest.

Deirdre liked the idea. She and Tomas had been upset when they first heard Frank had set upon the Cuthbert boys last summer. But the priest explained to them that the Cuthberts had been bullying a girl. He said in a delicate tone that he would not name the girl, but Frank had preserved her honour. That made Deirdre proud. If only she'd known a boy like Frank in Galway. A boy to beat those British soldiers. A boy to save her from Galen's clutches. A man.

She imagined her own son driving Galen's son from her door. His fists flashing, bringing Brendan to his knees. Yes. Frank, who must never know who Brendan was, should be the very one to run him off for good.

3.4

FOR NINETEEN YEARS, VON HAS SLEPT EVERY NIGHT WITHOUT knowing where Kyle was, but tonight she finds it intolerable. Where did he go? When he first walked out, she told herself it was for the best. Then, when she started to worry, she tried to convince herself he'd merely gone for a walk to blow off steam. He'd be back soon enough, probably wanting a midnight snack. But it's past midnight now. He's been gone three hours, and it's Brooklyn, and he has no money. Her chest feels tight, as if there's not enough air in the apartment. She stands at the open window. Looks up and down the street. Finally she goes down to the basement and takes Rosheen's bicycle out of the locker.

She cycles through the dark streets in the direction of the hostel, but when she arrives there, she sees it's not a hostel. She'd been picturing a youth centre for adventurous backpackers, but this is a homeless shelter. This is "The Way," according to the sign above the door. The sign is not lit up. The bulb in the corner streetlamp flickers, ready to burn out. The adjacent streets are deserted. She can see a blue light of some kind in the interior. But the door is locked. She places her hands on the window glass to cut the reflection and peers toward the blue light. At the far end of the room, a man and a woman are watching television. They don't look homeless. Their clothes are too fashionable. Von knocks on the glass, but they won't come near her. They point at a sign that says they close at nine o'clock. Homeless people have go to bed at nine? Kyle would have missed that deadline tonight. Where might he have gone?

She rides around the nearby streets, looking for any open coffee shops, and before long she spots him at an all-night bakery. She can see him through the big windows. Relief washes through her lungs. She's alarmed by how relieved she is. The thought crosses her mind that she's not alone anymore. No matter what happens from now on, she is no longer alone. He looks paler under the fluorescent lights, young and unprotected, sitting in a booth with the war scrapbook open on the table before him. His feet must be sore, walking all this way in those thin sneakers. She should buy him some shoes. She should bring him back to the apartment and fix him a proper bed in the spare room, give him a set of keys, take him shopping. Take an interest. Ask about his girlfriend.

She locks the bike to a post and walks in and sits down across the table from him. He looks up, surprised, and she can tell he's glad.

"I'm sorry," she says right away. "I'm so sorry."

"It's okay," he says. "I know you weren't expecting me, and then I go and sort of invite myself into your life and — I do that sometimes. Dumb. Sorry." He cringes in a comical, friendly manner. Exactly like Rosheen. Exactly.

The server comes with coffee and they sit for a while, sipping. Kyle leafs through the scrapbook, puzzling over maps of Europe with dotted lines and arrows and dates pencilled in, and a route from Normandy up to Antwerp marked in red ink. Then page after page of black-and-white photographs of soldiers carrying rifles and binoculars. Stretchers heavy with maimed bodies. Flamethrowers, burst dikes, Nazi tanks. Muddy soldiers lined up, eating from mess kits or smoking cigarettes and smiling for the camera, their names written carefully in white ink above their heads.

"Why did she keep all this stuff about the war?"

"Part of her art project."

"She was interested in war? Isn't that kind of weird? I mean, for a woman?"

"Our dad was in the war," Von says. She points to the scrapbook. "World War Two."

He nods, very serious. Bends his head and reads some more. She realizes for the first time how lost he must be. He doesn't know his own history.

"What's this?" he asks. "Is this German?" He turns the book around and places the page in front of her. A letter to Rosheen with the heading, "Amsterdam, December 14, 1994."

"That's Dutch, I think," Von says. The letter is from a woman named Marijke Haas.

"Who is Marijke Haas?"

"I'm not sure. One of her contacts in Holland."

"I was thinking," he says. "About Amsterdam. Meredith and I should go and, like, you don't have to *take* us. You don't have to pay our hotel or anything. But we'll be there. If you need any help. Maybe you don't. But if you do. You know."

"I understand," she says. He's saying she can't stop him from travelling wherever he wants to travel. The money is his. His mother gave it to him. He'll spend it how he pleases.

"It's late. We should go home," she says.

"To the apartment? You don't mind?"

"I want you to stay with me," Von says. "As long as you're in New York."

"Thanks." He's sleepy. So is she. They have twenty blocks to cover and one bicycle. Kyle pedals, and Von perches on the handlebars, calling out "red light!" or "sewer grate!" to guide him. Halfway home, they both start laughing, though Von doesn't know exactly why. Maybe it's sheer relief. She didn't lose him, she didn't let that cold, scared streak inside her drive him away.

Without warning, she is visited by the memory of Bobby, before he was old enough to drive, riding her double on his racer. He liked to pedal standing up, while she sat behind him on the seat because, he said, he loved to feel her arms around his waist, holding onto him.

3.5

FRANK HAD NO SUCCESS CONVINCING HIS FATHER TO LET HIM QUIT school. After Martha Waters got married and moved away, Frank's father said he was old enough to get himself to classes. But Frank rarely did. He had other things to learn. Mr Edison was teaching him joining and framing. Mr Gray gave him regular drawing assignments, and critiqued his work on Sunday afternoons. Last week Frank had gone to the piers and sketched the long curves of a sailboat's bow and the frayed rope that moored it to the iron ring and the way the planks of the dock had cracked around the bolt that held the ring. Mr Gray told him to draw it again when the water was choppy and show the iron ring lifted upright and the strain on the rope when the wind pulled it taut.

Father Madden said talent was God's way of showing a man who he was meant to be, and Frank should practise the things he was good at. Father Madden meant boxing. But Frank prayed for guidance with his other talents as well, and it was soon revealed to him that the more he practised drawing, the more closely his pictures resembled the objects he drew. It was a matter of seeing, Mr Gray said, when he and Frank sat together, drawing one of the still-life scenes he liked to set up on the table, for practice. Frank needed to be silent and concentrate on looking. He soon discovered that this kind of looking cast a spell on him, and set him free from his own thoughts. But at home, Tomas insisted Frank must practise the things he was *not* good at, reading and arithmetic. Frank must stay in school, Tomas said, through grade nine. Then Tomas would see about getting him on at the factory. Father and son working side by side. But Frank knew he couldn't survive that long in school. And he didn't want to work in the factory, which seemed the same as school, only dirtier, working all day in a set place, where you couldn't see the sky.

Sometimes Frank thought his life would be perfect if only it weren't for his parents, but then a heavy guilt descended swiftly upon him, threatening to crush his spirits, and he told himself to be grateful. His parents supplied him with a warm, safe place to live and a bed to sleep in, even if it did have Junior in it. Still, he could barely wait for the day he would be a man and discover for himself what it was God wanted him to do.

Mr Green was closing for the day when the telephone rang with an odd request, an order so small it was barely worth delivering. But Mr Green insisted. "It's Paolo Madero. A good customer. You can do one more."

It was January, the temperature so low Frank could see his breath. He pedalled hard down Kent Avenue, searching for the address, which turned out to be the closed-down boot factory, a strange place for a person to live. Frank rapped on the door, calling, "Green's! Delivery!"

From somewhere inside, a man's voice told him to enter. Frank stepped across the threshold, taking off his cap and gloves. He walked through a kitchen into a large open space. Two thick shafts of winter sunlight poured in from the storefront windows. A table ran along one wall, holding dishes of colour — he counted five different shades of yellow — half-filled bottles of blue and black ink, a jumble of knives and little trowels and paintbrushes of all sizes — new ones with sleek bristles and old ones with splayed bristles and some with their bristles soaking in jars of oily liquid. An intoxicating smell. Three tall easels stood by the windows, each holding a different picture. The first was a painting of a blonde woman. She was smiling, her slightly parted lips level with his eyes, and he lowered his gaze to take in the rest of her. A shock, like a spray of hot water prickling beneath his skin, rushed through his body. She was very nude. Naked. Quickly, he turned away, so as not to be caught looking.

But Mr Madero didn't seem to care. He came forward, jingling coins in his hand. He was in his thirties. His white shirtsleeves were rolled up and his arms were brown. His face was brown too, and crinkled into a smile, revealing clean white teeth. He was cheerful and unashamed of the painting. He took the bottle of linseed oil from Frank's hand and tipped him a dime. "For candy," he said. He took the bottle to the table and began to open it.

Outside, dazed by the sunlight and the cold and the memory of that painting, Frank opened his palm. A whole dime? For delivering one tiny bottle he could carry in his pocket? He wondered if Mr Madero was right in the head.

———

The linseed oil, Frank found out later, was for mixing oil paints. Mr Madero had been a successful artist in Spain, but said he'd moved to New York because of "all that's going on in Europe." Frank nodded, wondering what that meant. He made many deliveries that spring to Mr Madero's studio and met many people there. Mr Madero knew a lot of women — loose women, his mother would call them — and men too, foreign men of all sorts, coming and going. Frank liked to come inside and look at the paintings on the easels, which were always changing. He liked to see who was there and listen to their conversations. He had never met such odd and interesting people before. People who talked about ideas as if they were important.

One day, as Frank waited, studying one of the oil portraits, he realized the artist was watching him. "That interests you," Mr Madero observed.

"Yes," said Frank.

"Sit down with me and have a drink." He gave Frank a glass of water and poured red wine for himself. "So, you like paintings?"

Frank told him Mr Gray was teaching him how to draw still-life arrangements, though he could not explain how it felt. Gradually, he was understanding how to let himself slide into a kind of daydream, right there in Mr Gray's living room, and let the shapes of the things he was drawing travel through his body. But he could not put that into words, so he told about the flowers and the fruit and the kinds of pencils he used. "But your paintings," he said. He swept his hand to indicate the whole room. "All this is…swell." It was a stupid word, but he had no better one. Embarrassed, he picked up a box of tin tubes and turned it over in his hand.

"These are oil paints. You have never tried them?"

"No. I tried some watercolours once but — Mr Madero?"

"I'm Paolo. Call me Paolo. You want to try?" He offered Frank a clean, dry brush and a scrap of wrapping paper.

"I don't know how," Frank said.

Paolo laughed. "Nobody knows how without trying. You just… try." He took a wooden board from a shelf and set it in front of Frank. He picked out some tubes of colour and squeezed dabs of paint onto the board — a copper colour and a red and a yellow. He added a blob of white and a small puddle of linseed oil and set down a thin metal trowel. "Go ahead, mix them up."

Frank was afraid he'd make a mistake, ruin something, but when Paolo left the room, he became brave. He patted the puddle of white paint with the back of the trowel and loved the noise it made, a lush little splat. Dipping a brush into the copper paint, he was surprised that it stuck to the bristles and did not drip. When he added oil, he saw how it thinned the paint but didn't dull the colour. He wiped the brush and drew it through the yellow, making a fat swirl that touched the blob of red. He saw how the yellow could merge with the red yet not get lost within it. Not right away. Oil paint was different from watercolour. It mixed, yet didn't mix completely unless Frank wanted it to. He blended the yellow into the red and added a little white and a little more white, each time making a wisp on the paper like a small flame. Six different shades of orange. He saw that if he had enough paint he could play with the colours endlessly. They swirled and blended like the colours he'd seen in puddles of spilled gasoline in the street. He looked closely at the sun-browned back of his own hand and turned it over, examined the pink and yellow palm, the pale blue veins in his wrist. Everything was multi-coloured. Everything in the world. You only had to open your eyes.

When summer came, Frank was too busy working to hang out at the docks with Corky, though sometimes when the city air was muggy and sweat dripped from his face as he pedalled through traffic, he daydreamed of diving off the docks again, into the cool waters of the East River. He only saw Corky at the gym, telling dirty jokes and bragging about his brother, Simon. Corky didn't have a job, but scrounged charcoal bits and scrap metal and often rolled dice or played cards for money. Gambling, according to Frank's father, Tomas, would lead a man straight to the grave. But Corky said it was fun, and if you were smart you could get rich that way.

Frank was riding down Chambers, in Manhattan, delivering packages for Dr Green, when he saw Corky horsing around on the steps of the Court House with some tough-looking boys. Corky sauntered over, hands in his pockets, as if for a casual chat, and then, without warning, he lifted himself onto the handlebars and whispered harshly over his shoulder to Frank, "Let's go!"

"Go where?" asked Frank.

"Hey," called one of the boys. "Get back here, you!"

"Go!" said Corky.

Frank heard the angry shouts of the boys as they gained on Corky. Without looking back, he pushed hard on the pedals, and he was away — standing tall so he could peer over Corky's shoulder.

The boys gave chase, trying to grab the back fender, but Frank ditched them by zigzagging in and out of traffic until he neared the waterfront.

Corky hopped off and looked down the street. "Looks like we lost 'em. Thanks, Frankie. Hey, what's in the bags, your lunch? How many lunches you got?" He grabbed one of the paper bags out of Frank's carrier.

"What did they want?" Frank asked.

Corky shrugged. He reached into the paper bag and screamed with joy as he pulled out a set of false teeth. "Choppers!"

"Put those back," Frank said. "I have to take them up to Fifth Avenue."

"Fifth Avenue? Lah dee dah," said Corky. He held the upper teeth in one hand and the lowers in the other and clapped them together as if they were talking. A young lady passed by, and Corky launched the teeth into a monologue. "Why Mabel, did you see the get-up that girl had the gall to wear to church? Well, I never!"

The young lady giggled. Frank couldn't help laughing too.

Corky turned his back on his audience and when he turned around again the teeth were in his mouth, huge and chattering, and he was braying like a donkey. The young lady covered her mouth with her hands and hurried away, doubling over with laughter.

"Corky!" said Frank. "Take those out!"

They climbed the fire escape of a warehouse on the waterfront and sat on the rooftop, sharing the corned beef sandwich Frank had made and the thick slices of watermelon Mrs Green had given him. After he finished eating, Frank stretched out on his back and looked up. Maybe it was going to rain at last. He thought about painting the sky in oils, its blues and greys and different shades of white, and the yellow cast of the clouds on summer days like this when they seemed to trap the city's heat within them. After a while he stood and stretched and walked the length of the roof and rested his wrists on the railing, watching a white sailboat wend its slow way under the Brooklyn bridge, to sea. What was it like out there, beyond Long Island? Where the water stretched as far as you could see? It must be like sailing into the high, impossible arc of the sky.

"Did you ever think of going out in a boat?" he asked Corky. "Crossing the ocean?"

"What for?" asked Corky. He chucked his melon rind as far as he could toward the river, but it fell short, landing below with an unheard splat on the pavement, startling a scavenging seagull into flight.

Then next day Frank came home to find Corky on the stoop outside his building, with two black eyes and a swollen, bloody nose.

"I won at craps," Corky said, by way of explanation. "They didn't like it."

Frank winced. "You won fair?"

"Can I come in and get some ice?" Corky asked.

Frank hesitated. But the bruises on Corky's face were truly ugly. "I guess so. My father is home, so Ma won't give us too much trouble."

Deirdre was sweeping the kitchen when the boys came in. She raised her broom as if to sweep Corky from her house like vermin. But Frank called out for his father right away, so she simply shook a warning finger at the boys.

Tomas was outraged when he saw Corky's face. He wrapped some ice in a handkerchief and applied it to Corky's nose. Frank's cousins came in, and Tomas took the opportunity to give them all a lecture. A man should avoid fighting whenever possible. He should only throw a punch in an emergency. Frank figured this advice was wasted on Corky, who probably hadn't put up much of a fight of any kind. But it was good advice. A man should fight only for a good cause, said his father. To protect the weak or stop an injustice.

Once he cleaned Corky up a little, Tomas insisted he and Frank must walk Corky home, in case the bullies were waiting for him, and sure enough, as they rounded the corner onto Wythe Street, they saw two punks leaning against the bridge pilings, watching the front of Corky's building. One of them had his shirt sleeves torn right off at the shoulder and carried a piece of pipe that he banged against the iron railing of the bridgehead — clang, clang — a low sound that echoed off the underside of the bridge and carried through the street.

"Are those the ruffians who hurt you?" Tomas asked.

"No, it ain't," said Corky.

Frank didn't recognize the two boys, but he could tell that Corky was lying. Maybe he was afraid to rat in case they beat him worse. The burly one with the pipe looked as if he weighed twice what Corky did.

But Tomas was already striding across the street, determined to have a word with them.

Corky leaped after him and grabbed his sleeve. "No, Mr Garrison, that ain't them. Please!"

Tomas turned, frowning. "Why, Corky, are you certain?" He took the time to look directly into Corky's eyes, to see if he were telling the truth. The punks seized that opportunity to run away. Frank saw them go. By the time Tomas turned around again, they had vanished.

"Those are just some kids live down the street," Corky said quietly.

Tomas stood watch on the stoop while Frank walked Corky up to his apartment.

"Your dad's nice and all," Corky whispered. "But he doesn't understand."

"If those are the guys who beat on you, you should admit it," said Frank.

Corky threw up his hands. "I took their money, Frank."

"But if you won the game, then —"

"I *took* it," Corky said. "The fat one, he had a wad of bills in his wallet. I saw how much it was when he took it out to pay his debt, and later he left it on the step behind him while we were playing craps. When I saw you coming by on your bike, I grabbed it and ran."

"Jesus, Corky."

"Don't tell your dad," he said. "I don't want your dad to know."

"The best thing," said Frank, "is to give the money back."

Corky filled his cheeks with air and blew it out. "I spent it."

Frank didn't know what to say to that. They had reached the Higgins' apartment door, so he said good night and went downstairs.

Tomas put his hand on Frank's shoulder and led him away. They walked silently until they reached the end of the block. Then Tomas turned and looked back. The two punks were nowhere to be seen.

"If you see those boys hanging around here again, you let me know," said Tomas.

"Yes, Dad." They continued walking.

"Two against one isn't fair. It isn't honourable."

"No, Dad," said Frank. He walked home beside his father, subdued and thoughtful. He thought of all the things he'd seen Corky take over the years. Candies from the corner store, an apple from the lunch-cart man, pennies from a beggar's cup. He remembered the dynamite from the construction site. Frank had been in on that himself. He tried to tell himself that was different, but he knew it wasn't. It was stealing. Worse, he could have hurt someone. He could only comfort himself with the thought that he'd been young. He and Corky were only kids last summer. Now they were fourteen. Soon they would be grown. It was time for them to decide what kind of men they wanted to be.

"Mr Madero? It's Frank from Green's." Frank stepped into the kitchen and set the box of bread and fruit on the kitchen table. Paolo didn't answer. Frank removed his cap and walked through to the studio, expecting to find the artist at work. Instead, he found two women. The blonde one sat on a chair, wearing a cloche hat and a faded pink dress. She was resting her heels on the edge of an empty easel, and Frank saw the ruddy soles of her bare feet. The other woman stood in the corner, wearing only a bed sheet. Her shoulders were bare, her skin deep brown, darker than the skin of anyone he'd ever met before. Her head was bowed, and a strip of blue cloth held the curls of her hair off her face. The white sheet and that blue cloth. The sun through the west window cast a rectangle of light on the floor, framing her shadow. The blonde woman smiled at him in a lazy, bored way, and he recognized her from the nude painting he'd seen on his first visit here. She yawned loudly, without covering her mouth, and her tongue curled up like a cat's tongue. The dingy strap of an undergarment slipped off her shoulder. He could not speak.

"Paolo's gone down to the corner for some ice," said the standing woman. Her voice was low and warm, and he knew she had moved here from the South. A charcoal drawing on the easel showed her long back, her spine and shoulder blades.

Paolo returned with a block of ice, unconcerned that the delivery boy had happened upon his half-dressed models. He cheerfully attacked the block with a pick and they all drank, ice water sliding down their throats.

"This is Wendy," Paolo said of the blonde woman. "And this is Tina, my new model."

Frank and the women said hello. For a few minutes they chatted about the heat. Paolo rinsed some grapes and passed them around, and Wendy smoked a cigarette.

"Frank's learning to draw," Paolo told them. "He's pretty good, too."

"You're his teacher?" Tina asked.

"Not exactly," said Paolo. "We're friends." He bumped Frank's cup with his own. "But maybe I should give him the odd lesson. What do you say? Can he sit in with us?"

Tina shrugged, and Wendy said, "Why, sure."

Frank backed away, startled. A sudden memory of his mother slapping his face in the soda shop when he looked too long at a picture of a woman in a movie magazine.

"Don't worry," said Paolo. "Wendy won't show you anything too grown-up. And Tina is a modest, married lady. She always keeps the sheet on. It would be good practice. Do you want to stay? I have some paper, and —"

"Yes!" said Frank. "I will."

Whenever he could that summer, Frank sat beside Paolo in the rich, creamy light of his studio, trying to capture that drowsy smile of Wendy's. But more often it was Tina, for Paolo was working more extensively with her. Frank spent hours tracing the contours of Tina's head and neck and shoulders onto sheets of paper pinned to an easel, while she turned and twisted into the postures Paolo requested. Sometimes she was so still and the room so quiet Frank fell into a trance, his pencil moving as if it were drawn across the paper by his eyes. Drawing. To draw. It was a good word. He was drawing the world in at his eyes the way he drew breath, pulling it through his body, and then letting it pour out again through the muscles of his arms, his hands and fingers. Through drawing he had learned to love the shapes of apples and vases and the leaves of trees. To draw a live person was even more exciting, a way to worship the human beauty God had made. Of course he never took these drawings home. He was afraid of what Deirdre might do, if she saw even one of them.

"You should take proper lessons," Paolo told Frank one evening as they packed up their art supplies. "You know Oskar? He has an art school on Grove Street in Manhattan —"

"I can't afford that," said Frank.

"You're still young, but your work is good. He might take you in a year or two. He did it for Max long ago. You pay what you can, clean the brushes, wash the floor."

Frank said no more, but for the rest of the night, while Paolo spoke of other things, and later at home, he thought about taking art lessons. If Oskar would show him how to get the shading right, how to handle the difficult watercolours. He thought about having a truly nude model to draw from, to look long enough at a woman's body to absorb it fully, to memorize the way it was constructed. Even in the privacy of his own mind, he found those imaginary bodies dangerous to look at. That wasn't the reason he loved art. Was it? He crossed himself. He thought about Jesus, Joseph and Mary, how pure they were, and he vowed to dedicate his art to God.

Frank delivered Paolo's orders at the end of the day, because that was the time he was most likely to get invited in. Late in the afternoon, Tina put on her regular clothes. Paolo cleaned his brushes and put away his paints, and one by one his friends dropped by. Abe the etcher and Oskar Johan the art teacher, and Giuseppe, a sculptor from Italy, and Paolo's girlfriend, Sue. Sue was a French Canadian who cooked in a restaurant on the lower East side and always brought leftover pastries and meat and sometimes a bottle of wine. Then Tina's husband, George, would come to take her home, and if the house was full of food and friends, George could be persuaded to stay a while and play songs on Paolo's guitar.

When every chair in the house was full, people sat on apple crates or the rungs of the ladder or the floor. They took up collections and sent Frank to the corner bar with a handful of coins and an empty bucket to be filled with beer. Paolo often poured him a bit in a mug and welcomed him to sit and then forgot all about him. The others ignored him, too. It felt good to be ignored. It meant he could be quiet and listen. He watched George's long fingers tune the guitar, listened to his deep, open voice, and the drumming of Tina's palms on an upside-down soup pot, and if it wasn't too hot the friends spilled into the street out front and danced and laughed until the neighbours called out for them to shut up.

Frank often sat on the bottom rung of the library ladder, sipping from a mug of beer, listening as Paolo and his friends spoke of artists they knew who had fled Berlin for Paris and then fled Paris for London or New York. They said the climate in Europe was bad. Frank didn't know exactly what that meant, but he knew they weren't speaking of the weather. Many of Paolo's friends had come here from Europe for this reason. Bad climate. Abe and Oskar were from Germany and Max, a painter who slept in Paolo's back room, was from Austria, and most of them were Jews. Frank had never thought about what made a person Jewish. Now, listening to the conversation at Paolo's, Frank learned more. He heard Max and Oskar speak about their parents, the temples where they studied as boys, the books they read. They spoke with reverence of God. He remembered his Aunt Lucy saying the Jews hated God. How did she get things so wrong?

A lot of what the artists said about philosophy and modern art was hard to understand, but Frank loved to listen. There was a tone to their voices he'd never heard before, a way of arguing, intense and low and often passionate, but never cruel, never out of control. He thought with shame of his mother's screeches as she chased him with the broom, or his cousins and uncles who would punch other men over nothing, a stupid pool game or a snub at a funeral. He leaned back against Paolo's wall of books and thought of his parents' apartment, the one book of poems. Maybe his father would like to see Paolo's books. Maybe he would be interested in the new ideas discussed here. But Frank knew his father would never enter this place. He would be shocked by the way the women dressed, how they sat on the floor with crossed legs and entered the conversation freely. Tomas was polite to everyone he met, and would not speak a word against any race, even if others goaded him. Yet Frank was sure his father had never shared a meal with a Jew or a Negro. Had never laughed or taken a drink or sung a song with anyone but Irish Catholics.

Europe, the artists said, was now a perilous place. In Germany, Jews were no longer allowed to practise law. Jewish books were burned in public bonfires. Jewish shops were vandalized and boycotted. Jewish teachers at the universities had lost their positions. This was to keep them from teaching the truth, Oskar said, and to keep them poor. The Nazis kept records, said Abe, of where the Jews lived, where they kept their shops, so they could evict them, confiscate their belongings. So they would know where to find them, said Max. When the time came. Nobody complained out loud, said Paolo. No one protested. These things seemed impossible, yet they were true. Frank thought of his mother nodding to Mr Green in the store and buying his meat and then later, at home, agreeing with Aunt Lucy that Mr Green was a dirty money grubber. He remembered that his mother was expecting him for dinner. She would be furious. He should go home. He slipped over to the bucket and dipped his mug in and gathered another two inches of beer. Everybody saw him do it and nobody told him not to.

George sat for a long time fingering the frets on the guitar. Then he said very quietly he'd learned a new song at his grandmother's church. The tune he played was not for dancing. It was a slow, sorrowful song, and George's voice dipped lower than Frank had ever heard it before, singing about a soul passing through the world of woe and going home to God. It was like nothing Frank had ever heard at church, and he knew Father Madden would consider it sinful. Yet at the heart of the song was a longing that was, well, beautiful. It was beautiful, sometimes, to want something, just to want. The beer must have addled his brain because he felt tears sting his eyes and he had to hang his head and pretend to inspect the sole of his shoe.

———

Frank had failed grade seven. It was a hard defeat, when September came, to return to school. It was degrading, after spending the summer with artists and intellectuals, to sit in a grade seven classroom with twelve-year-olds, reciting the capitals of the forty-eight states. It was painful to walk past groups of boys his age and hear big Don Cuthbert calling him retarded and singing the ABC song. To have Nancy Gray, who used to look up to him — who used to have a crush on him — now asking with a social-worker smile did he need any help. Even Corky Higgins was ahead of Frank. Corky — who couldn't put two thoughts together — was in grade nine. But even though Frank begged to be set free, Tomas would not relent. Frank must get an education, no matter how miserable it made him. He gave Frank a card for the teacher to sign every day to prove he had attended.

A neighbour boy, Tim Burke, had come out of reform school, where he'd been sent for stealing a policeman's motorcycle and crashing it into the Williamsburg Savings Bank two years ago. Tim and Corky were best of friends now, smoking cigarettes and getting up games of poker. Corky ran errands for the men who hung around the beer parlour, carrying messages and taking bets and keeping watch at the door when they ran illegal gambling in the back room. Corky told all of this to Frank with pride. He offered to get Frank in on it, if he wanted some easy money. But that was exactly the kind of life Frank was determined to resist.

———

On a cold Saturday in November, after finishing deliveries for Dr Green, Frank saw Paolo's girlfriend, Sue, standing beside Abe in a line of people on West 53rd. They were going into the museum, they said, to see an exhibition of the works of Vincent Van Gogh, the Dutchman Paolo talked about so much. Did Frank want to come along? Abe asked the question casually, as if it were common for them to take Frank on outings in Manhattan.

Frank hesitated. The sign on the door said admittance cost twenty cents.

"It's all right," Sue said. "We'll buy your ticket."

The museum of art was the cleanest, emptiest space he had ever entered. With its echoes and hushed voices, high ceilings and long, clean walls, it seemed as sacred as the church. People stood in front of the pictures in quiet groups of four or five, looking. Someone who knew Abe silently lifted a hand to acknowledge him and Abe lifted a hand in return. Abe nudged Sue toward a line of people waiting to view a display case. Frank followed, but was disappointed to see only a collection of handwritten letters under glass. He moved on.

In the next room, the walls were hung with drawings in pencil and charcoal and ink. Frank admired the cross-hatching and the lines of perspective. He saw how the artist had made the moon and the horizon both from one thin line and how quickly he'd done it. He thought of the things Paolo had said to him, about eyes and hands and translating things, how each person saw things differently. He wished Paolo were here. He wanted to ask a lot of questions but he didn't know the words for what he wanted to know, and anyway, he sensed that words would not help. Words were not always needed. There were ways to know things that the schoolteachers didn't understand. There were things in the world beyond what his parents knew. Maybe even beyond what Father Madden knew. That thought scared him, but he kept moving past the drawings, seeing what the artist was showing him. Yes, yes. When he reached the far wall, he walked around the room again. He thought he was seeing the most beautiful art a person could imagine. But that was before he moved into the larger room and saw the paintings.

The trees lifted their arms and their upper branches rippled like green flames against a swirl of thick white clouds, and the whole sky blazed, and Frank saw, in a small lower corner of the field, far below the treetops, two young girls, two thick smudges of white and cadmium yellow, holding their bonnets against the wind. How insignificant they seemed, so far below the living sky. In the next canvas, the sky churned with giant stars and a brilliant, spinning moon, above blue hills cradling a dark and sleeping town. One church spire rose above the horizon to touch the edge of the clouds. The next painting showed a restaurant, outside, tables and chairs on a cobblestone square and buildings rising high above the street and above the buildings a pocket of deep, deep sky and those stars again, bright whorls and white and yellow pinwheels, reflecting off the surface of the street and the tables and the white coat of a waiter, scattering colour everywhere, lighting the world. So this was painting. This was what paint could do.

The sky is alive. It moves and breathes, and this painter knew it. What was his name again? Frank glanced around, looking for Sue or Abe, but didn't see them. That was all right. He wanted to be alone with the paintings. In some way they belonged to him. They were presents given to him by a stranger.

Afterwards when they stood together on the street, Frank wondered that New York still looked the same. When Sue asked if he had liked the paintings, he could only say they were beautiful, and he felt keenly how stupid he was. But Sue smiled lightly and punched Abe's arm and said, "See? I told you he'd like them." So Frank thought maybe she understood.

He wanted to say something more, something about the artist, but he wasn't sure how to say the man's name out loud, or whether he was still alive. He hated his own ignorance, hated that he didn't know how to find out what he wanted to know. That he was imprisoned in school, where there was no learning about the world, where people were barely awake.

But for a glorious hour, inside the gallery, he had forgotten all about those things.

3.6

KYLE WANDERS INTO THE BACK ROOM AND WATCHES VON LIFT A stack of scrapbooks from a shelf and set it on the floor. She stretches and rubs the aching small of her back. She has now emptied half the shelves. But the emptier the shelves look, the more cluttered the inside of her head feels. When she first approached this room, she didn't know what she'd find here, the whole apartment one vague, frightening mass. Now she knows the contents of each box and biscuit tin. A jumble sale of disarticulated memories. Tugging at her. Testing her resistance.

"Need some help?" Kyle asks.

"I can handle it."

"But I want to help. Are these my mum's scrapbooks? I want to see more of her stuff."

"Yes, of course you do. I'm sorry. How about you look through this pile? Alex says — " She laughs. "Alex says some of these scrapbooks might be valuable."

"Yeah," says Kyle. "Ingrid said the scrapbooks show how she got into making collages. How she developed her sense of composition."

Von is impressed. "I didn't realize you were listening to all that."

"I always listen," Kyle says. He crouches down beside the box of scrapbooks.

At lunchtime, Von makes a spinach omelette and coffee. She listens to Kyle's description of the rooming house, the tomatoes he grows in the backyard, the birdfeeder he made from an empty soda bottle. He tells her of the jobs he took at the age of sixteen, when he dropped out of school. He cleared snow in winter and worked the fields in summer for the local farmers. In fall, he helped with the harvesting.

They return to work for a couple of hours, sorting and stacking, each absorbed in a different corner of the room. Von is piling books into empty boxes when Kyle calls her over.

"Von, come and look at this." He's holding a very old sketchbook, with an ink-stained cover. Where did this come from, she wonders. A second-hand shop? She opens it, curious to see if Rosheen had found it usable. On the first page, a pencil sketch of North First Street surprises her. It's the view from this very window, on an early morning in winter. The next page shows the nearby church with its statue of the Virgin above the door and the fake owl on its eaves to scare away pigeons. But something's wrong. The street isn't paved, and the chestnut tree in the churchyard is missing. Then she sees the signature, *Frank Garrison*.

These are his drawings? She's never seen any of his drawings before. She studies them now, in awe, as Kyle looks over her shoulder. This was what he saw, once. Williamsburg, the 1930s. Barges on the East River and workmen crossing the bridge and a horse-drawn feed truck in the nearby courtyard. She turns the crinkly pages carefully. Two girls skipping rope on the sidewalk, a gang of ragged, barefoot boys fishing off the Navy pier. Three musicians gathered on a street corner, rendered in loving, sensitive detail — a boy blowing a trumpet, a woman strumming a homemade guitar, and a fat man on the saxophone bent backwards in a long and graceful curve, his eyes closed in bliss. And here is a charcoal sketch of Deirdre, on the cusp of middle age. She stands in front of her building on a summer's day. Her hair tumbles out of the kerchief that's meant to keep it tidy, and her apron is rumpled. Her arms are crossed, and smoke curls up from a cigarette between her fingers. It's a quick sketch, smudged and almost careless, but you can feel her anger. She's burning with it.

3.7

THE BLACK AND GOLD SINGER SEWING MACHINE IN MACY'S window, the latest model, mounted on a wooden table with a fold-out shelf, six drawers, and best of all a light bulb on top, cost more than the remainder of Deirdre's savings. Much more. The combination of Lucy's tuberculosis, Junior's cough, and Brendan O'Nolan's thirst for whisky had nearly emptied her tobacco tin. But now that Lucy was gone — God rest her soul and Deirdre would never speak any ill of the dead or let slip a word to suggest Lucy's death was a burden lifted — and Junior was much improved, and Brendan O'Nolan was miles away in New Rochelle, perhaps she could try to fill up the tin again.

Deirdre walked from Macy's to the subway station and boarded the train, her mind occupied with economics. She had just picked up her pay from the glove factory and spent half of it at the downtown market. The other half she would hide away. She was taking in more piecework, now that she had the time for hand stitching. John Junior, who rarely went out to play and wasn't strong enough to get a job after school, kept her company as she sewed. He sorted the sleeves and cuffs and folded the shirts into the basket when they were done. Recently she'd hit upon the idea to teach him how to sew. She was pleased by how careful he was. He managed one piece for every three that Deirdre finished, but his stitches were tight and straight. Illness had made him patient. With Junior's help, she was steadily increasing her income.

Frank was bringing home earnings too, from his delivery jobs. He was fourteen now. Mr Edison was keen to take him on full time as an apprentice, and Deirdre could not for the life of her understand why Tomas wouldn't allow it. Carpentry was good respectable work for their son. The best he could possibly do in life. If he stayed in school too long, Mr Edison would take on another boy and Frank would lose his chance. If only she could make Tomas see. All his talk of education and ideas only turned Frank's head the wrong way around. He was becoming a dreamer. Why, yesterday she'd heard him asking Tomas to let him take lessons in the city. On how to draw pictures, of all fool things. He was too old to be drawing pictures. But Tomas had bought him a pad of drawing paper. Paid good money for blank sheets of paper.

Deirdre got off the subway at the Bedford station, carrying two bags heavy with late-summer vegetables. One weighed more than the other, and she was forced to lean to one side as she walked. She was picturing the Singer sewing machine tucked into the alcove off the parlour and herself seated at the wooden table, sewing seams late into the night, by the light of the cunning little built-in lamp. She heard a burst of laughter from across the street and looked up. Half a dozen people were loitering outside the old boot factory. A strange lot. Mrs Heintz had told her that artists and jazz musicians sometimes congregated there.

As she passed by, she was horrified to recognize among them her own son, her only son, in the midst of these ragtag Gypsies and Bohemians. Talking away with them, easy as you please. She set her grocery bags down on the sidewalk. The women were drinking out of a flask, like men, passing it between them and laughing too loudly. One of them wore an outrageous turban-thing on her head and a dress that was too short — it was obscene. Deirdre knew the times were changing. Had already changed. She'd seen plenty of women like this on the streets of Manhattan. But she didn't like them speaking to her son. Her first impulse was to storm over there and twist his ear and make him come straight home. But there was something about the way he moved in the small crowd that seemed to forbid her to do it. He was so tall and stood so straight. She felt she could not cross the street and claim him as if he were a child.

As she stood watching, the people began to disperse. Frank mounted his big grocery store bicycle and came riding down Kent toward Deirdre.

"What are you doing with those people?" she asked, when he stopped beside her. She could barely suppress the urge to slap him.

"Delivering groceries to Mr Madero."

"What does this Mr Maderry do?" Deirdre asked.

"Madero. He's an artist, Ma. He makes paintings."

She sniffed. "Paintings of women, I suppose."

Frank looked her steadily in the eye. "Sometimes." His chin was lifted and his head held high, so that he was looking down upon her. It almost seemed he was daring her to disapprove. She was alarmed to find she could not maintain her gaze. She dropped her eyes, confused.

Her son possessed a kind of strength she could not understand. It didn't come from his height, or his muscles. It didn't even come from his growing reputation, among the local boys and men, as a champion in the boxing ring and a hero to the parish. It came from someplace inside him. She had glimpsed it from time to time, as he was growing up. His power. She didn't know where he had gotten it. But she felt now that if she wanted his favour, she should not say anything against his friends.

"I've just bought a pumpkin at the market," she said. With both hands, she pulled the enormous pumpkin out of her bag. "Could you take it home for me?"

"Sure, Ma. I'll take all your groceries." He loaded her bags into the bike's large baskets.

"It's good to have such a son," she said. "A son who will help and protect me."

He eyed her suspiciously.

She smiled at him, and the painful lump in her throat, which must have been the rage she was forcing herself to swallow, brought a tear to her eye.

When Deirdre saw Brendan O'Nolan again, it was spring, over a year since he'd gone to New Rochelle. He was leaning against a post at the end of her street, watching her approach. He knew very well she couldn't avoid him, for she was on her way to church, and many in her congregation were walking that way as well. If she turned back, everyone would see and wonder why. As she reached him, he tipped his hat, as if he were a gentleman, and began to stroll along beside her.

"How are you faring this morning?" he asked, with an insolent bow.

"I am well," said Deirdre. "Why are you not at your job up in New Rochelle?"

"That's done," he said. "I'm back at the Polish church and living at Wolnski's place. Wolnski is letting me stay there until I get my first pay. But I need some money —"

"I've given you enough," she said. "I owe you nothing more."

"You owe me plenty, and don't forget. Wolnski is moving to Florida, so I need new lodgings. He's sold the building and all his tenants must be out by the first of next month."

"That's no concern of mine," said Deirdre. "Hello, Mrs Heintz."

"Hello, dear," said Mrs Heintz, who was walking in the opposite direction, to her own church. She paused, expecting Deirdre to introduce the young man. But Deirdre hurried past her.

"I suppose these people all think you a respectable mother and wife," said Brendan.

"That I am." She stopped. They had reached the corner across from her church, and she could see Tomas and Frank in the yard. They had gone early that morning to help Mrs Casey. It was Palm Sunday, and Mrs Casey liked to hand out the yew branches, though she was crippled so badly now she couldn't walk without assistance. She sat in a chair by the door, giving a branch to each person who entered, with Tomas and Frank beside her. Deirdre hoped neither of them would speak to her. She didn't want Brendan to learn who they were.

"You'll give me a hundred dollars or I'll have a talk with your neighbours," he said. "You know where I live. Make sure to come by and pay up before the end of the month."

Would his demands never end? She thought of her own father, how he had pawned off her clothing piece by piece when she was a child, until she was naked. And in later years he had taken her boots and her coat to sell, and finally he'd taken her very body and sold it to Galen O'Nolan. And now here was O'Nolan's son, wanting more.

"End of the month," he repeated.

Deirdre looked him in the eye. "Go to hell," she said. She meant this literally.

She crossed the street. She guessed he would not dare follow her, and he did not. But as she entered the gates to the churchyard, she looked back and saw him watching. The first bells rang, and Tomas hurried toward her. She turned away, but he came directly to her side and took her arm. She could feel Brendan's eyes on her, and his malevolent thoughts.

Throughout the Mass, Deirdre counted in her mind the amount she had already given to Brendan. One hundred and eighty dollars all told, a fortune. If she kept giving in to him, he would take all the money she had, and then what was to stop him from telling Tomas everything? She stood with the rest of the congregation for communion. She must get Frank to give him a thrashing, scare him away for good. She would tell her son that Brendan O'Nolan had stolen her pocketbook. Or she would say he had insulted her. Surely Frank would come to her defence. For no matter what, she must hold on to her money. If Tomas were to cast her out, she would need it all. She would not give Brendan another dollar, she vowed. She stood before Father Madden and opened her mouth for the host. Not a dime.

3.8

SUGAR DUST SIFTED INTO THE LUNCH ROOM THROUGH THE ventilation system. The men carried it in on their clothing, and the refinery fans winnowed it in through cracks in the walls and windows. The tables and the coal stove and the water pipes that ran below the ceiling beams were coated with sugar dust, and when a man walked into the room you could hear the layers of dirty sugar crunch beneath his boots. Tomas used his sleeve to clear a spot on the bench so his son could sit down. Frank sneezed, and the other workers laughed. They lived with the brown and white dust every day. It settled into the seams of their clothes and the creases in their necks. It coated the inside of their nostrils and their throats and some said it encrusted the lining of their lungs.

Tomas thanked Frank for the lunch, a clean syrup tin filled with chicken stew, and asked him to stay while he ate. "Tell me again about these art lessons. Your mother didn't like it, but I went to Grove Street, Saturday, and saw the school. I have to say it looks proper enough. I couldn't talk to Mr Johan. He had a room full of men and boys all listening to him. He looks very teacherly. Perhaps I'll talk to him someday, when he's not in class." Tomas unwrapped the spoon and began the work of prying the lid from the syrup tin.

Frank's knees were jumping up against the bottom of the table, his fingers drumming on the table top. He'd been talking to Tomas about Oskar Johan for over a year now, trying to convince him that art school was a good investment. He'd told his father many times about the money Mr Gray earned by drawing magazine illustrations. He'd listed every other opportunity he could think of — pictures for billboards, book covers, Christmas cards, labels for goods of all kinds. Somebody had to draw the sardine on the sardine can, he said.

"You have to go on in school until grade eight at least," Tomas warned. He dipped his spoon in and tasted the stew, giving Frank the little nod of thanks that meant it was still warm.

Frank would never make grade eight, and he knew it. Still, this was a victory, better than Tomas's previous insistence on grade nine. Frank would not fall as far from the goal Tomas had set and so, Frank reasoned, Tomas would be less disappointed.

"It would take that long to save the tuition money anyway," Tomas said.

Frank's heart thumped hard. He'd been waiting for Tomas to mention the tuition. "Mr Madero said if I take my drawings to show Mr Johan, he might give me a scholarship."

Tomas nearly spit out his stew. "A *what*? For *you*?"

"Honest," said Frank. "Every year he takes in a fellow on scholarship and lets him work for his fees."

Tomas simply stared, unbelieving.

"It's a scholarship for fellows who can draw," Frank said. "You know I can draw."

Tomas spooned stew into his mouth and chewed. He seemed to be looking far off in the distance. He didn't say anything, but maybe he was considering a change of mind.

As Frank left the lunch room, he was nearly stepped on by a beefy, fair-haired fellow, puffing on a cigarette. Probably a bum, taking shelter from the wind. It was an icy April. The fellow tried to push past him, into the lunch room. But Frank stopped him. "Say, you can't smoke in there."

"I smoke where I want," the man said. He had an Irish accent, but slurred his words.

Frank smelled the liquor on him. He grabbed the man's sleeve and led him away. "You can talk to the foreman if you want work," he advised. "But don't come back until you're sober."

Frank walked on home. When he got to his building, he stopped on the sidewalk, listening hard and looking up at the window for Deirdre, a habit he'd developed over the years, for any clues to the mood she might be in. As he waited, he saw that the beefy man from the factory had followed him home. Did he need help?

"You Frank Garrison?" the man asked.

"Frank!" Deirdre called down from the window. "Get up here. I need you."

The man came closer. He lifted a chubby, arrogant chin and stared at Frank with red-rimmed eyes. "That's your mother, isn't it?" He shaded his eyes and looked up, but Deirdre had disappeared inside. "I know your mother from back home. Know her well."

"Who are you?" Frank demanded.

The man's lip curled up on one side. "I'll decide when to tell you that." He ambled away.

Frank let him go. His boxing coach had told him that drink makes holes in the brain, makes people forget who they are. That's what must have happened to this Irishman. When he got upstairs he asked his mother, "Do you know that fellow?"

"Who?"

"That man with the yellow hair. He was talking to me in the yard. You saw him. He said he knows you."

"He's nothing but a tramp," said Deirdre. "Don't tell your father, but he came right inside the building one day, begging. Why, he insulted me."

Frank rushed to the window and looked out. The man was gone. "He insulted you?"

"It would only upset your father if he knew," Deirdre said. "He's not young anymore, and he can't stand a shock. But you're a strong boy, Frank, and a good fighter. Everyone says so. If that tramp comes around here again, you teach him a lesson. You hear me?"

"Yes, Ma," said Frank. She had given him many lectures before about protecting the family. But this one had a new urgency to it. He wondered who the stranger really was.

By the end of the week the air was warmer. Early rain had melted the ice, and the roads were wet and muddy. Puddles filled every hole in the ground, and people stepped carefully, trying to protect their shoes. Friday evening, Tomas came out to watch Frank win the parish title in the boxing ring at the city clubhouse, and afterwards he took him to Reilly's for a glass of beer. Frank, sore from the pounding his opponent had laid on his upper body, was succeeding in keeping a smile on his face and joking with the men and boys who congratulated him. Tomas was a good companion, helping Frank refuse the excess beer the others pressed upon him.

"He's an athlete," Tomas told Kelsey the butcher. He pushed the beer glass away from Frank and along the bar toward Kelsey. "You drink it. Raise your glass and drink to the boy, but don't poison him."

"Ah, you're a good daddy, you are," said Kelsey. "I b'lieve I will." He soaked it up.

"That'll help him sleep," Tomas whispered into Frank's left ear.

Frank laughed. Then, on his other ear, he felt hot air and wet lips. "Brother," a voice whispered. "I will collect what's owed to me."

Frank jumped down from his stool, wiping his ear with the back of his hand. He turned to face the speaker. It was the pale Irishman again. He grasped Frank by the wrist.

Frank pushed him away with one arm. Despite the man's bulk, it took little effort to send him reeling across the floor and crashing against the door.

"Out with you," commanded Reilly, from behind the bar. "Leave our champion alone." Everyone laughed and cheered, and called for more beer. The blond man staggered outside.

"Good riddance," said Reilly. But Frank was curious. After a minute he opened the door and peered out. The man was lurking under the street light. Frank took a good look at him.

The Irishman stared back with squinty, penetrating eyes. This man whose speech was so much like his mother's, who claimed to know her from "back home," had some reason to hate Frank. Surely a hatred so strong could not come out of nowhere. Even if the man was raving mad, there must be something to his story.

"Who are you?" Frank asked.

The man opened his trousers and began to piss against the side of the building.

"Jesus Murphy," said Frank. He shuddered and went back inside. He wasn't afraid of the fellow physically. The man was intoxicated every time Frank saw him, his balance so poor he likely couldn't take aim any better than a baby could. But the knowing look in his eyes was frightening. What did he know?

"Who is that man?" Frank asked Reilly. "I saw him the other day at the factory."

"The sugar factory?" asked Tomas.

"Looking for work, I think."

"He'll get no work around here," said Reilly. "That's Brendan O'Nolan. He's a thief, he is. Just out of jail. Sentenced to ten months for stealing the cash box out of the New Rochelle rectory."

"Stealing from the priests!" said Tomas. "He'll come to a bad end."

"That he will," said the barman.

As Tomas and Frank headed home, O'Nolan came out from the alley and stumbled deliberately into Tomas. "Tell your wife you met me," he said. "Say I tol' you about the nuns."

"Get away from me, you damned liar," said Tomas.

Frank looked from O'Nolan to his father. They had obviously met before, and O'Nolan had given Tomas some reason to accuse him of lying. Frank raised his fist.

"Hold back, Frank," said Tomas. "I'll not have you throwing away your honour on the likes of him."

Frank drew his elbow back, preparing to punch O'Nolan's flat, freckled face.

"I said *hold back*," Tomas shouted. He tugged at Frank's sleeve.

With difficulty, Frank forced himself to hold back. He didn't want to disobey his father.

O'Nolan smiled. He moved closer to Tomas, muttering, "Seven of us, and she dumped us like a dustman taking out the —"

Tomas hit him in the jaw. The blow didn't budge O'Nolan, but he looked offended. He lowered his head and stretched both arms before him and charged at Tomas's chest, knocking him flat on his back in the mud.

"Hey!" Frank rushed forward, and O'Nolan, seeing him coming, ran off down the middle of the dark, wet road.

Frank took after him. O'Nolan was awkward, flat-footed, his legs sticking out on either side of him. In two minutes, Frank could catch him up and wallop him. He was dying to do it.

"Frank!" Tomas called. "Help me!" He was lying on his back in the muddy road. A yellow car drove past, swerving sharply to avoid running him over.

Frank gave up the chase and returned to his father. "Dad. Give me your hand." He got Tomas out of the mud and helped him home.

Deirdre came to the door when they entered and saw the mud plastered on Tomas's head and coat and trousers. "What happened to you?"

"No harm done," said Tomas. He walked past her into the living room.

"It was that Irishman," Frank told her. He looked her in the eye. "The one you said you didn't know."

Deirdre caught the tone of his voice and cuffed him on the side of his head.

Later, in the kitchen, she berated him. "You let him knock your father in the muck? You should be ashamed of yourself. Next time he comes around, I want you to give him a good beating. Do you hear me? Next time you fix him so he never comes back."

———

On Monday, when Frank went to the factory with his father's lunch, O'Nolan was there again. He was leaning against the factory wall, rolling a cigarette, while Tomas, red in the face, tried to walk past him. But O'Nolan stepped into his path. Smug. Licking the cigarette paper.

Frank rushed forward and grabbed O'Nolan by the collar. "What are you doing here?"

"Frank," said Tomas. "No fighting."

"I'll break your neck," Frank said to O'Nolan, "if I catch you around my mother or my father again. Now go on home."

"You can't touch me," said O'Nolan. "Your da doesn't want any trouble." But he was backing away as he said it. He didn't want to get hurt.

"Come on, Frank," said Tomas. "Come inside." He turned toward the building.

Frank didn't move. He was still watching O'Nolan. *Fix him so he never comes back.* Frank knew exactly how to do that. He wouldn't like it, the way he had liked beating Cuthbert, but he could do it, if it was necessary. And it seemed necessary. O'Nolan was crazed with rage. Frank saw it in his eyes, and he knew his mother had seen it too. O'Nolan was dangerous. But Tomas, who believed every man was good at heart and capable of reason, could not see it.

"Frank!"

Reluctantly, Frank followed his father inside. Tomas was handling this O'Nolan fellow all wrong. But Frank didn't want to argue with his father today. He wanted to talk to him about art school again. To tell him new classes were starting up next fall, and that Paolo felt sure Frank could get in on a scholarship with the new drawings he'd done. Frank had rolled up the best ones and brought them along. He knew they were good — a portrait of Paolo's girl, Sue, and a sketch of the Manhattan skyline seen from the pier, with boats on the river. He knew if he showed them to Frank in the lunchroom, the other workers would see them and praise them. It would make Tomas proud. It might make him change his mind.

Inside, the foreman stood watching out the window. The lunch whistle hadn't blown yet, and no one else was in the room.

"Who is that fellow out there?" the foreman asked, as Tomas entered.

"He's a bum," Tomas said.

"What's he doing here?"

Tomas shrugged. "Looking for work. I wouldn't advise you hire him." He sat down and wiped the table with his sleeve.

"You fellows should clean up in here," the foreman said. "This is a hazard." He handed Tomas a rag and he took one himself, and the two of them began to wipe the white film of sugar dust from the table.

When the door opened, the wind blew in and sent glittering, grimy crystals swirling through the room. Frank began to cough. The flying sugar stung his eyes and he held his handkerchief against his face, so that when O'Nolan came inside, Frank did not see him.

"Hey, fella," said the foreman. "Close the door."

Frank lowered the handkerchief and saw O'Nolan place his unlit cigarette in his mouth.

"You can't smoke in here," said the foreman.

"You have no say what I do," said O'Nolan. "I do what I want. And nor you, nor *you* —" He pointed at Tomas and then at Frank. "Can stop me."

Frank was standing beside his father at one end of the room. O'Nolan and the foreman stood by the exit at the other end. Between them stretched the lunch table, three feet wide and twelve feet long.

O'Nolan drew a match out of his pocket, and Frank began to move.

"Stay here, Dad," he said. His mother was right. His mother had been right all along. Quickly, deliberately, he strode the length of the table, planning to take O'Nolan down.

"See here," said the foreman. "You can't light that cigarette in here."

"Put that match away," Frank said. "Or you'll be sorry."

O'Nolan looked Frank right in the eye and said, "I'm not scared of you. You won't do nothing. Your old man won't let you touch me." He lifted the wooden match high.

Frank dived across the table. But he was too late. O'Nolan struck the match on the rough metal of the water pipe above his head. Particles of sugar seemed to come alive mid-air, popping and sparking. "Jesus Christ," said the foreman. "Get out!" He ran out the open door. A gust of wind blew it shut with a bang, dislodging the thick, sugar-glazed layer of dust that coated the pipes. Pale, shiny motes of sugar drifted down on O'Nolan, settling in his hair and clothes and spinning in the air above his head like snow.

O'Nolan stood still, his mouth shut at last, burning match in hand, distracted by the flashing sparks that danced before his eyes.

"Get out, Frank!" Tomas was running toward the exit now, too.

Frank obeyed. He slid off the table. Lunged at the door, heaved it open. Heard behind him, a sudden, powerful *whoosh*. Turned to see a long tongue of flame lick out for Tomas. He reached for his father, but at that moment the sugar dust ignited and the blast threw Tomas backwards, into the corridor that led to the boiler room. Frank couldn't see his father. The space between them was burning, the very air on fire, and then the windows blew and the walls burst outward and Frank was thrown through the air.

When he woke in the yard, to a hideous screaming, he recognized it as the voice of Brendan O'Nolan, trapped under the collapsed roof and burning. Men came running from all parts of the plant, carrying pails of water. The foreman, with a hose in one hand and a shovel in the other, was searching the pile of broken planks and shingles, calling for Tomas.

Frank tried to shout, "My dad's not in there," but his voice didn't work. He tried to stand, but his legs wouldn't work either. He crawled toward the foreman, pointing. "Around back," he croaked. "The boiler room." The foreman ran around the corner, followed by two other workers. Frank crossed himself and kneeled in the dirt and prayed for Tomas.

O'Nolan was still screaming while Frank began, "Most merciful Jesus." Frank could hear him screaming all during the prayer. It wasn't until he said "Amen" that O'Nolan fell silent.

They carried Tomas out on a door that had blown clear of the fire. Frank got control of his legs and was able to limp behind the men as they carried his father to one of the company trucks. They'd called an ambulance, one man said, but it hadn't arrived yet, and Tomas looked bad. He needed a doctor. The men loaded the makeshift stretcher into the back of the truck. The foreman climbed in and helped Frank in, and they sat on either side of Tomas. The driver started off with a lurch. Frank held his father's hand. He could see a big hole in Tomas's head, where his ear should be, and he didn't want to see it. He concentrated on looking into Tomas's eyes. His eyes were wide open, which Frank thought must be a good sign.

"Dad?"

"The things he said," Tomas muttered.

"He's dead," said Frank. He felt he was in a dream. The world had rushed forward very quickly in time and now it was slowing down. Now, when they had to get Tomas to a doctor, everything moved with brutal slowness.

"He knows things," Tomas said. "Things he couldn't know, unless —"

"Jesus, Frank, your arm," said the foreman. His voice dragged, like a record played on low speed. Frank looked down. A long shard of glass was jutting out of a slash above his elbow. Blood ran in a thick rivulet over his forearm and onto the charred front of Tomas's shirt. Frank saw the glass, but he couldn't feel it. He was numb, his whole body leaden.

His father was moving his lips, trying to speak. "Frank?"

"Yes, Dad."

"You've been a good son to me," said Tomas.

Frank covered Tomas's hands with both his own. Why was the truck moving so slowly?

At the hospital, Frank tried to follow his father when they carried his stretcher down the hall, but a nurse stopped him.

"You're not going anywhere," said the nurse, "until the doctor looks at your arm." She sat him down in a chair.

The doctor grasped the long splinter of glass with some kind of medical pliers and pulled. Blood gushed forth, and the nurse was ready with a piece of cheesecloth, which she wrapped tightly around Frank's arm. He felt the pain then. His head was beginning to clear.

The foreman came rushing in, and Frank saw he was crying, wiping tears from his eyes with the back of his hand. "Frankie," he said. "You got to come and see your father."

Frank stood then, and the nurse could not hold him back. He followed the foreman to a hospital bed, where Tomas lay pale and still while a priest prayed over his soul and a doctor examined the wound in the side of his head.

"Dad?"

Tomas's eyes flickered open and then closed. Frank kneeled at the bedside while the priest continued in Latin and blessed Tomas. Then the priest left the room. The doctor looked at Frank and asked, "You're the son?" Frank nodded. The doctor called in a nurse and held a quiet, rushed conversation with her that Frank couldn't hear. Then the two of them left the room. Frank was alone with his father. The light in the grimy window pane faded and night fell. Frank stroked his father's hand and said a prayer.

Tomas stirred and opened his eyes. A smile of recognition crossed his lips as he looked at his only son. Then his eyes grew cold and turned to stone, and Frank knew that he was dead.

On the long walk back to Brooklyn, Frank relived many times the events
of that afternoon and the days leading up to it. He remembered the
day O'Nolan had first accosted him outside the factory and followed
him home, saying strange things about his mother. If only Frank had
clocked him that day. Or the next time, when he was harassing Tomas.
If Frank had fought back that night, he could have scared O'Nolan
off, but Tomas had told him not to. Why had Frank listened? He had
known in his gut that Tomas was wrong, that O'Nolan was dangerous
and should have been stopped. Yet he had listened and obeyed. Why?
Out of love? Or was it because he was afraid to make Tomas angry?
Hoping Tomas would give him what he wanted. Let him go to art
school. He groaned out loud, feeling his own selfishness like a hot coal
in his stomach.

Why learn to fight, he berated himself, if you're not going to fight?

He should have flattened O'Nolan's ugly face, pounded his body
to a pulp, driven a knife into his heart. Yes. He wished O'Nolan were
still alive, so that he could murder him.

It was midnight when he climbed the steep rise of the
Williamsburg bridge and began to cross the river. The temperature
dropped, and a dirty, bitter wind assailed him. The men who had come
along from the factory had driven home hours ago. They'd offered
Frank a ride, but he'd needed to stay to make arrangements. He
reached the highest point of the bridge and looked out over the river.
A few boats were crossing, lanterns blazing far below, and the banks
on either side were visible only as loose clusters of lights. He had never
before seen the city from the bridge in darkness. Tonight he had stood
over his father's dead body. He had spoken to a funeral director on the
telephone and arranged for the body to be washed and made ready for
the wake. He had spoken to the doctor and the priest and the driver of
the hearse. People had asked him what he wanted them to do, and he
had decided. He had made promises of payment and written his name
and address on pieces of paper, all the time feeling his activity meant
something, but now he couldn't think what it was. When he'd walked
out of the hospital and down to the subway station he'd realized he
had no carfare. Now, as a wave of exhaustion washed over him, he
wished he had borrowed a few coins. He wanted to stop and rest, but

it was pointless to sit or lie down on the bridge. He would only freeze. He forced himself to keep walking.

When he reached home, his cousin Davey leaned over the banister in the hallway and called out to him. "Frank! The hospital phoned. Something terrible's happened."

"I know," said Frank. He pushed past his cousin and opened the door.

Davey placed a hand on Frank's arm, saying, "Wait!" But Frank wouldn't stop.

He walked through to the kitchen. Deirdre sat rigidly, hands clenching her teacup. Junior had been crying. Paul sat with his arms folded, watching the door. When he saw Frank enter, he jumped up. At the same time, Davey rushed in. But Frank's cousins could not protect him.

"Ma," said Frank. He held out his arms for her.

Deirdre stood and stepped forward and slapped him hard across the face. "Where were you?" She slapped him again. The action seemed to calm her. "Out with those, those *people*, God knows where, while your father was in a horrible accident." She paused, watching him.

Frank saw that she was waiting for him to ask what had happened. She wanted to punish him with the brutal news.

"Ma, don't —"

"He's dead, Frank." She watched him greedily.

In her desire to make someone pay for her loss, she was turning on her son. As always, he was the person closest to her, the first person to blame. But this time he truly was to blame. This time he did deserve it. He turned away. Tomas was gone, and all she had left was her anger. Let her have it, then. She seemed to need it. He wouldn't be the one to tell her he'd gone with his father to the hospital, held his hand while he died. *You've been a good son to me.*

He looked at Paul and Davey, fatherless a long time, now. He remembered Tomas's other words: *He knows things.* What did that mean? What had Brendan O'Nolan known? Why had he hated the Garrisons? Frank knew he had to forget those questions. He would never get an answer from his mother. And he didn't have time to speculate on the past. He was fifteen years old, and he had a family to support.

3.9

MEREDITH IS SURPRISINGLY LARGE. SHE IS TALLER THAN KYLE, with broad shoulders and a sense of gravitas in her deep brown eyes. Von had expected a flighty teenager, but Meredith, at eighteen, is a woman. She wears a fringed deerskin jacket, with traditional Manitoba beading on the pockets, a pair of jeans and well-worn brown suede boots. Her luggage is a denim and leather backpack, adorned with overlapping patches in many colours and a fuzzy baby-duck toy, attached to the zipper toggle. Except for the duck, she is very adult. She has brown, shapely hands, long fingers and neatly trimmed nails buffed to a sheen. Even her nose ring is sedate, a small rhinestone nestled behind the flare of her left nostril, and her hair, though it hangs past her waist, is tamed into two neat braids.

Von has agreed to come to the airport, because Kyle said that would make Meredith feel more welcome. Meredith sits in the middle in the back of the taxi, and Kyle does most of the talking until they get home, describing with enthusiasm Rosheen's glass collage *The Winter Garden* and quoting Ingrid on its artistic significance. Meredith turns to Von and says it must have been fascinating, growing up with an artist like Rosheen. Von pastes a welcoming smile on her face and agrees. She's aware of a mild panic going on somewhere inside her body. More and more people are entering her space. Opening her up. The private stories of the Garrisons, once firmly under her control, are spilling out.

Back at the apartment, Von adopts a hostess role, offering towels and pillows and inquiring about Meredith's preferences for dinner. "We're all stocked up on fresh vegetables," Von says, "from the farmer's market. Beets, carrots, green beans..."

"That sounds great," Meredith says. "Kyle and I will cook."

"That's not necessary," says Von. "I can manage."

"We'll cook," says Meredith. "Right, Kyle?"

"Meredith's an expert," Kyle says. "She took cooking classes in night school."

So while they prepare the meal, Von sits in the living room and picks up the magazine Alex gave her. Since she's agreed to help put together Rosheen's show, she needs to educate herself. Vaguely, she'd always considered her sister's artwork a hobby, a childhood habit she never outgrew. But it's clear to her now, now that it's too late to talk to Rosheen about it, that people in New York have been taking her work quite seriously, for at least the past five years. Critics have written about it and galleries have displayed it and students have been influenced by it. These are facts Von should have known, would have known, if she hadn't tried so hard to shut Rosheen out of her life.

She opens to the article "Translucent Memory" and reads about the process of making *The Winter Garden*. Glass, according to the article, plays a significant role in the work of Róisín Dubh.

As a girl, Róisín worried about the birds that flew into the greenhouse windows. One summer morning, when a cedar waxwing slammed into a window and fell to earth, dead, and Róisín began to cry, Manuel quickly wrapped it in a tissue and said he was taking it to the bird hospital. A few hours later, when a robin crashed into the glass, Siobhán held her breath, hoping Róisín wouldn't see it die. But the robin only lay on the lawn for a minute, stunned, and then flew away.

"Maybe their nests aren't warm enough," said Róisín. "They want to come inside."

"The winter birds never bump into the glass," their mother said. "It's only the summer birds who make that mistake. So the robin isn't doing it because he's cold."

But Róisín opened the door of the greenhouse and stood there, calling the robin, the way you might call a dog. "Here, birdie! Come in the *door*, silly."

Siobhán and her mother, watching from the kitchen, shared a smile.

"Could we make blankets for them?" Róisín asked. Her mother tried to reassure her that the birds were perfectly all right. She explained that birds have cold blood, so they stay warm. This violated Róisín's seven-year-old sense of logic.

Von giggled. "They're warm because they have cold blood? Yes, Mum, that *does* sound backwards!" Their mother laughed too. She tried again, saying that birds see their own reflections in the glass and think they're seeing other birds. They just want to make friends.

"But it's their own selfs they see?" asked Róisín. "Not a friend?"

"That's right, honey."

"Oh," said Róisín. She looked outside, where the robin was pecking at the wet grass, looking for worms. "That's sad."

Above her head, Siobhán and her mother exchanged rueful glances and shrugged, in twin gestures of defeat.

"The thing is," said Siobhán, "the birds are not very smart. They have wee little brains. But they do learn to tell the difference between their own reflection and the other birds. They make lots of friends. By the time they're, oh, in bird grade two, they have it all figured out."

Róisín screwed up her freckled nose. "Bird grade two? Oh, Siobhán, there's no such thing as bird grade two!"

"How do you know? Come on back in the kitchen and wash your hands, and you can help me make a pie out of those plum preserves."

"If you girls make a pie, we can take it with us on our picnic tomorrow," said their mother. She'd been planning this picnic all week, and Róisín was excited, though Siobhán wasn't counting on it. Her mother was always planning picnics, but few of them actually took place.

The sisters worked on the pie together, with Róisín standing on a stepstool. Siobhán showed her how to sift the flour and how to cut the dough and how to put everything back in its very same place when you were finished with it.

A car pulled up outside, and their mother came back into the kitchen, saying, "It's your father. Manuel picked him up early from work today. He isn't feeling well. So you girls be good."

The girls moved to the kitchen table, where Siobhán showed her sister how to make the pie top pretty by weaving strips of dough into a pattern over the fruit. As they were bent over this task, Frank pushed hard on the swinging kitchen door and came striding toward the sink for a drink of water.

"Hi, Dad."

"Hi, Dad."

Siobhán knew, by the fact he didn't answer and by the sound of his movements, too fast, that they should get out of his way. She put an arm around Róisín and said, "Maybe we should go check on that robin." But before they could escape, she heard a *bang* and knew instantly what it was. They had left a cupboard door open, one of the cupboard doors above the sink, and their father had walked right into it.

He swore. Siobhán drew Róisín up tight against her. She hoped her mother would not come in and scold him for swearing, *Please, Mum, let it go*. Bam. He punched the cupboard door shut with the side of his fist, so hard it bounced and flew open right back at him. It hit him again in the forehead, and he punched it again, this time holding it so it could not move, and his fist made a hole right through it. Von pulled Róisín backwards, through the kitchen door that was still swaying from the force of his entry.

She heard a great creak and a splintering, as if he were ripping the cupboard door from its hinges, but she didn't see him do it, because by then she was in the front yard, with her little sister's arms wrapped around her waist.

The girls could see their mother on the porch, poised to run, one hand on her heart, uncertain which way she should go. She looked out at her daughters hugging each other under the elm tree. Then she looked back toward the kitchen. She took one more glance at her daughters and then hurried toward her husband.

From the elm tree, the robin sang a little song, cherroo cherree. It was the song the parents sang when they were getting the baby robins ready for their bath, or at least that's what Siobhán had often told Róisín.

When Kyle calls her for dinner, Von is impressed by the way the table is set. "Where should I sit?" she asks, feeling like a guest. Kyle has picked up bread and fresh flowers at the corner store. He's put a vase of daisies on the table, and set each place with a napkin folded like a swan, and a glass of cold water, complete with an ice cube and a lemon twist.

Kyle pulls out a chair for her, and Meredith brings her a bowl of hot soup.

"This is very nice," Von says. "It's been a long time..."

Meredith brings soup for Kyle and herself and they sit down, begin to unfold their napkins. Meredith waits politely for Von to continue and then prompts, "A long time?"

"Since anyone's cooked for me," says Von. Good God, now she's getting sentimental over vegetable soup. What is happening to her?

The soup turns out to be delicious, and the conversation is good. The three of them sit together and laugh, tell stories and pass the salt like family. Not like the family Von grew up in. More like the family she'd once planned to have, a peaceful husband, happy children. She'd lost her only chance for that a long, long time ago. But this evening she's grateful to be with Kyle and Meredith, to hear their stories and watch them smiling at each other, the way people smile when they're in love and know they're loved in return.

3.10

DEIRDRE WENT DOWN TO WOLNSKI'S BUILDING WHERE BRENDAN O'Nolan used to live and knocked on the office door. He was not in, and the tavern was closed. She decided to wait in front of the building for him. If anyone saw her there, she would think up a quick lie. She no longer felt the terror that used to grip her when she imagined Tomas finding out about her past. Strangely, having no husband to lose meant having no fear of losing her husband. God certainly worked in mysterious ways, as Father Madden was so fond of saying.

Mr Wolnski took off his hat when he saw her waiting for him in her mourning dress, in front of his building. He juggled the hat, along with a loaf of bread and a newspaper and a black umbrella, and bowed to her with great dignity.

"My condolences, Mrs O'Nolan."

"I thank you, Mr Wolnski," Deirdre said. She did not correct his mistake about her name. She knew he was selling his building and moving away. Even so, she did not want her true name connected with Brendan's in any way. It was unlikely he would ever speak to anyone she knew, given the divide between the Irish and the Polish. But you never knew what people might overhear by accident. This was how she had learned of the thefts at the Polish church. She had overheard in the butcher shop that the collection money had gone missing and a gold crucifix had been stolen from the nave. They said it was Jews that did it. But Deirdre had a different theory.

"Please come in," said Mr Wolnski. "Bring the baby."

Deirdre demurred. She had brought a covered baby carriage with her, borrowed from Mrs Heintz, but it had no baby in it. "I'll leave the carriage here in the fresh air."

Mr Wolnski peered under the hooded cover and saw a bundle of blankets. "Nice and cozy," he said. He led Deirdre into the office beside the tavern and settled her into a chair. "You want to attend to your son's affairs, of course," he said. "Give me a moment while I get the key." He set his things on a shelf and hung up his hat and coat.

Deirdre watched him closely. He was a plodding sort of man. Slow and simple-minded. He did not seem to suspect she was anything more than a grieving mother came to collect her son's belongings. She guessed he had not heard the rumours of Brendan's crimes. Deirdre herself had only heard them after Tomas's funeral, when Frank told her Brendan had been jailed for stealing from the priests in New Rochelle. She doubted Mr Wolnksi would knowingly rent one of his rooms to a convict. He was a decent man, she thought, no matter what anyone said about Polacks. She was starting to realize that people said a lot of untrue things.

Now he was opening a drawer in his desk. He took out a ring of keys. "I have left his room as it was," he said. "I expected you would want to attend to it."

"Thank you." She followed him upstairs. The other doors along the hall stood open, the rooms empty. Everyone had moved out. Only Brendan's room was still locked.

The room was as she remembered it, except the bed was not made. A jumble of socks and underclothes lay at the foot of the bare mattress.

"I'm sorry," said Mr Wolnski. "The maid has been dismissed."

"That's all right. It's my own son's room. But if I could have a wee bit of privacy?"

"Naturally." He backed out of the room. "Call me if you need some help."

She got down on her knees and looked under the bed. Only dust. She crawled under and prodded every floorboard and peered into every crack. Only dust and dirt. She sat on the bed and sorted through the soiled sheets. Only a bad smell. She lifted the mattress from the frame and searched between the bed slats and found a silver knife and a silver letter opener. She put these in her purse. She pulled the candle from the candle holder and the soap from the soap dish. She held the Bible by its spine and shook the pages. The Bible yielded five twenty-dollar bills.

She opened the dresser and searched the pockets of the shirts and pants and unrolled the socks. The socks were full of dollar bills. She wanted to count them, but fearing Mr Wolnski's return, she simply scooped them into her purse. In the second drawer she found a bulky cloth bag, which she emptied onto the bed. She blinked. Then she counted. Seven silver spoons, two pocket watches, a diamond brooch, and four rings she thought were gold, each inlaid with different jewels. For a few moments, she bowed her head and prayed. Then she reached to the very back of the drawer and found the crucifix. It was swaddled in butcher's paper and a tablecloth. Deirdre unwrapped it and held it in her arms. It was heavy, definitely gold, with spots of red paint dabbed into the wounds under the bony ribs and on the scalp beneath the crown of thorns, and on the palms and soles of the feet. A hook on the back of the cross scraped Deirdre's arm. Brendan must have stolen this sacred treasure off the very wall of the Polish church, the twelfth station of the cross. He must be howling in hell this very minute.

But Deirdre's prayers had been answered at last, her fortune returned to her sevenfold. Maybe more. She would find out from the pawnshop man in New Jersey, where she had long ago taken Lucy's things — who would have suspected Lucy's trinkets would fetch so much? She felt a warm glow rise through her body as she pictured the sewing machine she could buy. Shiny new scissors and a girl to help her, and enough left over to rebuild her savings. She never felt entirely well unless she had some hidden savings. For you never knew what might happen in this world, and when God decided to favour you it was only right to take advantage.

Finally, she stowed all the bundles in the carriage. Last of all she laid down the Lord Jesus in his swaddling clothes and tucked a baby quilt around him. For it was a very chilly day.

3.11

THERE WERE NO MORE QUESTIONS NOW, ABOUT FRANK'S education. Since Tomas was dead, there would be no more grade seven, and no art lessons, either. Mr Edison took him on full time as a carpenter's apprentice when he was only fifteen. After work and on Saturdays, Frank continued his bicycle deliveries for extra money. In this way, he supported his mother and his cousins for three years.

Frank's oldest cousin, Davey, dropped out of high school when he made a girl pregnant, and now he worked in the sugar factory and lived with his wife and baby at his father-in-law's house. Paul got on at the factory as well, but he didn't move out. Loyal to the memory of Tomas, Paul stayed on to help Frank with the household expenses. Junior, the youngest of Lucy's boys, was the only one who stayed in school, as Tomas had wanted them all to do.

When he was not too tired, Frank rode past Paolo's house late at night. If there was a gathering, the artists welcomed him in. Often, Paolo was alone and invited Frank in to his studio to look at his paintings and experiment with the oils. He talked to Frank about the history of painting and the new work artists were doing now, how they were breaking free of the past.

Paolo's friends said the Germans had put on a massive exhibit of modern art in a museum in Berlin, not to honour the artists but to shame them. The Nazis hated modern art and hated artists, especially the Jewish artists, Max said, and anyone who did not paint the way the Nazi party thought they should paint. The German public was invited to come and mock the paintings. The artists were condemned. Many were exiled from the city of Berlin; others could not get work. They were not allowed to teach or even to paint. Abe told a story about a painter in München who stuffed rags in the crack under his apartment door, so nobody could smell the paint fumes in the corridor. To ventilate the apartment and keep his family from suffocating, he had to keep the windows open all year long. In winter, his children wore their coats and hats to bed. Some artists left the country but still could not get work. Once they were labelled degenerates, no one in Europe wanted them. Jewish professors and lawyers lost their positions too. Frank sat and sipped the coffee Sue had given him. He drank slowly, wanting to linger and listen. There were bullies everywhere in the world, it seemed. Right here in Brooklyn and all the way across the ocean too. A long time ago he had looked at a map on the schoolroom wall and seen where Germany was. How small it seemed, to have all this turmoil. Frank did not think very many people could live there, and yet at the movie house he had seen masses of Germans marching and thousands of people filling the streets, waving Nazi flags. Nazi ideas were spreading all over Europe, Abe said. He read out loud from the *New York Times* about a speech a man had given to the Chamber of Commerce downtown. The man had denounced Hitlerism and the Nazis, and called for the United States to unite with Britain and France to defeat Germany.

"War," said Abe. "It's coming and it's time."

"At what cost?" Max asked. "Too many will die."

"Too many will die anyway," said Abe.

Frank walked home thinking about all these things. Some people wanted to stand up to the Nazis but others did not. Would the President go to war? Would the other countries join together? It kept him up late, imagining the battlefields and remembering the exciting stories Mr Gray had told about the action he had seen in the Great War.

The next morning, he slept late and hurried to get dressed and make lunch for Mr Edison and himself. In the kitchen, Deirdre was trying to start a fire in the stove with damp woodchips.

"Did you take that paper out of the kindling box?" she asked Frank.

"Just a piece of cardboard," he said.

"Well, I need it."

Frank went to his room and retrieved the cardboard, on which he had been practising drawing Junior's bare foot while Junior was sleeping. Deirdre glanced quickly at the dozens of disembodied feet that covered both sides of the cardboard. Then she tore it into pieces.

"That's a waste of good time," she said, "and good kindling. Those artists have got your head turned backwards, thinking anything good will come of scribbling like this. I don't want you associating with them, Frank. I won't have you living like that, in that...squalor."

Frank concentrated on opening a tin of sardines and slicing a loaf of bread. He wrapped two sandwiches in wax paper and placed them in his lunch box with a couple of apples.

Deirdre got a fire going and mixed a batch of hotcakes while John Junior and Paul waited at the table to be fed.

"Aunt Deirdre," Paul said, "my tooth hurts whenever I touch it."

"Don't touch it then," said Deirdre.

"Could I have carfare, Aunt Deirdre?" John Junior asked. "They're interviewing boys for that business college over in Queens, and I need to get there before noon."

"You've got two feet," she said, "last I looked."

Frank reached into his pocket and gave Junior two bits. "For carfare — and so's you can get a bowl of soup somewhere later, if you're hungry."

"Gosh, Frank," said Junior. "That's good of you."

"And you, Paul," said Frank. "You come with me this afternoon to Dr Green's office, and he'll take a look at your tooth."

"We can't afford a dentist," said Deirdre.

"It's all right, Ma," said Frank. "It's Mr Green's son. He took out my sore tooth last year, remember? And he let me pay on time. He said he'd do the same for anyone in our family."

Deirdre turned her back on her son. She flipped the hotcake with a force that sent it flying out of the pan and into the flames.

"Ma! Ma, be careful." Frank leaned forward and rescued the cake from the fire with his bare fingers and returned it to the pan. "He's a good man. The Greens are good people."

Deirdre sniffed. She mumbled something about working for Jews.

"Yes," said Frank. "I have been working for Jews for many years, and I'm glad of it." He looked her in the eye. "I'm grateful to them."

He felt something break, and break free, inside him.

Deirdre's shoulders tightened. But he knew she would not dare to hit him now. Even the familiar, deliberate curve of her shoulders as she turned away did not sting him as it used to. He realized he did not fear her anymore.

In the spring of 1939, when Frank had his eighteenth birthday, the talk at Paolo's gatherings was all about the mass burning of paintings in Berlin. The Germans had piled up thousands of paintings, Abe reported, all the works they deemed to be degenerate, and doused them with gasoline and set fire to them, creating the biggest public bonfire in all of Germany. This was not done by criminals but by government officials, in a square in front of the firehouse in Berlin.

"They will burn the artists next," Abe said.

Everyone was silent. Frank guessed they were remembering friends they had left behind in Germany. Some of these friends were trying to send their children out of the country. Abe's sister had managed to get her son into Paris, but he was now stranded there.

Abe couldn't get him into the United States. He didn't have the right papers, they said. Frank never heard what happened to the boy, who was nine years old. How would it feel to be exiled from home, to have no home? Last winter, Mrs Heintz down the street had shown him a newspaper with photographs of German synagogues in flames and Jewish shops with their windows smashed and their goods pulled off the shelves and stolen or destroyed. The police had done nothing to stop the vandals. What would happen in Brooklyn if someone did that to Mr Green's shop? He thought of the time a man had spit on the ground deliberately, right in front of two Jewish scholars coming from Beth Jacob synagogue, and he and Corky had watched and said nothing.

In the fall, England declared war on Germany, and now it seemed everyone was talking about Hitler. Father Madden publicly condemned the preparations for war, but his heart didn't seem to be in it. After church, a group of boys and young men stood around boasting that they would join up and go after Hitler if the United States declared war.

"I'd sneak into Hitler's house at night and shoot him in the heart," said Corky.

"Go on," said one of the older boys. "What army would have you?" He gave Corky a good-natured shove and Corky grabbed Frank's arm to keep from falling over.

"What about you, Frank?" Corky asked. "Would you go?"

Frank said nothing. In Corky's family, the war had caused a blowout so bad that Corky's brother Simon, the boxer, had left home and gone up to Canada to join the army, and his mother and his uncles said they would disown him. Simon had stormed into the gym the week before and handed around recruitment posters from the Canadians and pinned one up on the board in the gym, and the owner had torn it down and ripped it to pieces in front of everyone, cursing the British. A number of fistfights had broken out over this controversy, and Frank had slipped out the side door of the gym, not wanting to become entangled in the high emotions. He knew more about Hitler, he thought, than most of the other boys and men at the gym. He'd learned, from people who'd lived in Europe, how mad Hitler was, how dangerous. If the United States joined the war, Frank thought he would go. But he was keeping that decision to himself. In his neighbourhood, there were many who took the side of Germany only because, as Irish nationalists, they were sworn to hate England. Frank was ashamed of their ignorance.

As they left the churchyard, Frank and Corky saw Annie Taylor coming toward them, carrying a prayer book. This was the street where she lived.

"How are you, Annie?" He removed his cap. She was a young woman now.

Down the street, the door of her house was open. Her brother Henry stood on the front step and called her name.

Frank waved, but Henry did not wave back. He stood with his arms folded across his chest. Annie turned away without a word of good-bye and hurried home to her brother. Frank watched as Henry held the door open for her and followed her inside.

"He won't talk to me," Frank told Corky. "Neither of them hardly says hello. It's like they've forgotten me."

"We're not kids no more," said Corky. "We got to stick with our own kind now."

"That's stupid," said Frank.

"Lots of things are stupid," said Corky.

Frank had arranged his life so that he could support his widowed mother and his orphaned cousins. His days were spent on carpentry jobs with Mr Edison, and his evenings and weekends on deliveries for the Greens. But he still tried to practise drawing and painting, when he could, and he continued to attend gatherings at Paolo's house, late at night. After one long session of music and talk, Paolo asked Frank to come outside and share a smoke with him. Frank didn't smoke. It was bad for your health, he said. Paolo laughed. That was an old wives' tale, he told Frank. A cigarette wouldn't hurt him.

"No, thanks," said Frank. "But I'll come out and talk."

They put on their overcoats and stepped outside. The sky was clear. The stars seemed sharper in the cold air, and Paolo's burning cigarette smelled harsher.

"Did you ever talk to Oskar Johan about those art lessons?" Paolo asked. "You should. There's something new, now. Night classes. They're beginning soon, if you want to attend. You should take your sketchbooks over to the school and make an application for that scholarship. Now that you're older your chances are very good." He gave Frank a handbill from the school. "You have three weeks to apply."

Frank took the handbill home and calculated his income and expenses. He was eighteen, and just when most young men were taking on more responsibilities, his were lightening. Deirdre had somehow managed to purchase two new sewing machines and hire two girls to help her. Junior, who surprised everyone by becoming the first member of the family to graduate from high school, was enrolled in a business course. Paul was helping to pay Junior's tuition and the household bills. Thanks to Paul, Frank didn't need to continue making deliveries in the evening. He could go to night classes. But only if he got that scholarship.

He pulled his sketches and paintings from under the wardrobe in the bedroom he shared with Paul and Junior. He remembered the two drawings he'd taken to show his father on the day of the sugar dust explosion. They were destroyed in the fire, but he remembered them well. He had improved a lot since then. As he set aside his best work, he dared to let his hopes rise. He decided he'd create one more, something special.

For three weeks, he worked every minute he could spare, giving up his Saturday deliveries to take advantage of the daylight. His new piece, the hardest one, the one that took him the longest and used up the most paper — good, expensive paper — was a watercolour painting of the big copper kettle in the kitchen, with the late winter light coming in from the window and the reflection, distorted by the curves of the kettle, of the shelf of teacups of all colours. He was beginning to understand how light worked. He felt sure Mr Johan would see that.

———

Two days before the deadline, Frank readied himself to go into town to Grove Street and see Mr Johan at the art school. He counted out coins for the fare. He put on clean clothes and polished his shoes and combed his hair. Then he bent down under his wardrobe to pull out his sketchbook. He couldn't feel it, so he got down on his knees and looked. It wasn't there. The cardboard folder of loose watercolour and ink drawings wasn't there either. He slid his hand far to the back, but found nothing. Even the dust was gone. His mother must have cleaned his room.

"Ma?" he called. He found her in the alcove, sewing. "Ma, did you see my drawing books? Did you move them somewhere?"

"Those books are a waste of time," she said. "I told you the paper's more use as kindling."

Frank waited, but she said nothing more. She resumed her work. She had a brand new electric Singer sewing machine, the latest model, and she was making a whole set of clothes for the wedding party of a policeman's daughter. Frank watched her work for a while. The truth came to him slowly. "You didn't," he said.

"I certainly did."

He sat down heavily on the couch. "Ma. You didn't."

"I did. That book was grubby and dusty. And those paintings, too."

"But Ma —" He felt sick to his stomach. The art school was closing in two hours. He could never replace the pictures in two hours. Not even in two days.

"You take those pictures too serious, you hear? It's not right."

Frank put on his coat and walked out of the apartment and down the stairs and through the door into the cold sunshine. But once he was outside, he did not know where to go. He flung himself down on the stoop to think. At first he was fixated on remembering the pictures — the buildings and trees and boats and people he had sketched. All the people. Mr Edison with his nervous grin, his forehead wrinkled from frowning while he measured. Frank had drawn him measuring, one eye shut as he read the ruler. Mrs Gray in her winter hat, her mouth closed in a tight line so her broken tooth would not show. The copper kettle. Three Saturdays and three Sundays he had worked, making eight, nine watercolour sketches of that kettle, trying and trying again to reproduce the glare where the sunlight hit hardest, and the dent in the handle and the reflections of those five teacups, the blue one with the white rim and the one with the buttercups that had driven him mad with its scalloped edges. But soon he tired of this brooding.

He thought bitterly that the pictures themselves did not matter. They were mere pieces of paper. He could always make more. No, it wasn't the drawings and paintings he cared about. They never turned out the way he wanted, anyway. What he loved was the act of *making* the drawings. The way time and language vanished and the physical

objects of the world took up life inside his body. That was what she
had taken from him. The chance to win a scholarship that might have
let him spend his days exploring where that way might take him. Did
she hate him so much she couldn't let him have a life of his own? He
imagined the great flames rising from the pyre of paintings the Nazis
had burned in Münich, thousands of paintings on fire, the air so
clogged with smoke the people could not breathe or see the sky.

The next day Frank went to the bank and took out all his money. He
purchased a life insurance policy with his mother as beneficiary. He
bought a canvas duffel bag, the kind he'd seen the sailors carry down
at the piers, some new socks and a sketchbook. He went to church
and confessed to Father Madden, who did not try to stop him from
leaving. He went home and packed. Everything he owned fit into the
one bag, and on top he folded the poster Corky's brother had handed
out at the gym, with the address of the recruitment office. He told his
mother he was leaving home. She did not believe him, and he did not
try to convince her. He went to his room early and lay on his bed and
thought for a long time about Tomas.

    He should have used the strength God gave him to defend his
father. He had tried to atone for that failure by taking Tomas's place as
provider for the family. How proud he had been, all this past month,
thinking he had done enough. Thinking he was free now to practise his
other talents, his art. To share with people what he saw in the world,
share with them *how* he saw the world. But God was telling him it was
not yet time for that. There was still a debt he had to pay. God gives a
man talent, Father Madden said, to discover what his destiny will be.
That's what he said when Frank won his first boxing match, and he
said it again the night Frank won a fat purse for the parish. Frank was
good at fights, everyone said so, and right now he was furious enough
to dive headfirst into a big one. A fight is honourable, Tomas said, if it's
a fight against injustice. Frank heard those words now, in his father's
voice, and he knew he was making the right decision. To go where he
was truly needed. He could think of no fight more just than the war in
Europe, and no place farther away from his mother.

    In the evening, he ate the supper Deirdre served and then took
the subway to Grand Central Station. By midnight, he was on a

passenger train, rolling north to Montreal. All night he drifted in and out of sleep, lulled by the rhythm of the wheels on the tracks, and jolted awake whenever it stopped. Just before dawn, the track veered west, and from his window Frank could see the front of the train, moonlight shining on the engine and the cars ahead of him. As they rounded the long curve, he had a wide view of the sky over a flat plain. More stars than he'd ever seen in the city, but already they were fading. The predawn light absorbed the constellations until only two stars, then only one, remained. He saw in the north a thick scarf of black clouds and knew the train would soon pass under them, as if entering a tunnel. Above the clouds he saw a vast expanse of blue sky, with the one star still shining. He wanted to remember that star, while he was travelling under the rain clouds, wanted to remember that the sky still stretched wide and blue above the world, beyond the depth of any knowing. When he came back from the war, he would be a man. He would need nobody and nobody would be able to tell him what to do.

3.12

THE ONE THING DEIRDRE REMEMBERED MOST VIVIDLY FROM THE day that Brendan O'Nolan first arrived at her door was the bargain she'd made with God. *Take my husband*, she'd said. *If you must take one of them, please, take my husband.*

She walked into her empty bedroom and opened the closet and unwrapped the Lord Jesus. He was the only one who knew of this bargain, and she felt she could confide in Him. Years ago she had taken Him, along with Brendan's other treasures, to a New Jersey pawnshop, and been handsomely rewarded. But in the days that followed, she'd begun to feel it wasn't right to leave the Lord Jesus in that dusty shop among the hocked candlesticks and silverware. So within the month, she had returned with her pawn ticket and redeemed Him. She was keeping Him hidden for now, wrapped in the baby quilt, lest by rare chance a member of the Polish parish should ever come into the apartment and recognize Him. But every few days she unwrapped the quilt and engaged Him in a little conversation. He was very understanding, and she was glad of the company. The apartment was too quiet. Davey and Paul were both married now. Junior was always off to his day job or his night course. Frank had deserted her entirely. He had gone to Canada. What was Canada? A British colony, said Mrs Heintz. But that only reminded Deirdre of the British soldiers who had beaten Daniel and the rebels who had ripped his leg off with their bomb. If Frank went to war…she could not think of it.

How noisy the apartment used to be. How hectic, with Lucy and her little boys. So many chores to do and Mrs Gray, the social worker, nosing around. Tomas wanting his dinner, a clean shirt, a new baby. It all seemed a muddled dream, now.

Back then, all Deirdre had wanted was peace and quiet and more money. Now she possessed all of those things. And yet…

Beside the alcove, the three silent sewing machines gleamed in the lamplight, casting three hump-backed shadows on the wall. In the bank, her money grew and grew. She no longer had to hide it. She could look at the sum in her bankbook as often as she wished. Why didn't her new wealth please her? Perhaps because she'd never truly longed for it.

Ever since she came to New York City, she'd been afraid of losing the little she'd managed to salvage in her escape from Ireland — her freedom and her son. But fear was not the same as longing. She'd been afraid Frank would be run over by a car, drown in the river, tumble off the roof. Or he'd never learn to read, he'd fall in with the wrong crowd, waste his talents daydreaming and drawing pictures, sink into the filthy poverty she knew so well from childhood. The money wasn't something she wanted for itself. It was only for safety, in case Tomas fell ill or was injured or found out about her past and threw her out.

She'd nearly forgotten how it felt to want something good and beautiful, how desire had once gripped and shaped her, flooded her body with strength. Once, she'd risked her life for what she wanted. That cold, wild ride in the currach, the swell of the river beneath her, the whipping squall. Had it been too much to ask? she asked Lord Jesus. To live with an illiterate Irish fisherman on a barren island, imprisoned by the northern sea? It seemed a meagre thing enough. But it had been denied to her.

4

Fire

4.1

AT CAMP ALDERSHOT IN NOVA SCOTIA, A MAN DIDN'T HAVE TO make decisions. A man was clear of all that. He had made one decision, to commit himself to the regiment, and that one commitment set him free. Frank belonged to the Black Watch regiment of Canada now. The Black Watch was his family, all members bent to the same purpose. Days were for exercise, the training of limbs, building of muscles. All day Frank marched in the snow and ran and performed push-ups and chin-ups on demand, along with everyone else. In the evening, instead of reading or playing cards, he joined the small boxing gym the officers set up. At night he had no time to dwell on memories, because he fell instantly asleep. Hard work lifted from his mind the burden of his guilt, and from his soul all doubt, and made him feel he was on the right side of things again. It was as Father Madden said. By serving God, he learned his own strength. He welcomed every challenge. The more difficult it was, the more eagerly he lost himself inside it.

The obstacle course worked that way. At first it was a tangled maze with fresh trials at every turn, confusion and pain. But each time he ran the course, he learned something new. After the tunnel came the

barbed wire and then the frozen marsh and then the sheer climb up
to the lookout tower and the long slide down. Once he knew what to
expect from the course, his time improved. Frank was often the fastest
man in his unit, Frank or the tall, red-haired Canadian named Connor
Flynn. But when the exercise became routine, thoughts drifted back
into his mind, the acrid smell of Tomas's scorched shirt, his own
burned drawings. He was always relieved when the officers changed
the obstacle course, making it strange again, so that it required all
his concentration. This was what it would be like in the war, every
day a different terrain, new enemy tactics. The will sharpened to one
direction.

———

Frank watched the Canadian men in his company, gauging their
strengths, their reflexes, their common sense. He was aware they
watched him, too. Some were jokers, who mocked his accent and
nicknamed him "Brooklyn." But most were decent and said outright
they admired his boxing skill. In time, the name "Brooklyn" was spoken
with respect.

The Canadians flooded a large area behind the camp and made a
skating rink. Frank, who had never worn a pair of ice skates, watched
them play hockey. Red-haired Connor Flynn was the fastest and the
most sure. He skated in and around the other men with ease, carried
the puck as long as he wanted to, and sent it with great force exactly
where he wanted it to go. He was disciplined and did not hesitate. He
was someone you could trust to make the right moves, someone you
wanted near you if you were heading into battle. Connor did not box,
but came to the matches and observed Frank closely, as if to learn from
him. Frank wanted to speak to him, but didn't know how.

On a Saturday in spring, when they both had passes to go into
town, Connor and Frank stood shaving in front of the mirror in their
tent. Connor said he and his friend Dickie Lassiter were going to a play
in Halifax. Did Frank want to come along? Connor was nonchalant,
covering his handsome freckled face with shaving cream. "It's *King
Lear*," he said.

That meant nothing to Frank. But he was drawn to Connor.
"Sure," he said. Their eyes met in the mirror, and Connor smiled, as if
Frank had done something right.

A friend of Connor's drove them into Halifax and dropped them at the theatre, saying he was going to the pub and he'd pick them up at the same spot at midnight.

In the theatre lobby, the women filing in to watch the play wore fancy evening dresses and the men wore pressed black jackets and ties. Frank was glad he and his fellow soldiers were in uniform. Nobody, looking at the three of them, could tell that Frank was any different from Connor or Dickie. As long as he didn't speak out loud and give himself away. Men and women smiled and nodded to the soldiers as they passed through the lobby, and some of the men came over to shake their hands. They settled into their seats at last, good seats near the front, and after the curtain went up, Frank became immersed in another world.

When they stepped into the street afterward, he was glad the night was dark.

"So, what did you think?" Connor asked.

"Splendid," said Dickie. "Just the thing to make you glad you're away from your family!"

"Frank?"

Frank couldn't speak. His chest was sore. He didn't know what to say. He had watched stories acted out before, at the picture theatres back home. Comedies and cowboy stories. But nothing like this. Never anything like this. He could think of nothing to say. *King Lear* was about a man cut to the core. It was about being alone. But Frank had no words for talking about things like that, and he knew he had understood only part of the play. As they walked the streets, looking for something to do, he was silent.

When they passed a dance hall, with its doors open to the street, they stopped a while to listen to the music, and Frank stepped over the threshold to look inside. It wasn't a fancy place. Just a big room, with the lights turned low and a little stage at the front where four musicians in dark suits were playing "Stardust." There were about a hundred people inside, slow dancing or sitting at the tables that surrounded the dance floor. A dark-haired girl was sitting alone at a table near the entrance, with her hands clasped in her lap and her eyes downcast. When a young man stopped to speak to her, she looked up and shyly shook her head, and he moved on. She turned toward the doorway then and looked directly at Frank. Her eyes were dark and shining, and though she seemed shy, she did not turn away. They remained looking at each other until Frank began to grin. He saw the corners of her pretty mouth turn up in amusement.

"Let's go in," said Frank.

"After you," said Connor. He and Dickie followed Frank inside and established themselves at a spot near the canteen. They leaned against the wall with their arms crossed, watching the band. But Frank watched the dark-haired girl, who had turned away from him when two of her friends came to sit at her table. The other girls had prettier dresses, but Frank was not interested in them. The three girls whispered together, and within minutes, the two new ones began to turn their heads to smile at the soldiers. Connor and Dickie exchanged a glance before ambling toward their table. Introductions were made, but Frank listened only to one word. Her name was Lenore. Then the band started up with "Pennies from Heaven," and Connor and Dickie each took a girl onto the floor for a spin. But Lenore touched the chair beside her, inviting Frank to sit, and he was glad.

She spoke freely, as though she had known him a long time. He liked her laugh and the little rasp in her throat when she talked. She said "wif" instead of "with" and "ain't" instead of "isn't," and never mentioned Frank's accent, except to say, "You must be from New York." She told him she liked to play cards and go to the movies, especially if there was singing in them. She said she lived with her mother and her little sisters just west of town. Her father had died last year. She described the funeral, how hard it had rained, giving her mother a chill she had never gotten over. "She coughs even now, and it's been over a year. I'm afraid for her."

"I lost my father early, too," Frank said. "A few years back."

Lenore placed a hand on his arm. "I'm sorry." The pupils of her eyes were open wide in the soft light, and her eyelashes were long and black. She wore a delicate silver cross on a chain around her neck and a thin silver band upon one finger.

Frank touched the hand with the ring and stroked it gently. "What's this?" he asked. "You're engaged to be married?"

She giggled. "No! This ring was a prize at Sunday school, for reciting Bible verses."

Connor passed by and winked at Frank. But Frank only smiled. While Connor and Dickie drank beer and danced with as many girls as they could, Frank sat and talked with Lenore for over two hours. She told him she worked in a hotel in Halifax and that soldiers from Aldershot often came into the hotel restaurant or beverage room. Soldiers were welcome there, she said.

"Maybe I'll come sometime," Frank told her. She lifted her face to his, her full lips parted slightly, and he could not help himself, he had to kiss her.

"Frank!" Connor was calling. "It's time to depart! Where's Dickie?"

While Connor searched for Dickie, Frank and Lenore walked out onto the sidewalk. He kissed her again, under the awning of the dance hall, and she told him the name of the hotel where she worked.

"I'll come to see you," he said. "Your boss won't mind?"

"I'll look for you," she said. Then one of her friends came out and called her name, and she ran back inside.

On the ride home, Connor and Dickie exchanged funny stories about the girls they had danced with. Frank laughed at everything they said, and sometimes he laughed for no reason, just giddy with freedom and already half in love with a girl he didn't even know.

In June, when Frank had a weekend's leave, he hitchhiked from Kentville to Halifax and asked directions to the hotel where Lenore worked. He went into the hotel restaurant and sat at a table and Lenore came along in a uniform of pale yellow and a pale yellow cap on her head and asked what did he want. When she saw who he was, her feet left the ground for a second in a jump of excitement. "You came!"

"I did," said Frank. "May I have a cup of coffee?"

He drank two cups of coffee and waited for her shift to be over, and she invited him home to her house. She lived on a small farm. Nothing more than a henhouse and a field of pumpkins. A horse, well into old age, stood grazing on grass in the front yard. The house was in need of paint. Country poverty was different from city poverty, but he recognized it. When they entered the house, she did not call out. They stepped directly into an untidy kitchen, and he followed her through to a parlour, where she invited him to sit on a worn sofa. They were alone.

"My mother takes my sisters every afternoon to visit her mother and make her supper," she said.

"And you don't go along?"

"I stay home to clean the house and do my typing," said Lenore. "I'm taking a typing course in town and we have exercises to practise." She lowered her head and a mass of dark curls fell across her forehead, obscuring her eyes.

"And what do you need to learn typing for?" Frank asked. He reached across and pushed some of the curls behind her ear.

"I'm getting away from here," Lenore said. "Away from the farm and this..." She waved her arm toward the kitchen with its dirty breakfast dishes and ironing board. "As soon as I finish my course I'm going to Toronto to find a job. There's lots of jobs for girls now, with the war on. I can earn a lot of money."

Frank chuckled softly. He liked this girl with her crazy optimism. "What will you do with all that money, then?"

"I'm going to save it up and go to university."

Frank coughed to keep himself from laughing. He knew that some girls, rich girls, went to teacher's college. Or nursing school. Still, he didn't think a farm girl, even one who took a typing course, had any place in a university. But he didn't want to be unkind.

"Good for you," he said. That was a phrase he had picked up from Mr Green back home.

"What about you?" she asked. "Will you go to university? After the war?"

"Why, sure," said Frank. She had surprised him into the lie.

"The University of Toronto?" she asked. "Is that where you'll go?"

Frank cleared his throat. He hadn't intended to deceive her, but now he was embarrassed to back down and tell her the truth, that he hadn't even finished grade seven.

She didn't notice his silence, but only said, "Me too. It's the best school in the country."

"Well, I'll see you there, then," he said lightly. He turned her gently to face him and then he kissed her.

All summer, whenever he could get away from camp in the evening, with leave or without, Frank met Lenore in Halifax. They went to picture shows, or to the dance hall, where he met her girlfriends, who were bold and funny, and loved Lenore as if she were their sister. They warned Frank, more than once, to treat her right. Most of the boys Lenore knew were the sons of fishermen or miners, and most had recently enlisted in the Navy. They punched Frank on the shoulder and made jokes about the superiority of the Navy to the Army. But they were good-natured. They liked to ask Frank about American baseball and boxing, which they followed on the radio.

After these evenings, Frank would walk Lenore to the end of the road that led to her house, where her mother kept a light burning on the porch for her. He would kiss her and cling to her until she wriggled away, and then he watched her as she ran up the path and entered her house. She always waved before she closed the door, though he knew she couldn't see him there, in the dark.

———

In the fall, Frank accepted an invitation from Connor Flynn to come home with him to visit his family in Toronto. Dickie Lassiter was going to Toronto, too, on his way to visit his own parents, so they arranged to take the train together. Connor's family had lived in Toronto for three generations on his father's side, he said. Dickie's family came from the prairies, but now they lived outside of Toronto, where his father ran a tree farm. Dickie and Connor had gone to the same private school in Toronto, and had done a year at university together, before they both joined up. They seemed to go everywhere together, though Frank didn't understand why they were friends. Dickie was pale and thin and slow. He often failed to understand exactly what was going on. His droopy eyelids made him seem perpetually on the verge of nodding off to sleep. Frank did not trust his judgement. But Connor seemed attached to him, so Frank assumed that Dickie must possess some hidden value.

Dickie's father met them at Union Station. He was a small, meek man, overjoyed to see his son. He shed a few tears and held Dickie in an embrace so long that Dickie, embarrassed, had to push him away in order to introduce his friends. Mr Lassiter dropped Frank and Connor at Connor's parents' house on McKenzie Avenue. He politely refused Connor's invitation to come inside, saying he had to get Dickie home to his mother. She worried so.

Frank got out of the car with his bag and followed Connor through a tall iron gate into a small park and up the wide stone steps of a lodge of some sort, attached to a conservatory. But after he'd been inside for a few minutes, taking in the polished wood-panelled walls and the high ceiling with its elaborate chandelier, he realized this was Connor's home. The whole, entire building was his family's house.

A maid came to take their duffel bags to their rooms, but Connor told her no, they would do it themselves, and he led the way up the curved staircase with its carved oak balustrade. Frank followed more slowly, examining the paintings on the wall. Traditional portraits of distinguished men in dark oils. Solemn faces. Connor led him through the spacious upper landing, past open doors, through which he glimpsed lamps and framed mirrors and beds laden with tasselled pillows. Connor entered a small room with a dresser and a cot and large windows that overlooked a long green lawn and a forest in the distance. The leaves were turning now, the forest a bright quilt of red and orange and green and yellow.

"You can sleep here. This was my summer bedroom when I was a kid."

Frank grinned in thanks. He stood at the window, wondering what it must have been like to be a boy here in this airy space. He could see the conservatory below, and through its glass ceiling the plants, exotic trees with split leaves and ferns of all shapes and colourful flowers and a pond. From a room somewhere below, he was aware of piano notes, first a light trilling climb up the scales, then a faltering echo, repeating over and over. He heard a truck somewhere in the distance. Otherwise only birdsong and the wind stirring a pile of fallen leaves on the lawn.

After they washed, Connor's father, Dr Flynn, took them into a room he called the study, with glass-fronted bookcases lining every wall, and gave them each a short drink of whisky. Dr Flynn was tall and stout, with a long moustache. He wore a vest and a black bowtie and a white shirt with the sleeves rolled up.

"You boys will see action soon," he predicted. "I know it's hard to wait, but you must take heart." He raised his glass. "To Canada." They all drank to Canada.

When Connor's mother came in to greet them, she immediately enveloped Connor in a hug. He lifted her off her feet and spun her around.

"Mother, you've become so small!" he teased, as he set her down.

Frank tried to imagine treating Deirdre in this manner.

"You've grown two inches at least," Mrs Flynn said. She was laughing, a little breathless, and very beautiful. She had the same colouring as her son — the rust-coloured hair and the brown eyes — and the same warmth. A soft lilt to her voice. "And this is Frank Garrison?"

"Yes," said Connor. He introduced Frank, and Mrs Flynn asked about his mother. She said Connor had told her Frank's father had passed, and she touched his hand as she spoke of it.

She ushered them into the parlour, where two girls sat at the piano, wearing white dresses with matching sashes tied in bows at the back. The older girl, about sixteen, was leaning over a music book and pointing out something to the little one. But she jumped up and threw her arms around Connor the minute she saw him. "I didn't hear you come in! We've been practising scales, and Charlotte insists on banging so! I've been wondering and wondering when you'd get home."

"This is Eileen, my sister," said Connor. "Eileen, meet Frank Garrison."

The girl kept her left arm draped around Connor's neck and extended her right, offering Frank her hand. Cool fingers, the scent of lavender. White sandals on her shapely feet. She had hazel eyes and hair the colour of marmalade that fell smooth and straight to her shoulders and then curled up in a little flip at the ends. Frank had never been so close to a young lady as refined as Eileen. He shook her hand very carefully, a little awed by the clean, pink fingernails.

The smaller girl looked up once and, not interested, returned to her scales.

"This little ragamuffin is Charlotte," Eileen said. "She's nine. Say hello to Connor and his friend now, Charlotte." To Connor, she whispered, "Stubborn today. Missing her mother."

Charlotte looked up and graced them all with a sad smile. "Hello," she said. "I'm glad to meet you."

"There's a good girl," said Mrs Flynn.

Connor said quietly to Frank, "Charlotte's our little foster-sister now. Mother sent away for one as soon as the war began. Her parents are still in England."

Mrs Flynn began a story about how she had found Charlotte. When she read in the newspapers about the dreadful treatment of the Jews in Europe, she said, she made some calls to discover what could be done. She put in her name to the Canadian Embassy in London, and offered her home as a refuge for a little Jewish child. It took ever so long, and they never did send a Jewish child, she explained. But as soon as the bombing began in London, they sent Charlotte, the daughter of a London banker. They were ever so pleased to have her — and here Connor's mother smiled at Charlotte and patted her curls — and so long as the war continued, they would keep her, safe and sound, in Toronto.

"Now go and get washed for dinner," she told Charlotte, and the little girl obeyed.

So this was the kind of people they were. While others tsked and gossiped, or ignored the news from Europe, Connor's mother had telephoned the Canadian government and tried to help. He couldn't imagine himself, or anyone he knew, even thinking to telephone the government — how did a person telephone the government?

At dinner, Frank reminded himself to speak quietly and eat slowly. He admired the heavy linen tablecloth, the crystal goblets of cold water, and the pats of butter on a plate, set upon a bowl of crushed ice. The china, even the gravy boat and sugar bowl, seemed rimmed with gold, and he could hardly believe his luck when he saw the food. The maid set a beef roast on a platter before Dr Flynn, and he carved it into thin slices and passed it down the table to everyone. Eileen and Mrs Flynn handed round roast potatoes in a covered pan and carrots and asparagus arrayed in a silver vegetable dish with ivory handles. Frank watched the way they passed the food, excusing their fingers and smiling at each other and keeping up a conversation about the party that Frank was to attend tonight with Connor and Eileen. Connor had shown Frank the shirt and jacket he would lend him, and a tie. The party was at the home of "Connor's girl," Eileen said.

"You mean the girl who used to be my girl," Connor corrected. He explained to Frank he was very fond of this girl, but he had set her free when he joined the Black Watch. It wasn't fair to make her wait when he was shipping off to war.

Connor's parents knew all about this girl and the party, and the girl's parents, too. Connor must take Dr Flynn's Lincoln, they decided, though Connor expressed a preference for the Dodge coupe. Connor must remind the girl's mother, said Mrs Flynn, that she was to join her for tennis next Saturday afternoon, doubles, at The Lawn, and that they were trading courts with the Philopotts, who were off to Niagara-on-the-Lake for their daughter's anniversary brunch, and not to mix that up.

"Not to worry, Mother," said Connor. "I shall deliver the message with impeccable clarity."

"Oh, you," said his mother.

After dinner, Frank climbed the stairs to the second floor and stood in the large upstairs hall while Connor lingered in the entryway below — the vestibule, they called it — conferring with his father about automobiles and tennis courts. Frank counted five doors leading off the hall, all of them ajar. Which one led to the porch? He chose the first and found himself in a room with long glass-fronted bookcases lining every wall. A wide wooden desk faced a window overlooking the park-like backyard. There was a shrine of some kind on the desk, a tall box of inlaid walnut and marble marquetry, with mechanized doors. But when Frank opened it, he found no saint inside. Only a candlestick telephone with a polished chrome dial. Beside it, a medical book of some kind, thicker than a Bible, lay open to a complicated drawing that he guessed was a human heart. The heart looked ordinary and bloodless, sketched in ink with letters of the alphabet marking its different parts. The text was full of impossible words.

Beside the desk stood a wooden cabinet, as tall as Frank, with two doors, an upper and a lower. It didn't match any of the other furniture. The wood was unfinished, and each door had a latch that was strangely simple and rough, merely a metal hook and eye. It was an old clothes closet, he guessed. But why two doors? Shirts on the top, perhaps, and trousers on the bottom? It wouldn't hurt to look. He wanted to find out as much as he could about how these people lived.

With one careful index finger, he lifted the upper latch and the upper door swung quickly toward him. Frank stepped back, then stared. He was face to face with a toothy skull. Through its empty sockets, he could see right into its hollow head. The skull was attached to a spine. A rib cage. Frank opened the lower door and saw the whole skeleton. Pelvis and double-boned legs and long white toes. He stifled the laugh that bubbled up inside him. The fun he and Corky could have had back home with a find like this!

Connor's voice sounded on the staircase. He was coming up. Frank slipped back into the hall. It was time for them both to get dressed for the party, together, as if they were brothers.

The party, crowded with Toronto people, flowed through the house and into the garden, where coloured lanterns were strung among the branches of the trees and couples danced on the wide stone terrace. The guests all spoke and laughed as easily as Connor and Eileen did, gliding from place to place in clothing that seemed sewn to their bodies. Eileen's filmy blue dress floated around her legs as young men twirled and dipped her to the music. She and Connor were leaders here, without even trying, or being aware of it, and because Frank was with them, everything about him became acceptable. When the hostess giggled at his Brooklyn accent, Eileen said lightly, "Now, Helen, I'm sure we sound just as strange to him!" This was what they called good manners. Making him feel comfortable. Still, he worried he might break or spill something. And he didn't dare ask Eileen or any of her friends to dance. They fluttered past him, creatures from another world.

In the garden, a serving girl offered him some punch, and just as he accepted it, Dickie Lassiter appeared and slapped him on the back so hard he nearly dropped the punch glass.

"Punch is for girls," Dickie told him. "That's why it's pink." He removed the glass from Frank's hand and placed it back on the girl's tray. "Come out to the gazebo. Connor and his friends have some real liquor out there."

Frank followed Dickie across the lawn toward a little screen house at the bottom of the garden, where Connor and a couple of other men were passing around a bottle. This was the gazebo. Frank was learning many new words this weekend: *vestibule, study, terrace, gazebo.* The size of these people's homes! You needed a map and a dictionary to find your way around them.

Connor introduced Frank to his friends, who were called Reggie Dunsmuir and Trent Williams. They had not enlisted, though Dunsmuir said he wanted to. His father was making him go to law school.

"No school for Williams, though," said Dunsmuir. "Williams has to mind his old man's stocks and bonds."

Connor poured Frank a glass of whisky. "Williams here has funds," he said. "Tell us about your funds, Williams."

"Shut up, Flynn."

"A secret buried treasure, isn't it?" Connor turned to Frank. "They say Williams's grandfather was some kind of a pirate."

They all laughed. Frank laughed too, though he didn't know why.

Trent Williams's cheeks were pink. "Every family has a few skeletons in the closet," he said. "We've got our fair share, that's all."

Frank was surprised. Every family? He had imagined Connor's father kept the skeleton because he was a doctor. But Williams's father was in bonds. Or was it stocks? Why would he keep a skeleton in the house? Perhaps it was some kind of custom. A Canadian thing.

The laughter died down, and in the silence, Frank turned to Connor. "That one in your dad's study," he said. "Where did it come from?"

Connor raised his eyebrows and studied Frank's face. Then he said, "Oh, you mean Yorick. Now, where *did* he come from?"

"Alas, poor Yorick," said Dickie.

"Nefarious midnight raid in a moonlit cemetery, I expect," said Williams. "Some are pirates and some are grave robbers." He gave Connor's shoulder a friendly shove.

Surely there had been no real raiding of graves. But what did Williams really mean? And why did they call the skeleton by name? Surely they hadn't known the poor dead man. That seemed too gruesome. For the rest of the night, Frank nursed his one glass of whisky and watched the others drink. The drunker they got, the more witty they found each other. But Frank understood very little of what they said. He admired Connor's Toronto friends and envied them their parents, with their glamorous, carefree lives. But he felt he'd never be able to decode their conversations.

Frank felt more at ease with Lenore and her friends than with the people in Toronto. When he returned to camp in Nova Scotia, the training schedule was heavier, the discipline stricter, and it was harder to get away at the weekends. But he managed it twice. Once there was a square dance and a fall supper offered at the dance hall, where Frank now felt he belonged. Lots of joking and roast turkey and pitchers of beer. It was fun, but all night he longed to be alone with her, and as he walked her home, she confessed she felt the same. That night he lay in his bunk, remembering every detail of their good-night kisses and the warm, round curves of her body, until he fell asleep, exhausted. After a day of hard training and the long trip to Halifax, his body craved sleep. He sometimes wondered if he could keep his body satisfied, with all he was demanding of it.

When he went again to see her, it was a Sunday afternoon. She took him to a little bunkhouse in the bush where she said the farm workers used to stay when her parents had money to hire farm workers. She lit a fire in the stove and then she lay down and let him lie down beside her and kiss her and hold her. She told him all the news of her week, and he loved her whispery voice and Nova Scotia accent, the way she spoke too fast. Her typing course, he learned, had paid off. She had quit her job at the hotel, she said, and gone to work as a typist for a shipping company. She had bought new clothes for her little sisters and shoes for her mother. She had gone to the picture show and seen John Wayne and still she had enough left over to put into her savings account. She was happy.

The old clock in the bunkhouse was broken, and Lenore had no wristwatch, so he showed her how to measure time by the position of the sun on the rough planks of the floor. He counted the number of planks that were in full light, and checked his watch.

"The sun's at the fourth plank now," he said. "And it's one o'clock. So you watch next Sunday. I'll be here at one. When you see the sun creeping up on the fourth plank, you'll know I'll be coming through the door any minute."

She stood in the doorway, smiling at him, her thumb turning the silver ring on her finger around and around.

But six nights later the orders came. The Black Watch was shipping out for England.

———

Next morning he woke at sea. The churning in his stomach prevented him, for the first time in his life, from eating. But he managed better than some, who were confined to their beds. He did his chores and nibbled some biscuits at lunch, and during the free time he was granted, he stood at the railing and watched the high waves roll across the surface of the ocean. Finally, he was following all those boats he had seen when he was a boy full of childish wishes. He thought of Lenore. He checked his watch. It was one in the afternoon. She'd have been home from Mass for a while now. She'd have hurried through her chores and now she'd be lying on the bed in their bunkhouse, watching the sun crossing the floorboards, waiting. He thought of writing her a letter, even though he was no good at writing, but he didn't know where to send it. Her house did not seem to be on any particular street, but out past the edge of the town. The path they had walked through the bush did not have a name. He had known how to get there. He had thought that was enough. He pictured Lenore lying on the lower bunk, counting as the sun beam passed the fourth floorboard and then the fifth and the sixth and the seventh, and she would know he was not coming.

4.2

IN THE EVENING, MEREDITH SITS ON THE COUCH, KNITTING WITH her long, graceful fingers. She has a fat ball of pink wool in a basket at her side, and from between her clicking needles, a long scarf of many colours is rapidly unfurling. Kyle sits at her feet, looking at an atlas.

"It's not far from Amsterdam to Paris," he says.

"How far is it to Rouen?" Meredith asks. "They have a fantastic cathedral there."

"How do you spell that?"

Meredith tells him. She sets down her needles and pulls another ball of wool from her basket. Neon orange. When Von was a girl, everyone said orange clashes with pink. Never wear orange and pink together, or pink and red, or red and orange. The rules must have changed, or Meredith doesn't care about the rules. Von remembers that she had never cared about the rules at that age, either. Not the rules of fashion, anyway. She'd had other things to worry about.

Kyle holds up the atlas page to show Meredith where Rouen is. "If we're in Paris, we could take a train there and back in a day," he says. "Or do you want to stay overnight?"

Von still thinks they're being rash. They'll spend too much money. Money Kyle could save for college. But she can't help admiring their excitement. They're having fun planning this trip, figuring out the budget, the time zones, the tickets. Von wants nothing to do with such discussions, which make her anxious and irritable. Why is that? she wonders. Because in her childhood all planning was fraught with arguments and tears, all plans in danger of interruption? She remembers the light-hearted normal families she used to see on television, those rare times she went to a friend's house after school. She studied those families — with amazement and longing — to see how they did it. But she never caught on to the secret.

The day before their flight leaves, Von is packing, trying to cram her new blue travel journal into her carry-on, when Leif appears at the apartment door. He's come to say good-bye.

"Sorry I never called you back," says Von, who's been avoiding him.

"Hey, I understand," he says. "You've got a lot going on in your life right now."

He has brought a guidebook to Holland for Kyle and Meredith, who pore over the pages together, arguing over which section they want to read first. They decide to start with the map of Amsterdam and begin to search for the street where Rosheen was living.

Von offers Leif a drink, but he says no. "Thanks, but you've got enough to do."

When she walks him to the door, he hands her a small gift, a flat, square package, wrapped in sparkly tissue paper. "Open it when you get there," he says, "and think of me."

"You shouldn't have," Von says. "You're too generous."

He smiles. "You can bring me a souvenir."

"Sure. What do you want?"

"Surprise me," he says.

"I will."

"Phone me when you settle in?"

"If I get a chance," she says. She can tell he's disappointed. He wants more from her than she's giving. She knows this isn't fair. She is even sorry. If she'd known he was going to be around so long, she never would have gone out with him in the first place. But she can't say that. That would sound — what? How would it sound? As if there were something wrong with her.

He says, "All right. Good-bye." He kisses her, just a short kiss on the cheek, before he lets himself out the door.

As soon as he's out of sight, she opens the package. It's a recording made by the same band they enjoyed on their two carefree nights of dancing. The card enclosed is small and simple. The message "Bon Voyage" above a tiny bluebird with open wings. She smiles. Then she reads the note inside. "With love from Leif."

Love. Such a small word. An ordinary, everyday word. Yet she can't recall the last time she might have written it on a card or a letter to anyone.

4.3

ENGLAND WAS COLD AND DAMP. FRANK AND CONNOR WERE surprised to discover that training could be harder and more vigorous than before. They expected to see action soon, but weeks and months and finally a whole year unfolded and still they had no orders to cross the Channel. It became a bitter joke among the men, the interminable delay, their keen desire to enter the real battlefield. Instead, they engaged in constant exercises. Commando training, weapons and tactics, inspections, practice drills at sea, work parties. Frank took courses in first aid, German artillery, hand-to-hand combat. He took a three-inch mortar course, learning to assemble, load, and fire the mortar guns.

Sunday afternoons were filled by polishing belt buckles and boots, cleaning weapons, and writing letters home. When he first arrived in England, Frank had written a letter to Lenore and addressed it to the Halifax hotel where she used to be a waitress, on the slim chance someone there might remember her and care enough to get it to her. But he never received a reply. He wrote each week to Deirdre, out of duty, though she didn't answer. John Junior answered once in a while with news of the family and to reassure Frank that, yes, Deirdre was receiving his army pay, as he'd arranged.

Connor received a lot of mail and many packages. His sister sent letters with flattened flower petals folded inside them, and his mother sent biscuits and hand-knit slippers, and his father sent advice. He also had an aunt, in Dublin, who sent books to him regularly, and he shared these with the other men, often pressing his favourites on Frank. Frank liked novels, but it was the poetry that truly moved him, and Shakespeare's plays, which most of the men found difficult. He laughed when they called him "Professor." If only Tomas could hear that!

Frank lay on his back, holding *Hamlet* above his head, reading the graveyard scene, astonished. When Hamlet lifted the skull from the ground and called it "Yorick," Frank let the book fall onto his chest and stared at the tent ceiling. At the party in Toronto, when Frank had asked about the skeleton in Dr Flynn's study, Connor had called it by that name. Yorick. And Dickie had said, just exactly as Hamlet had said, "Alas, poor Yorick." This was no coincidence. Connor had been talking about this very play, and everyone had laughed. They had all read this play. Even Dickie. It had been like a joke in a foreign language, one that everybody knew. Except Frank. He'd thought he would never understand the world of Connor and his friends, their quick nods and jokes. But as he brooded on the problem, it occurred to him that if their easy, knowing manner came from what they read in books, then it wasn't something they were born with, but something they had learned. And if they could learn it, Frank could learn it too.

Any leisure time he had, Frank read or sketched scenes from life in the camp. When the men noticed his skill, they began to ask for portraits of themselves to send home to their wives and sweethearts. Frank was glad to oblige. He also discovered ways to make them laugh, by exaggerating aspects of camp life in his pictures. Their CO, Captain Aidan, pinned many of these up on the cork board outside the mess tent. Soon the men expected to see one of Frank's cartoons there every week.

In a small tent beside the mess tent, Captain Aidan set up his phonograph, an RCA Victor Special in a felt-lined aluminum case, edged with shiny chromium. Aidan had a deep, melodious voice, and he liked to sing along with the records when he wasn't belting out orders. He said his men could use the phonograph when they had leisure time, and it seemed to Frank there was always someone in there, listening to a song. One afternoon Frank was in the cook tent, enjoying the smell of roasting lamb while he pared a hundred apples for the cook to bake into pies. Someone in the music tent next door was playing Frank Sinatra's "I'll Never Smile Again" over and over. Finally, when the song finished playing for the fourth time, Frank yelled over, "Hey! Play something else, will you!" There was silence for several minutes. Then finally they heard the opening bars of "Smoke Gets in Your Eyes."

"Tsk," said the cook, "some broken-hearted bastard," and they both laughed.

Frank was nearly finished his kitchen duty when Captain Aidan stopped by and called out, "Garrison! You're needed on a work party!" So Frank was sent off with a dozen other men from different regiments, to a site twenty miles up the road, where a bridge had collapsed.

———

After five hours of clearing debris, the men were delivered to their home camps. By the time Frank was dropped off, supper was long over. Too tired to ask the cook for leftovers, he climbed into his bunk and fell asleep.

He woke in the night, thinking of the meal he'd missed. The roast lamb he'd smelled that afternoon, the apples he'd pared for the cook. Apple pie. Hot mashed potatoes and beans. Even a slice of bread. He heard the crunch of boots on loose stone as the guard passed on his rounds. Bread and jam. The huge tin of strawberry jam on the third shelf in the mess tent. There was time. Fifteen minutes before the guard would return. He threw off his blanket and left the tent. Blackout meant he had to feel his way along the guide-ropes that stretched from the tent post of one bunkhouse to another, all the way to the end of the row. From there he walked toward the mess tent with nothing to guide him but memory and starlight.

Inside the mess tent door he waited in vain for his eyes to adjust to the dark. A flying insect bumbled into his forehead and he swept it away. He inched forward, running his fingers along the counter until he felt the bread box and reached in. Luck. Two whole loaves left over. Searching the pantry shelves, lightly, so as not to make noise, he found the tin by touch, its sides tacky with spilled jam. He pried off the gummed lid and with his pocket knife slathered jam onto a hunk of bread. Something crawled onto his hand, and he brushed it off gently. If he broke any dishes, if the guard came to investigate, he'd be in trouble. He stuffed jam and bread into his mouth and chewed, rolling the sweet strawberries over his tongue until he bit into something sharp. A needle? Suddenly his mouth seemed full of pins and needles. They pricked his tongue and the inside of his cheek. Shocked, he spat the food from his burning mouth. He reached wildly overhead for the hook that held the water dipper, knocking his wrist bone hard against an iron skillet in the row of cooking pots suspended from the ceiling. A pan came clattering down. Desperate for water, wanting only to put out the fire in his mouth, he lit a match. In its brief flare, he saw the dipper hanging on the lip of the water barrel and before him the open jam jar, its viscous surface crawling with yellow wasps.

He gulped water, one dipperful after another, but his tongue began to thicken. Air. He couldn't suck in enough air. He lit another match and found the ice box, chipped madly with the pick and shovelled ice into his mouth, praying he would not suffocate. For over an hour, he crouched in the mess tent, sliding chips of ice between his bruised lips to keep his airway open. Suppressing his desire to groan. Finally, the swelling began to subside. And then the bugle blew. A night drill of some kind. Bad timing. He crammed his mouth with as much ice as he could hold, and ran back through the darkness to his bunkhouse.

The boys were scrambling into their uniforms, grabbing their rifles. Dickie, already dressed, tossed Frank his belt and boots, and by the time the whistle blew, they were all standing rigidly in single file, ready for inspection. The CO shone a flashlight down the line, across the soldiers' faces. Frank imagined his own face, puffed and ruddy. When the CO looked sharply at him, he was afraid he'd be accused of fighting. He kept his eyes front. Within his mouth, the wasp stings pulsed, as if alive. One inside his upper lip, one on his tongue, and one on his inner cheek. Hot sparks radiated through his jaw, and he began to shake, as if with fever. Luckily, the CO satisfied himself by giving Frank a stern frown and deciding to let it pass. He had other things on his mind. He ordered the men to march outside to a convoy of trucks waiting down the road. They were driven to the seashore and piled into boats.

"Not the Channel again!" moaned Dickie, who was often seasick.

Frank hunkered down among the others in the belly of the boat, crouching above the floor to keep the seat of his pants dry. His lips and tongue throbbed, and his stomach twisted perversely with hunger. The Channel was choppy, a night wind stirring the surface into peaked waves the men could hear but not see.

When they were halfway out, the CO stood and addressed them. This launch was not another drill, he said. The men were going to see action at last. The beaches of France. A place called Dieppe.

4.4

"Where's Dieppe?" Kyle asks. He doesn't have enough room on his lap to lay the scrapbook flat, so he's resting the spine between his knees and holding the covers open, just wide enough so he can see inside, with one elbow on Von's armrest and the other on Meredith's. He went to some trouble to get seats in the same row as Von on the airplane, so they could all fly to Holland together. Von has the window seat. Dream fragments flit beneath her eyelids, rows of budding roses in the greenhouse…and then she's gazing at the deep, shadowed contours of the cumulus clouds below. She needs to sleep, but every time she drifts off, she's woken as the airplane dips and shudders through turbulence over the Atlantic.

"Dieppe?" says Meredith, without looking up. "Germany, I think." She's studying an intricate pattern in one of her knitting magazines.

"France," says Von. "It's on the coast of France."

"France?" asks Meredith, interested now. "I thought it was Germans we attacked at Dieppe."

"That's right," says Von. "The Germans had occupied France."

"I thought they occupied Austria. Like in *Sound of Music*."

"Austria too," says Von. She closes her eyes. She wants to glide again into the dream of roses, but now the word *Dieppe* recalls the answer to a childhood question: *What happened to Daddy's arm?* In the centre of a patch of pale, roughened skin on the upper arm, a sunken knot of hard, discoloured flesh. That was Dieppe. Their father's body one long map of scars.

She wakes as the plane is landing in Amsterdam. Schiphol is enormous and severely clean compared to American airports. It teems with travellers. For a few minutes, she stands with Kyle and Meredith in the middle of the arrivals deck, a little stunned. None of them has even been to Europe before. But they follow the directions Alex gave them in New York, find the elevator that takes them to the subway station below, travel by train, then transfer to a tram to the Leidseplein. Von has booked into a hotel a few blocks away, close to the studio where Rosheen had been working. Stepping off the tram into the square is disorienting. Hundreds of people are shopping, strolling, drinking beer under white umbrellas, or lounging on the wide ledge surrounding the fountain. A thin layer of clouds barely mutes the sunshine. Light bounces off the gleaming sea of handlebars in the bike racks. Slowly, Von navigates through the crowd, pulling her wheeled suitcase behind her, while Kyle and Meredith follow with their backpacks. When a clown on stilts approaches Von and tries to give her a flower, she shies away. But Kyle, laughing, hands the man some American coins. Finally, they consult a map, and Von points, because it's too noisy to talk, in the direction of the street where her hotel's located.

Her room overlooks a wide canal, spanned by a bridge that leads to a small park. Kyle's idea of independence was to book a room for Meredith and himself across the park. A one-minute walk from Von's hotel. They'll be able to wave at each other from their balconies. Houseboats line the canal, flowers blooming in their window boxes and bicycles hanging from hooks beneath their eaves. From the banks, magnificent silver willow trees lean over the water.

The next day, they all walk to the studio together and are greeted by the co-ordinator, Durgan MacLeod, a lean, long-legged young man who needs a shave. He says he's from Northern Ireland. He's been here two years, and he knew Rosheen well. Spent a lot of time with her, he says, in the four months she was here. He plunges into a long story about travelling by train to Russia with her.

"Russia?" Yet another chapter of Rosheen's life that Von knows nothing about.

Durgan tells of getting lost in St Petersburg and losing his friend's address. Missing a train and sleeping under a bridge with Rosheen. In the rain. His voice is full of warmth and nostalgia. The good old days. Sleeping under bridges with Von's disturbed and drug-addicted sister.

"No wonder she ended up with pneumonia," says Von.

But Kyle is intrigued. He wants to hear more. "How did you get home?"

Durgan tells of being questioned and nearly thrown in jail by the Russian police. "But Rosheen was such a good liar. She told them —"

"That's enough," says Von.

"What do you mean?"

"Enough of that story. We need to start packing. Can you show us where my sister's work is?"

Durgan looks hurt. As he leads them upstairs, he says to Kyle, "I'll tell you later."

The room where Rosheen worked last winter is small but flooded with light. Durgan leads them inside, asking, "Do you know which pieces you want?"

"We'll be shipping everything back to New York," Von says.

"It's all the way she left it." He points to an assortment of boxes, each labelled "Garrison," in Rosheen's handwriting. One plywood crate, the size and shape of a public mailbox, is already sealed and addressed to the Northside Gallery in New York. Three smaller crates are partially full. Shopping bags and cardboard boxes and packing paper litter the floor. "She didn't come in much those last few days," he says. "She was pretty sick."

Von shoots him a withering look as she gets down on her knees among the mess. It's becoming a familiar task, sorting through Rosheen's effects. But now she has two helpers. Kyle and Meredith get down on their knees, too, and begin looking.

The first thing Von finds is an airmail envelope containing a hand-written letter and four photographs of her father that she's never seen before. The black-and-white photos are small, only two by three, but well preserved. The envelope is addressed to Rosheen at this studio in Amsterdam. So it must have arrived fairly recently, while she was working here. The return address is a Mr Lassiter, Blake Street, London, England. In the photos, Frank looks about the same age Kyle is now, though Frank is much heavier, more muscular. In a pressed uniform and beret, he poses at the edge of a cliff, peering through binoculars into the mists rolling off the sea. The caption on the back reads, "Adolf, where are you?" The other photos are all simply captioned "Frank Garrison, 1942." In one, he is chinning himself on a bar in an outdoor gym. In another, he pretends to bite the pin from a grenade. In the last photo, he stands shirtless, wearing one ammunition belt, loaded with bullets, around the waist of his army pants, and another strapped diagonally across his bare chest. He carries a Tommy gun and a bayonet, both pointed at the camera. In his mouth, he holds a hunting knife, unsheathed, between his bared teeth. Parody of a mad warrior. But she guesses the comic pose is only half in jest. Her mother had told her how long the young soldiers waited, how badly they wanted to leap into battle, beat back the enemy, kill Hitler. How their frustration built as they waited and waited to go to war.

She passes the photos to Kyle, who says, "Hol-ee."

"I've never seen these before," Von says. Her father was handsome, and this revelation surprises her. She's never thought much about his life when he was young. She never asked. He wasn't exactly approachable. "These must have been taken in England," she tells Kyle. "At training camp. Before he saw action."

"Rosheen got these photos from a guy she met at a reunion," Durgan says. "There's a pamphlet about it somewhere. Here it is. The Black Watch. Your dad's regiment, right?"

Kyle has turned to a series of framed prints, stacked on the floor. "Oh man," he says. "Meredith. Come look."

Meredith moves to join him, and Von follows. "More pictures of my grandfather," Kyle says. Each print is made from a collage of drawings based on these photos of Frank, with additions of text and paint. Kyle lifts them out and leans them against the wall in a row. Rosheen has used pictures of Frank at different ages, scraps that seem to be torn from hand-written letters, army memos, maps. In one piece, she has deliberately set Frank's pre-war face beside his post-war face, and the difference is dramatic. Kyle holds this one up for everyone to see.

Durgan asks, "Is that the same person?"

"Yes," Von says. She examines the two faces. "Sort of."

Kyle eyes her sharply. Then grows quiet, absorbed in studying the contrast.

Durgan offers to start wrapping the prints, but Kyle wants to see them all first. He's excited to discover newspaper clippings from stories about Frank. One features a full-colour photo on the front cover of a Winnipeg newspaper, taken on Remembrance Day when Frank was in his fifties. He's wearing his Black Watch beret and dark glasses. A row of medals on his chest. He holds his head high, with the arrogance that used to drive Von wild with anger, and clutches his white cane with black-gloved hands. The white glare of snow on the legislative grounds behind him.

"He was a hero," says Kyle to Von. "You didn't tell me he was a hero."

"More collages!" Meredith calls out, as she opens another box.

"Hey, these are ready to hang," Durgan says. He helps her lift them out — a series made from layers of pencil sketches and paintings, then varnished and mounted on board.

To Von, there is something familiar about them. She's seen these raggedy kids somewhere. Also these musicians. Then she remembers. These are figures from Frank's sketchbooks, back in New York. Rosheen had traced his drawings, leaving some whole and cutting up others, transforming them with paint and glue. Frank's kids on the pier are now on a boat, sailing out to sea. His street musicians have been transported. His ecstatic sax player still blows strong, more vibrant than ever in solid colours and foregrounded against a repeating pattern of paler musicians in modern clothes, with microphones and amps, all washed over with a haze of ghostly blue.

"Look, Kyle," says Meredith.

But Kyle is entranced by the handwritten airmail letter that was in with the photographs. He doesn't stop reading until he's finished. Then he hands it to Meredith.

4.5

AT FIRST LIGHT, THE LANDING CRAFT APPROACHED THE BEACHES OF Dieppe. It was one among hundreds, a flat-bottomed steel barge, coming in for a surprise raid on the Germans. In the crowded hold, Frank and Dickie tried to make their way toward Connor and the other members of their mortar detachment. But movement was difficult. The barge held eighty troops, three Churchill tanks and a scout car, tins of mortar shells and stores of TNT. High on both sides of the bow, the Toronto Scottish manned the Vickers guns, while a crew on the bridge manned the Bofors. The British Air Force buzzed overhead. Frank's stomach was tight. His blood vibrated in his veins. The soldiers in the tank crews called out last-minute jokes and encouragement to each other before they lowered themselves in and closed the turrets. The drivers warmed their engines as Frank pushed past them, squeezing his body against the side of the barge. Once the tanks rolled out, he and the mortar men would follow on foot, packing four dismantled mortar guns and 600 rounds of ammo, 250 yards up the shale beach. The mortar teams had assembled and loaded hundreds of guns in training. But never in action.

Frank peered over the gunwale. He could see their objective, the cliff to the left, where they were to set up gun positions. Enemy fire from the shore seemed light, occasional flares and anti-aircraft shells. A lot of smoke.

Squeezing past the last tank, Frank reached the scout car just as the boat hit the beach hard. He looked back down the narrow space between the tanks and the hull. Dickie was coming toward him. Men were turning the winch, lowering the flat steel door of the bow that would serve as the landing ramp. Frank was ready. All the way across the Channel, readiness had been swelling in his heart, and now it surged through all his muscles and nerves. It tingled in his hands and feet. Two years of training, two years of longing for action. The ramp began to descend, *at last, at last*, the bow opened up, and then, from the beach, the enemy let loose with a massive barrage of fire power.

Exploding shells bombarded the ship. Frank crouched low, but there was no cover. The air was alight with tracers, their red tails whizzing over his head. Bullets hit the deck and ricocheted off all sides. Bullets pierced the canvas cover of the hold. He peered out again. White flare of machine gun fire from every window on shore — not just the pill boxes on the beach, but every building on the waterfront. The Germans had been expecting them.

From the bridge and bow, the Canadian gunners answered, starting up the steady clatter of the Vickers guns and the thundering Bofors. The ramp came down. The first two tanks rumbled off the landing craft, drawing fire and stalling a couple of times, but progressing up the beach. Frank watched eagerly as the first two tanks demolished a wall of barbed wire and crushed it under their treads. Then he was shocked to see the flattened wire pop back up again, after the tanks passed over it, looking as impenetrable as ever.

Now the mortar men had room to get ready. They knew what they had to do. Scoop bombs out of the tins as fast as possible. Load the bombs into knapsacks. Throw off their life jackets to hoist the heavy knapsacks onto their backs. They checked their watches. Thirty-eight minutes left to do a job that should take an hour. To move all the ammo, they'd need to make two, three treks up the strand. Gunfire pounded the foreshore. Shale and rock flew upward. The air filled with sand and smoke. Straight ahead, an Allied tank and an enemy tank fired at each other until they both burst into flames. Frank and Connor exchanged a look. This was the terrain they were to cross on foot.

But they couldn't go ashore yet. As the third tank rolled out, towing the scout car, it stalled. It hung there, its front half on the beach and its rear half caught up on the landing ramp. Blocking the way. The skipper reversed the craft, easing back into deeper water, and managed to set the stalled tank free. The tank moved forward, and then, just as the scout car cleared the ramp, mortar shells rained down upon the bow — one two three four hits — and smashed the chains that held the ramp in place, breaking them loose from the winch.

Dickie said, "How the hell —"

A massive shell hit the ship's bridge up above.

The Bofors guns fell silent.

"Gunners down!" someone shouted. "Stretchers! Stretchers!" Men raced across the deck, straight into the heavy fire, to haul the wounded gunners down below.

The skipper was steering forward again, to try a second landing. But the broken ramp now hung straight down from the bow. Connor and Dickie turned the winch, but the chains were broken. The ramp would not budge. Its edge had caught on the sea bottom. The barge could not move forward. They were stuck.

Frank struggled with the chains. Above him, the young gunner on the starboard Vickers gun got hit in the chest and fell. He landed, sprawled precariously on his back across the gunwale. One of his comrades tore through the fiery hail, scrambled up a ladder and grabbed the legs of the wounded man before he could fall overboard. Another man brought a stretcher and together they strapped the wounded gunner in and began to cart him down the steep ladder to the hold, while bullets flew at them from all directions. One of the stretcher-bearers, hit in the hand, let go. His cargo, the young man bleeding from his chest, began to slide headfirst into the hold.

"Jesus," said Connor. He leaped forward, streaked through the deadly onslaught of fire, and caught the sliding man in his arms. Others helped him, and together they eased the stretcher down below. Above the Channel, air battles tore up the sky.

Frank and Dickie tried to fix the winch, while all around them, everything spun in rapid motion. Up on the bridge, new men, barely knowing how to load the Bofors, took over the unmanned guns. The signaller punched the radio, trying to connect with a station. The door of the ammunition locker blew off, and high explosives burst out of their cases and rolled across the deck like logs let loose from a woodpile. Everyone expected them to blow, but by some miracle they did not. A bullet tore through the arm of the last trained gunner on board. The medic called for help. The skipper pulled out deeper. Water rushed in at the open gate.

"We can't land," Frank yelled at Dickie. "Let's go above."

"What?"

"Above!" He pointed toward the deck.

They took off their heavy packs and set them on a bulkhead. The water was now a foot deep in the hold and rising. They waded toward the stern, where men were yelling for help to plug holes in the hull.

Dickie was hit first. He went down face first in the flooded hold, six feet in front of Frank. Blood leaked from his left shoulder blade, spreading over the back of his shirt. Frank bent down to grab him, just as Dickie was hit again, this time in the leg. Blood gushed from his thigh into the water. Frank turned him over. Dickie sputtered and coughed and drew a breath. His face, in less than a minute, had turned white. He closed his eyes and groaned.

"I got you," Frank said. He checked Dickie over. The leg was the worst. Pumping blood. He needed a tourniquet. Frank glanced up. Chaos on the bridge. No use calling for help. He sloshed to the bulkhead to get his pack, ripped open the first-aid kit, and found the tourniquet. He grabbed a life-jacket. By the time he turned around, Dickie had floated closer to the open gate. Frank waded back to him and held him fast. "I got you," he said. He wrapped the tourniquet above the hole in Dickie's thigh and tied it tight. He wrapped a life jacket around Dickie's torso and fastened it.

The water rose. Frank turned Dickie around, aimed his head in the right direction, and pushed him toward the stern. At that moment, off the starboard side, an Allied ship exploded, sending shrapnel everywhere and setting off a powerful wave that rocked the craft. The wave washed in, slamming Frank to his knees, and sluiced out, carrying every loose, floating thing — canteens, backpacks, tins of ammo, and Dickie's skinny body — into the sea.

Frank saw his friend drifting into the dangerous stretch of water between the bow of the barge and the beach. Bullets strafed the water's surface. He pressed the palm of his left hand against the inner wall of the hold and pulled himself to his feet. He felt a bullet go straight thorough his left arm, just above his elbow, heard it pang against the steel wall as it came out the other side. He kept moving, wading toward the edge of the open bow. He had to reach Dickie, pull him back in. Directly overhead, a German plane let loose a long barrage of cannon fire, splitting a British Spitfire in two. The broken fuselage spiralled down into the Channel, spewing debris, its flaming tail falling almost right on top of Dickie. Dickie was still face up, but his legs were sinking, pulling him down. The tail of the Spitfire floated beside him, still on fire, sending up black plumes of smoke. Taking a deep breath, Frank dived from the edge of the barge into the open water.

The bullet hole in his left arm burned, though immersed in the cold sea, and his nostrils burned from the sea's salt. Under water, the sound of battle dimmed to distant thunder. As he swam, he could hear his own heart, *bom* ba *bom* ba *bom* ba, sure and strong. And his soul was pure and his brain was clear. One thought only: *I got you. I got you, Dickie Lassiter.* He manoeuvred himself behind Dickie, wrapped his injured left arm around Dickie's neck in a loose hug. He raised his right arm high, reached back behind his own head, and brought his arm down into the water and up again, powering toward the barge with a one-armed backstroke, kicking his legs like mad. He judged he was fifty yards away from it. He swam and swam but could not gain on it, and finally, as his breath became ragged, he realized the skipper had given up. He was hauling out to sea. Leaving Frank and Dickie behind.

Frank searched the water for any Allied ships, but the only one close by was on fire. He saw two landing craft on the beach, one on fire and one with its landing ramp blocked by a mound of dead soldiers. He rested, turning in a circle to survey the scene. He saw there was only one way to go. He struck out for the open Channel, toward England.

Frank can't die, not now when he's holding Dickie Lassiter's life in his arms. Not now when his own life is just beginning. Not after the weeks, months, years of training, when he's at his peak, more prepared than ever before. When he finally understands his purpose. This can't be the end. Not yet. He must live. Save Dickie. If God will let them both live, Frank will give anything, dedicate his life to. Prayer. Our Father. Who art in Heaven, hallowed. Salt water washing into his mouth, absurd pain of the wasp stings even now when he is beyond wasp stings. The swelling. Be thy. Give me this one thing and I will give You all of my life, everything, every. Name. Thy Kingdom. Come. Loose, Dickie is slipping loose. Dickie's neck is sliding out of the crook of Frank's left arm, and Frank tries to clench him tighter, but he's losing control of that arm. It has no strength. Thy will be done. On Earth. With the force of his own will, Frank flexes his torn left bicep and wrestles Dickie back into place. His right arm keeps up its steady backstroke. His legs kick, kick. Somewhere out here, an Allied ship will come along, will pick them up. As it is in Heaven. As long as Frank does not quit. He will never quit. Even when he blacks out and slips under, the salt water in his throat wakes him, and though he's drowning he sees far above him a green shaft of dirty daylight and follows it up, up into air, yes. He vomits seawater from his belly, coughs it out of his lungs, and here is Dickie, still floating, the jacket holding him on the surface, and the sounds of the battle on the beach are dimmer and then he sees the ships. Ships far and high, tall shadows. He swims toward them, towing Dickie, and finally somebody sees them. The captain of a Polish destroyer sends out a sailor in a rowboat to pick them up. And Dickie is still alive, still breathing, when they haul him on board. Amen.

4.6

PROGRESS ON SORTING AND PACKING ROSHEEN'S WORKS IS SLOW. Both Von and Kyle are slow. It's hard to focus on the practical business of wrapping things in cotton and paper, especially when those things are exactly what they want to examine and explore.

Von has read the handwritten letter. It's from Dickie Lassiter's son, who met Rosheen at the Black Watch reunion and thanks her for "the lovely lunch." Then, "as promised," he provides a detailed account of Dickie and Frank at Dieppe, "as told often by my father." His father's hands, he says, shake too much for him to write, but he sends his best regards. The son wishes Rosheen well with her project and asks her to let him know when her show opens in New York.

Von has never heard this story of Dieppe. Not a word of it.

She has read articles about the stoic vets of World War Two, notorious for their silence. A reticent, macho lot, one article said. But is that true? When Von and Rosheen were little, of course, their father had tried to protect them.

"Does it hurt?" Rosheen would ask, running her fingers across the bullet hole in his arm, and he'd say, "No. It doesn't hurt. That was a long, long time ago."

When Von was older, however, he did speak of it. Yes, he did, though she didn't listen.

"I killed people," he said to her once. A quaver in his voice. A sound she couldn't bear to hear, didn't have time for.

"Dad," she admonished, dismissing him. "It was war."

As if she knew what "war" meant. She only wanted him to leave her alone so she wouldn't have to listen. Wouldn't have to know.

She's always thought of her father's suffering as intensely private. An embarrassment to be kept within the family. A Garrison thing that set the Garrisons apart, made them different. She folds Mr Lassiter's letter into her purse. She'll write to him, tell him of Rosheen's death, and tell him the date of the opening. He deserves to know. It's his history, too. It takes a lot of people to tell these stories. These stories belong to all of them.

"I can't believe my own mother made this," Kyle says. He's holding a small oil painting, two nightingales on a twig. The male is lifting his full white throat to sing, while tilting his head at a crazy, comical angle, his black bright eye almost human, yet utterly wild. How did she *do* that? It's humbling. The little bird is a marvel, from its every feather to its eccentric personality.

"She always loved birds," Durgan tells Kyle. "She'd go in the woods with a bag of seeds and a camera and just wait. I have a book of her nature photographs. You want to see?"

Kyle follows him eagerly down the hall.

When he reappears, he's carrying a pair of field binoculars. "These were my mum's," he says. "Durgan says I can keep them. Hey, did you know they have free bicycles in Amsterdam, all painted white? Durgan says you can just hop on one of those white bikes, for free!"

Meredith is interested. "You can?"

"Yeah, and did you know you can smoke dope here? Durgan says you can buy it right in a *coffeeshop* or, like, even grow it in your own house."

"So I've heard," Von says. "We should go for dinner now, Kyle. I made a reservation." But he wants to wait for Durgan. He insists on bringing Durgan with them to the restaurant.

Over dinner, Durgan finishes his tale: Escapade in St Petersburg, Part Two.

"So Rosheen points under the bridge," he says, "where there's a rusty old cistern, and tells the Russian cops we were down there looking for her gloves, which she dropped from the bridge, and how do they think that crate of vodka got into that cistern, could it be smugglers? So the cops hustle down the riverbank, paying no attention to us, and we turn and run. Hightail it down the street and hop on an early-morning tram. Before they even notice we're gone." He tilts back his shaggy head to drain his beer. "She was so brave."

Von tries to turn the conversation toward the historic sites of Amsterdam. But Durgan knows Kyle is dying for more stories of Rosheen. He tells them how Rosheen once took a train to France on a whim, without any luggage, or food, or even money. How she stayed up all night, outside, on the windy cliffs above Dieppe, in order to photograph the beach exactly at sunrise.

"Why not set an alarm clock?" Von asks dryly. Durgan snorts, implying she doesn't understand. But she understands all right. She understands her sister had to take her enervating lifestyle to the limit, in the most dramatic, dangerous way possible.

"You prefer to stay indoors, I guess," says Durgan. "Under glass." He accepts another beer from the server and downs half the bottle.

"Who wants dessert?" asks Meredith brightly. "Look at those pastries."

"Just watching things grow," Durgan adds. "Like watching paint dry."

"Believe me, there's a little more to it than that," says Von.

"Oh? Getting your hands dirty?"

"Kyle likes getting his hands dirty," Meredith says quickly. "When he worked on my brother's farm last summer, he was covered with dirt every day from the hair on his head right down to the socks on his feet. I think he still has dirt in his ears."

"And my back's still sore," says Kyle. But he's grinning. "Digging those potatoes. I never saw so many potatoes in my life!"

"He brought in the whole crop," Meredith tells Von. She begins a long story about her brother and sister-in-law and their baby, and potatoes and lentils and berries.

After dinner, Durgan departs, unsteadily, down the dark Amsterdam street. No doubt seeking more beer. Kyle and Meredith walk Von to her hotel.

"I have to phone home," she says. "It's six in the morning, now, in Manitoba. Jeanne will be starting her day. I should check in. She's all by herself, and...it honestly *is* hard work."

"We understand that," Meredith assures her.

"Sure, and I don't mind hard work," Kyle says. "It'll be a blast working in a greenhouse!"

"Oh, you don't have to work in it," Von says.

"Of course, I won't know everything. I'll make mistakes. You'll have to show me —"

"You won't be working in the greenhouse, Kyle," Von tells him.

He looks at her. "What do you mean? Carol said my mum left me her share of it."

"Yes, but...didn't she explain? I've arranged to have your share deposited every quarter, right into your bank account."

Kyle looks at Meredith. Meredith looks at Von.

"You mean...pay him, without...without any work?" Meredith asks.

"That's right." Von smiles. "That's the advantage of owning a business."

"But that's not fair," Kyle says.

"Maybe you two can talk about this later," Meredith suggests, delicately, as if Von must be handled carefully. She pulls Kyle away, telling Von to "Sleep well."

Von goes to her room. She hopes Kyle understands. She's sure he will, once he realizes what a good deal it is, the deal Von made with Rosheen long ago: Von does the work and Rosheen gets the money. That was her way of looking after Rosheen — giving her money. Ever since her mother died, Von had supported her father and sister by running the greenhouse. Now that they're gone, she'll do it for Rosheen's son. But she can't have him actually inside the greenhouse, physically present. He'd only get in the way, asking too many questions, making mistakes. The hothouse flowers she works with require expert, specialized care. It's her responsibility to protect them.

4.7

—

Two years after the landing at Dieppe, Frank's left arm was healed and strong. He bore a patch of grafted skin over his bicep muscle, and a puckered mark at the site of the exit wound, like a knot in wood, above his elbow. But the arm worked. He was glad to be reunited with his old company, led by Captain Aidan.

Dickie was not so lucky. After the wounds he sustained at Dieppe, he was confined to a wheelchair. He was home, or close to home, in a Toronto hospital, and would never return to the front. Frank had saved his life, that was certain. Dickie's father mentioned it in every letter he wrote, and he wrote often, detailing Dickie's progress. Dickie would have to learn to walk all over again, he said, like a baby.

Frank read these letters to Connor and to Dickie's other friends — Roger Towne and Jack Sinclair and Charlie Tanner. Dickie's father was a good writer, descriptive and interesting and even funny, and he always added a message from Dickie and a box of cigarettes or candy. Dickie's mother always added a P.S.: "God bless you, Frank."

———

In June of 1944, Frank's unit was back in France, pushing through Normandy.

Early in July, he huddled with Connor's platoon behind a burned-out mill on the banks of the Orne, studying his map. For days they'd been pinned down under heavy fire, unable to advance. Now, finally, they were on the move, driving the Germans east. Tonight, their orders were to raid a command post — a boarding school occupied by Hitler Youth in a village outside Caen. The job was to get inside the school and take the post before the Black Watch attacked the village at dawn.

"Kill every guard outside, but hold your fire," Connor told them. "Total silence. Don't give the Krauts inside any warning."

He checked their silent weapons. Bayonets, knives, garrottes.

Frank had a garrotte tucked into his belt. He had never used it. It wasn't a weapon you could practise with. It consisted of two rough wooden handles strung together with a two-foot length of sharp wire.

"Once we take out the guards, we go in shooting," Connor said.

"What if they outnumber us?" asked Jack.

"They do," Connor said. "So that's when you make noise. Go in with everything you've got. Smoke, guns, grenades. Yell and scream. Make it sound like the whole company is coming down on their heads."

"What if —"

"And no surrender," said Connor. He looked each of his men directly in the eyes. "Hitler Youth don't take prisoners."

They split into two groups. Connor took four men with him to handle the guards in front.

Frank, Roger, and Jack were to take the single guard in back. They crept through the heavily wooded grounds, which smelled of wet earth and tree bark. Wind in the leaves sent showers down upon their heads. They waited for Connor's signal that the sentries in front of the school were dead. When they heard it — a single cuckoo call — they advanced through the woods.

A lamp above the back door illuminated a paved square where the guard stood, his spine rigid and both hands on his rifle. He was small. Frank judged his weight at a hundred and twenty. If they could get his rifle, he'd be easy to take. They crept closer. Roger picked up a stone and tossed it high over the sentry's head, into the bushes behind him. When the sentry turned, Roger surged forward, leaped on his back and brought him to the ground. Jack whistled, and the rest of the unit came out of the bushes and rushed the back door. Connor glanced at Roger, saw him rolling in the gravel with a man half his size, and kept running. He beckoned Frank to follow him into the school. But Frank stayed where he was. The sentry was small, but he was somehow wriggling out of Roger's grasp. He was taking his radio out of his belt, while Roger seemed barely able to rise to his feet. Roger swiped the radio from his enemy's hand, and it rattled away into the darkness. Then Roger staggered hard against him, as if drunk. The sentry raised his arm high and that was when Frank saw the knife in his hand, its blade red with blood in the lamp light. He saw the dark patch of blood at Roger's throat. The sentry drew back the knife, aiming at Roger's heart. Frank pulled the garrotte from his belt.

He grasped one handle in each hand and looped the wire over the boy's head. Yes, he was a boy. As he held the sinewy body close against his own, Frank knew the sentry was no more than sixteen. He almost hesitated, but the kid had slashed Roger's throat. Frank pulled back with both hands, and the kid gagged. He pulled again. The kid's whole body jerked and spasmed, but he didn't let go of the knife. Rain fell. Roger lay still on the pavement. He needed help. Needed someone to stop his bleeding. Frank pulled harder. The kid fought for his life, kicking the steel heels of his boots into Frank's shins. Frank tugged and jerked but could not break his neck.

When the first shots sounded from within, Frank was still grappling with the sentry. A gun battle raged throughout the school, while he struggled on, choking, hacking, slicing. By the time the boy's mangled body dropped lifeless to the ground, the battle was all over. The surviving members of the platoon came out. Jack wrapped Roger's throat with his own shirt and stole a car to drive him back to camp. Connor and two men stayed to gather intelligence and set up a base inside the school. The others ran, and Frank ran after them, through the woods and into the village, where the invasion was just beginning.

———

They fought on through June and July and into August, crawling through the mud during the day, digging in to slit trenches at night. The noise of the guns made them all deaf and crazy, and they all had small injuries — bruises, blisters, powder burns, broken fingers, infected feet. Many sustained serious wounds. Some went to the field hospital to be patched up and sent back into battle. Roger Towne was one of these. He came back to camp with a line of stitches holding the skin of his slit throat together. He couldn't talk, but he could fight. Others were shipped home, or died and were buried where they fell.

Still, at times, a patina of normal life descended temporarily. Connor and the others traded books they got from home, and when a battle wasn't imminent they read. Sometimes in camp they read aloud to each other. They teased Frank, saying Tennyson and Shelley weren't meant to be read with a Brooklyn accent, but Frank didn't care about that. He felt the meaning of the words coming to him readily now, felt the world opening wider as he turned the pages.

And the men openly admired his drawings. Jack Anderson nicknamed him "Picasso," and Frank felt warm inside to know Picasso made a kind of art vastly different from his own, and to know he shouldn't show Jack up by saying so. He didn't need to prove he wasn't stupid. He was accepted. When he got out of the war, he could make something of himself. Connor and his friends had given him confidence. He was certain now he could get a decent job and pay his own way at the art school he had waited so long to attend. Connor even thought the University of Toronto would accept Frank into their school of fine art, if they could see his drawings. Frank tried not to hope that was possible, but he couldn't help it. He saw himself at university, which he imagined as a larger version of Connor's house, walking across wide lawns with Connor and his friends, an easel strapped to his back. With a degree in art, he could earn a living. Teach others. Maybe even show his paintings in a gallery one day.

The chaplain's office gave out paper books of prayer so small they fit in a man's palm, and most of the men carried one at all times. But the books that came in the mail from home were hardbound and bulky and couldn't be carried on the battlefield. On one slow day, a rare day without rain, they set up a proper camp and got some rest. The Captain ordered a bath parade, and everyone was glad to wash in the cold creek nearby. Afterwards they built a fire and heated water for laundry. All afternoon they set about chores, repairing tents and cleaning guns. Frank sat in a corner, sketching quick studies of the men as they went about their tasks, mending socks and changing bandages. Roger Towne, whose voice was getting stronger as his throat healed, was sewing a patch to the knee of his pants. Having no camouflage material, he used a scrap of green satin from the lining of a worn-out cap. Connor sorted through his books, trying to find a volume that would fit into his knapsack.

"I can't carry *Paradise Lost* into the field," he said. "It weighs six pounds."

"Rip it up then," said Jack Sinclair. "That's what I did to Dreiser. Look." He reached into his kit and held up a sheaf of dirty, crumpled pages. "*An American Tragedy*, chapter one."

"That *is* a tragedy," said Connor.

"It's practical," said Jack. He passed the sheaf to his buddy, Roger. "Now Roger can start reading it, see? While I go on to the next part."

He thumbed through the battered volume to the place he wanted, and with his knife he sliced another section from the spine.

"You've ruined the book!" Frank cried.

"Hitler ruined it," said Jack. "Don't blame me. Anyway, our books are no good to us sitting here in the tent if we're out in the mud."

"True enough," said Connor. He turned *Paradise Lost* over in his hands, stroking the leather cover. "But this was a gift from my mother, for my twenty-first birthday."

"Then I'm sure she wants you to read it," said Roger. "Give him the knife, Jack."

Connor held the knife in his hand for a long time, but he didn't use it.

It wasn't until the following day, when they all had to leave the comfort of the tent and go out again into the muddy trenches, that Connor acted. He used a pair of scissors from the first aid kit and snipped the pages of *Paradise Lost* neatly, an inch from the binding. He handed the first batch of pages to Frank. "Ever read this?"

"No."

"Then you must," said Connor. He clipped another section for himself, and left the gutted leather covers behind.

———

That night, during a long bout of shelling, Frank got separated from his unit. When darkness fell, and he came upon a deserted farm, he scrounged items from the house and yard, a rope and a pail of water, a metal pot and a cooking grate, and candles.

He climbed to the loft in the barn and spread his jerkin over the straw. He could hear the shelling, about five miles away. He would look for his unit in the morning. For blackout, he hung a horse blanket in the window. He made a fire in the grate and boiled water for tea and heated a tin of stew. After eating, he lit a candle. He pulled from his knapsack the crumpled pages of Milton's *Paradise Lost* and smoothed them flat. Lying on his side, he propped up his head with one hand and began. He read the first long sentence five times, consulting every footnote, before he understood it. Then he went on, sentence after sentence, letting the story build in his imagination.

Against the distant groans of the German mortars and the crash of artillery shells, *Paradise Lost* held him fascinated. Satan's fiery fall from Heaven was terrifying, and his reaction to his punishment more terrifying still. Waking on the lake of fire, cast out from goodness and the grace of God, Satan refused to repent but vowed to commit himself with all his might to hating the God he once loved. *Better to reign in Hell, than serve in Heaven.* Frank shuddered. He wanted to ask Connor about this Milton. How did Milton know so much, *feel* so much? Father Madden's sermons about evil seemed feeble in comparison. Frank knew the will to do evil existed in human beings. Some people had an absolute lust for it. But he had never before thought that those people might feel miserable inside, might be tormented, that they might feel wronged.

He blew out the candle and for a long time lay with his eyes open in the darkness.

Outside of Falaise, as the troops marched through a sodden, moulding vineyard, Roger Towne stepped on a mine and in less than an instant his body was ripped to pieces. In the confusion, the hidden, waiting Germans lobbed grenades down on the rest of them. Jack Sinclair, his legs running on instinct toward his friend, though his eyes had witnessed him blown apart, was nearly caught in a second explosion that blasted Roger's remains high into the air. Frank and Connor saw it happen.

"Jack!" called Frank. "Don't —" The leg of Roger Towne, still dressed in its army pants with the shiny green satin patch at the knee — the left knee, Frank thought stupidly — came flying up from the ground, its broken thigh bone bloody and sharp. The bone came spinning through the air end over end toward Jack's face. Jack's head snapped back and he fell to the ground. When Frank reached him, Jack was sitting up, holding his jaw, his teeth jagged and broken, his eyes dull with disbelief.

But he lived through it. Do you live through these things? A voice had begun to speak to Frank at such times, asking questions with no answers. After the dead, splintered femur of your best friend smashes out your front teeth, do you live?

On the last day of August, they reached Rouen. The Germans had fled. The citizens were celebrating. As the trucks and tanks drove through the streets, the people of the town came out to wave and throw kisses.

Girls tossed daisies and roses and apples to the men, who caught them, or missed them, with joy. Frank watched the rain of fruit and flowers and listened to the cheers, as though in a dream. A young woman ran out to the truck and handed him an apricot, saying something to him in French. He accepted it and thanked her, all the while wondering what was happening. What was happening?

4.8

KYLE COMES BY HIMSELF TO VON'S HOTEL THE MORNING AFTER she told him he won't be working in the greenhouse. He wants to talk about the business, he says. His phrases sound rehearsed. He says he wants to make a contribution. Participate fully.

She explains to him gently that he'll have a steady income from his share of the profits. Not enough to live on, but enough to make a difference. The greenhouse is successful. Rosheen wanted him to have what she had. A cheque four times a year.

He turns away from her and gazes out the window. Clouds are gathering. He says, "I'd want more than that."

Von isn't sure what he means. She says, "We can do it monthly then, if you'd like. It'll be more paperwork, but if you —"

"It's not the money." He turns to face her. His lips are trembling, two pink spots reddening high on his cheeks. This is hard for him. Standing up to his new aunt.

"Now wait a minute," she says. "Don't start —"

"It's a partnership," he argues righteously. "The lawyer showed me the papers. My mum had an equal partnership and that's what she left me. Fifty percent of the business, meaning fifty percent of the vote and a say in every decision."

"Yes, but Rosheen never took part in any decisions. I've run the business all on my own for years. In fact, for all intents and purposes —" She stops herself. Why is she using these stuffy words? She begins again, "What I mean is, I've been doing everything, making all the decisions, the hiring, the buying and selling, ever since my mother died, oh, twenty-five years ago. Rosheen never lifted a... Rosheen didn't take part at all."

"But legally," he says, "she had a right to."

"Listen," Von says. She slows down. "You. Don't. Understand. She didn't *want* to be involved."

"But I do." He looks at her steadily. "I want to."

"No, you don't," she says. But something's happening. Something's slipping away from her. He's not listening.

"I like gardening. Growing things. At home, a bunch of us dug a garden in the backyard and we work in it every day. We supply everyone in the house with lettuce and veggies. We even canned tomatoes last year. I *like* doing it."

"This isn't the same thing, Kyle. This is a big operation."

"I worked on a farm last summer. That's a big operation."

"You did?"

"We *told* you. Meredith's brother has an organic farm in Saskatchewan. I helped him bring in the lentil crop and the potatoes. Practically broke my back digging those potatoes. And in summer, when Meredith's sister-in-law had her baby early, Meredith and me, we went out there and picked all the strawberries. I drove every load into town all by myself and sold it."

"You got everything to market on time?"

"Of course I did." He's indignant. "They were *counting* on me."

He's defending himself. This isn't what she wants, to interrogate him, question his character. She's losing control of the conversation. And maybe of her business.

"Look," she says. "We'll talk about it later. Once you understand what's involved."

He waits for her to say more.

"I'd have to talk to Jeanne. She's the manager."

He crosses his arms.

"Maybe you can come and see the place this fall," she concedes.

He isn't satisfied. But at least she's managed to defer the issue. When Meredith arrives to take him out for breakfast, Kyle says goodbye in his usual friendly voice. Not the type to hold a grudge. He trusts that she will make this right, eventually.

But how?

Once she's alone, she brews a strong pot of coffee. She can't let Kyle come and work with her. And she has to admit that it's not because he's inexperienced. She has hired and trained inexperienced people before, and she has never minded their questions, or their mistakes.

It's because the greenhouse is her home. Her sanctuary. And Von values her privacy. She likes the peace and quiet. With Jeanne, it's different. Jeanne's used to her ways — well, all right, her moods. Face it, Jeanne puts up with her. Jeanne feels sorry for her. Because Jeanne knows what the Garrisons are like. Jeanne knows their story.

Last month, when Von phoned Jeanne from Brooklyn, to tell her she'd found Kyle, Jeanne wept. "How much will you tell him?" she asked.

"I *want* to tell him the whole story," Von said, letting the rest of the sentence dangle. But that isn't true. She doesn't even want to remember the whole story, let alone have to tell it. And it isn't true that Von found Kyle. He found her. He sought her out.

———

After the protest strikes in the spring of 1943, the Germans ordered the Dutch citizens to turn in their radios. So the people resorted to making their own radios, crystal sets they concealed in all manner of locations, so they could listen to Radio Orange. At the Dutch Resistance Museum, where Durgan has taken them today, Von and Kyle and Meredith listen to the tape-recorded voices of elderly men and women who lived through the Nazi occupation. They view models of houses with secret compartments for hiding Jewish families or Dutch boys old enough to be drafted into the German army. Kyle is fascinated by a tiny matchbox, displayed half open and stuffed with radio parts. It's like something they got out of a spy movie, he says. Durgan reminds him it's the other way around. War first. Movies later.

Durgan has recommended a lot of places to see, most of them related to the war. "Rosheen immersed herself in the history of the war while she was here," he says. "She wanted to know all the details, whether they showed up in her work or not."

Later, at a café down the street, Kyle takes out his mother's yellow scrapbook. He has never returned it to Von, never actually placed it in her hands. He keeps it in his backpack, as if it belongs to him. He shows Durgan the pasted-in letter from Marijke Haas, asking, "Do you understand Dutch?"

"Sure." Durgan leans over and reads. "This person, Marijke Haas, says she met Frank Garrison during the war. She says here she has photographs for Rosheen's art show. But I don't think Rosh ever got them. She never mentioned them to me. Have you met Marijke yet?"

"No," says Kyle. He looks at Von. "Aren't you going to contact her? Her address is right here."

"Yes," says Von. "I meant to. I will."

She is not as eager to learn about her father as she was to learn about her grandmother. She felt a closeness to Deirdre as she uncovered the story of her past. Was it because they were both women? Or was it because Deirdre's life had been at a good safe distance? Her father's life, so fiercely tangled with her own, seems far more dangerous. What does this Marijke know? Von fears the discovery of a long-lost sibling, or some such awful revelation. She has to face it, but thinks it better if she faces it alone. Maybe while Meredith and Kyle are in France.

Later that evening, Meredith knocks on the door of Von's hotel. She's been caught in the rain, and she's tired and wet, burdened with too many packages. She has a blister on her left heel from the second-hand shoes she bought at the market yesterday.

"Where's your umbrella?"

"We only brought one with us, and Kyle's got it."

Von gives her a towel and a bathrobe. She tosses Meredith's clothes in the hotel dryer, then brings her a basin of warm water to bathe her sore feet, and a bandage for the blister.

Meredith has bought cheese, pears, a packet of cold pancakes, and an expensive bottle of organic orange juice from Spain. Von makes an impromptu dinner from these groceries and takes it into the sitting room, where Meredith is drying her feet and applying the bandage.

"Did you walk far?"

"From the museum all the way back to the studio," Meredith says. "Then I went shopping."

"Was Kyle with you?"

"He came to the studio with me, but then him and Durgan took off for the *coffeeshop*."

"Oh, no," says Von. "They're scoring dope?"

"It's legal here, Von."

"That doesn't mean it's healthy. Durgan is not a good influence. Can't he see how *young* Kyle is, how impressionable? Durgan tells him these wild stories —" She remembers that Meredith is just as young as, in fact a little younger than, Kyle. But Meredith seems older. Even now, she is watching Von patiently, waiting for her turn to speak so she can impart her adult knowledge.

"Kyle likes Durgan," Meredith says, "because Durgan talks to him about his mother."

Von shifts uncomfortably, stands up. "He's talking to Kyle about the wrong things, showing him the worst side of his mother."

"If there's another side to her," says Meredith, "you should tell him about it."

"You should stay out of this," says Von. "Believe me, you don't know anything about Rosheen."

"You don't know anything about Kyle," says Meredith calmly.

"How long have you known him?" Von counters.

"Only a couple of years. But that doesn't matter. I understand him. Kyle and me share a bond. I'm adopted. I know what it's like to not know your birth family."

Von tries to interrupt, but Meredith won't let her. "It's hard when you don't know who you are. It's hard to have no one who looks like you. Sounds like you. Walks like you. No blood relatives."

"I'm a blood relative," says Von.

Meredith shifts her eyes down, looks at the floor through her lashes. Her shrug is so subtle Von isn't even sure if she's seen it.

4.9

In Holland, the Canadians couldn't replace their casualties fast enough. Reinforcements arrived untrained. Cooks and truck drivers pulled from duty. Young kids who only a few months ago were still in high school. Sent into battle with no knowledge of field craft, no understanding of the weapons. An eighteen-year-old from some small town in the Canadian North arrived at noon and lasted until two o'clock. He pulled the pin on a grenade and lobbed it so straight into the air it fell back into his slit trench, blowing both his hands off his wrists.

The farmland of the Netherlands, north of Antwerp, resembled a lake. The Germans had bombed out the main dikes. In many fields the tops of the remaining dikes were visible only as dark lines beneath a skein of water, roads the men could march, knee-deep, in single file, surrounded by flat open water — targets lined up for target practice.

In the pouring rain, Frank steered Connor and a boatload of new recruits across a flooded polder, searching for a place to set up a temporary training camp. A cluster of treetops to the east marked the edge of a farmer's field that had become a river, and in the middle of the river, a barn was visible, perched on a slight rise and possibly dry inside. Frank headed toward it. The boys in the boat had never loaded a Bren gun, and wouldn't survive a day if they didn't learn. When the boat ran aground, Frank tied it to a tree, and they all waded up the rise into the shelter of the barn, where Connor demonstrated how to load a Bren. He ran each of the eight new recruits through the process in turn. How to fill the gas piston. How to fit the magazine so it wouldn't jam. How to replace the barrel if it overheated. How to clean the gun. How to aim and fire it. Connor glanced at his watch and cursed. He had aged. His freckled face was lined with tension. His brown eyes had lost their warmth. "We're out of time," he said grimly to Frank. His red hair was filthy and too long. He pushed it out of his eyes and scratched his head angrily with both hands and then put his helmet back on and said, "Let's go." They loaded the men and the guns back into the boat and drove them to headquarters, where Captain Aidan divided them into pairs, gave every pair a Bren, and sent them into the field. Each man had loaded the gun exactly once.

That night, shortly before sunset, Frank saw three men go down in a row before their comrades could return the fire. The three bodies lay in the ditch until two men arrived near dusk to fish them out and carry them on stretchers to the waiting trucks. The men got the first two bodies out all right. But when they came back for the third and loaded him onto the stretcher and began the march back, slogging along the top of the dike, the blanket of cloud pulled apart along the horizon and let through a last thin ray of light as the sun descended, so that the shapes of the men stood out in black relief against the rose-grey sky, and a sniper picked them off. Two shots and they went down, first one stretcher-bearer, then the other, and their burden too, leaving again three corpses submerged in the silt. And then it was dark.

They fought on. The guns got plugged with mud and would not fire. The tank treads got plugged with mud and would not turn. Jeeps slid off the roads. In a thick mist, a tank caved in a slit trench with three of their own men in it, killing all three.

Frank splashed along behind Connor. Their collars, caked with mud and grizzled with frost, chafed their necks. Their boots scraped the skin from their ankles. They waded through mist, a place no longer part of the world. The absurd daily numbers of the dead, 50, 119, 81, held no meaning. There were only the names of those you knew and the faces of those you'd seen and the stories your friends had told, when they used to tell stories, and the dog tags you untangled and removed from their necks and placed into the Captain's outstretched hand. It was becoming impossible to remember they were men. They were the residue of men, the ghosts men left behind. They marched through grey mud under grey skies.

They had been in Europe four months.

One day, when Frank was lagging behind, Connor turned around and waited for him to catch up. They had been out scouting that morning, assessing the terrain north of Ossendrecht, and had found an abandoned factory that could serve as a munitions magazine, as the troops advanced north. It was an old candy factory, and the smell that lingered within it reminded Frank of the sugar refinery in Brooklyn, and of his father, Tomas. He hoped this was a good sign, a sign that the place would be safe, protected by Tomas's spirit. But he worried it might be a dire warning, seeing as Tomas was fatally wounded in the sugar dust explosion. Then he worried he was becoming superstitious, like his mother, and he realized he hadn't thought of his mother for weeks. All this introspection slowed him down as he and Connor crossed yet another polder, slogging ankle-deep through matted, soggy straw. He saw Connor waiting and hurried up.

As Frank drew close enough to hear him, Connor called back, "Say, did you ever finish reading the Milton?"

An aircraft buzzed on the horizon. A British plane. Connor lifted his head, shielding his eyes — not from the sun, for there was no sun, but from the general glare of the clouds — and took one small step backward. A mine exploded beneath his foot.

The explosion sent up mud, straw, stones, and thick grey smoke. Frank dropped to the ground. But it was over. The mines were quick.

A crack, a burst of smoke, and nothing. Frank leaped to his feet and tore across the field.

Connor's body lay in two separate pieces on the ground. Frank kneeled above him and looked into his eyes. Connor looked back. He was sorry, terribly sorry. But then Connor's gaze shifted. His brown eyes widened. He was captivated by whatever it was he was seeing over Frank's shoulder. Amazed.

Frank said, "No." He leaned across Connor and spread his arms wide, as if to prevent him from leaving. But Connor was already gone. There was nothing to do but repeat the words of prayers and cover Connor's face and mark the spot where he lay with an upright rifle and a helmet, so he wouldn't be crushed by a tank. Then send the stretcher-bearers to collect his remains.

———

An hour after Connor died, Frank was driving twenty men and a store of ammunition to the candy factory, to make it ready in advance of Captain Aidan, who would come with the rest of the company the following day. The building was the size of a New York department store, with four floors. It had been empty, Frank guessed, for two or three years. At some point, it had been hit by a bomb, which felled its big chimney, and hundreds of bricks littered the main hall by the front entry. Yet the smell of candy, like some childish ghost, still haunted the rooms, making everybody sick with nostalgia. As the men cleaned the two large rooms in the centre of the building, setting up a makeshift kitchen and dormitory, he heard them talking.

"Remember candy floss?" they asked each other. "Remember Mackintosh toffee? Sweet Maries?"

Frank secured the main floor and loaded the ammo into the factory's storage tanks. While the men cooked and ate, he worked, but when they spread their sleeping bags on the floor to sleep, he lay down too. All his muscles ached. His throat and ears burned, and white lights flashed behind his eyelids. He fell into feverish dreams, and at midnight, when two enemy soldiers killed the Black Watch guards outside, Frank didn't wake up until they were inside the building.

The two Germans unloaded a machine gun into the dorm, killing three and wounding seven, before Charlie Tanner killed them both with his Bren. Frank and Charlie quickly turned the room into an infirmary, unpacking the first aid kits and moving the wounded to the centre of the room, where the medic could attend to them. Jack took to the roof, to see how bad it was and came back to report Germans were lined up behind the long fence facing the factory, at least a dozen of them, and four smaller clumps, three and four Krauts together, behind the four outbuildings in the back. And more might be coming. Only Frank, Charlie, Jack, and four other survivors, besides the medic, were able-bodied enough to fight. Jack got on the radio to Captain Aidan.

Trapped in the factory, outnumbered, and with wounded men to protect, Frank remembered the strategy Connor had proposed at Caen. Make noise. Make it sound like the whole company was here, a hundred strong, armed to the teeth. He stationed a man at each of the four corners, armed them all with as many guns as they could carry, and told them to run up and down the stairwells and shoot from different floors. "Try to hit as many as you can. But fire, even if there's no one in your sights. Fire and fire again. Keep moving." He stationed Jack above the main front door, the north entrance where they were most vulnerable.

Then Frank covered the north and west sides and Charlie took the south and east. They knew the building only from their earlier exploration of it. In total darkness, but for the flare of the weapons and the scant moonlight that came and went with the windblown clouds, they raced from room to room, pulling pins and tossing grenades out windows and sprinting like hell up and down stairs and tearing back to the storeroom for more.

Jack yelled for help. He'd been hit in the knee, and the Germans were gaining on the front entrance. They'd broken a window and were throwing grenades in through the hole. Jack had been tossing them back out before they exploded, but he needed help. Charlie gave him fresh ammo, and Frank boarded up the broken pane. Then they left Jack to fend for himself while they toured the building again. From outside, they hoped, the factory looked to be occupied by a hundred men. They had a crack sniper doing damage from the third floor, moving from one position to another, as if the Canadians had six snipers. The Germans retreated, and while they regrouped behind the outbuildings, Frank and Charlie re-armed all their gunners. The medic bandaged Jack's knee, and Jack wedged himself between two windows above the front door, with two machine guns.

The Germans advanced again, storming the main entrance. Two of them battered the front door with a steel rod, and the door quaked in its frame. Jack lifted the upper half of his body out the window and aimed straight down, shooting them both in the top of the head. But others replaced them.

Out of grenades, Frank picked up a Bren gun. A German crawled through the broken glass of a ground-floor window, and Frank shot him dead. A second one followed and Frank shot him dead. A third followed and the Bren jammed. Frank chucked the gun at the man's head, knocking him unconscious, and for a few minutes the inert body blocked the window, protecting those inside.

Frank armed himself with bricks from the broken chimney. He stood in the main floor entry, guarding the infirmary, a brick held high in his right hand, and another ready in his left. Total blackness. Every time he heard a sound, he turned and hurled a brick in its direction. He toiled like this through the darkness, hour after hour, holding the enemy back and keeping alive the wounded until reinforcements finally arrived at dawn.

Exhausted, feverish, grief-stricken, Frank slept all the next day. But he did not rest. His brain replayed the movements of the night. His nerves sang like taut telegraph wires, alert for the slightest noise or movement, as he hurled brick after brick into a void from which Nazi soldiers poured like maggots from a rotting corpse. For days afterwards, he jumped at every sudden movement. But all the men jumped at every movement. They were all inflamed with adrenalin, ready to detonate.

In October, after devastating casualties at Woensdrecht, the surviving members of Frank's unit were dispersed. Frank was assigned to a small detachment, twelve men. They drove north, to a farmyard at the edge of the town of Bergen-op-Zoom and divided into search parties.

Frank's orders were to clear this sector of the town and set up camp. He took three men with him and put Jack Sinclair in charge of three men and Charlie Tanner in charge of three others. Each team moved through the bombed homes and shops with their rifles drawn, searching for Germans. They found nothing but ruined, smoking buildings, some still burning. Shattered windows, collapsed roofs, broken stone. Frank had practically forgotten what a town looked like, what a simple house was. The last street ended in a hay field, and across the field they could see a barn and the remains of a farmhouse, bombed. The farmers had abandoned the place — recently, and in a hurry, for a pig remained in a pen beside the barn, rooting in the mud.

Frank's soldiers, farm boys from Quebec, volunteered to slaughter the pig. They stunned it with a heavy hammer between the eyes. They tied its feet together with rope and threw one end of the rope over a sturdy hook in the arch of the barn door and hoisted it into the air. Two men held its front legs apart while a third thrust a sharp knife high into its chest and sliced upward, deep into its neck. A river of blood gushed from the wound, splattering the grass and pooling in the dirt, a thick, red puddle. Frank turned away. The men promised to butcher the pig and have it ready to be roasted for a feast tomorrow.

A short row of damaged shops and houses at the edge of town, close to the farm, offered good shelter, and Frank decided to make camp among the ruins. He radioed Captain Aidan and gave him the coordinates. On the corner, a deserted café remained virtually untouched, its whitewashed walls gleaming in the sun. Out front, on a cobblestone patio, four white tables and chairs still stood upright, waiting for customers. Frank thought of Connor, how he might once have performed a great parody of manners for this occasion, using his ten-dollar words to make them all laugh.

Captain Aidan drove up to the café in a truck packed with rations, books, whisky, vodka, and cigarettes. He had hauled along his RCA Victor Special, no longer shiny, and a crate of records, Bluebird labels and V-discs he'd got by trading with the Americans. Aidan reported that Jerry had left this sector and headed south to Beveland. Aidan didn't believe they would return tonight. The men took this as an occasion to celebrate, or was it an opportunity to mourn? There was no name for these rare, crazy moments of freedom. Charlie and Jack unloaded the rations and the phonograph. One of the older guys, a veteran of the Great War, climbed into the jeep with Aidan and they drove off in search of some beer.

"Boys," said Jack, "let's make ourselves at home." He carried the rations inside and investigated the café's kitchen. The power was out — it was out all over this sector of town — and the pantry had been raided of every scrap of food. But all the equipment seemed to be in place. He pulled pots and china dishes from the shelves, in preparation for a dinner that would be, in its settings anyway, stylish and refined. He found bleached white tablecloths, which he spread on the tables. He gathered far too many drinking glasses and set these out as well, along with a bottle of vodka.

Frank was uneasy. He had always trusted Aidan, but right now he feared the Captain was making a mistake. There were too many directions from which the Germans could return in the night, and not enough sentries. If Jack and Charlie drank too much, and that looked to be their plan, there would be even fewer. He would have to work out a schedule for tonight's watch that didn't depend on the drinkers.

In the meantime they needed firewood, never easy to find in flooded, rainy Holland. But he had to find it fast. They needed to cook before nightfall, as they couldn't risk a fire after dark. He left Jack and Charlie pouring vodka and headed across the dull yellow stretch of hayfield, toward a small copse of trees. Tank tracks criss-crossed the hay field in deep gouges that had filled with water. He mucked his way through them to inspect the trees. It was October, and they all stood leafless, cold and bleak, their bare branches shaking in the wind. He touched a thin wizened oak. Its bark was damp, but when he kicked it, the bark flew off in chunks, and the trunk caved in.

He returned to the barn and entered, stepping around the massive pool of pig's blood. Inside, he found an axe and a whetstone. He sharpened the axe, and back at the copse, he chopped open the oak, finding it desiccated. The first dry wood he'd seen since Antwerp.

It felt good to throw himself into physical labour with some reasonable expectation it would be worthwhile. He chopped the logs into lengths and split the lengths until he had enough firewood for tonight's dinner and a start on tomorrow's pig roast. Now he needed a way to haul it back. Against the side of the farmhouse, he saw a pile of tools and machinery, partly covered by a tarpaulin. Maybe there was a wagon or a barrow underneath. He walked across the yard, swinging the axe, eyeing the fence, measuring his distance from it. He aimed at the upright fencepost and flung the axe straight at it. Missed! The axe flew past the post and embedded itself in the

ground at the edge of the tarp. He was tired, losing his edge. He
needed a drink of water.

He approached the rain barrel and leaned against it. Filled his
canteen, drained it and refilled it. Then he bent down, grasped a corner
of the tarp, and threw it back, uncovering a human being. A young
woman. Crouched in the mud on her knees and elbows, her back
arched high and her face pressed to the ground. She covered the back
of her neck with her two dirty hands. She was shaking.

"Jesus." He had nearly thrown the axe down on this very spot.
He might have beheaded her. He touched her shoulder and she jerked
away as if burned.

"I'm Canadian," he said, the first time he had said those words
without hesitation.

She lifted her head. When she saw he told the truth, she began
to sob, kneeling in the dirt. Beneath her body, she had been concealing
a small boy, no more than two years old. He crawled into her lap and
thrust his head into her belly as if to hide inside her. They both had
pale, straight hair that needed cutting, and their clothes were tattered.
Hans, she said his name was. And she was Marijke.

Frank pointed at his heart and said, "Frank."

"Frank," she repeated. "Frank, van Canada."

"Yes." He asked her about her parents but she didn't speak English
well enough to tell him much. Her father and mother had gone away.
She pointed at the railway tracks.

Frank asked her, with gestures, if she was hungry, and she nodded.
She followed him back to the café, carrying the boy. The men were
unloading beer and dinner rations.

Captain Aidan knew some Dutch. He talked to Marijke and
learned her parents had been arrested by the Germans. Her house had
burned down. She and her brother, Hans, were caught in crossfire in
the street and almost killed. She had taken shelter in the farmhouse.
When the battle ended and the neighbours left their smoking houses
to seek refuge elsewhere, Marijke was too frightened to come out. So
she and Hans were left behind. This morning, when she heard the
soldiers drive into the yard, she'd hidden under the tarp.

They heated tins of corned beef and veg and opened bottles of
beer. Captain Aidan presented a box of apples he'd brought up from
Antwerp. Jack peeled and cored one apple after another, stabbing

them through and coring them whole with his knife. Marijke chopped
them into chunks and baked them. They were delicious. All four men
handed over their chocolate rations for the little boy.

The butcher shop next door had been destroyed. Its white and
blue tiled floor was enclosed by walls of broken brick no more than
three feet high. But its counter was still standing. Charlie set the
phonograph and records there. Jack broke out the whisky.

Jack and Charlie looked through the records. They called Frank
to join them, but he shook his head, no. If the Nazis returned tonight,
there would be open battle, gunfire everywhere. He wanted to find a safe
place for Marijke and Hans. Crumbling concrete blocked the caved-
in entrance to the house across the street, but the cellar might still be
habitable. He walked over to investigate. No entry was possible on the
main floor, and the open window on the second floor was too high to
reach. He circled the house, searching for something to use as a ladder.

While Frank worked, Marijke rested on an overturned washtub,
holding Hans on her lap and watching Jack and Charlie in the shop
across the street. Jack placed a record on the phonograph and turned
the crank. Music rose from the rubble, and soon Sinatra's voice came
in, singing "Shake Down the Stars."

Frank found a dead tree trunk and tried to lean it up against the
side of the house.

"Give me a hand, you bums!" he called.

His friends paid no attention. Jack took Charlie in his arms, and
with a deep mock tenderness he led him in a dance around the butcher
shop. Hans stood on Marijke's thighs and bounced up and down to the
music. She picked him up and carried him through the bombed-out
yard, dancing, twirling in circles to make him laugh.

The tree trunk was too heavy for Frank to raise by himself. Jack
and Charlie were now performing a tango and Burt was singing along
with Sinatra, loudly and off key. Frank couldn't help smiling. But he
had to return to the farm yard to search for something to use as a
ladder.

Inside the barn, he found the perfect thing: a ladder. He hauled
it down the street to the house. Hans was quieter now. Marijke was
rocking him in her arms, and Sinatra was singing a slower song. Frank
propped the ladder against the wall and shook it hard. It wobbled,
but didn't break. He climbed six rungs to the top and looked in the

window. He saw a small upper room with an open door that led to a staircase. He climbed inside and crossed the floor, descended the staircase slowly, gun drawn. But the building was empty. The kitchen was intact, with a stack of wood beside the stove, and by good luck a barrel of rain water stood outside a hole in the wall, where it could be reached. The cellar was small and dark, but it was dry. If he brought some straw for warmth and some rations, they could be safe here, for as long as a week. He went back outside to tell her.

"You go up." He pointed at the window. "Then down." He pointed at the cellar, moving his fingers like little legs down the slope of his arm to show her what he meant.

He put the boy in his duffel bag, along with the rations, and tied the bag to his chest. He rested his chin lightly on Hans's blond head and inhaled the scent of soap. In the midst of chaos, flame and brimstone, she had found or hoarded a scrap of soap to wash his hair. Frank delivered the child to the top and deposited him on the floor with the supplies.

"Tommy Dorsey!" cried Jack.

"Glenn Miller!" countered Charlie. They began a loud argument over which record to play next.

Frank climbed back down. "Come on," he said to Marijke. "You will be safe inside."

The little boy called out for her from behind the wall, "Marijke!"

Marijke hiked her skirt above her knees so she could climb. Frank stood below, holding the ladder. When she got to the top, she stretched her arm toward the window, but could only graze the ledge with her finger tips. She wasn't tall enough to pull herself inside.

Frank turned around, his back to the ladder, and climbed up, between her legs, until his face was level with her waist. Bracing his feet against the rung, he wrapped his arms around her thighs and lifted. The ladder swayed. Marijke gasped.

"I've got you," he said. "Reach up, up. Good."

"Nee," she said. "Nee." She kicked her legs, to shake him off, but he persisted.

"You have to get inside," he told her. "Reach up. Come on."

Charlie and Jack must have come to an agreement about the record, for the first sweet horns of "Moonlight Serenade" came wafting from across the street.

Slowly, Frank raised his arms, hoisted Marijke higher. She was light as a child, but his arms shook with the effort to maintain his balance and his grip on her. She wriggled, and the hem of her dress worked itself ever higher up her thigh. He couldn't understand why she was so reluctant to accept his help until he saw, as he lifted her, finally, above his head, that she had no underpants on. Underpants were a luxury she couldn't afford. Frank knew he should turn away, but he looked. As her body passed above his head, he saw her belly button only inches from his eyes and then the fringe of blonde hair, so sparse and pale he could clearly see the cleft between the two delicate lips, plump and rounded, though the rest of the girl was so thin, and two small moles on her inner thigh, and then her legs and she was free of him. Just before she slid inside the house to safety, her hips got caught on the edge of the sill and she lay on her belly, the white curve of her bare bottom exposed and her legs dangling out the window. With one last effort she pulled herself inside the house. From inside, she called out, "Zank you." But she did not show her face. She must be mortified, he thought. He heard her speaking to the boy. She would see the stairs and go down, as he had shown her, and they would be safe in the cellar, with firewood and water. He climbed back down the ladder, thinking of nothing but that tender white cleft, how vulnerable she was, and then from the direction of town came the boom of bazooka gun fire and the ground shook, the ladder rattled and slid and he was falling.

At first, there was no pain. He believed he was still upright. He tried to take a step and felt the sharp cobblestone stab his shoulder blade. He realized he was flat on the ground. Night had fallen. He must have been lying here for hours, unconscious. But no. From the butcher shop across the street he could still hear the gramophone. Glenn Miller's orchestra still playing the "Moonlight Serenade." No time had passed. The explosion, he reasoned, had created a cloud of debris so thick it had turned the air black. He was afraid to breathe.

He tried to rise, but managed only to turn over and push himself up on his hands and knees. Then he half rose, kneeling in the darkness. As soon as he lifted his head, he felt the blood pour from his face, soaking his neck and chest. Quick memory of that pig hanging in the dooryard, life streaming in a torrent from its slit throat. He raised his hands to his face, explored the torn flesh. Gingerly, he traced the curve of his jaw line and his bare fingers touched bone. He reached higher, to his upper lip, but the lip was gone, replaced by a sharp metal fragment embedded in the upper gum. He moved left of his mouth and found a mass of jelly suspended there, a huge gelatinous teardrop clinging to his cheek, and he knew it was his own left eye. His right hand, tentative now, reluctant, moved to his right eye. His fingers, slippery and wet, slid easily into the empty socket. He lowered his arms slightly and remained kneeling, his hands open before his chest. Blood filled his cupped palms until they overflowed. For a moment longer, he still felt no pain.

Afterwards, he would remember that brief, peculiar sensation: the absence of pain. Or rather, he would try to remember it. For it was a gap he could never recover. Over the days and months and years to come, the memory of painlessness receded until finally it became as distant, and as inconceivable, as light.

Darkness

5.1

COOL AND DIM, THE BAR ON BLOEMENSTRAAT IS ALMOST EMPTY IN the middle of the afternoon. A bearded student scribbles in a notebook, drinking beer. At the bar, a young man polishes the draft taps. There is no sign of Marijke Haas, the person Von is supposed to meet here. She raises her coffee to her lips, then remembers how bitter it is and sets it down again. She is alone. Kyle and Meredith have gone to Paris. Von expected to feel relieved, away from Kyle's questions and Meredith's disapproval. Instead, she misses them, wishes they were here.

The woman who enters the bar is beautiful, dark-skinned, about thirty, wearing a patterned kaftan and headscarf. She looks at Von. "Are you Rosheen's sister?"

"Yes," says Von. "You're not… Marijke Haas?"

"I'm Marijke's niece," she says. "I'll bring her in." She steps back into the street and returns, pushing an impish, grey-haired Dutch woman in a wheelchair.

Marijke's eyes are blue and lively, though her face is heavily lined. The first thing she says is, "I'm sorry for your loss."

They talk about Rosheen for half an hour. Marijke's English is precise but limited. Her niece provides translation when needed.

0

Marijke says she will miss Rosheen's letters, and her stories about Frank. She wanted to give Rosheen these photographs long ago, but it's taken a while to gather them all and make copies. She pulls an envelope from her bag.

"So, you knew our father?" Von asks. "During the war?"

"For a moment," says Marijke. "A brief moment in life, but an important one. I have thought of him many times since that day."

"And you have pictures of him?"

"I'm sorry, dear. I've no pictures of Frank himself." She fiddles with the metal clasp on the envelope, then asks her niece to open it.

"We need a larger surface here," says her niece. She crosses the room to drag back a second small table.

"It was the day your father was wounded," Marijke tells Von. "He hid me and my brother in a cellar, just before he got hit. Instead of protecting himself, he protected us."

Her niece borrows a cloth from the bartender. She wipes the table tops and dries them thoroughly. She tips out the photographs and begins to sort them.

"After your father was hit," says Marijke, "the hell broke loose."

"All hell," says her niece.

"All hell broke loose. Gunfights in the streets and in the shops, even in the church. And the bombing! Every building on that street razed to the ground. The house where your father hid us was destroyed. But we were safe. We huddled in the cellar and ate the food and chocolate that he gave us."

Marijke's niece hands Von a photo, saying, "I'll show you who is who. Here's Aunt Marijke and my Uncle Gregor on their wedding day."

Von accepts the photo. It's unremarkable. Marijke, young, in a rather plain traditional wedding dress, beside a handsome blond man in a suit and tie.

"Their four boys." Four ordinary kids, blond and gap-toothed, in their Sunday best.

"Her grandchildren." Now Marijke's niece begins to spread the photos on the table top, like a poker hand, as Von counts, one two three…nine grandchildren.

"Here's my dad, Hans. He was born during the war. He was only two when your dad saved him. And here's my mum—she was born in Morocco — and my sisters. That one, Vera, she never married, but the others all did — look, here are my twins, Elke and Salma." She pulls over a third table and keeps spreading out photographs. Marijke beams proudly, as if she's performed a magic trick.

Von studies the metre-long display of smiling faces. Surely these people can't all be so happy in their everyday lives, but in their poses, gazing up at Von from the polished table tops, they're all content, angelic.

"I don't understand," Von says.

"My family," Marijke explains. "I have written all the names on the backs."

"But why did Rosheen want all these pictures?"

"I wanted her to have them. This is all — my family."

Her niece says, "Marijke wanted Rosheen to see everyone who wouldn't have been — me too, I wouldn't have been born, if not for your father."

Von counts. Forty-six people. She's starting to get it.

"I looked out the window that day, to tell him good-bye," says Marijke. "And I saw. What happened to him." She shakes her head, closes her eyes. "I have never forgotten it."

———

Marijke readily agrees to be filmed as she tells her story. She talks for a long time, describing the events of that day, and Von, shaken by what she hears, is grateful she doesn't have to ask questions or prompt her, because she's speechless. She barely manages to say good-bye when they part, but she gives Marijke a long hug and says, "Thank you, thank you so much."

After leaving the bar, she walks several blocks without knowing where she is or what she's doing. Eventually, she finds herself gazing into a gift shop window and remembers she's supposed to buy a souvenir for Leif. He never said what he'd like. *Surprise me*, he said. The bell tinkles when she enters, and the scent of sandalwood incense brings her back to the present. She wanders, browsing, and comes upon a shelf of assorted notebooks. Her own is almost full. She wants a new one, with a soft cover. The hard cover is too difficult to pack into her bag, its corners too sharp. She chooses a beauty, the right size, with unlined pages and a soft, flexible cover, a deep poppy-orange. Then she spots another. It's identical except for the colour of its cover, a rich, earthy brown. It reminds her of Kyle, his proclaimed love of the soil. He should be keeping a journal, too. His first trip to Europe. Possibly his only trip to Europe. He should be writing things down. She buys both books, and an umbrella for Meredith. Although she searches the entire shop, she doesn't see anything that reminds her of Leif.

On the way back to the hotel, she passes the home of Anne Frank. People are waiting in a long line to enter the tiny house and attached museum. A babble of voices, babel of languages. Japanese and Dutch and Portuguese. A lot of English with American accents. A noisy bunch of teenagers spills off the sidewalk into the street, laughing, pushing each other and talking non-stop, all of them at the same time, it seems, in a dialect she recognizes. French-immersion French. They're Canadians. Rich Canadians. Here on a school excursion of some kind. One of them, a freckled girl in a pink baseball cap and overalls, boosts herself up to sit on the railing and balances precariously there, holding on with one hand. In the other, she clasps the strings to a fat bouquet of blue and yellow helium balloons. She and her companions are giggling so hard Von's afraid she'll fall. Then they all break into song — a mock-soulful version of "My Heart Will Go On." Their raucous behaviour is apparently an affront to the dour pair of nuns in the line behind them. The girls take no notice but continue with their song. Are they indifferent to the solemn site they are about to enter? Disrespectful to the memory of the young writer who lived in this house? Or have they come here with some deeper purpose, their laughter and balloons the only way they know to honour her? The girl in the pink cap jumps up to greet a newcomer, squealing in welcome. One of the balloon strings slips between her fingers and a blue balloon escapes, disappears into the blue-grey bank of clouds that hangs so low above the house it seems to graze the shingles on its roof.

5.2

FRANK DREAMED THE WAR WAS A DREAM. HE LAY WITH HIS CHEEK flat against the cold chalk floor of the slit trench, his face numb. He was in the dentist's office in Manhattan, and all his teeth had been pulled out. Dr Green explained that the war was a hallucination, it was only the ether addling his brain, and then the Panzer engines woke him and he raised himself from the trench and fumbled to set up the mortar. He cranked the elevating handle, but he couldn't see, and he tripped on the tripod and felt the mortar collapse on top of him, the muzzle pressed tight into his chest, and as he lay there he realized that all around him the mud walls of the trenches were caving in, burying his friends alive. He heard their wet, bubbling murmurs in the darkness. Too many men, too deep in the mud to save.

Someone took Frank down, wrenched his arms behind his back and shoved him to the ground, he was a prisoner, and then he was lifted — strong hands under his armpits, and English words: "Garrison! Wake up! Garrison, what the hell are you doing? Are you drunk?" He tried to answer but his tongue filled his mouth. He needed water. They dragged him across the floor, sat him on a bed. He was aware he was warm and dry and in a quiet place. He was saved. For a moment, he was grateful, and then he rested his head in his hands and felt again the bandages that veiled his ruined face.

When he would not speak they sent a priest to visit him, a man who chanted above the beds of the wounded men in nasal Latin and distributed rosary beads. But Frank would not pray. He would not think about God now. He thought only of Satan, cast out, chained on the burning lake, fuck you.

Both eyes, the surgeon said, had been excoriated. Frank had never heard the word before but he understood instantly what it meant. He remembered Jack, leaning against the bombed-out wall of the Dutch butcher shop, peeling apples, how he'd slashed an X across the stem and plunged the blade in, quick flick of the wrist to pluck out the core.

They evacuated him to a hospital in England, where Captain Aidan came to visit, speaking in his smooth, radio voice about God and family, and insisting Frank write to his mother. He wrote down the few words Frank wanted to send and promised to mail them. Frank said he worried because he could not find his locker by himself. He was concerned about his things, his gun and tool-belt, his wristwatch and his wallet. When the Captain came again, he brought new handkerchiefs and chocolate and a Mass card from Deirdre. He brought a metal strongbox with a lock and key and set it on Frank's blanket-covered legs, and patiently waited while

Frank learned to lock and unlock it by himself. He fetched Frank's belongings and placed them in the box and hid it under the bed. With a long string he fastened the key to the bed frame and tucked it out of sight under the mattress.

After the Captain left, Frank dragged the box out a little. He wanted it near at hand. He had to lie perilously close to the edge of the high bed in order to reach it, but he felt better when he could touch it, and he fell asleep that way, his fingers grazing the metal lid. He remembered the blind man who used to cross the Brooklyn Bridge every morning and stand on a corner of Wall Street with a tin cup while the businessmen passed by. He remembered that Corky had once or twice reached into the cup and stolen a few cents and the blind man, feeling the pressure of Corky's hand in the cup and hearing the clink of the coins, had thanked him.

Frank had lost his left eardrum. A shrill whine sounded all day inside his head and rose in pitch whenever he especially needed to concentrate. The surgeon said he would try to reconstruct the eardrum. But first, he worked on Frank's jaw, cheekbone, eye sockets, wiring him together with metal plates and pins. Patching the holes with grafts of skin he peeled from Frank's thighs. Each time they stripped the bandages from his face, the nurses praised the great skill of the surgeon. But Frank understood, by the tone of their voices, that he had become a monster.

Captain Aidan encouraged Frank to take heart. Aidan was a good man, but he did not recognize the way things truly were. He told tales of men who had lost their eyesight and yet led productive lives, made brooms and baskets, even operated weaving looms, all manner of fool things. But "productive lives" was a term he used too often, and Frank knew he must have read it in some book. Faith was the key, Captain Aidan said. It had brought many a man back from the brink of despair. Did Frank want to pray?

Frank often woke in terror and several times found himself standing upright before he realized where he was. One night he got all the way out of the ward and into the corridor before the nurses caught him, but usually he collided with something first, and the commotion brought the nurses running. The doctor prescribed pills to keep him asleep at night, and Frank held these under his tongue and later spat them into his hand. He did not want to sleep deeply. He hated the nightmares and was afraid to sink so far into them he could not wake. He had already lost too much control. He wanted at least to know what was going on around him.

The men on this ward were all badly injured. Frank heard them groan and gasp, and at night he heard them whimper. One poor son of a bitch could not speak. He made noises in his throat, unshaped vowel sounds, like an animal might make, but he could not form words. His tongue must be gone, Frank thought. He cringed when he heard this man pleading and the nurses answering in soothing tones, telling him everything was all right. One night when the man sounded most despairing, Frank cried out to the nurses, "Get him a pencil and paper, for the love of Christ," and a nurse must have done so, for she said, later, that the patient had written down that he had a fierce headache and wanted a priest. He died the following day.

Frank wondered whether the nurses watched the patients at all times. He tried testing the staff by sitting up in bed and waving an arm in the air to see if anyone would come. Soon he learned that the nurses gathered in a lounge down the hall very late at night to drink coffee, and at that time there was no one supervising the ward. The other men were sleeping or lost in their own misery, and the staff did not enter the ward unless someone called out or rang a bell.

After he discovered this, he sat up listening in the night and judged the length of time the nurses were gone. It seemed long enough. Three nights after they buried the tongueless man, Frank stayed awake and when all was still he reached under his bed and fumbled with the metal bed slats, trying to find the string. When he located it, he pulled, but his own weight was trapping it beneath him, and he feared the string would break. He got out of bed. Crouching on the cold floor, he tugged at the string and retrieved the key. Opened the strongbox. Found his pistol and ammunition. Set the gun on the bed and inserted the magazine. No one was awake. He did not want to do this thing in the room with the other men, but he knew he couldn't get himself outside without rousing the staff. He remained kneeling beside the bed, and the posture recalled him to his childhood, when he knelt to say his prayers before he slept. I served You well, he thought, and look how You've repaid me. He pulled back the slide on the pistol. He knew it was a sin and did not care. He would not ask forgiveness. He had thought already about his mother and the shame this sin would bring on her. He was through thinking about that. It could not be helped. He would bring shame to her blind or dead. He held the pistol in his right hand and positioned his head against the wall. It was an exterior wall, he knew. He had planned this. No one would get hurt. He leaned his deaf ear against the cold plaster. The phantom whine rose in pitch. I'll never have to hear that damned noise again, Frank thought. He placed the muzzle against his right temple and then bam, his head was shoved down, his right arm seized and twisted behind his back, and the gun clattered to the floor.

"Sergeant Garrison," said the orderly, who was sitting on top of him. "You don't know what you're doing, Sir."

The orderly kept a firm hold on the back of his head, grinding a newly stitched seam on his right cheek into the floor.

They drugged him, sent him spinning deep into a whirlpool where he was assailed by new sounds, strong winds, giant bed sheets flapping on the line, a paralyzing thunder in his brain. He made a great effort to dislodge the noise, but could not move his head. For days, it seemed, he fought to come to consciousness, and finally, high above the storm, he heard a voice, a Scottish woman, singing. He struggled toward the sound. A song about the Isle of Skye. He felt a hand on his forehead, a cool wet cloth. The woman was bathing him.

"Where are we?" he asked.

"Ah, you're awake." She told him he'd been transferred to a rehabilitation unit at the military hospital in Bramshott. He was to be trained and made ready to go home.

"Don't stop singing," he said. She continued, and he let himself drift a while in the twilight sleep of the drug. But he knew that soon he would be forced back into life.

An intake nurse came to interview him. She had drenched herself in a strong perfume that tickled his nostrils. She gave a rehearsed speech about rehabilitation and independence, describing in a bored voice the programs for veterans, exercise classes and confidence building, as though they were children's games for a rainy day. When she was done, she asked if he had any questions.

He had only one. "When can I get my gun back?"

She rustled some papers. "You won't be getting your gun back, Sergeant. That wouldn't be advisable. But I heard from your Captain you've got a sweet tooth. Here." She placed a box in his lap. "He sent some Christmas cookies and a bar of chocolate."

He ate them. He was twenty-three and already getting fat. No matter. They couldn't keep him here forever. He would cooperate, do what he was told. He would become mobile and independent, like Captain Aidan said. He would learn to feed himself and dress himself and even use a cane if he had to, and once he learned how to get around on the streets and shop for himself, they would have to let him go. He would find an apartment somewhere, all by himself, and then he would buy himself a gun and put an end to this sham of a life.

———

The difference between night and day, which he had once thought lost to him forever, was perfectly clear, after a week or two of experience. He knew what time it was by the routines of the hospital. The scraping open of the windows, every morning at nine, no matter how cold the air. The smell of disinfectant when the janitors washed the floor on his ward, always at noon, no matter how it turned the stomachs of the men as they were served their midday meal. Most of the practical things at hand could be understood, without being seen. He recognized the voices of the different patients, the dampness of a pillowslip not hung long enough to dry, the taste of stale bread. The smell of smoke one night made him call out for the ward nurse, who discovered a cushion had fallen on a heater and begun to smoulder. He was not entirely useless.

But he remembered the sky. Its ever-shifting shapes and colours. Its breath. Once he'd wanted to transform its passing moments into paint, to slow time that way. Always, looking up, he'd known he was open to the space beyond, that nothing held him down except the warm, benevolent embrace of gravity. Deep in the heart of Manhattan, surrounded by skyscrapers that hemmed him in, he could always lean back and glimpse between the rooftops some measure of the sky. Even on the worst, most suffocating nights in the slit trenches, when clouds or bright exploding shells obscured the stars, there always came that moment when the stifling cover lifted and dissolved at dawn. The pearl-pale light, its rebirth every morning. Grace.

He never imagined God would take that from him.

Now a lid was fastened down upon the world. The narrow slots of his lungs contracted. Trapped. He could not draw breath. His dry throat was closing up.

"Nurse!" His voice was weak, an old man's voice. Why couldn't he simply die?

"Sergeant Garrison?" It was the perfumed one, who had given him candy.

"Water."

Immediately, she pressed the cool tin cup into his open palm. He clutched it, but he could feel that she was holding onto it too. She was raising it toward his mouth. With his other hand, he tried to push her away, but he succeeded only in spilling water over his sheets.

"There, there, never mind," she said, as if he were a child.

Reckless now, he lifted the cup with both hands to down the rest of the water, but there was more water left in the cup than he imagined, and it spilled onto his chin and down the collar of his pyjamas. He cursed.

"There, there," she said. "I'll fetch some more." The empty cup was taken from his grasp. A warm hand rested on his shoulder and was gone. "It's all right."

He was angry — with her, for treating him like a child, and with himself, because a small, forgotten part inside him was remembering a childhood in which never, not once, had he been treated with such tenderness. He wanted to curl up in the nurse's arms and cry. He might as well be dead, really, because he was no longer a man.

———

Frank dreamed that Connor was marching ahead of him with his boyish, loping gait, and no matter how fast Frank ran, he couldn't catch up. One night, full of anaesthetic after an ear operation, Frank dreamed he caught up at last and Connor turned to ask him, *Did you finish the Milton?* When Frank said no, Connor twisted his hips. His upper half swivelled outward like the hinge on the door of the skeleton box in his father's study, and rotated slowly in a circle. When his face came round again, it was a chalk-white skull, its two black orbits staring at nothing.

Then Frank was behind the wheel of a jeep, driving through the streets of New York, swerving around skyscrapers at high speed, the tires hugging the curves of the submerged dike that was the road, narrowly missing the freighters and German naval vessels, as the captain drilled him on the types of German artillery, *Schmeisser, Nebelwerfer, Panzerfaust,* and the jeep left the road and became airborne, water spewing from the back wheels as he rose among a fleet of metallic aircraft, their wings gleaming in the sun, but someone was tugging on his arm, holding him back. He pulled away, wanting to soar above the clouds and then someone said, "It's all right. You're safe. You're here at Bramshott." The scene vanished. The ships and planes and shining sky were gone. He could not see.

On waking, he thought of the planet Earth as a crumpled ball of paper, set on fire and burning itself out. He thought again of Milton's Satan, and the words that described his hell: *A Dungeon horrible, on all sides round / As one great Furnace flam'd, yet from those flames / No light, but rather darkness visible.*

He received a card from Connor's parents, and a sweet note from Connor's sister, Eileen. And letters from Dickie Lassiter and his parents. But he didn't answer any of them. Connor had shown him a new way to live, but that way was closed to him, now. No point writing to Connor's sister, or Dickie, or anyone from that life. He cringed to remember his own ambitions of mingling with such people. Of going to art school! A cruel joke. To think he had imagined himself at a magazine office, at one of those slanted drafting tables, sketching scenes of city life or illustrations for a book. Imagined his own paintings on a gallery wall.

He couldn't return to his former life. Before Connor, there was only dirt and sweat and a longing so fierce he'd thought sometimes it would wrench his heart wide open, a life in which he felt, but did not understand. He could never enter that life again, even if he wanted to. What use would Paolo have for him, now? Or Mr Gray, who taught him to draw? Or Mr Edison, who taught him carpentry? Or Mr Green at the grocery store? Even Corky — but Corky was a little boy, someone Frank had left behind a long, long time ago.

And where could he live, in Brooklyn? His cousins had lives of their own, now. Paul and Davey had families to raise. John Junior was starting a business. There was only his mother. His bigoted, ignorant

mother, with her sentimental Mass card. There was a picture of Jesus
on the card, holding a lamb, Captain Aidan had said, and the printed
words, *The Lord shall guide you.* The Lord! Didn't she realize, even
now, that the Lord despised him, had sent him into exile here in this
cramped cell with no escape?

———

In the utter darkness, distant noises. Rattling. Enemies trying the
door. A thump. Another thump. Nazis coming in at the windows.
Frank grabbed the nearest weapon and was about to heave it at the
window, when he realized he was in bed. His hand, above his head,
was gripping a grenade, or brick, what was it? He lowered his arm.
His hand was wrapped so tightly round a coffee mug it ached. He was
in the hospital. A cart came rumbling down the corridor. It must be
morning — no, he smelled disinfectant and vegetable soup and vomit.
It was lunchtime.

"Here you go." It was the Scottish nurse, the singer. She took the
grenade away. "I'm setting a bowl of soup here, and in a minute I'll be
back to help you with it."

Frank sat up. He did not want her spooning soup into his mouth
as if he were an infant. And he wasn't hungry. Sick of the smells on the
ward, he was craving fresh air. When the Scottish nurse came back, he
said, "Take me outside."

"Not in this weather," she said. "It's all fog and spitting."

"I'm going outside," he said. He stood. Took a step forward.

"Very well," she said, "since you are determined. But not in your
bare feet." She handed him his slippers and waited in silence as he
found the right one for each foot and put them on. Then she offered
her arm and led him away, until the familiar sounds and smells of
the ward faded behind them, and he heard only brisk footsteps and
the muted tinkle of silverware and glasses under a murmur of calm,
ordinary conversation.

"The staff cafeteria," said the Scottish nurse. "The girls are taking
their tea."

Soon she was pushing open a heavy door. Frank tried to help but
he only stepped on her foot and then suddenly they were outside.

For the first time in weeks he felt the cool air on his face. He
inhaled deeply. "Cedar trees," he said.

"Lord have mercy, how do you know that?"

"I can smell them," he said. A drop of cold water fell on his forehead and rolled down his face. He tasted it, rain. He was under the open sky again. "Is it cloudy?"

"It's a world of mist and fog," she said. "I can't see a foot in front of me." But she did not turn back. She led him through the grounds, under the dripping trees, and she sang the song of the Isle of Skye, letting him know she remembered he had liked it, and as he walked he could feel the soft, moist air all around him, as though he were buoyed up by clouds.

Priests and counsellors and doctors came to talk to Frank, to cheer him up and talk about his future. But he had no future. The only visitor he respected was a blinded veteran from the first war, a man named Benjamin Hudson, who came once a week and was content to sit at the side of the bed and listen, no matter how angry Frank was, no matter what fears he expressed.

He began to visit Frank in the winter, and by VE Day, he had become a friend. Frank's only friend.

"It's hard," said Benjamin, after they listened to the Victory celebrations on the radio. "Everyone's dancing in the streets, saying the war is over, but for you it's not over."

Frank was sitting up in bed, with his head against the wall and his legs straight out in front of him. He said nothing. He was thinking of the death camps the Americans had found in Europe. Last week a young hospital volunteer had read the newspaper reports to him and said, "I can't describe to you the photographs. They are obscene." But Frank heard details on the radio. The bottom of the world had opened up and men had fallen into hell. Women and children tortured, starved. Gassed and burned. And now they spoke of victory! What victory could they claim? They who had fought through the continent for years, yet never stopped these horrors? Never came to the rescue of these people? This was not a time to celebrate, to speak of victory, but a time to bow their heads in shame at their defeat.

"Let's walk," said Benjamin. "We'll take a turn around the grounds. Frank? Are you there?" He reached out and gave Frank's knee a shake. "Did you fall asleep?"

"The nurses are busy," said Frank.

"We don't need a nurse," said Benjamin. "I know these grounds. I have my cane."

Frank didn't dare admit his doubts that Benjamin could lead him safely through the grounds. He put on the shoes that Benjamin had brought him as a twenty-fourth birthday present. "How do we do this?" he asked.

Benjamin placed Frank's hand on his arm. "Just hang on lightly and walk." They moved together through the corridor and out to the grounds, Benjamin's cane scraping the floor and the stone steps and swishing through the tall grass on the lawn.

They instituted a regimen of walking every day, a little longer each time, and Frank felt strength returning to his legs. The aches and pains in his back eased up. He began to work out in the rehab unit, lifting hand weights. The exertion — even the pain — reminded him he was a man.

One afternoon Benjamin announced he wanted Frank to meet some visitors. In the cafeteria, he introduced Miss Sewell and Mr Gillis from Brighton, who had come on the train together to speak to Frank. Mr Gillis shook his hand, and Miss Sewell poured him a cup of tea and gave him a biscuit. They were from St Dunstan's Institute for the war blinded. Benjamin had attended St Dunstan's long ago, and wanted Frank to know about it.

Miss Sewell smelled of peppermints. She placed her hand on Frank's arm while she spoke in a sandpaper voice about manly fortitude and lives remade at jolly old St Dunstan's. Mr Gillis also put a hand on Frank's arm, his other arm. Frank felt as if he were being arrested by two policemen. Mr Gillis spoke of occupational training and independence. Frank knew this kind of people. The kind who wanted to show you how wisely they had lived their lives so as not to find themselves in the spot where you were. He remembered how much his mother had hated the social worker, Mrs Gray, and finally he understood why.

There was more a man could do besides making brooms, Mr Gillis said. St Dunstan's men trained to be masseurs, to operate kiosks, to roll cigars, to work as poultry farmers.

"Poultry?" asked Frank. He suppressed a laugh. "You mean chickens?"

"We have a saying at St Dunstan's," said Miss Sewell. "There is only one thing a blind person cannot do. He cannot see."

"Why, we even have an archery range on site," said Mr Gillis. "For target practice."

When Frank heard this, he had to laugh out loud. It was the first time he could remember laughing since coming out of Holland, but he did not enjoy it.

Back on the ward, he sat on his bed, fumbling with his shoelace, trying to find an end.

"You should consider St Dunstan's," Benjamin advised. "Even if you don't want the job training, they teach social skills. Eating and drinking. Personal grooming."

"Grooming!"

"Can you cut your own fingernails?" Benjamin asked. "Can you shave yourself?"

Frank tugged hard on the shoelace, and it broke in two. Enraged, he ripped the shoe from his foot.

"They're good people," Benjamin said. "They can help you."

"I don't need their bloody help," said Frank. He pitched his shoe across the room and heard it hit the wall with a satisfying smack.

"Hey!" said Benjamin. "You could hurt someone like that."

"They'd better keep out of my way, then," said Frank. "You tell them to keep away."

Two days later, Benjamin was back. He said nothing more, at first, about St Dunstan's. The two men walked the grounds, and when they returned to the ward, Frank sat on his bed and removed his shoes.

"You know," said Ben. "There is no reason you should be in bed."

"That's all they have here is beds," said Frank.

"At St Dunstan's you use your bed only for sleeping at night. The rest of the day you are up and doing. Just like normal."

That frightened Frank. Up and doing? Doing what? "Like normal?" he mocked. "Nothing is like normal anymore. And I don't want those two touching me and lecturing me and telling me I can have a productive life. What do they know about it?"

"They are both blind," Benjamin said. "Totally blind, just like you and me."

At first, Frank felt tricked, betrayed. Benjamin was the only person he trusted, because he thought of Benjamin as the only person who understood what it meant to lose your eyesight. But of course he wasn't the only one. There were many, many others. He remembered that the social workers had come up from London on the train together, just the two of them. Totally blind. That knocked the fight out of him. He regretted his bad manners.

5.3

As soon as the sun comes up, Von carries her tea and her new orange journal out to the rickety table on the hotel balcony to write. She needs this time alone. She's never been as far from home as she is right now, or stayed away so long. Never had to engage with so many strangers.

She writes down the story Marijke told her, about the day of the blinding. What would that feel like? How would the shock affect you, down to your bones? Marijke spoke with such gratitude for Frank's kindness that Von had barely recognized him. The strong man who carried a woman and child to safety, eased their fear, was not the father she remembered. He was twenty-three that day, she reminds herself. Not much older than Kyle is now. Yet burdened with terrible duty. Willing to give up all that he had, his own body. Grief washes over her. Loss. This man she'd known and never known. She had sometimes pitied him when he was alive, but she had never tried to imagine who he was.

———

When she hears a knock at the door, she assumes it's the hotel housekeepers. She jumps up, leaving her notebook open on the table. But it's Kyle. Back from France. She asks him about the trip, but he only says, "It was cool. We had a good time." He says he's glad Von's an early riser, because he's been up all night and he wants to ask her something.

"I saw you out on your balcony," he says. "Are you working on something?"

"I'm writing in my travel journal," Von says. "Keeping track of the trip, where we go and what we see. You should do it too. Here, wait."

She rummages in her bag and finds the brown notebook. "I got this for you. It'll fit in your backpack."

"Gee, thanks," he says, without enthusiasm.

"I'll make us some coffee," Von says. By the time she returns, with two cups on a tray, he is standing over the table, turning the pages of her notebook, reading.

He looks up. "Why are you writing about your dad in your trip journal?"

"I've been thinking about him." She sets down the tray, closes the notebook cover. "After looking at all those pictures."

"Me too. Thanks." He takes a cup of coffee and spoons in sugar. "There's more about him in my mum's yellow scrapbook. A lot about the Battle of the Scheldt, in the south. I was thinking we should go down to that place where he was, you know, where he was wounded."

"Bergen-op-Zoom."

"There's a train that goes right there." Kyle is an expert, now, on the European rail system. "It's just a small town, but they have a war memorial, and a Canadian cemetery. There's directions in the scrapbook, and an article about a ceremony they had there back in 1995. Did you read it?"

"I read it," Von says. "Long time ago."

Rosheen had pressured Von to take their father there, although by then he was in no shape to travel. Rosheen phoned many times from Brooklyn, trying to talk Von into it. She said Von should call the DVA, rent a wheelchair, hire a nurse, do whatever it took to get him there. "You're not the one who has to look after him!" Von had shouted. And Rosheen had shouted back, "No! I'm the one who's *not allowed* to look after him!"

"So what do you think?" Kyle asks. "Shouldn't we go there? It's on my mum's list, to photograph Bergen-op-Zoom."

"Is that what you wanted to ask me about?"

He shakes his head. Exhales. "Meredith always says if you want to know something you should just come out with it." He places his cup on the table and moves to the balcony railing and leans over. From the street below, the sounds of morning traffic. A busker tuning a guitar. Without turning around, Kyle asks, "Did she ever talk about me?"

The busker strums a few chords. "Ode to Joy." Did Rosheen ever talk about Kyle? Certainly not to Von, who had refused to see her for nearly as long as Kyle's been alive. Even the few times Von had relented in recent years, Rosheen never mentioned Kyle. Or never dared to mention him... Why didn't she dare? Von has never asked herself that question. She listens to the music from below, exquisite movement, rising from note to note, a celebration.

"I think she wanted to talk about you," Von says. "But —" *She was afraid of me. I intimidated her, my temper...* She doesn't know where this sudden thought has come from, but it stuns her with its audacity, its truth. "Maybe you should ask Durgan," she suggests. "Or ask some of her friends in Brooklyn."

Kyle turns and faces her, fires the next question. "Why did she give me away?"

"It wasn't like that," Von says. "She didn't *give* you away. She was having a hard time, and everyone just thought it would be better if the Penners looked after you for a while, and then, later... What did they tell you?"

"They just said she wasn't well enough. And she wasn't married. They said she was too young to handle a baby all on her own. Why was she all on her own? Where were you?"

"I was — she felt that, that the Penners would be the best choice, being married and everything. They were a stable family. Registered foster parents. A nice home in the country, and then, when Rosheen was a little older and she had solved some of her problems, everyone thought it wouldn't be right to move you. The Penners were the only parents you knew. You were starting school. It wasn't a good time."

"Right," says Kyle. He places both hands behind him on the railing and hangs his head, as if interested in the balcony floor. "What kind of problems, the drinking?"

"Yes. And the drugs." She hesitates. "That can be inherited, you know."

"I'll be okay," he says.

"She loved you very much."

"That's what the Penners always said."

Von takes their empty cups back inside. She rests her fists on the counter for a minute, closes her eyes and curses under her breath. It's not his fault. All he wants is to know about his mother. To know Rosheen. Impossible desire. He has no idea what he's asking for. Then she remembers the envelope of photographs from Marijke. She pulls it out of her purse and beckons him through the balcony's glass door. He comes back in.

"Tell you what," she says. "We'll go to Bergen-op-Zoom. We'll go and see the cemetery, if you want. But for now, let's look at some of the people who *survived* the Battle of the Scheldt." She begins to lay Marijke's photos out across the table, and to tell the tale.

5.4

"There is nothing so unpleasant to the sighted as a blind man with his head lolling at an angle or staring at nothing," the instructor warned. "You must hold your head high. Chin raised. Face forward. Neck steady. Those who have been advised to wear dark glasses should do so at all times, even indoors. For if people are not comfortable being near you, smooth social relations will become impossible."

St Dunstan's instructors were full of this type of advice. Keep the lips curved upward when in public. Move slowly, lest you touch a person's body. Those who were totally blind should learn to say, "I am totally blind," for otherwise they could not be distinguished from those with partial sight. Those with missing limbs should wear their prostheses even in the home, for the comfort of spouses, children, and visitors. It was a kind of a monster school, Frank said to Benjamin, for learning how to be a monster.

"I'm glad to see you're getting your sense of humour back," Benjamin said.

"I never had a sense of humour," said Frank.

"There was a guy I knew," said Benjamin, "who got a bullet through the wrist. Shattered it. He was up in the Silver Street hospital with me. When the surgeon came on rounds, the guy asked him, 'Doc, will I be able to play the piano?' and the surgeon examined his wrist and said, 'Sure, you'll be able to play just fine, once the wound heals up.' So the guy says, 'Gee, Doc, that is a miracle. I always wished I could play the piano.'"

"Very funny," said Frank. "Help me with this blasted tie, will you?"

At St Dunstan's there were dozens of lessons: how to tie an ascot, how to polish shoes, clean fingernails, fold clothing, find the clothing you'd folded, and walk with the aid of a cane. Frank practised walking whenever he could.

St Dunstan's was built at the top of a long hill that sloped up from the sea. Long walkways, with railings at waist height, covered the hillside. The chaplain took Frank for a tour, providing commentary on the landscape, the ocean view, the impressive windswept cliffs. Beyond the walkway railings, he warned, was a steep drop to the sea. On stormy days, the waves crashed against the sheer rock walls, and a fine cold mist rose high into the air. Frank soon mastered the St Dunstan's grounds on his own. The network of walkways was simple. If you felt yourself descending, you were moving away from the building. To get back, you only needed to turn around and begin the ascent. The walkways stretched across the grounds in all directions, but all of them converged in the end at the doors of St Dunstan's. There was no way to get lost. And no escape.

Unless, perhaps, if he ducked under the railing at the spot where the chaplain said the cliff was at its highest point, he could step off the edge. But was the drop sheer? If you flung your body off the top of the cliff, would it fall into the sea? Or land on the rocks? He didn't want to wake up mutilated on the rocks. Possibly paralyzed or brain damaged. Worse off than he already was. He wondered if the tide would make a difference. At high tide, perhaps, he could be sure to drown. If only he could see the side of the cliff, he'd know. He imagined it often. It became his future. Middle of the night, full tide, clean drop into the sea.

Nevertheless, he attended the Braille lessons. If forced to concentrate on writing his name by punching a needle through little holes in a tin plate, he couldn't think about anything else. At night, when all was quiet, and he had to stay in bed, his thoughts tormented him. The wire had not sliced easily through the German boy's throat, no. He'd had to saw through. Hold the boy's body tight against his own, bend his leg and jam his knee into the boy's back. Grip the garrotte with both hands. Pull on one handle and then the other, again and again, saw and saw, while the boy's arms flailed and his torso squirmed. It was this death that had stamped itself most deeply into his own body, its physicality—the consistency of the flesh, like a tough rare steak, the sounds of the crushed throat and cracked bone, the gurgling and gushing and the stink of blood and shit. It was his most visceral memory and the one that always came first in the grim midnight parade. It would play itself over again like a scratched phonograph record, if he did not allow the other deaths to crowd it out. The man who stood beside him in the slit trench, how he'd lifted his helmet to wipe the sweat from his eyes and crumpled to the ground, a hole in his forehead. The way a man's guts squeezed out of his body when a tank, no he would not, the screams of the boy with no hands. Connor's eyes still looking at him, though his head was, no he would not think of that, he would think instead of the night sky, stars, and then came that moment when he'd placed his fingers into the eye sockets of his own skull. To remember that was to relive the certainty, the full understanding of what a man was. Live meat. For a short time. Then a slab like any other dead animal.

When he slept, he had vivid nightmares that ended with explosions so loud he woke with a jolt, as if fallen from a great height, his heart beating fast, and often when he woke he was not in his dorm. One night he regained consciousness in the lounge on the main floor. He only discovered where he was by crawling across the floor and bumping into the radio console. How had he gotten down the two flights of winding stairs and through the labyrinth of hallways he could barely manage in the daytime? It seemed as though his body was attempting to escape his mind. The chaplain was trained in psychology, and whenever he asked Frank if there was anything he wanted to discuss, Frank made sure to say no. He didn't want to hear the chaplain diagnose his condition. Maybe it was what they used to call shell shock or, more likely, he was plain crazy. If anyone found out the truth, Frank was certain they'd bury him so deep in the hospital system he would never get out. And he had to get out. He'd never find a way to put an end to himself in here, where he was always being watched. He knew now he couldn't find his way to a clear fall from the top of the cliffs, not by himself. He had to stick to his original goal. Learn enough skills to become independent. Then they would have to let him go. So he kept quiet about the nightmares and the sleepwalking, or whatever it was. The only people he told, in the privacy of his mind, were his father, Tomas, and his friend Connor. Being dead, they understood. They were waiting patiently for him.

When Frank had been at St Dunstan's eight weeks, the head instructor announced a field trip to a local fair on the weekend. Everyone was to go by bus to the fair, where there would be prizes for the fattest piglets and the fleeciest lambs. There was to be a music festival and the men could purchase cakes and pies at the baking table. They would get good practice at manoeuvring through crowds.

On the morning of the field trip, Frank begged off because of a headache. He always had a headache, though he rarely mentioned it. It normally began as a low ache in his jaw mid-morning, then ticked its way into his temples and thumped across his forehead all day long, veering close to a scream near dinnertime and subsiding again once he had eaten. On the day of the fair, it was especially vicious. He wanted only to do nothing and be nothing and think of nothing all day.

"You'll be alone in the building if you stay behind," the instructor warned.

"I'll manage," Frank said.

She gave him a bag lunch, and with a stylus she wrote the telephone number of her own parents, who lived nearby, in case he needed help.

The bus departed at eight in the morning, in the rain, leaving Frank with the gigantic building all to himself. He made his way to the lounge and turned on the radio. Right away he ate his lunch, a tomato and cheddar sandwich, an apple, and a cookie. Then he stretched his legs out on the couch and listened to the Ink Spots sing "If I Didn't Care." His headache eased a bit, and the music kept the dark thoughts in his mind at bay.

He woke to a knocking on the door, and a deep Cockney voice calling, "Hi! Isn't anybody home? Anybody home?"

He sat up. He lifted the crystal of his new watch and checked the hands. Ten thirty. Peggy Lee was on the radio—"It's All Over Now"—and the rain was drumming hard on the windows, a heavy downpour. He groped around and found his cane. The voice at the door called out, "I can't stop any longer. I got to get back to town."

As he reached the lobby, Frank felt a blast of cold wind, heard rain splash on the front steps, and then the door slammed shut. The man was gone. Had he left a delivery of some kind?

Frank heard a sneeze, the squeak and squelch of wet shoes. He said, "Hello?"

"Oh, hello!" A surprised voice. A young fellow. British and timid.

"Do you have some business here?" Frank asked.

"I'm... It's me. I'm the business. My name's Eddy Anderson? From London? Someone was supposed to meet me at the station."

"I don't know anything about that," said Frank. "What is it you want?"

"I, uh, don't want anything. I don't even want to be here." His voice broke, and he cleared his throat. "My doctor recommended it. My mother said I had to come."

"How old are you?"

"Nineteen."

"And you're a veteran?"

"152 Ambulance. Italian campaign. I waited a long time in the rain. There was no one there until the station opened at ten. Then the ticket agent came and put me in a taxi."

"A mix-up," said Frank. There was nothing for it. He slid his cane across the floor and touched something. Bending to examine it, he felt a duffel bag, soaked through. And a damp trouser leg, with a bony knee inside it.

The kid yelped. "That's my knee!"

"I figured that," said Frank. "Come on." He grasped the boy's clammy sleeve. "I'll get you something dry to wear."

Frank led him up to his own room, where he found a towel, trousers and a shirt. Socks and slippers, exactly where he'd stored them. The St Dunstan's method was paying off.

Frank's clothes were too big, so he helped the kid roll up the pant legs and shirt sleeves and found a belt so the pants wouldn't fall off. He even had to help him thread the belt through the belt loops and get the prongs of the buckle through the right holes. Who dressed this kid every morning? No wonder his mother wanted him out of the house.

"I'm kind of hungry," the boy said.

"Of course." Frank wished he hadn't eaten his lunch so early. The cooking staff was off for the day, because of the field trip. But he thought of the pantry in the practice kitchen. Just yesterday, he'd explored the layout, learning where the utensils and the food were kept, and how to place his finger in a glass while pouring, to keep from overfilling it. The men had practised with red wine, and had drunk it afterwards. The recorked bottle should still be in the fridge.

"Let's go and get some lunch," he said.

The kid gripped Frank's arm tight with both hands and hesitated on every step down the stairs. Even when they reached the main floor, he hung on, dragging his feet. Frank shook him gently. "Loosen up," he said. "Trust me. There's a kitchen right along here. It's part of the rehab unit." He ran his hand along the wall. The rehab kitchen was on the left. He hoped there would be some cookies or sliced bread in there, something easy to serve.

But he couldn't find the kitchen. He must have missed the door and got turned around somehow. He led the kid through the halls, blundering into the boiler room and the laundry room. When they ended up in a janitor's closet, he gave the kid a push broom. Slight improvement. The kid pushed the broom before him as he walked and didn't lean on Frank so much. Finally, after half an hour of wandering, Frank heard, in the distance, the voice of Perry Como. The radio.

He followed the music to the lounge and started all over again. This time he found his way to the rehab kitchen without incident. He settled the kid at a table and searched the pantry, lifting lids and smelling things. Cinnamon, flour, tea. Inscrutable tinned goods. His hands found a flat metal tin with a key attached to its side. Sardines! He could handle this. He broke the key off and set it down while he searched for the metal tab along the edge of the can. He found it, pulled it upright, and reached for the key. But he moved too fast. His hand pushed the key off the counter. He heard the dull plink as it hit the floor and bounced. Somewhere. He got down on his hands and knees and swept the floor with his palms. He found a dried pea or a bean of some sort, but no metal key, though it had to be right in front of him.

The kid was patient. He didn't complain or ask any questions, though he must have been starving. Frank remembered bitterly what it was like to have to wait to be fed. As a kid he'd sometimes begged on his knees for food. He'd sworn he'd never be in that position again. He ran his fingers again and again along the floor until he found the key at last.

Now the trick was to fit the tin's metal tab into the slit of the key blade. He had done this hundreds of times back in Brooklyn. He ran his thumbnail along the blade of the key until he found the slit. But it seemed impossible to get the tab into it. He held the can still with one hand and held the key in his other hand, feeling with his fingertips for the tab. Ah, the tab slid in. Damn, it slid out. In. Out. Finally he got it in and turned the key. Nothing happened. The tab had slipped out again. He wanted to scream, beat the wall with the sardine can, but instead he fit the tab back into the slit and tried to crimp the end of it with his fingers, so it couldn't slide out. Again, he turned the key. This time he felt the tension. He exerted more pressure and heard the tiny pop that meant he'd made a hole in the can. Now if he could keep turning it steadily, in a straight line, he'd peel a strip of tin off all the way around and — ah, he could smell the fish.

———

At long last, Frank and Eddy had a feast. Sardines, crackers, figs, and two glasses of wine — Frank had been tempted just to pass the bottle between them, but since he had already come so far, he went to the trouble to find the glasses and use his new pouring skills. He felt victorious. And ridiculous. It had taken him two and a half hours to get Eddy into dry clothes and feed him. He lifted the bottle and shook it. A few ounces left. He poured a little more for both of them.

"Cheers," he said.

"Cheers," said Eddy. "Can I ask you something? My mother sent me here to learn to read and write and count money, so I can work in the store. My family has a clothing store. In Chelsea. Is it true you can learn all that here? If you can't see?"

"Is that what you want to do, work in the clothing store?"

"I wanted to teach. I was supposed to go to Cambridge and read history."

"But you went to war."

"For six days. It happened six days after I got there. I was putting a load of stretchers in a truck. I never saw the sniper. The bullet went in the side of my face and behind my eyes. Came out the other side, right here." He thought about that. "In front of my right temple. Zipped in and out, just grazed me. But it took out both eyes. That was one month before the war ended."

"Jesus," said Frank. Every soldier here had a horror story. Eddy's was different only because he was so young. "You've been in the hospital all this time?"

"I wasn't in hospital long at all. I got sent home and that's where I've been, nearly a year. I never went out. Finally my mother said I could

come here and get training or go on the street and beg. So here I am."
Now that Eddy was warm and fed, his immediate distress relieved, his
basic terror was showing through. "Is it hard to learn Braille?"

"It wouldn't be hard for you," said Frank. He wanted to cheer the
kid up. "Say, there's some nice girls come to read for the men here." Then
he remembered the tape library. "Upstairs, there's a whole room full of
books already read on tapes. You can probably listen to any history
book you want. You could probably study to be a history teacher, right
here."

"I can't teach," said Eddy. "Look at me!"

"I wish I could."

They both laughed. Briefly. They drained their glasses. Frank
thought they should stay seated until the wine wore off. He didn't
want to get lost in the halls again.

"Some men do teach," Frank said. "There was a fellow came
through here who teaches now up at a school for blind children in
Scotland. He sent us a letter just last week."

"How does he live?"

"He has an apartment. Goes shopping. Makes his own dinner.
Like we just did."

Eddy was quiet. Maybe he was thinking about being a teacher.
Maybe he was thinking a blind person didn't have to be helpless.
Maybe this would help him. It had been a long time, Frank realized,
since he'd been able to help anyone. Since he'd even thought about
helping anyone.

———

When Frank had first arrived, they'd told him about the tape library,
but he'd been sunk so far inside himself he hadn't paid attention. Now,
when he wanted to get Eddy a history book, he asked the librarian's
help in searching the titles. It was a request that changed his life. He
discovered not only history books, but plays, philosophy, natural
science, poetry. He learned to thread the reels of tape into the big
recorders to listen to Shakespeare, Dickens, Yeats, the Brownings. He
read George Bernard Shaw and Albert Camus, excited that men could
believe in goodness and hope without believing in God.

"Have you ever considered going to university?" the resident
social worker asked.

Frank thought of Lenore, the Nova Scotia farm girl he had loved. How she had confided so easily to him her bold ambitions. He had not understood her, then. He hadn't known what it meant to study. He had barely read a newspaper. But Connor had given him an education. Connor and his friends had shared their books and their ideas with him.

"Yes," he said. "The University of Toronto. I'd like to study philosophy and poetry."

"Have you considered what profession you might enter?" the worker asked.

"I've always been interested in social work," Frank said.

———

Within a year, Frank was well read. He had passed two years' worth of examinations in high school history, mathematics, and science. He could make soup, count money, and shave himself. He could even do some carpentry. They gave him a brass bowl with the St Dunstan's insignia on it, and sent him to Canada. He was scheduled for plastic surgery, in Montreal, to reconstruct his left ear. When he recovered from the surgery, he could live at Baker Hall, a home for the war blinded in Toronto. There, he could finish upgrading his education and apply to university.

He could not return to the United States. He was to be discharged from the forces. Unfit for service. But he was a veteran of the Canadian army, so eligible for a veteran's pension, and the Canadian government would cover his medical expenses and tuition. If he went back to the States, he'd be on his own. He'd have to rely on his family. Was that possible? a social worker asked him. Frank shook his head. No. He had lost his country and adopted a new one. He was in exile now.

5.5

———

DEIRDRE STOOD IN THE FALLING SNOW ON A SWANKY TORONTO street, a week before Christmas. She had not seen her son for seven years. She consulted the paper on which Father Madden had written the address. Yes, this was the place. But it didn't look like a home for the blind. It looked like a rich person's house on a rich person's street.

With Christmas decorations in all the windows. What did they need so many windows for?

A young lady answered the bell and asked who she wished to see. As Deirdre spoke her son's name, the lady smiled, very politely, without judgement or pity, and invited her in. Deirdre was nervous. She didn't want to meet any blind men and certainly didn't want to be surrounded by them. They were bad luck. But Father Madden had shamed her into coming. He said her son needed her. The son who had abandoned her to run off to the wars.

The young lady asked her to wait in the long, carpeted front hall, which was gaily decorated with pictures on the walls and pretty furniture. A fancy place, this Baker Hall. She supposed they kept it nice for the visitors. She was relieved to be the only person here. She sat on the edge of a chair while the young lady went up the wide staircase to fetch Frank.

Minutes later, a stream of blind men entered the room, completely unsupervised. They were talking loudly of something—sports of some kind, she thought—and laughing. Why were they laughing? They began to take seats, and she jumped up, terrified lest one of them might sit on her. She could think of no way to let them know she was there. Appalled and somewhat sick to her stomach, she tiptoed to a corner, where she stood and watched them from a distance, keeping one eye on the staircase where she expected the girl would soon appear, escorting Frank.

But suddenly Frank arrived, running recklessly down the stairs, all by himself. Had he been cured? He hugged her briefly and made her sit beside him on a sofa and asked about her journey from New York. She stared at the dark lenses of his glasses. Could he see her?

"I want to see your face," she said.

"Go ahead, then." Frank sat up straight and perfectly still.

She removed the dark glasses and looked at him. Holy Mary, Mother of God. What had they done to her son? She forced herself to examine the damage. The glass eyes were the wrong colour. A dull, dark blue. And his poor face. The skin beneath the left eye pulled away from the socket, like bread dough stretched too thin, leaving a gap below the glass eyeball, where mucus gathered. A strip of colourless skin extended down his cheek, curved around what used to be his upper lip, and disappeared inside his mouth. This strip of skin was too short. Like a hook, it tugged up the corner of his mouth, holding it open, displaying the teeth and the gum. He looked as though he'd been torn and mended by one of her sewing assistants, one of the clumsy ones.

She peered again into the glass eyes, but they were opaque, revealing nothing. Was Frank even in there? She realized she could not really see her son. He was lost to her. The light of Daniel Mac Michael, the lively blue-green light that Frank had carried within him all those years, was gone from the world.

He told her of his goals for the future, his plan to study social work. Social work! Was there no end to the shocks she must endure? As he spoke, she watched the other blind men in the room. One of them had only one leg. Yet for some reason, he persisted in pacing back and forth, telling some tale to the others. Each time he passed, she drew back to avoid him — luckily, the blind were easy to avoid. But he veered close to her, again and again, swinging by on his crutches, his empty pant leg flapping. She couldn't help but interpret his presence as a sign from God. A reminder of Daniel Mac Michael. But what such a sign might mean she could not tell.

5.6

Before he moved to Canada, Frank had written to Connor's sister, Eileen, telling her his news. She wrote back to say she was glad for him. But she was in mourning. Her father had died, and her mother, inconsolable, had sold the big house and moved back to Dublin to be near her brothers and to help look after her own aging parents. Eileen was the only member of the Flynn family left in Canada. She planned to study English at Victoria College, at the University of Toronto, and live in residence there. She was lonely, she said. She missed her family, and she missed her childhood home, with its beautiful conservatory, which had been a comfort to her in her grief. Frank must come to see her when he arrived.

Baker Hall was walking distance from Victoria College. On the first few mornings after Frank arrived, Eileen came to call for him and walked with him to the College until he learned how to find his own way. When he told her the story of Martha Waters, who used to shepherd him to public school in Williamsburg, she laughed. "I won't let you get away," she said.

She reminded him of Connor, with her easy attitude, her confidence. He felt drawn to her, though he knew he was not of her class, not on her level. Without the presence of her father, and her father's big house, she seemed somehow more approachable, and gradually, with her gracious manner, she made him feel he was her friend. She brought the campus alive to him, describing the layout of the buildings, the walls of brick and stone, the ivy and the stained-glass windows, the types of flowers in the gardens, the black squirrels in the trees — and he constructed a model of it in his mind. They discovered they were in the same English class, with Professor Frye, and arranged to lunch together on the days of their English lectures.

On a late October day of his first year as a university student, Frank stood on the steps in front of Annesley Hall, the woman's residence, waiting for Eileen. The autumn sun was warm on his face, and the wind whisked the fallen leaves across the grass, a slight whisper, and across the brick walkway, a crisp rustling, and across the stone steps, a louder scraping sound. He listened to the students passing by, the low murmur of earnest voices, words caught on the wind, *football, hamburgers, anthropology*, the light steps of girls and their laughter. He felt his lungs expand and understood suddenly that he was alive. He had decided to live. He had survived the war, the painful medical procedures, the indignity of rehabilitation. He had learned to read Braille and carry a white cane. The doctors had given him a new face, and he had practised hard to speak with a Canadian accent. He'd sweated in the gymnasium to rebuild his muscles, learned a different way to swim, to walk, to wash the floor, to cook an egg and open a goddamned sardine can. How to hammer in a nail and saw a board straight, even use power tools. Most of all, he'd studied. He'd read Shelley and Sartre and Bertrand Russell and understood a lot of it.

He was here. The University of Toronto. A place name he'd first heard long ago, on the lips of Lenore, the Canadian girl who'd pronounced it with such longing she had made it seem like some enchanted castle. He wondered if she had ever earned enough money to take classes here. He felt sure she'd managed it. She'd been so determined. He wondered how long it might have taken her to get here, and if she were here still. He dared not imagine meeting her again. What would she think of him, now? Would she even recognize him? He barely recognized himself. Sometimes he felt he was not himself at all, but some lesser creature, pieced together from the broken ruins of Frank Garrison, some usurper who had seized control of him while he was at his weakest, used his blindness as an entry to the upper-class life. Deep within himself, he felt this creature gloating.

Frank managed his studies with the help of Eileen and women volunteers at the university, who read to blinded veterans. Frank was surrounded by women volunteers. Women came to Baker Hall from the Junior League and the Volunteer Aid Detachment and various churches and clubs, and they devoted long hours to the residents. Women volunteers escorted the men to doctor's appointments, took them shopping or bowling, drove them to church and read to them and took dictation. These last services were especially important to those who were students. Frank knew he could never get through his courses without the help of these women. If ever one of them was slow, or made mistakes, he tried to keep his temper in check, reminding himself that he should be grateful. He should put on a cheerful disposition. But it was a struggle.

Frank worked hard at all his studies, except for the poetry course that he and Eileen were taking. That wasn't something he had to work at, but something he loved. When Dr Frye read the poems out loud, Frank remembered how he used to feel in church. He no longer went to church. God had banished Frank, and Frank had not forgiven Him. Yet poetry moved him the way the music of the church service used to move him. The best poems reached in deep, past the mass of scar tissue that entombed him, and in every class, Dr Frye read poems out loud. He read Blake and Milton and John Donne. In their own way, Frank thought, all these men were angry with their God. He didn't think Professor Frye was likely to agree with that idea. But Frank could hear the anger, in the pauses at the ends of the lines and in the images — that tyger burning bright, that darkness visible, that battered heart. Yes. Frank knew exactly what those poems were all about.

When Dr Frye spoke of vision and prophecy, Frank remembered the long fluttering cypress trees of Vincent Van Gogh at the New York Museum of Modern Art. He would never again see those branches flicker like green flames, yet he could feel them. They were still inside him, like a slow shudder through his body. And when he stood alone, outside, in an open space, he felt the sky, its depth and undulating rhythms. He could sense its infinite expanse above him. He came to understand that he possessed an inner vision that could not be taken from him. He remembered the long dark eyelashes of Lenore, the curls that fell across her forehead when, feeling shy, she looked down at her hands, twisting on her finger the little silver ring she'd earned at Sunday school, by memorizing Scripture.

———

He did not know, could not imagine, what he looked like. He remembered his embarrassment, at twelve, on catching a glimpse of himself in the mirror at the Grays' house back in Brooklyn, skinny and dirty, gobbling pie. A boy who took whatever he could get as quickly as he could, before someone snatched it from him or chased him or beat him or called him a retard. He remembered, at twenty, seeing his own face beside Connor's and Dickie's in the shaving mirror, proud to stand among such honourable comrades, to be a man with a purpose. And now? He was neither that boy nor that man. He didn't know, yet, who he would turn out to be. All he knew was to keep on reading, to memorize, recite, to push himself to follow the difficult arguments of the philosophers, to listen in history class to the dates and the names of the generals and the names of the cities they burned and pretend that such facts provided a knowledge of war. He knew he must never, ever speak of what he had seen and heard and smelled and most especially what he had felt, what he felt now. He mustn't speak of those things even at Baker Hall, where he was not the only one who woke up screaming or in unfamiliar places on occasion. One blinded vet had been stopped by a policeman in the middle of the night for walking down Admiral Road in his pyjamas. Another put his fist through the wall in the bathroom. Many drank alcohol until they vomited or passed out. And poor Jones, a quiet man whom Frank had barely known, managed to hang himself with a bed sheet from a rafter in the cellar. Officially, it was said that he had "died suddenly." Nobody spoke of the cause.

Sometimes he felt within his body a hunger sharp as the hunger he'd known as a boy — not for food, or for a better life, but for freedom from the prison of this silence. On Remembrance Day, the vets of Baker Hall marched to the cenotaph, medals on their chests. They made their way through the Toronto streets with canes and dogs, a parade of the maimed, and afterwards Frank heard that the neighbours had grumbled, on seeing them return. "Why should we have to witness such a pitiful sight, here in our own homes, from our own front porches?" But the newspaper described them as blinded heroes, and they all knew what it meant to be a hero. It was a job description, a role the country allowed them to play. Being a hero was much preferred over being a pitiful sight that spoiled your neighbours' day. So the men were stoic, or daring, or jocular, or sometimes rough and angry, but above all, on the topic of nightmares or crying or hanging themselves, they were entirely silent.

Frank never forgot Lenore, though he tried not to think of her. He remembered her warm body and her high ambitions. He remembered her Nova Scotia accent and her husky voice, and although he had not heard it for six long years he recognized it right away when he heard it again on campus one spring day. He was standing outside the Dean's office, and he heard Lenore distinctly through an open window. She must have been working there, as a typist, because she said, "I left the carbons wif the letters on your desk. I'm goin' to lunch now."

All along he had hoped and feared that he might meet her here. Now, any minute, she would be coming out the front door of the college. She would pass right by him. He waited, with the cold March wind stinging his face. He remembered to raise his chin and lift the corners of his lips into a smile.

He listened to the students moving up and down the stone stairs, some shuffling, some running, some brisk and deliberate. A group of girls, their heels click-clacking together, all speaking at once, and among them, Lenore. Her innocent, too-loud laugh. She was telling a story.

"Lenore?" Frank called. "Lenore, is that you?"

She stopped talking. He heard whispers, a nervous giggle.

"Lenore?"

A hand on his shoulder. A man's voice. "Say, who are you? Lenore, do you know this fellow?"

"It's me," he said. He tried to step forward, but the man's hand pressed gently, firmly against his chest. "Lenore? It's me. Frank Garrison."

He recognized her cry. "Oh, no. No!"

"See here," said the man. "You're upsetting the girl."

He heard her friends rally round her, purring, "Are you all right? Lenore, what's the matter? Who *is* that?"

He heard the muffled sound of her crying become distant. Her friends must have hustled her away, and then Connor's sister, Eileen, was there, oblivious, saying, "Sorry I'm late. Shall we go to class?"

Frank took Eileen's arm and walked with her to the lecture hall, grateful for her chatter about her morning tea and her new spring jacket and the latest letter from her mother.

For a long time, he waited, expecting Lenore to seek him out. He knew he was easy to find. He walked past the Dean's office every day on his way to lectures. All she had to do was come out the door and say hello to him. He would tell her that he understood. It must have given her a shock, seeing him so unexpectedly, seeing he was blind. He could forgive her for that. But she did not give him the chance to forgive her. She kept her distance. Perhaps she wasn't allowed to leave her desk, he thought. But he knew from other girls who worked on campus that the Dean was not so very strict. Besides, Frank and the few other blinded veterans were well known on campus. She would only have to make a few inquiries, or telephone Baker Hall. So he knew she was avoiding him.

Naturally, she would want a normal man, not a monster. And naturally, she would not want to remember the intimacies she had shared with him. He had never violated the virginity of her body, but he had kindled in her, and himself, a fervent desire. He thought of those ardent hours and how innocent she'd been, wanting them to be true, to be forever. Whenever he passed her office, he was conscious that she might be looking at him from her window. He clenched his cane tightly, felt his hands coil into fists.

As graduation approached, newspaper reporters began to come to campus, or to knock on the door at Baker Hall, wanting an angle for a human interest story. As though they had all read the same book on how to interview the blind, they invariably asked the same question:

"What was the last thing you saw?" Then Frank would remember the rising hem of the Dutch woman's dress, her white thighs. Marijke. He wondered where she and her little brother, Hans, might be now, whether they'd survived that day and the long winter of hunger that followed, whether she ever thought of him. He remembered how the "Moonlight Serenade" played on while the light of the world went out.

"Moonlight," he said. "The last thing I saw was the moonlight shining on the Scheldt."

Dickie Lassiter, who was walking like a normal person now, brought his parents to visit Frank at Baker Hall. Dickie's father grasped Frank's hand and held it a long time before embracing him. "I can never thank you enough for what you did at Dieppe," he said. "You saved our son. So many dead —" He choked a bit. "If it weren't for you, our boy would be among them."

"We were all in it together, Mr Lassiter," said Frank. He could feel the man's warm tears against his own cheek. "We looked out for each other."

"Let me hug him, too." Dickie's mother. Her small hand on his sleeve, the scent of her perfume. "Thank you for saving my boy."

Frank would never hear those words from Connor's mother.

"I only did what any of us would do, Mrs Lassiter." He ushered his guests into the parlour, and one of the volunteers brought them tea. Baker Hall was known for its hospitality. Frank told Dickie and his parents about the concerts and lecture series the men hosted. Mr Lassiter said he thought it was splendid the way the men in the house all got around. He was very impressed that Frank was going on to a master's program in social work, and pledged to help him however he could.

It was the volunteers who helped organize most activities at Baker Hall. Their aim was to improve the social skills of the men. When Deirdre came for a second visit, and saw the men all dancing, so gracefully and with such well-dressed women, she believed at first they had miraculously regained their sight. But Frank explained it was all about practice.

"There is only one thing a blind man cannot do," he told her. "He cannot see."

Deirdre was quiet for a moment. Then she said, "Why, that's true, isn't it?"

Perhaps, he thought, his mother was maturing. He should be patient. He reminded himself that she had little education. And that he needed her.

It was when sighted visitors came to call that the men were at their best and most reckless. Charging down the stairs at top speed was a favourite trick, or dropping a casual mention of their fencing lessons. They delighted in the horrified gasps of the ladies and the forthright admiration of the men who came to visit.

Eileen came at least once a week, even after she graduated with her English degree. She made friends with many of the residents, played cribbage with them, and took an interest in their future plans. She had a gift for making the men feel at ease, teasing them light-heartedly, until even the surly ones had to laugh. She arranged for a number of girls she knew to come to the Hall, and introduced them to her favourites. Several men, convinced no woman would ever want them, found themselves the objects of attention, invited to picnics and church suppers and sometimes even home to meet a girl's parents.

Most parents were opposed, at first, to their daughters dating the mutilated, although many a girl's father was intrigued, despite his misgivings, by the daring feats and eerie knowledge of the blind, how they could detect, by vibrations, the presence of nearby objects. "Like a bat," said the father of a girl Frank dated one summer. Frank liked to exaggerate these powers. On a car trip to the lake, he claimed he could tell how far they had travelled by sensing each milepost that they passed. The family was impressed. No matter that Frank, not knowing the girl had closed the car window, tossed a handful of cherry pits hard against the glass and sent them flying through the vehicle's interior, bouncing off people's heads.

"The window was so clean," Frank said later, "I thought it was open."

The sighted people laughed nervously, unsure whether that was a joke.

Frank was never very serious about the girls he dated in Toronto. But as the years went by, he felt his friendship with Eileen grow deeper. They shared their memories of Connor, Eileen relating humorous anecdotes of his childhood and Frank relating tales of Connor's service in the war, tales that emphasized his bravery and intelligence, never his suffering, never the dull, defeated look in his eyes those final weeks, never his death. They took long walks and attended plays and concerts. She read to him from his social work textbooks, and he dictated notes for his thesis while she typed them up. He was studying the impact of sudden blindness on the adult male, and preparing himself to work with people who had disabilities of all kinds. Eileen was proud of his accomplishments.

One evening, after five years of friendship, she stood on her toes and kissed him on the lips as she was leaving Baker Hall. He was so surprised at first he couldn't move, and then he held her to him and kissed her thoroughly until she claimed that she was dizzy.

In the months that followed, he began to court her. At first he did not dare believe she'd have him. The daughter of a doctor, raised in a cheerful, airy home of polished wood and silver, a woman with elegant manners. She was wealthy, though she never understood that, claiming she had very little money. And she was beautiful. Of this he was certain, though he carried no clear image of her from those few days before he went to war. Only impressions — fluid gestures, layers of sheer, gauzy clothing. He had not felt entitled to look directly at her. But now she seemed so close, so present. She often touched his face with her cool fingers in a way that told him she loved him. When she spoke to him at length one evening on her ideas of marriage, he realized she was telling him she'd have him. She wanted a family, she said. Children. She wasn't meant to be alone. She wanted to create again the warmth and laughter she knew as a girl within a charmed circle of loved ones, a real home.

When they became engaged, Dickie Lassiter and his parents invited them to a celebration supper. Mr Lassiter told them he owned a property in Manitoba he was willing to let Frank have for the asking. After all, Frank would need a place to live, now that he was graduating. It was outside St Boniface, a little French town, just across the river from Winnipeg. A couple of acres, a house and greenhouses. Low taxes. A fine place to raise a family. Frank thanked him and said he would certainly think about it.

With the help of his academic advisor, he sent out applications all winter long, hoping to find work in Manitoba, and finally, after many rejections, he found a part-time job in St Boniface. He and Eileen agreed it was time to be married and to accept Mr Lassiter's kind offer. Frank hoped to find full-time work before too long. Once he gained experience, he was sure his chances would be better.

Mr Lassiter told them the history of the property. It was the place where his own father had started his nursery business, specializing in roses. He had worked with a group of botanists in a nearby town, and still held the patent on some hardy prairie varieties. Eileen liked flowers, didn't she? It was an ideal time to reopen the business, if she was interested, with so many new suburbs planned in the nearby city. It might be an enjoyable hobby for her. Something a wife and mother could manage at home.

"Isn't it cold there?" asked Frank. He had heard of tremendous blizzards on the prairies.

"Isn't it hard to grow roses out there, in those cold winters?" asked Eileen.

"Well," said Mr Lassiter, "Yes."

BOOK III

Von and Rosheen

The Greenhouse

6.1

LASSITER'S ROSES, FOUNDED IN ST BONIFACE IN 1912, HAD FOLDED during the Depression. But nobody ever bothered to remove the old sign that marked the turnoff at the side of the highway. This sign was often hidden, by the snowdrifts of winter or the tall green weeds of summer, and many of its letters had been washed away by decades of wind and rain. It used to say LASSITER'S ROSES, one word above the other. But for years before the Garrisons moved in, the property had been known to the locals by the letters that were left: LAS ROSES, as if it dreamed of becoming a Mexican ranch.

"There's a couple moved into Las Roses," said a woman in the grocery store.

Frank and Eileen heard this remark the first time they went shopping. Two women were chatting in the next aisle over.

"Have you met them yet?" one asked the other.

Eileen tugged on Frank's arm, moving him forward, eager to round the corner so they could meet their new neighbours.

But then the first woman said, "The husband's a blind man. Can you imagine? Has a white cane and everything."

"Is the lady his wife?"

"Mm hmm. Imagine!"

Eileen stopped. Frank stood still beside her. They listened in silence.

"I saw them walking at the side of the road. My John wanted to offer them a ride, but I said, let them be. Why, I'm sure I wouldn't know *what* to say!"

"Imagine, taking him everywhere."

"What a life for her!"

Frank went home and hung up his new punching bag in the basement. It was a burlap bag, the size of a man, stuffed tight with sawdust. He had bought new boxing gloves, too, and when he felt the need he pounded the bag until his muscles were sore and his hands stung.

The house was in need of repair. But it was roomy and tall — three storeys, topped by a long attic. Frank and Eileen made their bedroom on the third floor. The second floor had two smaller rooms that Eileen thought perfect for children. She wanted children soon, he knew, though he preferred to wait until they were more settled. He wasn't sure what he meant by that. Money in the bank, perhaps. He wasn't sure his nerves would ever settle down.

They walked the grounds, inspecting the rundown greenhouses and the double garage, and the American elm trees that bordered the field. They ran ropes between the buildings, so Frank could find his own way. They turned the garage, which was heated and spacious and close to the house, into a workshop. They purchased power tools — a table saw, a drill, and sander — so Frank could start the necessary renovations. He hung his hammers and screwdrivers on the wall, lining them up by size with military precision.

Frank reported to his job at the Disability Agency, and clenched his jaw when the supervisor admitted that he, personally, did not believe in the blind leading the blind, but the decision to hire Frank had been made at the head office, and he hoped Frank would be reasonable and not expect to be eligible for advancement. The agency's policy, he explained, was for all social workers to hand in their typewritten case notes every Monday. He hoped Frank had a typist? And naturally, all workers must wear business attire and maintain impeccable grooming. "It lends a tone," he said. He hoped Frank's affliction would not prevent compliance with that policy? Frank assured him evenly that it would not.

Three days a week, he climbed a narrow staircase to the Agency's suite of offices above a hair salon on Marion Street. An ancient freight elevator clanked up and down at the back of the building, but it was faster to take the stairs. The suite was overheated, even in winter. The office assigned to Frank was a stale, windowless square at the end of the hall, with a vent in the floor that let up the scent of hairspray and the sound of dryers shutting on and off. He had his own small desk, three chairs, and a file cabinet that barely fit into the room. Clients in wheelchairs had to be seen in the lobby. He served about sixty clients, seeing each of them once a month. Mostly he encouraged them to try new things and take more risks, and they resisted. He took Braille notes on their progress or their difficulties, and on weekends he dictated the notes to Eileen, who typed them up and came in Mondays to file them in alphabetical order.

During the early years, they survived on his DVA pension and his small paycheques. Eileen used her own savings to get Garrison's Greenhouse started. She began as a wholesale florist, and later, after her mother died and left her some money, she expanded, adding new, more modern greenhouses and raising bedding plants as well. It was unfortunate she invested so much time and money in the long-stemmed roses she bred in the old greenhouse off the kitchen, for there was no profit in them. But Frank tried not to criticize. The roses were her one indulgence.

In all other matters, she was practical and economical, an excellent homemaker. In summer, she bought baskets full of apricots and peaches when they went on sale, and in the fall she picked plums and apples from the surviving trees in the old orchard. She processed and preserved all this fruit in glass quart jars she kept in the kitchen pantry, so they could have real fruit when winter came. She cheerfully taught herself to bake bread from scratch, mend clothing, cut weeds with a machete — skills her own mother had never needed to learn or even think about.

But when the children came, Eileen seemed overwhelmed. She took a long time to recover from each birth, and since her own mother was gone, Deirdre had to fly in to help with the babies. Frank had still not forgiven Deirdre for her cruelty when he was young. But he had learned it was better to get what you needed than to let resentment hold you back. It was a lesson he tried to impart to his clients.

He had hoped for a son, but in some ways felt it was only right he should have fathered girls. He couldn't teach a son to ride a bike or pitch a ball or drive a car. He couldn't afford to send a boy to college. It occurred to him the girls might want to go to college. Well then, once he got full-time work, perhaps he could save for college tuition. For now, he barely earned enough to heat the house and keep them all in food and clothes.

He didn't know how to relate to the girls when they were small. Their mother looked after them. Some evenings she placed a baby in his arms, and he touched its face, gingerly, with his fingertips. When they got bigger, she persuaded him to tuck them in at night and tell them stories. So he told of his adventures with Corky in Brooklyn or with Uncle Connor at training camp. But he was so worn out at the end of the day he fell asleep before the story's end. When Siobhán poked him in the ribs one night to wake him, he sprang up with a yell, knocking her off the bed. He had to speak to her sternly to make her stop crying. He could not stand it when they cried. Just as he'd feared, the children were too much for him. He didn't have the patience or the know-how. Caring for children was women's work.

He helped Eileen with other things, building fences and a tool shed and insulating the attic. He could perform simple tasks in the greenhouse, like wrapping flowers for shipping. But as the business grew, she needed more help than he could give. That was when they hired Manuel. Frank first met Manuel, the son of a client, because the boy was in trouble. He and some friends had broken into their school at night and stolen sports equipment. His parents, not knowing what to do with him, had asked Frank for advice. Frank spoke to the boy at length and later explained to the parents that their son lacked confidence. He was trying to prove himself to the tough kids in his neighbourhood by stealing. If they would encourage him, spend time with him, praise him for the things he did well, he was sure Manuel would be fine. He also said he thought the boy could use a job. Could he drive a truck? Would he like to work in the greenhouse?

Manuel started out on weekends and holidays, shopping and making deliveries and learning, slowly, how to care for the plants. By the time he graduated high school, Eileen needed him — and could afford to pay him — full time. He worked in the greenhouse domes most days and took his lunch at noon with Eileen and the girls, like part of the family.

Manuel's father had lost his right arm to a hay baler just before the war, and considered himself useless. But with Frank's encouragement, he had attended night school and learned bookkeeping. At first, he had balked at the work. He was right-handed, and complained he couldn't write with his left hand. He wrote like a child, he said. But he persevered and now he ran his own business from his home, keeping accounts for other small businesses. He was so successful the Agency cut off his disability payments. He still grumbled that the work was too hard. He was too tired. The work took him twice as long as it took a two-handed man. But Frank reminded him he was independent now. That was the important thing. To keep your dignity. Your pride.

Frank liked to enumerate these facts in his mind, especially when he woke in the middle of the night and could not get back to sleep. He sometimes woke mid-dream to find himself on the porch, or in the greenhouse, not knowing how he got there. Then he'd make his way to the armchair in the living room and try to lull himself back to sleep. He counted up the buildings on his land, the many talents of his wife, the people he advised. He was a property owner, an employer, a professional who used his training to help others. He was a husband and a father. He was not a truant slum kid. Not a beggar on the corner with a tin cup. And he was not a soldier. The war was over.

Or he was dreaming that the war was over. He was still lying in the slit trench, half-buried in the Dutch mud, dreaming he was free and married with two children. A home with pine logs blazing in the fireplace, cups of tea and a quilt-laden bed, warmth in the aftermath of a winter storm. A squadron of ploughs and graders moving in to clear the snow. No! He forced himself to wake. He lifted his head, heard the grinding gears and engines of the Nazi tanks, their treads churning the frozen sludge. A barrage of machine-gun fire without pause, and beyond the machine guns, the moaning Minnies falling in the distant woods. Tanks closing in. He had to set up the Bren. Where was the gasoline? In the crucible of winter, he strode across the frozen polder, the soles of his feet burning with the cold.

6.2

FIVE O'CLOCK IN THE MORNING WAS THE WORST TIME OF DAY, especially in winter. In her second-storey bedroom, where she lay taut and vigilant, eleven-year-old Siobhán heard the snowploughs in the distance. Harsh gears shifting, motors roaring. Her father's heavy tread in the downstairs hall, crack of the telephone table tipping over, clang of the telephone bell as it hit the floor. Flinging off her covers, she leaped across the room, throwing a flannel housecoat over her pyjamas. Screech of the unoiled hinge on the rear door, clatter of shovels and brooms on the landing, winter boots and ice skates tumbling down the basement steps. If he fell he could break his neck.

As she flew down the stairs, the cold air rose to meet her. She felt for the wall switch, snapped on the hallway light. He had left the rear door open to the January wind. Winter swept into the house, seeping down the hallway toward the kitchen, threatening the roses. She shoved her feet into her mother's boots and stepped outside, closing the door behind her. Winter nights were rarely dark. The clouds reflected so much light off the white field she could easily find her way. But the wind cut through her housecoat. She couldn't survive long out here, dressed as she was. Where did he go? A crash came from the direction of the garage, and she hurried down the short shovelled path to the entrance. A snowplough gunned its engine as it came up the road. She entered the garage. Total darkness. She groped for the trouble light that hung from a crossbeam and switched it on.

The light revealed the cause of the crash. Glass jars of nuts and bolts knocked from the shelves, smashed to pieces on the floor. A stack of toppled paint cans. What was he looking for? He was kneeling on the cold concrete, trying to unscrew the cap on the gas jug. His ungloved hands were white with cold but steady. He got the cap off and held it between his teeth as he began to pour, aiming very precisely at an invisible spot on the floor. The gas trickled down an incline toward the space heater at the back of the garage, toward the pilot light beneath the heater. She knew how dangerous this was. He had explained it to her himself.

"Dad?"

In one motion, he rose and pinned her to the wall.

His elbow tightened against her throat. She couldn't make a sound. But her arms hung free. Acting on dream logic, he had pinned her neck but forgotten to hold her arms. Should she hit him? She imagined her spinal cord splintering, the individual vertebrae skittering across the floor like necklace beads. But the stream of gasoline was on the move. She thought of sparks, explosions, pictured her mother rising from her bed, finding Frank missing, coming out to look for him. Or her little sister. What if her little sister came in?

She slapped her father hard across the face, and he loosened his grip.

"Daddy, it's me! Siobhán!"

He let out a sob, sank to the floor. She covered her mouth and warmed her fingers with her hot white breath, quietly, so he couldn't hear. The heavy machines had cleared the road. They rumbled down the highway, back toward town. All was silent, except for Frank's ragged, indrawn breaths and the winter wind. Gradually his breathing slowed and grew steady and he regained control. He stood and stretched out his arm, groped until he felt the shelving and took a step. He walked across the broken glass and across the hard-packed snow of the pathway in his bare feet, following the rope to the house. Siobhán threw an old rug over the puddle of gas, to stop it from spreading any further. She followed her father into the house and stood in the hallway at the bottom of the stairs to watch him climb up to her parents' bedroom on the third floor. His feet left bloodstains on the carpet. She would wash those quickly now, before her mother or sister could see them. Then she would dress properly and clean the garage. Throw the gas-soaked rug into a trash barrel, far from the house, and mop the floor with plenty of soap and water. Upstairs, Eileen and Róisín slept, each curled in a flowered nightgown, covered with quilts. The wind picked up and slammed the rear door shut. High above them all, the roof beams cracked as the attic filled with an upsurge of wind so strong she thought the house and everyone in it might lift off into the sky.

———

Von closes her notebook. She is approaching the most dangerous part of the story now, the years when she and her father were both alive at the same time, both conscious in the same house. The new orange notebook is supposed to be for the present, not the past, especially not these parts of the past she's worked so hard to forget. But Rosheen's project, Marijke's story, Kyle's questions, Meredith's reproach — all have drawn her to the brink of memory. It's like running a finger over the edge of a razor blade to see if it's still sharp.

It is.

She walks to the railing of the hotel balcony and looks down at the park below. Kyle is sitting on a bench by the canal, under a stand of silver willow trees, with a pencil and his travel journal. Head bent over the pages. Apparently he takes after his Aunt Von. Every once in a while he looks up into the branches above him, as if trying to think of the right word. She wonders what he's writing about. His grandfather the hero, maybe. Meredith is right. He doesn't know who he is. Von is the only one left who can tell him about his family, his parents, his origins. For the first time, she feels a twinge of doubt. Maybe it's not right to keep him from his own history. But the alternative, telling him the truth, still seems worse to her.

———

Kyle carries with him a photograph Von gave him in New York, the picture of his mother on her eighth birthday, wearing a party hat. He said he wanted to keep it to show the Penners and to show his friends in Winnipeg. He looks at it every day, and he shows it to everyone he meets in Amsterdam. "My mum," he says. "She was an artist."

"She was a cute little thing," says Durgan, peering closely.

It's a small snapshot, but you can see the creamy complexion, the rosy cheeks, the front teeth, newly grown-in, even and white. A perfect smile. Róisín Dubh before the fall.

———

"Why didn't you show him any pictures of her when she was older?" Meredith asks Von. "There must have been some in the New York apartment." This is later, when the two of them are alone in Von's hotel room, waiting for Kyle to join them for dinner. Meredith seems suspicious, seems to know Von is holding something back.

"The Penners might have told Kyle," Von says, "that she...had some facial scarring?"

"Yes, of course," Meredith says. "From the accident, I assume. But that's no reason to —"

"It was…maybe rather worse than they let on," Von says. "I didn't want to shock him. I'd like to prepare him first."

"Durgan told us *he* has recent pictures of Rosheen. Kyle's gone over to his place to see them." She looks at her wristwatch. "He should be back here soon."

Von stands up too quickly, making her head spin. She clutches the arm of the chair.

"Are you all right?"

"Yes." Von opens the balcony door. She needs air. It's happening. It's going to happen. She's drawing closer to a memory she's been circling for weeks, a scene that's buried incompletely, images and sounds that still flash through her brain.

Siobhán should have known Róisín was right behind her. Róisín followed her everywhere. After breakfast, when Siobhán washed dishes, Róisín stayed at the kitchen table. When Siobhán moved into the living room to dust and vacuum, Róisín moved after her. Even after Siobhán got Róisín bathed and into her boys' pyjamas — she preferred firemen and spaceships to kittens and flowers — and made up the kind of stories she liked to hear, about adventures in outer space, and kissed her and turned out the light, Róisín often followed Siobhán — mere minutes later — into her bedroom. When Siobhán grew desperate for privacy and locked her door, Róisín camped out in the hall with a sheet and pillow and her comic books, making herself a nest, leaning her little body against the door and talking to her sister through the keyhole. Sometimes she fell asleep that way, and when Siobhán finally pulled her door open, Róisín tumbled in.

When Siobhán was thirteen, she could rarely find time to read. All day she was needed for one task or another. At night, when she should have slept, she read. In summer, when heat gathered in the upper storeys, she often snuck downstairs, after Róisín fell asleep, to lie on the sofa by the open window and read by the light of the floor lamp, with the breeze coming in through the screen. What was she reading that night? *Rebecca*? Whatever it was, she fell asleep with the book lying open, face down on her chest.

Early in the morning, a muffled sound made its way into her dream, disguised as the sound of a baseball, *whump*, landing in a leather glove. Instantly, she was awake, though still locked in the paralysis of sleep. Her eyes were open, fixed on the living-room ceiling. Her hands lay heavy on the cover of her book. The lamp was on. What was that sound?

She willed her hands to move, and with great effort managed to wiggle a finger and break free of sleep. She sat up straight, listening. A sound from the kitchen. Then silence. She was about to lie down when she heard it again, something soft and solid, like a ball of wool, hurled against the house. Immediately, as if in answer, came a hard crunch. Something was wrong.

She swung her legs off the sofa and felt, under her feet, the warm mass of little Róisín, wrapped in a bed sheet, curled up on the rug. She must have followed Siobhán downstairs in the middle of the night.

Róisín rolled over and mumbled, "Siobhán?"

"Shh. Go back to sleep."

"Whatsa matter?"

"Nothing, Róisín. Just getting a drink. Go back to sleep."

Kitchen laced with shadows. Pale, pre-dawn light, dappled by the long fronds of the ferns in the window, the forest of long-stemmed roses in the greenhouse, their blooms still closed against the night. Her father, in his blue pyjamas, stood before the pantry with his back to her. The pantry door was open. Groceries had been swept from the shelves and lay on the floor around him, cereal boxes, jars of preserves, tins of vegetables. At her feet, Siobhán saw the source of the crunch: a box of coarse salt lay crumpled against the baseboard, salt crystals spilled all over the floor. He must have thrown the box against the wall, thrown it hard, and it had exploded on impact. A crushed package of oatmeal cookies lay on top of the stove, half the cookies pulverized to dust, and the face of the stovetop clock was cracked in two. She stayed perfectly still. She heard a rustle behind her, just a whisper, maybe the wind in the curtain, but she did not look back. She kept her eyes on her father. He was waiting. But for what?

The sound came at her, *whump*, against the window, inches from her right ear. She jumped. Turned her head in time to see a brief, brown flutter of wings bounce off the pane and drop out of sight. In the split second she'd taken her eyes off her father, he had moved. He'd grabbed a quart jar of peaches and now stood, tense and ready, holding the jar above his head, aiming it at the window. He was looking straight at

Siobhán, or straight through her. She did not move. Her father did not move. He was clenching the jar so hard she thought he might shatter it. Wake himself up. Then the bird flew at the window again, a feathery, muffled thud, and Frank let go. He hurled the glass jar hard into the void.

———

Sometimes in her dreams she feels it still, the tingle as the hairs lift from her scalp, as the jar of peaches hurtles toward her skull. Then she wakes, blood pulsing in her ears like ocean waves.

He must have looked scary in that moment, his face contorted in a murderous rage. But Von didn't see his face because she ducked.

God help her, she ducked.

She dropped and flattened herself against the tiled floor and let that jar go whistling past above her, through the empty space where she should have been standing, the space she was supposed to occupy, in front of her sister.

———

When Kyle comes back to the hotel, with the photo of his mother, he hands it first to Von, without a word. It's a full-colour close-up, eight by ten. The photographer, Durgan, has not tried to spare the viewer. The lighting is perfect. Sunshine turning Rosheen's hair a golden red, like maple leaves in fall, warming her skin. You can see the intricate design of her strange and pretty eyes, sky blue with little emerald slivers, and you can see the scar in all its grotesque, vivid detail, a garish red serrated seam across her right cheek and her chin. As if someone has recently taken a whip to her face. The lump of scar tissue, like a bubble of blood on the deformed lower lip. Durgan has caught her in one of her rare moods of mad joy, laughing. Her mouth wide open. Von hands the photo back to Kyle, watching to see how he's taking it. He hands it to Meredith.

Meredith says, "Wow." She studies the photo closely, then lays it on the table, where they all can look at it together. She glances up at Kyle. "Wow," she says again.

"I know," says Kyle. Their eyes meet.

And then, at the same moment, they both say, "She's beautiful."

———

Siobhán ducked and the jar of peaches smashed into her sister, crushing her cheekbone and slicing her face in two. Róisín lay still and white on the floor in her spaceship pyjamas, arms and legs outflung, spilled salt around her body like stars on the dark tiles. A bed sheet crumpled at her feet. Her eyes rolled back in her head. White eyes. White, white skin. Slowly, in the silence, blood rose and gathered along the cut. Then the blood began to overflow.

He couldn't see this, of course. He thought Siobhán was hysterical when she screamed for her mother. He thought Eileen was overreacting when she bundled Róisín in a blanket and carried her out to the car, and he yelled at Siobhán when he realized she was leaving with them.

"You stay here!" he shouted. He barred her way to the front door, forbidding her to leave. But she heard her mother starting the car. She had to go. For the first time in her life she deliberately eluded him. She dodged his groping arm and ran out through the greenhouse.

Róisín lay face up on the back seat of the car. Siobhán crouched on the floor and held her, as Eileen sped around the hairpin turns of the gravel road, calling out first-aid instructions, telling Siobhán to pinch the wound closed. But the wound was too big, it was everywhere. It was bad. Siobhán knew it was bad, though at the time she had considered only two alternatives: either Róisín would live or she would die. She hadn't been able to imagine the complicated future.

6.3

AT FIRST IT WAS DARK, AND RÓISÍN KNEW ONLY THAT HER BODY was in motion. Then she opened her eyes and recognized the shape of Siobhán's bowed head above her, Siobhán's dark hair hanging down. She saw the frame of the car window and through the window the apple trees fluttering by too fast, dark trunks, pale flashes of sky between the branches. The car rounded a curve, hit a ridge in the road and lifted into the air. Róisín's stomach lifted with it. She closed her eyes. She didn't know why she was here, only that her sister was holding her and the car was speeding through the orchard. The sky was a funny colour, pink or white. She wanted to see it again, but she didn't want to be sick. The car wheels bumped and bumped. Like that robin trying to enter the greenhouse. Why did he hurt himself like that? Siobhán said the robin couldn't see the glass. He saw only the green plants and the sky. But why did he keep on trying, if it hurt? He couldn't remember the hurt, said Siobhán. His brain was too small. He had a bird brain. Was that yesterday? The pain was all around her. In the air, like weather. The car turned left, rounding a long curve, pulling Róisín headfirst along the seat, and only Siobhán's grip kept her head from slamming into the car door. Róisín's eyes flew open and the trees whipped past, faster now, and when she closed her eyes again, the rhythm of the trees remained imprinted on the inside of her eyelids, dark dark dark light dark.

A long time later she was being carried, as if it were her birthday and the party guests were lifting her into the air to give her bumps. She wanted to see where she was but she didn't know how to open her eyes. She heard her mother's voice, speaking about an accident, and the voice of a man, a stranger, but she couldn't hear what he was saying because Siobhán was too close to her ears, breathing too loud, in short, hard gulps, almost like crying, except Siobhán never cried.

She was hot all over. Above her a black dress and a silver cross. A wimple. Cool palm on her forehead. *Ne t'en fais pas.* Fire burning her skin. She tried to call her mother, but she couldn't open her mouth. Tall black crows around the bed. One gripped her feet with its claws. *I don't like the look of these stitches.* Stitches? *They look inflamed.* In flames. She rolled from side to side in the bed that was not her own. The nun caught both of her wrists in one of her giant hands and said, *Roy-zin, calm down.* The cross bounced wildly as Róisín tried to break free. A doctor with a grey mustache pierced Róisín's arm, in the soft crook of her elbow, with a long silver needle. Róisín screamed, and the scream seemed to rip her sewn mouth open. But they held her still for a long time, pushing the needle into her veins. From far away, the tall nun said, *There, there, Roy-zin.* The nun was up on the ceiling, spreading her wings. *You'll feel better now,* she said.

Róisín's mother was crying, *It's all my fault.* The nurses told her not to blame herself. Accidents happen. It was nobody's fault. It was God's will.

Róisín wanted to tell them about the bird, but she couldn't talk. Where her lips should be was only a blur, a buzz. She let her fingers rise to her mouth and tap on her lips. She felt there a soft pad of some kind, but in the place where her lips should feel her fingers tapping, she felt nothing. *Don't touch your face, Roy-zin.*

Siobhán sat beside the bed and read to Róisín from her book of constellations. On the background of a dark night sky, the artist had drawn a white line, connecting the white stars, creating outlines of the animals — the goat, the bull, the two bears. Siobhán read about Ursa Major, and Róisín drifted to sleep looking at the illustration, a grizzly prowling on all fours, its body a patch of bear-shaped sky, dark and full of stars. It was familiar to her somehow, the bear patrolling the hallways of her house, a low growl like a motor humming in its throat.

It was night. She drifted through the Milky Way, space-walking like Invisible Girl through cosmic rays. Then it was morning.

It was night. She woke in her own house, all alone. She walked from room to room, and every time she turned a corner, a shadow crossed her path, something wanting to pounce out at her. She called her parents and her sister, but no one answered. She traipsed the steep stairs from the cellar to the attic. Every room was empty. Quiet. Only the floorboards creaking and the wind chimes on the front porch and the dripping of the kitchen tap.

Siobhán later said that was a dream. But it was real.

By the time the bandages came off and she could talk, she discovered she had someone else's voice, all high and raspy. When Siobhán came, Róisín explained she was a different person now, since she had floated into outer space. They had given her a new name, Roy-zin.

"That's because they only saw your name written down," said Siobhán. "It *looks* like 'Roy-zin' to them, because of the way it's spelled."

"I don't have a new name?"

"No, sweetie. Of course not."

"Can you spell it different for them? So they'll know?"

"Sure, honey." So Siobhán wrote "Rosheen" on the hospital chart.

The doctor said she was healing now and didn't need so much medicine. He reduced the dose, saying her head would be more clear. He was right. Her head became as clear as glass. Her body became transparent, light and watery as the sunbeams coming through the dirty window. Even the needle piercing her arm did not weigh her down. The green bruise and the blood that collected in a dark crust under the bandage did not bother her. She remembered, vaguely, being afraid of the needle, but it was part of her now. It didn't hurt. Nothing hurt. As long as she was attached by the tube, like a cosmonaut attached to the spaceship, she could bob on the waves of the bed and never feel a thing.

Róisín developed super hearing powers. She heard the man from the Children's Aid all the way down the hall at the nurse's desk. *Poor little Roy-zin*, said the nurse, and he said, *Terrible thing for a girl. What are the parents saying?* And when he came in and talked to her and her mother, she could hear another voice, underneath his friendly voice, that was hard and sure like the voice of a policeman in a movie. Róisín could tell her mother was afraid of him, even though she acted calm. That was why her mother agreed to go away and let him speak to Róisín by himself.

The Children's Aid man had long yellowy teeth and a long yellowy tie and a brown suit. He had a board with paper clipped onto it and a pen. After he asked about her school and her stuffed rabbit and her family, he pulled his chair closer to her bed. "So, what happened to your face, here? Gee, looks like you got a bad knock of some kind."

A knock? Róisín tried to remember. Spots of light and darkness dancing on the kitchen walls. Scratchy salt or sugar under her bare toes, cool kitchen tiles, distant swish of her mother's fuzzy slippers on the upstairs carpet, and the robin. Flying into the window.

"Can you tell me what happened?"

She shook her head. Her thoughts jumbled, higgledy-piggledy, like thoughts in a dream. A tall figure in the shadows, a dark bear standing on its hind legs, one arm raised high — no. No, it must have been the bird, the bird broke the glass and the glass cut —

"A bird," she said. She saw again her sister turning toward the sound, dark hair swinging.

"Tell me about the bird," said the man. He tried to bunch himself up small, drawing his shoulders close to his neck, letting his arms dangle between his knees. "What kind of bird?"

"A bear," she said. "A bob." Where was the word? "A robin."

"What did the robin do?"

"Bashed the gash." Her mouth hurt. She needed more medicine.

"A bird broke the glass? A little robin? Where were your parents when this happened?"

"Seeping," said Róisín, though she felt sure she'd heard her mother's footsteps on the stairs, and her father … but that could not have been her father, that black hole in her memory, like a cave from where a dark wind — "I want my mother," she said.

"We need to talk a bit longer." He patted her hand. "It's my job to make sure little kids like you are safe. You want to be safe, don't you? You see, there's a law to help —"

"No!"

"All you need to do is tell me who —"

"No! Leave me alone! Don't touch me!"

A nurse came running in. "What's the matter?" she asked Róisín. "Who are you?" she asked the man. "Did you touch her?"

"Children's Aid," he said. He sounded angry. He showed the nurse a piece of paper, and she went away, looking back over her shoulder as if she didn't like the man at all.

"There are places kids can stay," he said, "while we make sure —"

"Don't touch me!" Róisín screamed. He wasn't touching her. "Don't *touch* me!"

The nurse hurried back in. "Now, see here —"

Róisín's mother ran in. Then another nurse and the doctor, the one with the mustache, Róisín's favourite. He told the nurse to fill the empty bag with medicine, and told the man from Children's Aid to go away.

While everyone was making a big commotion and bustling around, Róisín's mother sat on the bed and held her hand. She looked deeply into Róisín's eyes and nodded, smiling, to let Róisín know she'd done the right thing.

That night the nurse and her mother encouraged her to pray to God to help her get better. She stuck her palms together and closed her eyes to please her mother. But she knew God wasn't going to help.

The law wasn't going to help, either. The only thing that helped was the needle.

———

After a while, the nurses said Róisín's mother should go home at night. She might get sick, they said, if she didn't go home and get a good night's rest in her own bed. Look how cramped that chair is, they said. Your mummy can't sleep sitting up like that.

"Would you mind very much, darling?" her mother asked. "I'll come to see you every morning after breakfast, or Siobhán will come. All right?"

"Yes, Mum."

"You be good," her mother said. "Don't give the nurses any trouble."

Every night, after her mother went home, when the other children were asleep and the nurses were busy at the desk, Róisín woke up. Her spine was sore from lying too long on her back, and she'd shift over onto her left side. Sometimes pictures drifted across her brain, wispy as spider's webs. Chalk drawings on lace. That was in another world. There were different worlds, far apart, each pale as onion skin, and sometimes she hovered between them. Sometimes she was looking down at her own body in a white room, with harsh lights and doctors in white masks bending over the case she had burst out of and they were sewing her back in. Once she woke up in her grandma's apartment in New York, but she was a different person there, a person from long ago. Then the worlds reshuffled and she was stuck hard to the hospital bed again, in the lowest desert on Earth, with the tube stabbed into her arm and the awful dry headache, and she knew she was dying.

Dying was nothing to fear, her mother said, because God loved her, she would go to heaven, but she'd heard her father say there was no heaven. Both her parents said that death was a long way off, nothing for children to worry about. But she had seen a boy in the corridor yesterday, attached to a long tube just like hers. His eyes were sunk deep in his face, surrounded by bruises, and she could see his skeleton under his yellow skin. She told herself she would get out of the hospital soon, like the nurses said, and skip rope and swim at the beach. She conjured in her mind a long funnel of years ahead, full of music and friends, opening into a summer sky, but the funnel looked too much like the cardboard horn of plenty her class cut out and glued together last Thanksgiving, with apples and pumpkins spilling out of it, and she knew she was making it up. She could taste the cardboard in her mouth.

Near morning, she could always feel the stitches tightening. Her skin stung and itched. Her nose throbbed. She wanted to throw up. If she had to wait too long for a nurse, her face seemed to go up in flames again. She tried to be quiet, but early, early in the morning she often heard her own thin moaning, as if from some place far away.

When the nurses finally came to sit her up and wash her with cool cloths, and give her medicine, the relief nearly made her cry. But it was really her mother and father she longed for. She wanted both her parents and her sister holding her, all their hands touching her at once, until she fell asleep. Or died.

She thought of Siobhán, always saying that she wanted to be left alone. Siobhán didn't know what it was to be alone for real.

6.4

VON HAS TOLD THE STORY OF THE ACCIDENT TO KYLE AND Meredith, and it was almost as terrible as she'd expected it to be. At one point — describing that moment from hell when she realized her sister was behind her — she couldn't speak. For years, she had managed to stop the memories at those early morning sounds — dull thud of bird on glass, soft rustle of bed sheet dragging on floor *why didn't I turn around?* Sounds that cycled through her brain, warning her not to go any further.

But after she made herself remember those details — bird, bed sheet, blood — she didn't die. The world didn't fracture into pieces. Even during the brief halt in her story when she huddled, shaking, hiding her face in her arms, she'd felt the strong and gentle hand of Meredith, rubbing her back in small, warm circles, letting her know she wasn't alone.

The three of them wiped their eyes and talked and tried to understand. They stayed up late in Von's hotel room and spoke of blindness, nightmares, war. Von spoke of her anger at her father, and Meredith said she had good reason to be angry. Von said she wasn't sure anymore if that was true. But telling of her anger seemed to loosen something in her. They all stood up and stretched. They stepped out on the balcony to feel the warm night air. Below them the houseboats swayed, nearly imperceptibly, in the canal, their windows casting rippled squares of light upon the water. Then Kyle and Meredith returned to their hotel. Von watched them stroll across the bridge and through the park, holding hands and leaning, very slightly, on each other.

The first evening, as soon as Róisín came out of surgery, Eileen hurried to the telephone to let Frank know she was all right. Then she sent Siobhán home to make his dinner. Siobhán didn't want to make his dinner. She never wanted to speak to him again, but her mother said, "Please, Siobhán, *please*. I can't take any more trouble today. I just can't." So Siobhán went home and boiled potatoes and made a hash with tinned corned beef and sat at the table with him and pretended to eat. Every time she moved a forkful toward her mouth, she pictured Róisín's shredded lips, and she felt sick.

"How is she?" Frank asked. For some reason he was wearing one of his ironed white shirts and a suit, though it wasn't an office day.

She scraped her fork across her plate. "Mum says she's going to be fine."

"Good," he said. "Well. Good, then." He drained his glass of milk.

After a few minutes, while Siobhán pushed the food around on her plate, Frank said, "That was a very nice dinner. You're just as good a cook as your mother."

"There's ice cream in the freezer," she said. "If you want dessert."

"That would be wonderful. Is it chocolate?"

When Von remembers that dinner now, so many years later, it occurs to her for the first time that he was making small talk to ease the tension, ease his own fears. He must have been terrified, she reasons now. But at the time she was disgusted by his selfish appetite, feeding himself while Róisín lay torn up and unconscious in a strange bed and her mother wept. He was thoughtless and cruel and Siobhán despised him. She washed the dishes and said good night — coldly, but not coldly enough to allow him to comment on it. Upstairs, alone in her room, she whispered, "I hate you, I hate you," and felt a hot blush stipple her neck and face.

Róisín was in the hospital for twelve days. Her mother told her father not to visit, because Róisín needed her rest. But Siobhán skipped school to spend every day on the children's ward with her mother and sister. Róisín's eyes — glazed irises, constricted pupils — followed Siobhán as she performed her futile rituals of atonement, changing water in the flower vase, fluffing pillows. Bobby Sullivan came to the hospital every day and brought Siobhán her homework so she wouldn't fall behind.

Outside, on the lawn of the hospital, Siobhán sobbed, and Bobby wrapped his arms around her. He let her rest her head against his chest, and didn't ask her any questions or say anything stupid.

On the tenth day, the doctor said Rosheen could go home soon. They all called her Rosheen now, a harsh approximation of her original name, but better than Roy-zin.

Rosheen still looked monstrous. The skin around the cut was swollen, the black thread of the stitches clearly visible. Green and yellow bruises ringed both eyes. Eileen told Siobhán to go home and get rid of the mirror in Rosheen's bedroom. "Take down all the mirrors," she said. "I don't want her to see herself until she's healed. And whatever you do, don't tell Dad what she looks like."

When Eileen first brought Rosheen home, Frank greeted them at the door. "Are you feeling better, honey?" He hugged her close and whispered, "I'm sorry, little rose. I'm so sorry." That was the only time Siobhán ever heard him admit he was to blame.

"I'm sorry, Daddy," said Rosheen. She began to cry. Frank patted her narrow shoulder, saying, "Shh. Everything's going to be all right."

He knew the scar existed, but no one ever described it to him fully. With subtle signs, Eileen persuaded Siobhán, and somehow even Rosheen, to protect him. From the day Rosheen came home, the three of them entered a silent conspiracy never to let him know, by word or deed or tone of voice, how ugly the scar truly was. So in later years, as it became apparent the scar was permanent, there wasn't any way to speak about it honestly.

6.5

It wasn't until she was split in two that Rosheen understood who she was. The accident was like noon, or midnight, dividing her from herself. Dark and light, before and after. Róisín/ Rosheen. A member of the family and yet not. She felt it when she first went home again. Her mother and sister weren't the same. They seemed to move about behind a sheet of wax paper. She wasn't sure if they could see her. They spoke to a spot in the air above her head, in new, cheerful voices, talking about nothing. Rosheen listened to other sounds, ones she'd never noticed before. The tick of the clock and the gentle whir the clock hand made between the ticks, the siss of juice mist when her mother peeled an orange, and her own heart beating, a thud and its echo, all day long and into the night. What was keeping it going?

She no longer had a body like she used to have. She remembered her arms and legs had once been solid and stayed put unless she made an effort to move them. When she used to lean her head on her hand, she had felt its hard bulk. But now it was weightless, floating by itself above her. Her fingers drifted toward the ceiling if she didn't clasp them together. And she didn't need to eat. The inside of her body was empty and perfectly clean. Warm and light as air.

One night she felt so light her head got dizzy and she fell down. When she woke she saw her father high on the stairs above her, saying, "Who's there?" He moved his head like an animal, lifting his nose, seeking the source of a scent he'd caught.

Siobhán ran out of her room. "It's all right. Rosheen had a tumble, that's all."

He grunted. He was all tangled up with his night self, the part trapped inside him. Rosheen could see it, a creature in the shape of a bear, its dark form spangled with white stars. It turned and lumbered back upstairs, and Siobhán helped Rosheen into her bed.

Someone had taken the bathroom mirror off the wall and hidden it, not very well, in the basement laundry room. Rosheen went down and stood before it, placing her right hand over the right side of her face, and cupping her chin. Some day soon, she'd be herself again, her mother promised. Once the swelling went down. Once the cuts and the needle holes healed up. Once the redness faded. And if she still had a scar, they'd get it fixed by a plastic surgeon.

"Not a real surgeon?" Rosheen asked.

Her mother laughed, as if Rosheen had made a joke. "Plastic surgeons are real," she said.

But Rosheen knew that even if they fixed her so she looked the same again, she'd never *be* the same. "Is it time for my medicine?" she asked.

"I just gave it to you," said her mother. "Remember?"

Some of Rosheen's friends sent cards, and two of them came to visit, with their mothers, but it wasn't any fun. First Mary-Kate came over, but she didn't want to play. She only stared and smiled in a fake way and talked about her new kittens and pretty soon she said she felt sick in her tummy and asked to go home. Katy-Ann was even worse. She looked at Rosheen only once and burst into tears. Katy-Ann's mother said to Rosheen's mother, "Heavens, Eileen, don't you think it's too soon? Poor Katy-Ann is *very* sensitive."

She was glad when the Ross family came back from their summer vacation and brought Raymond over to play. Raymond treated her the same as always. Sure, he winced when he saw her, but all he said was, "Does it hurt?" After that, he was the same as ever, chasing her around the yard, and playing lost in the bush. They pretended to catch fish and defend themselves from bears and they built a for-real fort in the bush by the back lot, with plywood and tarp. But Raymond only came once a week, on Sundays.

Late in summer, Rosheen's mother was called to the school for a meeting with the teachers. When she came back, she said the school counsellor thought it would be better, psychologically, if Rosheen were home-schooled for a while. So she didn't go into grade three with her friends in fall. Instead, a teacher came to the house with arithmetic books and readers and talked to her mother and sister about helping her keep up at home until she felt better. But Rosheen wasn't a kid anymore, like they thought she was. She knew she felt well enough to go to school. She knew she was staying home because nobody wanted to look at her.

When her mother asked if she wanted to visit her Grandma Deirdre in New York again, Rosheen realized even her own mother wanted her out of sight. But she was glad to see Deirdre, who welcomed her warmly and didn't say anything about her face. Deirdre gave her a box of twelve pastels, with rich colours and a deep, oily smell and wrappers to peel off as she used them up. She gave her fabric scraps, which Rosheen used to make collages and puppets. She taught her the lazy-daisy embroidery stitch, and Rosheen stitched daisies along the seam of one leg of her blue jeans. Deirdre and Rosheen went to the zoo in Central Park and took ferry rides and went with Uncle John Junior and his kids to Coney Island, where Rosheen rode the Ferris wheel and roller coaster with her cousins. She stayed two whole months in New York, and this time, when she was supposed to return for Christmas, she did come home.

After Christmas came a long, lonely winter. The only thing good about being out of school was that Rosheen finally learned how to read. Bobby Sullivan brought over a box of comics for her. Siobhán tried to interest her in the Classic comics, like *The Count of Monte Cristo*. But Rosheen's favourites were the superheroes, especially the ones with real-life concerns, like ordinary people — Spiderman's little Aunt May, or Invisible Girl's new miniskirt.

Rosheen put on her blue long johns and blue pyjama top, and wore a blue apron like a cape, tied at her neck. She knotted a bed sheet to the rail at the top of the staircase and swung down, the apron billowing from her shoulders, to land on the telephone table in the front hall. She was Invisible Girl, and the phone was her space radio, for contacting allies on other planets.

She dragged a dining-room chair into the hall for a lookout tower and spotted an enemy high on the Martian mountain. Stair by stair, she climbed to the summit. She was engaged in furious battle with the villain in the upstairs hall — and she was winning — when she heard a thud. The chair. She froze, a hard knot in the middle of her tummy. She had forgotten she was alone with him this Saturday. Her mother was working at the church bazaar, and Siobhán had gone out.

"For crying out loud!" her father yelled. "What the *hell* is this? Rosheen!"

He banished her to her room.

"You stay in there until your sister gets home. No sneaking out! And you be quiet. Find something quiet to do, for Pete's sake." He slammed her door.

She was lucky he was in a good mood. She wasn't supposed to move the furniture. Ever.

When her tummy stopped aching, she acted out the rest of the story. The rug was a raging river and the dresser was a Martian volcano that could blow at any minute. She was engrossed in the adventure, providing dialogue and sound effects, when her father thrust the door open.

"Rosheen!"

A loud rush, like the north wind in her ears, the shadow of a wild animal closing in on her. She stood still on the tall dresser, where she shouldn't be, holding a plastic sword in each hand, one blue, which was her own, and one red, which she had captured from the enemy.

"Rosheen? Answer me." The bear's voice.

"Yes, Dad." Still on the dresser, in a hero's cape and doubly armed, yet incapable of moving.

He turned his head toward the sound of her voice, as if wondering why she was so close to the ceiling. He stepped into the room.

She was afraid to look at him. Afraid to see him coming at her.

He took another step forward.

If she leaped onto the bed, maybe she could nip around behind him, run downstairs, and get out of the house, before he could catch her. She looked out the window. Deep snow everywhere and her feet were bare.

But he seemed to change his mind. "Keep it down in here," he said. "You're making a racket." He retreated, closing the door behind him.

Sick with relief, she lay on the bed, holding her tummy. She hated Siobhán for going out. Siobhán should not be allowed to go out. Ever.

———

In spring, when a blue jay flew into the greenhouse, Rosheen screamed and screamed, so loud and long she upset everyone, even herself. She didn't know where the scream was coming from.

The blue jay landed with a twisted neck upon the grass, and Manuel carried it away in a handkerchief, saying he'd take it to the bird hospital. But she knew it was dead. Later, Manuel told her his mother's trick of taping pictures to the windows so the birds didn't get fooled by the invisible glass. Rosheen rolled out the newsprint and with coloured pencils drew a string of life-sized blue jays, tanagers, cardinals, and cedar waxwings, the colours and the shapes of heads and tails so accurate her mother was astonished. She cut them out, and Manuel got the ladder and helped her put them up with painter's tape. Manuel and Rosheen stood in the yard admiring their work, a flock of coloured paper birds, suspended high above the roses. Not so many that they blocked the light, but enough to warn the real birds away.

"*Casa de las aves,*" Manuel said. "A house of birds."

Rosheen grinned. The paper birds worked and, for a while, made her feel safe.

And they were pretty. Everyone who came to the house remarked how pretty they were. Mrs Ross asked Rosheen to make some birds for the atrium at the church, and one of Mum's florists asked for some to decorate her flower shop. The birds made them happy, made them smile. It was the first time since Rosheen came out of the hospital that she had pleased anyone. She thought this was something she wanted to do, make beautiful things.

When grade four began in fall, Rosheen returned to school. Her face didn't look much better. But her mother was determined she should go, no matter what the teachers said. Rosheen had rights.

So there she was on the school bus again. As she walked down the aisle to find a seat, some of the kids said, "Hi," but they didn't look at her. One of the boys at the back said, "Holy monster movie!" and the others laughed. She wasn't sure, at first, whether he was talking about her. He was an older boy who didn't even know her. He kept it up, though, week after week. He covered his mouth, so he wouldn't get caught, when he called her names. But she recognized his voice. He called her Godzilla and Frankenstein and Creature from the Black Lagoon — and Cyclops, which didn't even make sense. But Rosheen pretended not to hear him.

Sometimes Rosheen wanted everything to be the same as it was before she got hurt. She remembered going to Katy-Ann's house and listening to her brother's Beatles records and dancing. But there were bad things about her old life, too. Like how stupid she used to be, believing Katy-Ann was her friend or that Manuel took dead birds to a bird hospital. How ignorant she'd been at six and seven and eight. She looked back at her younger self with pity.

6.6

ONE OF THE IMPENETRABLE MYSTERIES OF GOD WAS WHY HE GAVE children to women too weak to raise them: the first Mrs O'Nolan and the second Mrs O'Nolan and then Lucy Keogh and now Eileen Garrison, all of them needing Deirdre to care for their children. At first, Deirdre had only been grateful that someone, anyone, was marrying her son. She had assumed Eileen's pallor and shaky hands were only due to the strain of the wedding. The awful bagpipes and all those blind men in the church. But sadly, Eileen turned out to be the delicate type.

She took weeks to recover from childbirth, and both times Deirdre had flown to Canada to help with the babies. The house was a mess, a muddle of pots and pans too big to fit in the cupboards, dirty boots and gardening gloves and piles of washing everywhere. At least when the first one was born, the yard was pretty, and the flowers blooming. Deirdre took Siobhán outside every day in the fresh air. But the second one was born in January, and it was then that Deirdre saw the full horror of Frank's new home. Darkness at four in the afternoon. A wasteland of snow, the wind like a shrill blade scraping the land flat. So cold that the inside panes of the windows — *the insides* — were coated with thick, white frost and sealed to the sills with ice. Household smells — frying onions, peat moss, dirty diapers — circulated through the stale and chilly rooms, with no release. When Deirdre bundled up Siobhán and sent her with the day's trash to the bin at the end of the driveway, she feared the girl would sink in the deep drifts. But when she exclaimed over the danger, Frank merely cracked jokes. He seemed resigned to his exile.

When the girls were seven and two, and the whole family came to New York for a holiday, Eileen only seemed more anxious. She grew flustered by the ordinary doings of the day, and often needed a rest. At these times Deirdre took the girls on outings. She made them new dresses and taught Siobhán how to bake cookies. She had always wanted a little girl.

A few years later, when Eileen needed an operation on her heart, Frank sent Róisín to New York by herself, for he couldn't possibly cope with a five-year-old on his own. Róisín was shy when Deirdre met her in Toronto. She hid behind the stewardess who had flown with her from Winnipeg. Her hair, bright as orange peel, fell in curls across her forehead, and she would not meet Deirdre's eye. On the flight to New York, she ate the grapes that Deirdre gave her, but she kept her head down and didn't say a word besides "Tank you."

Her first morning in Brooklyn, Róisín still wouldn't speak and couldn't be coaxed. She curled up in a corner of the sofa with her flannel rabbit, shutting her grandmother out. It wasn't until noon, when Deirdre baked muffins, that she came silently into the kitchen, clutching the rabbit, and finally looked up, letting Deirdre see her eyes.

Oh, those eyes. From somewhere far away, Daniel Mac Michael was looking at Deirdre again through those beautiful blue-green irises. Questioning and friendly. Not seeming to blame her. His mild gaze travelled around the kitchen, settling on the muffins. When Deirdre buttered one and gave it to Róisín, the eyes lit up, forgiving her for everything.

Deirdre had telephoned Eileen and told her how exactly the colour of Róisín's eyes matched Frank's when he was a boy. But of course she didn't mention Daniel's eyes. She couldn't even mention Daniel's name. A lie was a horribly long-lasting thing.

Deirdre wasn't lonely. She had the girls who came to sew and she had Lucy's boys still living nearby. God had been merciful, in the end, to Lucy's children. They had all done well. Davey and Paul at the sugar plant and Junior with his own music store. And bless their hearts, Lucy's boys did not forget their Aunt Deirdre. Each of them came by once or twice a week, to tighten the washer on her kitchen tap or take her trash down to the street. John Junior brought presents, a beef steak or a warm scarf and even a radio. That was how Deirdre had discovered, in her fifties, that music was a pleasure. Strange that a mere song could change her mood. Stranger still, the sad songs, even those that brought tears to her eyes, made her feel lighter, as if she had loosened the buttons on her clothes. John Junior was her favourite nephew, though he wore his hair too long and listened to some dreadful jazz. He took her to Mass every Sunday, thank goodness, because the other widows all had dutiful sons to take them.

But the most precious person in her life was her granddaughter, Róisín. The older one, Siobhán, was very pretty, to be sure, if a little grave. But Róisín had a freshness about her, a way of looking at things with a kind of wonder, that made Deirdre want to laugh at her and protect her at the same time.

Róisín had been heartbroken that year, because she couldn't go home at Christmas, and Deirdre had tried to distract her with Lucy's old nativity scene. She set up the little plaster figures, the holy family in the stable, three kings, a camel, a donkey, and a dog. Róisín had taken one look and scampered into Deirdre's room, climbed on the bed and stretched her arm as far as she could reach to grab from the dresser — and Deirdre didn't know how she knew it was there — the little driftwood seal from Ireland, carved by Daniel Mac Michael. She placed it in the stable, between the baby Jesus and the donkey, and though a seal at the nativity didn't seem quite proper, Deirdre didn't have the heart to object.

Now, three years later, Deirdre was glad Róisín was coming for another visit. But she was worried, too. Eileen said the girl had been hurt. An accident, she explained on the phone. Frank had broken a jar and Róisín got badly cut. Let's not get Frank upset about it, but the scar might last a while. Deirdre should try not to be too alarmed when she saw her. Eileen would send a photo in the mail, so Deirdre could prepare herself.

Deirdre did not believe in accidents, and when she saw the photograph, she knew the truth. God had brought down his jealous wrath upon Róisín. It was a family curse. It had fallen on Daniel and on Frank, and now it had fallen on Róisín. God's punishments were logical and absolute. *If you try to run free, I will break your legs. If you dare to make pictures, I'll tear out your eyes. If you want to be loved, I will strip you of your beauty.*

Sunlight streamed through the window, illuminating the golden crucifix on the kitchen wall. Deirdre had taken the Lord Jesus out of hiding, since the Polish priest was long dead and the theft likely forgotten. She kept Him out in the open, where she could pray to

Him, and now she was asking Him how to help Róisín, for if anyone understood how cruel God could be it was the Lord Jesus. He counselled Deirdre to be kind. He reminded her she had turned her back on Daniel and on Frank, and it was time, now, for her to be braver than that, time to learn what Jesus meant when He spoke of love.

For a long time, Deirdre had felt endings closing in on her from all directions. Her glossy hair had faded to a cloudy white, and the steady hands she'd once been proud of often faltered. She had accepted that her work was done, her life completed. But now she felt something tugging at her, pulling her into the future. She wanted to help Róisín.

So when she met Róisín at the airport, Deirdre did not act shocked. She hugged her granddaughter and kissed her cheek, right on the horrid scar, and didn't say a word about it. She only remarked how tall she was, now that she was eight.

"Almost nine," said Róisín.

In the taxi, Deirdre felt a pang of grief at the destruction of Róisín's pretty face. She could only thank God for sparing the eyes. She squeezed Róisín's hand, and the girl looked up at her, grateful. Glad to be here. And Deirdre saw that she was still beautiful.

6.7

KYLE IS STUDYING A COLLAGE ROSHEEN MADE OUT OF THREE different portraits of Deirdre: Frank's quick charcoal sketch of her leaning in a doorway, Rosheen's pencil sketch of her holding baby Kyle in her lap, and Rosheen's more professional watercolour painting of her in her final years. The pencil portrait is impressive, considering Rosheen was barely out of her teens. You can see her love for her subjects in her effort and attention to detail, even though Deirdre and baby Kyle are both slightly misshapen, the drawing overworked. But the later painting is an accomplished, graceful thing, the culmination of years of study. Deirdre looks to be at least ninety. She's sitting up, quite straight and strong for her age, in her kitchen. A very different woman from the angry one in the doorway. Her face is composed as she gazes at the artist with tenderness. Her eyes are compassionate and Von can almost see in them a glimmer of humour. On the wall above her head hangs the gold crucifix Von had found in a shoebox in the Brooklyn apartment. The edges of the three portraits are ragged, the background made up of interwoven strips of paper torn from sheet music, recipes, dress patterns, and hymn books.

"What was she like?" Kyle asks. "Was she, um, *Catholic?*"

"Definitely Catholic. A bit eccentric. She had a hard youth in Ireland, but she was tough. She lived to be ninety-two, and your mum looked after her. They were always close, those two."

"I like this collage," Kyle says. "Deirdre and me are in it, and Frank and Rosheen made it. Four generations. Do you think I could have it, after the show? To keep?"

"I'm pretty sure that's up to me," says Von. "So, yes. It's yours."

"Thanks." He sets the collage reverently on a sheet of brown paper, wraps it the way Durgan has taught him, before placing it in the crate. For a few minutes he is silent, folding the paper and taping the package. Then he asks, "So, is the whole family Catholic?"

————

On Sunday mornings, when Siobhán and her mother got Rosheen ready for church, they tried very hard to be quiet, so as not to annoy Frank. He had no use for church, he said. Eileen argued that the girls needed the guidance. They needed to be taught how to behave. Did Frank want them running wild? Growing up to be loose women? With no respect for themselves? No, Frank had to admit, he did not want that to happen. So he suffered them to go to church. When Siobhán was younger, she thought that was a funny term, "loose women." She imagined women with watery bones, arms and legs as floppy as cooked spaghetti. But now she knew what it meant.

Siobhán had little use for church herself. Church was only good for getting out of the house, away from Frank. On Sundays, he listened to the preachers on the radio and swore at them. Once, when a preacher urged his listeners to lay their hands on the radio to be cured of their afflictions, Frank had thrown the radio against the wall, cracking the plaster and leaving a hole that was still there because Eileen was too nervous to mention it to him. He didn't believe in God or heaven and told Eileen that when he died he didn't want any rites or prayers or even to be buried in a churchyard.

"When the time comes," he said, "give me to the medical school and let them cut me up."

"Really?" Eileen's voice, cold as the north wind. "And I presume you want the children to know of that plan. Because they're in the next room and can hear every word you're saying."

The day the missionaries came, Eileen was out shopping for azalea bushes, a new line she wanted to try out. She specialized in cut flowers, and had developed friendships with florists, wedding planners, and funeral directors in the city. Her seasonal sales were good — Valentine's, Easter, and Christmas — and she supplied more weddings every year. But the funeral business was dying. During the sixties, families began to decline funeral wreaths and bouquets, asking for donations "in lieu of flowers." Eileen thought this was a shame, that it robbed the ceremony of its beauty. Besides, she said, if people wanted to donate to charity, they could do it without anyone having to die. But the trend caught on, and soon "in lieu of flowers" appeared in most obituaries. So Eileen was turning over one dome to bedding plants and digging up the side lot with a motorized tiller so she could plant and raise ornamental shrubs. She didn't have much time, that year, for her daughters.

Frank was at the far end of the greenhouse. All afternoon he'd worked at spiral wrapping long-stemmed roses. The backs of his hands were red with scratches from the thorns, and his forehead was bruised from an encounter with an open door that morning. In the kitchen, Siobhán was chopping carrots. At fourteen, she was used to making the entire supper on her own. Rosheen was decorating an old math book. She had long ago filled the margins of the text with dragonflies and hummingbirds. Now, with the coloured pencils Deirdre had sent for her birthday, she was studiously covering whole pages with birds and butterflies and diaphanous fairy girls flying across a yellow moon. She had perfected a technique of outlining the figures and then colouring them in with the slightest pressure of the pencil lead — pink-breasted robins and lime-green Luna moths with wings so pale you could read the geometry theorems right through them. She hummed happily to herself. They were expecting Manuel to arrive to pick up the bouquets for delivery. So they were not surprised to hear a vehicle pull into the gravel driveway. Siobhán dried her hands on a dishtowel and turned the heat down low. When the doorbell rang she was already at the front door.

But it wasn't Manuel. On the porch stood a sombre man with a small girl, about eight. He wore a dark suit and a starched white shirt and carried a book in the crook of one arm. The book was thick, with gilt-edged pages and gold letters on the cover, and Siobhán knew it was a Bible. The girl wore a pink dress and patent-leather shoes and carried a wicker basket. They both had dark skin and black hair. Siobhán didn't know many Black people. There were only three in her entire school, all from the same family, and they spoke French. Nobody Black had ever come to the door before. She smiled at the girl and said, "Hello. Bonjour."

The man said, "Good evening," with a British accent, and the girl offered her a pamphlet. Not wanting to hurt the girl's feelings, Siobhán accepted it.

"Are your parents at home?" the man asked. "I have some good news for them."

The title of the pamphlet was "God's Plan for You," so Siobhán knew her father would not consider it good news. But she could already hear him entering the kitchen and asking Rosheen about dinner, and the missionary could hear him too.

"My father's working," she said, but her father entered the hallway, where the man could see him drying his scratched hands with a dishtowel.

"Dad?" Siobhán said quietly. "There's a man here at the door."

"Who is it?"

"I don't know him. He's here with his daughter. I think he's going door to door?"

"Salesman?" Frank asked. He went back into the kitchen.

Siobhán smiled at the visitors. "Sorry," she said. "I guess he's too busy today." She stepped back, giving them a chance to leave, but instantly, her father returned. He had only gone back to the kitchen to hang up the towel.

"Good evening, sir," said the Christian. Siobhán left him alone with the lion.

Back in the kitchen, she told Rosheen to put away her pencils and set the table. Rosheen made as much noise as possible, clattering with the soup spoons, but they could still hear the men's voices. Siobhán turned on the radio. For a few minutes, "Bridge over Troubled Water" created a sense of peace and beauty in the kitchen. Then Frank's voice, deep and angry, rose from the hallway. Rosheen set the butter knives beside the spoons, her body tense, ready to run. But she said nothing — she seemed to feel safer pretending she didn't know what was going on. The screen door creaked open and slammed shut. Frank cursed. On the radio, Anne Murray sang "Snowbird." But not loudly enough to mask the sound of Frank knocking over the telephone table. Rosheen flattened herself against the kitchen wall as Frank came crashing through the swinging door, yelling, "Get that damned supper on the table, will you?" He banged out to the greenhouse.

Siobhán ran to the front porch and saw the man marching toward his car, his daughter hurrying beside him. She opened the screen door. The girl, hearing the creak, looked back over her shoulder, as if expecting Frank to emerge and throw a rock. When she saw it was only Siobhán, she stopped. The two girls gazed at each other. Siobhán raised a hand to wave goodbye. The girl's palm fluttered briefly before her father snatched it and led her away.

Just then Manuel pulled up and parked his truck. He nodded to the visitors and doffed his hat, but the man ignored him. He helped his daughter into the passenger seat of his car, crossed over to the driver's door with stiff formality, and drove away.

"Who was that?" Manuel asked.

Siobhán handed him the pamphlet. He nodded grimly. He'd been here once before when a missionary came to call. He gave "God's Plan for You" to Rosheen, and after dinner she decorated it with crayon swirls and sticky glitter.

6.8

A LONG NEEDLE OF PAIN ENTERED FRANK'S LEFT TEMPLE AND embedded itself in his right jaw.

They'd gotten in.

He leaped up, struck out with fists and feet. But he couldn't connect. He pivoted in a circle, throwing punch after punch, until his right fist hit a hard wall. Sound of shattered glass. He stood still, listened. Only his own harsh breathing. They'd retreated. Or hidden themselves in some black corner of the — what was this place? Would he die here, in the dark? He grabbed his head with both hands, as if to hold it in place. Explored his scalp with his fingers, looking for the hilt of the blade lodged there, but he found only hair, no blood. Then the pain came again, arcing across the interior of his skull. He stepped forward, tripped over something, threw out his arms to keep from falling and collided with a barricade of barbed wire or chicken wire or damn it he was in his own bedroom closet, tangled in wire coat hangers. They clinked as he flailed. The metal clothing rod clanged to the floor with all his shirts and trousers down around his feet.

Eileen's voice, calling, "Frank? Are you all right?"

He stumbled backwards, extricated himself from the mess, kicked the bundle of clothes and hangers back inside the closet and kicked the door shut before she entered the room.

"My goodness," she said. "What happened to the mirror?"

Mirror. Yes. The glass. Thank Christ he had not hurt the children.

"Your hand, oh Frank!" She was upon him, holding his hand tenderly, touching only the palm. "You need some ice."

A household accident, caused by plain clumsiness, incompetence. As he let himself relax into Eileen's care, he began to feel the throb of his knuckles, under the screaming pain of the headache. He had punched the mirror on the wall. He hoped he hadn't broken any bones. Eileen led him downstairs, wrapped ice cubes in a dishcloth and tied it around his swelling hand. She gave him three tablets that dulled the headache but did not take it away. He heard his daughters whispering in the hallway, the creak of the swinging door as they peeked inside.

"It's all right, girls," Eileen said. "Daddy's had a little accident. He has a little cut, but I've given him a bandage and he'll be right as rain if you just let him have a little rest this afternoon."

Frank heard *little, little, little.*

"Yes, Mum," said Siobhán from the doorway. To Frank, she said, "Does it hurt?"

"Not too much," said Frank.

"We'll be quiet," said Siobhán. "We'll go outside. Come on, Rosheen." The door creaked as it swung back and forth behind them.

They fled pretty fast, Frank thought. A high whine was rising again in his good ear, and the stitches behind his bad ear, where the surgeon had tried again to reconstruct the eardrum, itched ferociously. He also had a hangover from the general anaesthetic. It always took him weeks to recover from that. An especially troublesome scrap of shrapnel was pushing its way to the surface of the tender skin of his throat, just above the Adam's apple. He could tell the site was infected again. Periodically it caused his temperature to rise and gave him dizzy spells and chills. The tablets were mild, but they'd help bring the fever down. He'd wash his neck with rubbing alcohol and lie on the couch with the radio on to drown out the tinnitus and hope to sleep.

———————

He slept on and off, hearing through the screen the summer wind and the girls playing outside, laughing and then hushing each other. *Don't wake Daddy up!* Considerate. Or anxious? They were nervous children. He had warned Eileen many times not to overprotect them. Canadians spoiled their children, he had told her, shielding them from every little thing. Hearing this, Eileen had run from him, weeping, and locked herself in the bathroom. He had banged on the door and made her come out. "You're too sensitive," he told her. "You're behaving like a child." She had apologized, but he could tell she was still crying.

Of course it was true he had hurt Rosheen. That awful dream, like a hallucination, in which he was back in the dark candy factory in Holland, throwing bricks. He had destroyed the kitchen, sent Rosheen to hospital. He hated himself for that. Hated himself as soon as he came to, alarmed and confused. Siobhán screaming so much he'd thought it was she who was hurt. He had expected the Children's Aid to get involved, expected police officers to arrive that very day, to arrest him. He'd cleaned the kitchen as best he could and showered and shaved and changed into a suit and tie and sat in the living room all day waiting for them to come. But no one came. Eileen called to say the doctors had stitched up the cut, and Siobhán was home by dinnertime, saying Rosheen would be all right. Still, he hated himself for succumbing to the dream. He could hear in Siobhán's voice she hated him, too.

He knew, when he let himself think about it, that he would call the police himself, if the same thing happened to one of his clients. The first priority in social work was the safety of the children. But his own kids were fine. The family had gone through a rough time, especially Rosheen. But she was a tough little nut. She was fine now. He remembered the way she'd hugged him when she came home. She had stuck close to him for days, as if to comfort and protect him.

The other day, she'd come and sat beside him at the outdoor table when he was wrapping roses. She had lain her tiny fingers on the back of his hand and asked him if his scratches hurt.

"Little things like that don't hurt me," he had told her.

She brushed his hair back from his temples and asked about the new stitches behind his ear. "Does your ear hurt?"

"Not too much. The doctor had to cut the skin, so he could fix my ear. I can hear better now."

"Will the doctor fix your eyes?"

"No, honey. He can't fix my eyes."

"Maybe a different doctor could do it. In the future. They could invent a new procedure."

He didn't know where she got these ideas. Where she got that word "procedure." But he was touched. Rosheen was sweet, kind-hearted. She had forgiven him. Ironically, she was the only one who had forgiven him.

———

That evening, Eileen invited Manuel and Yvette to stay for dinner after work, to thank them for their help in getting the last of the wedding bouquets wrapped and delivered in time for the six weddings they had supplied yesterday. A record number, and Eileen wanted to celebrate. She had bought a pot roast, an unusual expense, and roasted it slowly all afternoon with onions and carrots and potatoes in their jackets. The smell had entered Frank's dreams and soothed him as he slept, anchored him on the living-room couch.

At dinner, Yvette and Eileen exchanged neighbourhood gossip. Frank barely listened. His headache had subsided and his appetite had returned. He was concentrating on his meal, trying to sop up gravy with a piece of bread. He knew he was making a mess because Siobhán had pressed a serviette into his hand, saying quietly, "Here, Dad." He wiped his face and chin and dried his sticky fingers. He picked up the bread again and brought it to his mouth, but only a few soggy crumbs reached his lips. He investigated the plate with his fingers. The bread had disintegrated into the puddle of gravy. He wiped his fingers on the serviette, which was now too wet to be any use, and picked up his knife and fork. He sawed off a piece of beef and chased it around the plate.

"When I was down at Mrs Allard's the other day," Eileen was saying, "this man came calling, a Negro man, with his daughter, the cutest little thing you ever saw. They were going door to door with religious tracts. Jehovah's Witness I think they were, or Mormons."

Frank cornered the piece of beef and lifted it on his fork. It was too big. But he was hungry, and the meal was getting cold, so he folded it all into his mouth and began to chew.

"Mrs Allard gave them some cold lemonade," Eileen said. "It was so hot and they must have had a long walk. I'm sure they don't live anywhere nearby. I've never seen them before."

"He had a car," Manuel said. "An old Dodge, good condition, except for a spot of rust."

"You mean they came to our apartment?" asked Yvette.

"No, they came here," said Manuel. "Last week. Gave Siobhán a pamphlet."

When Frank finished chewing, he set Manuel straight. "Those were different people."

"They must be the same people," said Manuel. "A man and his little girl."

"No," said Frank. "Those missionaries who came the other day? They weren't Negroes."

"Sure they were," said Manuel. "I saw them myself."

Frank dropped his fork. Gravy spattered his hand and shirt cuff.

"They came here, too?" Eileen was distracted, rattling dishes and cutlery. "He was an awfully nice man, very polite…"

Frank felt his face heat up. "You mean that was a *Black* man at the door the other day?" He stood up. "Siobhán? Was it?"

No answer. Frank waited. He knew she was there at the table. If she were not there, Eileen would say so.

"Siobhán," he said. "You answer me when I ask a question, you hear? Was that a Black man at the door?"

"Yes, Dad."

"Why didn't you *tell* me that?"

His daughter said nothing.

"For Christ's *sake*," said Frank. "Can't you *think*? Why, if I had known —" His own words came back to him *you people can take your filthy lies and get off my property*. Hot nausea rose in his stomach.

"Frank?" said Eileen. "What's the matter?"

She brought him back to himself. He tried to control his voice now, as he confessed the truth. "Eileen, I gave that fellow a real piece of my mind. I was … I swore at him."

"Frank, you didn't!" said Eileen. "Not in front of the little girl?"

"I didn't know she was little," he said. Eileen's disapproval made it all too real. "And I sure the hell didn't know they were Black! Siobhán, you didn't say one word. She said nothing, Eileen! She just let me — God!" He threw down his serviette, knocking over his water glass.

The room was silent.

Frank stood up.

Rosheen let out a cry. No one else made a sound. Water dripped from the table, into his right shoe, wetting his sock. Eileen had wanted a celebration dinner, he knew that. He was embarrassing her. He should leave. He wasn't fit company for anyone right now. He stood up, catching his foot in the rail of his chair. He leaned on the table to keep his balance, feeling the tablecloth wet and greasy under the palms of his hands. He kicked free of the chair. It tipped and fell with a loud clatter to the floor.

With one outstretched arm, Frank found the wall behind him and followed it in silence until he reached the hall.

"Good night, Mr Garrison," said Yvette. Her voice was small and tight. Frank wanted to say good night to her, to thank her for this small gesture, but he didn't trust himself to speak. He pushed the door open and went upstairs to bed.

Upstairs, he relived his conversation with the Christian missionary, hearing it all now from a different perspective. He sat at the foot of his bed, elbows on his knees, pressing his forehead into his hands. His face burned with fever and with shame. He had become what he most hated. What must that man have thought of him? Another ignorant racist, tearing his daughter's confidence to shreds. Making the world she lived in ugly. Frank slammed his fist against the wall and gasped at the pain that shot through his hand. He had forgotten about his damaged knuckles. But he welcomed the suffering. He deserved it. He lay flat on his back with his arms flung out at his sides and took inventory. His toe ached where he had kicked the chair. His right hand seemed to be on fire. His stomach burned, and the shrapnel site was sore. He lifted his hand to finger the metal fragment under the skin. It had not yet broken through, but soon it would work its way out as his body expelled it. He wished he could rid himself of this other thing too, this festering ulcer of shame and anger. Sometimes he thought he had succeeded, but then it would erupt again, poisoning everything around him. He willed his mind to be still, to stop thinking, to shut up.

6.9

WHY DIDN'T YOU *TELL* ME? CAN'T YOU *THINK?*

How, after all this time, do her father's words still have the power to hurt her? She understood what he meant. He was trying to say that if he'd known the man wasn't white, he wouldn't have been so rude. He would have been polite, so nobody would think he was prejudiced. At the time, she'd felt he was blaming her for not letting him pretend to be nice. She had lain awake, thinking up things she could have said, if she weren't such a coward.

She should have said, *They were standing right there in the hall beside us, Dad, what did you want me to say? There's a Black man at the door?* No. She had punched her pillow in frustration. She should have said, *I get it, Dad. It's wrong to judge people by the colour of their skin. But it's perfectly all right to hate them for their religion.* No. Too daring. He would have killed her if she'd said that, and anyway, that wasn't the point, though she wasn't sure what the point was. She brooded on the injustice meted out to the missionary and his little girl, to her mother and, as always, to Rosheen, who had vanished beneath the table as soon as the chair fell. She had spent a long time coaxing Rosheen to come out later for dessert. Not that anyone ate dessert. Manuel and Yvette left early, thanking Eileen profusely for the lovely meal.

Now, thirty years later, Von knows exactly what the point was. The point was, why did Frank feel so guilty, why was he so filled with regret over his rudeness to total strangers, when his cruelty to his own family didn't bother him one bit? That was the point.

Frank seemed to understand that he had hurt Rosheen the year before. Siobhán had heard him promise Eileen he'd see a doctor for his "sleepwalking" problem. But as far as she could tell, he never did. Didn't he care? Didn't he realize how serious it was? She tried to raise this topic, privately, with her mother, while her father was at work.

"Isn't there someone Dad could see?" she asked. "For his, you know, like how he *gets?*"

"He's much better, now. You know yourself, there's never been another incident like — " She looked behind her, to make sure Rosheen wasn't there. "Like that."

"But there could be. There might be. If he doesn't see a counsellor or — "

"Your father *is* a counsellor. What would people think — "

"He almost *killed* her!" said Siobhán. "Is that what you're waiting for? For him to — "

"Don't *say* that!" Eileen's hand was raised as if to slap her daughter's face. Her eyes told Siobhán she was sorely tempted. Siobhán's eyes told her to go ahead and try.

They stared at each other in horror. They had never treated each other so harshly before. Eileen's hand went down. Her voice was low but urgent. "I don't want to hear another word out of you on this topic, understand? You're growing up fast, but you are not as smart as you think you are. There is a lot you don't understand, and you should be *glad* you don't understand. You have no idea what your father's been through."

———

"There is only one thing a blind person cannot do," Frank often said. "He cannot see."

Frank said only inferior people needed light. This was supposed to be a joke, and he told it every time there was a power failure, though nobody ever laughed. How could they laugh? Once when Mr Ross and Frank were carrying a washing machine down into the basement, they had to stop and put the machine down so Mr Ross could turn on the light switch at the bottom of the stairs. Frank made the joke then, embarrassing poor Mr Ross. Siobhán knew her father appreciated all the things Mr Ross did for their family, especially the driving. But she could tell he also resented Mr Ross. He preferred to rely on his wife and daughters when he could.

When Rosheen turned ten, Frank gave her the job of helping him in his workshop. Every Saturday, he made her sweep sawdust and organize the nails and — worst of all — help him when he drilled or sawed wood. Rosheen hated the noise of the power tools and the sharp teeth of the electric saw. But she had to do her chores. Sometimes Siobhán took a break from her own chores and went out to the garage and watched them, Frank with his tongue between his teeth, concentrating hard as he measured with the Braille ruler or fed a two-by-four into the table saw, while Rosheen stood close by, gritting her teeth, following whatever instructions he called out, trying to be fast enough and not make any mistakes.

"It's good for you to learn about woodworking," Siobhán told her, when she complained. "Most girls never get a chance. You're lucky."

"You're the lucky one," Rosheen said. "All you have to do for Dad is read books, or go shopping."

Siobhán loved reading the books, though most of them were far over her head. But she dreaded the shopping. In Eaton's, when her father asked the clerk to show him the new power jigsaws featured in their catalogue, the young man took one look at him and blurted, "Ha!" Then he blushed deep red, as if embarrassed to have laughed at a joke in such poor taste. When he realized Frank was serious, the clerk appealed to Siobhán, asking with his eyes if Frank were insane. She remained noncommittal.

"You do carry the new jigsaws?" Frank asked. "I'd like to compare a few models."

"Sir. If you'll excuse me, sir, I have customers waiting."

"All right," said Siobhán. She turned away.

But Frank tightened his grip on her shoulders, as if she were the steering wheel of a car he was driving, and turned her around again. "We are customers too," he said.

The clerk hesitated. He tried to catch her eye, but she would not let him. She was a Garrison. No matter how angry she might be with her father, she was loyal.

"Very well, sir," said the clerk. "One moment." He glanced furtively up and down the aisles, no doubt afraid his boss might catch him showing electric saws to a blind man.

Frank waited silently. The only sign of his anger was the tightening of his grasp. After a shopping trip downtown, she often found purple finger imprints on her upper arm. She thought about showing these bruises to somebody, but that seemed tacky, a stunt a girl in a sordid soap opera might pull, to get attention. She waited silently beside him. Bobby Sullivan had asked her to meet him for supper, but by the time she got her father home and then went out again... She glanced around for a clock but couldn't find one. She couldn't see Frank's watch because his coat sleeve covered it. She couldn't look at her own watch because he was holding her left arm and he'd know if she did. Then he would ask her if she had somewhere else she had to be. Was he taking up too much of her time?

At home, Siobhán pressed the long white button of her father's tape recorder, and the reels began to turn. She read: *The trees are in their autumn beauty*. And for the next hour, she became a voice only, dispensing syllables in rhythms as required by the marks on the paper, reading whatever books her father asked her to read. She liked poetry the most, the chance to escape her own thoughts and slip into the mind of Yeats or Blake, feeling the flat black words lift from the page and come alive in her mouth as she found the rhythms. Sometimes she stopped the recorder and began again, rereading a passage once she felt more sure of its cadence, and even when the philosophers, Kierkegaard or Freud or Bertrand Russell, were incomprehensible, she could still discern the shape and emotion of their sentences, trace the movements of their thoughts, as if threading her way through a maze in the dark. But the best thing about reading for her father was the solitude. It was the only time nobody interrupted her.

———

Siobhán turned sixteen near the end of grade ten, and wanted to look for a summer job. But her mother said she was needed at home. "Especially now you're old enough to drive. You'll be able to do the shopping and —"

"I have to get Rosh ready, Mum." Siobhán set a cup of tea on the table beside the couch where her mother lay. Over the weekend, she had helped Eileen in the side lot, transplanting row after row of blue fox willow. But even though Siobhán had done most of the work, Eileen had exerted herself too much, and this morning she was complaining of chest pains.

In her room, Rosheen lay with the backs of her calves on her bed and the rest of her body dangling over the edge, her face more startling and crazier upside down. For reasons nobody could understand, the scar would not heal. It ran from Rosheen's right temple across the rebuilt cheekbone under her right eye, and then down through both lips into her chin. And it was crooked. Over the years, Siobhán had sat with her mother in the offices of a dozen different doctors while they examined Rosheen. None of them could explain to Eileen's satisfaction why the scar refused to shrink or even fade. The man who had sewn the wound was said be one of the best surgeons in the country, but the scar was stubborn. A keloid, one doctor called it. Attempts to fix it only thickened it and seemed to make it brighter. And the operations were painful, each one requiring more drugs than the last. Best to leave it alone. Rosheen was still young. Once she was an adult, they said, something might be done. They spoke of research and new procedures. Hope for the future.

Siobhán didn't believe any future surgery could fix it. Neither did Eileen, judging by the slump of her shoulders as she left those offices. They both thought it was hopeless. But they kept up the fiction. Rosheen could have an operation, Eileen told her. When she was all grown up.

"When I'm married?" asked Rosheen.

"Oh, *long* before you're married!" said Eileen.

She assured her daughter that once the scar was gone she would be pretty. She was pretty now, under the scar. The boys who teased her were ignorant. Eileen felt sorry for them because no one had taught them right from wrong. She was proud that her girls never teased another child. She kissed Rosheen and said she was beautiful on the inside. Yet more and more often she left her in the care of Siobhán.

This morning Rosheen wore only a blue undershirt and blue tights, because she was Invisible Girl. She was eleven now, and though she was small for her age, she was too old, in Siobhán's opinion, to be playing superhero. But Siobhán, like her mother, often indulged her.

"Let her enjoy being a girl," Eileen had once said bitterly, "because she'll get no pleasure from being a woman."

"Hurry up," Siobhán said. "Time to get dressed for school."

"I don't want to go!" Rosheen said. When Siobhán pulled her up, she wriggled away and climbed onto the bed. She bounced up and down, slugging imaginary villains. She had to rescue Mr Fantastic, she said, who was being held captive in the laundry basket.

"Hurry up and rescue him, then," said Siobhán. "I'm getting ready for school, and when I come back in here, you better be ready, too." She went into the bathroom and washed her face. When she came back in, Rosheen had disappeared. "Five minutes!" yelled Siobhán.

In her own room, Siobhán reviewed her choice of clothing. She was thinking of Bobby Sullivan, hoping he might come by the school today. He had dropped all his classes to take a job at the newspaper, but with his odd shifts he could often come by to see her during the day. She knew he liked her. He had taken her for two meals at the Blue Café and to two concerts in the park, and to two movies. Really only one movie, *Little Big Man*, but they had gone to see it twice. Siobhán wrote about these occasions in her diary. She didn't call them dates — she wasn't allowed to date yet, her mother said — and Bobby had never kissed her. But she knew for sure he was going to kiss her soon. Should she wear the turquoise blouse that tinted her grey eyes blue? Or the black blouse that hugged her body? She wanted to please him, wanted to make him laugh that sweet, private laugh, low in his throat. She pondered her lipsticks, white, cherry, and coral, wondering which to choose. The white didn't suit her, though it looked so good on the models in the magazines. So it was between the cherry and the brand new coral. As she compared them, she heard her mother coming up the stairs.

"Mum?"

Eileen came into the bedroom with her well-meaning smile.

"Mum, should I wear this new lipstick? Or is it too pink?"

"Let's see," said Eileen. "Show me." When Siobhán applied the coral lipstick, Eileen scrutinized her the way she scrutinized fruit in the supermarket, and then said, "Oh, honey, you look *so* pretty." She smoothed Siobhán's hair and tucked a loose strand behind her ear. "More than pretty. You're going to be a serious beauty some day, I can tell."

"What are you doing?" asked Rosheen. She was crawling out from under Siobhán's bed, with a plastic sword in her hand. "What's serious beauty?"

"Oh," said Eileen. "Good question. What is beauty, anyway? Why, beauty's in the eye of the beholder!"

"We're going to be late, Rosheen!" Siobhán left her blouses in the closet. Her flannel shirt would do. She combed her hair with her fingers and tied it back with an elastic. She packed Rosheen's school bag and wrestled her into a dress, and managed to get her to her bus stop on time.

Siobhán had recently taken to skipping class to read in the sugar shacks — the penalty boxes in the outdoor skating rink. One of the sugar shacks faced away from the school, and when the weather was warm enough, she'd spend her time out there with Jane Austen or Ray Bradbury instead of going to class. The other kids didn't disturb her. Sometimes they came out to sneak a smoke, but usually they just said "hi" and lit up at the other end of the bench and ignored her.

As it turned out, Bobby Sullivan liked Siobhán's turquoise blouse and her tight black blouse, and her flannel shirts, too. He liked her with or without the lipstick and did not care what books she read. He entered the long field of the schoolyard and walked under the football goal posts and through the baseball diamond and across the hockey rink — all puddles and gravel and weeds, now that it was June. She saw him coming, but pretended she didn't, even though it was hard not to grin or even burst out laughing for sheer happiness because it was summer and her whole body felt jumpy and light to know he was moving closer to her. When he leaned on the rail of the sugar shack and asked her what she was reading, she didn't look up.

She said, "*Nine Stories.*"

"All at once?"

She gave him a quick glance. "What are you doing here?" She had told him she planned to skip French today at two.

"Just passing by on my way home from work." He was an apprentice now, working for the men who ran the printing presses. He needed the money, because his grandfather was sick.

"I see," she said. "So this is a coincidence?"

"I call it fate."

She looked up at him. He had grown taller over the past year. His hair was cut shorter, and his shoulders were broader, his arms muscular from heavy lifting. She was proud of him. Proud that he liked her. He wore jeans and a white T-shirt and carried a white paper bag from the candy department at Eaton's. He said, "Can I sit with you?" He gazed solemnly into her eyes, but when she said, "Yes," he couldn't hide the smile that tugged at one corner of his mouth. He jumped over the gate. From the bag, he took out a snowball and offered it to her. She placed it on her tongue and tasted the coconut and smiled at him.

"Do you like it?"

"I like it."

He ate one too. A gang of boys ran onto the field and began a game of pick-up baseball in the diamond.

"How is your mother?" Bobby asked. Last week, she'd told him she couldn't go to the movies because her mother was suffering chest pains.

"Much better now, thanks. How's your grandfather?"

"He's having a bad time," Bobby said. "He's recovered from the operation, but the cancer treatments make him sick. It's hard to get him to eat. That's why I bought all this candy."

Siobhán liked his directness. Nobody else ever talked like that about cancer. Not that she wanted to talk about cancer. But he wasn't squeamish about things. Bobby's parents had both died young. His grandfather had moved in to take care of him when Bobby was ten, and now, six years later, Bobby was taking care of his grandfather. He wasn't like the other boys she knew at school, spoiled boys, who took their good fortune for granted.

While they watched the baseball game, he told her about the work he was doing on his grandfather's cabin, winterizing it, so the old man could live there year-round, as soon as he got his health back. "He's never liked the city," Bobby said. "He always planned to retire to his cabin. It's quiet there, in a hidden spot, on a bay on the north shore. He was getting ready to move there when, you know, he had to come and look after me. So some of my friends — guys that like to go out there fishing with us — are helping me fix it up — insulation, new windows and everything. It's fun." He turned away from the baseball game to look at her and lowered his voice. "You should come out with me sometime and see it."

Siobhán looked down at the ground, letting her hair fall around her face so he couldn't see her blushing or, worse, see her smiling at the thought of being alone, in a remote cabin on a remote bay on the shore of Clear Lake, with Bobby Sullivan…

"Hey," he said. He bumped her gently with his shoulder. He placed his hand over her hand. "Hey, what's the matter?"

She looked up then and he took her face between his hands and began to kiss her, and the book fell from her lap onto the ground, but she didn't notice. She didn't even notice the grade twelve track team come running out of the school and onto the field in their regulation whites, circling the rink, while the gym teacher marched toward the sugar shack, one hand on her hip and a whistle around her neck. She didn't notice the teacher at all until she heard the short, sharp whistle and the admonition, "Shame on you, young lady!"

6.10

EVER SINCE SIOBHÁN GOT CAUGHT KISSING BOBBY SULLIVAN, AND Rosheen knew this because she eavesdropped on the entire scolding, there was a wonderful new family rule.

Siobhán was sixteen and old enough to know better, her mother scolded. Siobhán was only sixteen, her father scolded, too young to be kissing a boy. It was a disgrace, he said, to behave that way in public, and it was a sin, she said, to behave that way in private.

"To think," Frank said, "that a daughter of mine would turn out to be that kind of a girl." He forbade her ever to be alone with Bobby again. Or there would be hell to pay.

This was the wonderful rule. Because now Siobhán and Bobby took Rosheen with them everywhere they went. Which was good, because Rosheen had no one else to take her anywhere.

At school, Katy-Ann and Mary-Kate had almost stopped speaking to Rosheen. They walked together, sometimes arm-in-arm with pretty Em Lowler in the middle, and when they passed Rosheen on the playground the two of them smiled and waggled the fingers of one hand, because their mothers had taught them to be nice. They said, "Hi, Rosheen," in identical high voices, like two girl robots. Rosheen waved back. She couldn't afford to snub them. She never smiled back, though. She knew she looked much worse when she was smiling. Like an overeager creature from the depths of the lagoon.

The word "nice" was a dull word, the teacher said. She had forbidden its use in composition class. But to Rosheen it was a vital word. It divided the safe kids from the ones who pinched and called her names or pretended to throw up when she walked by. Those were the mean kids. The ones who were neither nice nor mean ignored her, not wanting to take sides. This was what one boy told her in the winter, when she tried to get inside his snow fort to escape two boys who were chasing her. He didn't let her in because he didn't want to take sides. When the two boys caught her, they stuffed her underpants with snow.

It was no comfort knowing she was not the only one. She observed the shunning of short kids, fat kids, boys who looked like girls and girls who looked like women. That was Suzie Sam's problem. In grade six, when everyone else was eleven and twelve, Suzie was thirteen and developing what Rosheen's mother called "a body." Boys reserved for her a special kind of torment. When Rosheen tried to sympathize, Suzie told her to drop dead.

Rosheen could have given her advice. Suzie always sat up straight, looking all around her, trying to catch some nice kid's eye. Rosheen knew better. She would have told Suzie to get a book, a big hardcover from the library, and keep it on her lap on the school bus and at lunch. To clutch it to her chest when she was walking. It was best to keep your head down and pretend you didn't hear or see them. If they got too close, a heavy, hard-edged book could be used for self-defence. Rosheen herself had learned to carry a spiral-bound sketchbook everywhere she went. She uncurled the last wire spiral on the spine to make a sharper weapon, just in case, and concentrated on her drawing so she could ignore them.

The sketchbook turned out to be more powerful than she expected. Every so often, somebody taunted her for her constant drawing. Once on the bus, an older boy had grabbed the sketchbook and tried to pass it around, encouraging everyone to laugh. But nobody laughed. The first couple of kids just looked at a few pages and silently passed it along, and the third kid, a girl, handed it back to Rosheen, saying, "Sorry." Because even the stupidest kid could see her drawings were beautiful. That was what saved her. No one could ridicule her artwork without looking like a fool. This fact had silenced some of them for good. Not enough of them, however.

———

Rosheen's only friend was Raymond Ross, who went to a different school. So she rejoiced when her sister and Bobby started taking her along with them. They took her to the swimming pool and the movies and the park and the ice cream parlour. They included her in their conversations, telling her the names of the bands they listened to on the radio. They held her hands — one on each side — at the roller rink, until she learned to skate.

When winter came, they started a tradition of ice skating Friday nights. Bobby borrowed his grandfather's car, and they invited

Raymond Ross to come along, and the four of them skated outside the community club — or inside if it was too cold — to the upbeat songs in the club's record collection: "Knock Three Times" and "I Woke up in Love this Morning" and Rosheen's favourite, "Delta Dawn." Rosheen and Ray practised skating backwards and tried to spin while leaping in the air, usually landing on their bums. But Siobhán and Bobby danced. They were like two swans gliding together, so smooth and graceful that Rosheen wasn't the only person who stopped to watch them as they went round and round, their red cheeks glowing, the snow falling gently and catching in Siobhán's dark hair.

The best days were when Bobby came to pick up Rosheen right from school, and she didn't have to take the school bus home. Bobby would drive Rosheen to the high school, where they'd pick up Siobhán, and then they'd all go somewhere fun together. Just the three of them.

In spring, Siobhán got busy with other things, choir practice and editing the yearbook, and Rosheen went back to riding the school bus every day, her sketchbook balanced at the ready on her knees. She was near the end of grade six now. She was twelve and a half. Twelve was supposed to be the magic age, or so her mother had said, when the other kids would mature and cease to tease her. This prediction wasn't coming true. If anything, the kids were worse than ever.

But one day in May, Rosheen was invited out for a special occasion. Siobhán had permission to go to Bobby's house for dinner, as long as she took Rosheen. Bobby had bought his very own car and was coming to pick up Rosheen after school.

He pulled up at the curb in his new car and called her name, in front of everyone. He had bought a like-new, second-hand Mustang, black, with a silver horse on the hood. Rosheen wanted to jump up and down, but seeing as Katy-Ann was watching, she merely waved at Bobby and strolled casually toward him. She climbed into the seat beside him, though she knew she'd have to jump in back when they picked up Siobhán. Bobby showed her the tape deck and let her choose a tape to play. She took her time sorting through his tapes, and he waited for her before he started the car. She was glad of it, because when Katy-Ann's mother arrived in their family car, a clunky, fake wood-panelled station wagon, Rosheen was still sitting in the Mustang beside cute Bobby Sullivan, who was so cool he didn't even go to school anymore. She saw Katy-Ann staring and imagined her envy.

At Bobby's house, Siobhán carried in the groceries they had bought on the way home and put them on the counter as if she lived there.

"Hi, Mr Sullivan!" she said.

Rosheen saw a lump of blankets, possibly a man, scrunched up on a couch, and a table set with mugs and thick plates. There seemed to be only two rooms in the house, separated by a limp cotton curtain. It was partly drawn aside, and she saw beyond it an unmade bed.

Bobby said, "Grandpa?"

The lump on the couch stirred itself. An old man peeked out, the sparse hair on his head askew. He struggled to sit up.

Bobby gathered the blankets and began to fold them. "This is Siobhán's sister, Rosheen. She's joining us for dinner."

Bobby's grandfather put on his glasses and smoothed back his hair. "Welcome," he said. He reached out a hand to Rosheen and she gripped it, thinking he wanted to shake. But he needed her to help him off the couch, so she pulled. He groaned, a cheerful, friendly groan. "Stiff as a board," he said. "Lazing around all day." He didn't look sick. Bobby had said he was getting better. He was going to move out to the lake this fall.

They worked together, making salad and hamburgers, while Bobby's grandpa bragged about the fish he had caught and the ones he was going to catch this summer. He asked Rosheen about her visits to New York, and she described the giant bridges and the skyscrapers and Coney Island. Nobody had ever asked her so many questions before. "To think, a wee thing like you has been to the greatest city in the world," he joked, "while I've never left this province!" He sighed. "So, what are your future plans? Career girl? Or wife and mother?"

Rosheen squirmed. "Wife and mother."

"Oh ho! And how are the prospects looking so far?"

"Don't tease her, Tim," said Siobhán. "I told you, she's shy."

Tim? Rosheen looked up to see him wink at Siobhán, as if he knew her well. Siobhán shook her head at him in mock rebuke, and Rosheen saw they knew each other very well. Her sister must have been here many times. Without Rosheen. This was against the rules. Siobhán smiled, serving salad as if nothing was wrong. Rosheen tried to absorb this new information: her sister had lied, not just to Mum and Dad, but to Rosheen. Siobhán had never lied to her before.

After dinner they ate ice cream and played cards. Bobby and his grandpa had to teach the girls the rules, because all they knew was Go Fish. They never played cards at home. It was a waste of time, their mother said. Then Siobhán remembered that tomorrow was their mother's birthday, and she'd meant to pick some rushes to give her. For all the attention she lavished on hot-house roses, their mother loved simple wild plants too. Siobhán asked Bobby if he'd mind going to the river to look for some while she washed the dishes. It was getting late.

"Sure, Vonnie," he said. He often called her *Vonnie*, or just *Von*, making her sound like a model or a movie star. Then he turned to Rosheen. "Rosh, you want to come for a walk?"

Rosh! Rosheen jumped to her feet. That would be a perfect end to the day. "Ready in a flash," she said. She'd heard Doris Day say that in a movie once. Stylish and breezy. Cute.

As she washed her hands in the bathroom, Rosheen happened to look up. Ugh. In the mirrored door of the medicine cabinet, she caught a glimpse of her face. She was smiling like an idiot, her demented half-girl, half-monster grin. Doris Day? Who was she kidding? She threw open the cabinet door so she wouldn't have to see herself. Inside, wow. The shelves were packed, like drugstore shelves, with medicine. Curious, she checked the labels. All for Bobby's grandpa, "for pain." But they seemed abandoned. Maybe he didn't need any more medicine? On impulse, she shoved a thin tube of white pills into the front pocket of her jeans and untucked her shirt so the bulge wouldn't show. She dried her hands and came out of the bathroom.

Bobby pulled on his rubber boots, and Rosheen pulled on his grandpa's rubber boots, over her shoes, and they walked to the Seine. Bobby showed her where he'd seen a doe and a fawn just yesterday. They told each other about the animals they'd encountered on this riverbank. Deer, foxes, turtles, herons, woodchucks, owls, skunks, raccoons. Thousands of rabbits. And mosquitoes, said Rosheen. That made him snort. But they didn't find any reeds or rushes.

"Let's check the ditches by the highway," Bobby suggested. So they got in the Mustang and drove east. The ditches were narrow marshes, full of ducks and frogs. Bobby parked and for a few minutes they listened to frogs and crickets and buzzing insects. Then they walked to the edge of the marsh. Red-winged blackbirds darted among the rushes, calling. A crow flew down from a poplar tree, and immediately two blackbirds rose and hurled themselves at the crow, stabbing at it with their beaks and flapping their wings until the crow flew upwards.

"They'll escort the crow out of their territory," Bobby said. "Watch." The red-winged blackbirds followed the crow, each flanking one side of it, until it sailed out of sight above the trees, and then the blackbirds looped back to the ditch and settled in among the rushes.

"They have their nest in there," Bobby said. "They're protecting their eggs or baby birds."

"I don't want to scare them," Rosheen said. So they walked farther east.

In the tall grasses, Bobby found a long poplar branch, which he stripped and gave to Rosheen to use for a walking stick so she wouldn't sink into the soggy ground.

Soon, Rosheen spotted a patch of slender branches sprouting soft buds of grey fluff. "Pussy willows!" she called. She hurried down the shallow incline toward the ditch.

"Careful, now. Put your stick in the water. Make sure it's no deeper than your boots."

They waded in together and he cut the willow stems with his pocket knife, handing them to her one by one. Then he cut an armload of green bulrushes and they carried their harvest to the car.

When they turned onto Bobby's street, he parked and said, "That was fun, Rosh."

She walked ahead, her arms full of willow branches. A thrill of pleasure ran up her spine.

As she entered the house, she felt again the bottle of pills in her pocket and wondered why she had taken it. She didn't want to steal. She should return it. But once inside the bathroom, she hesitated. So many pills! Surely Mr Sullivan wouldn't miss one bottle. If he really still needed medicine for pain, he had plenty of others to choose from. But if Rosheen needed it, she'd have nothing. She decided to keep it. Just in case.

6.11

AFTER A YEAR OF LIVING UNDER HER PARENTS' EDICT, SIOBHÁN and Bobby had discovered many ways to slip away together without her little sister knowing. Siobhán had become adept at the art of the half-truth, telling Rosheen she was going to Sara's house and then going to Sara's house — for half an hour, before leaving to meeet Bobby. Today she had told her parents she was going to a concert "with friends," which was only true because she and Bobby knew some of the members of the audience from school. But they weren't sitting anywhere near them. It was July, summer holidays for Von, whenever she could get away from chores, and a rock band was playing in Memorial Park. She lay on her stomach in the grass, her chin propped on her hands, while Bobby, using the small of her back as a pillow, fell asleep, despite the loud music, because he'd worked all night in the pressroom at the newspaper.

Von didn't mind. She watched the young dancers as she felt the bass notes beat from the speakers into the ground and through her body. Bobby's head lay warm and heavy on her back. Idly, she'd been aware of rain clouds drifting in from the west, and then suddenly, the temperature dropped. Bobby woke up. The odd slant of the light, the green tinge of the clouds, warned of hail, or even a tornado.

The concert ended early. The band packed up their equipment and went home, the crowd dispersed. Everyone knew the storm was going to be bad. Bobby rode Siobhán double on his bicycle, all the way down Portage Avenue and over the Provencher bridge to St Boniface. She didn't have to go home yet. Her mother had gone out for the day, leaving a cold dinner in the fridge, so she didn't have to cook. She'd told her father she was going to Sara's house for dinner, planning to stay out late at the concert. But the weather had ruined that plan. The sensible thing to do now was to take shelter at Bobby's house, with his grandfather. But they were not sensible. They were seventeen. It was Saturday afternoon, and they'd been waiting for this day all week so they could be alone together. To postpone their parting as long as possible, he offered to ride her double to her house.

She sat on the bicycle seat and held on to his waist while he pedalled, standing, all the way up the highway and onto the twisting, pothole-riddled road through the oak trees and into the orchard. When he reached the small clearing, a patch of thin grass among the Manitoba apple trees, he stopped and let her off. He flung himself to the ground, winded and happy. "Almost got you all the way home without stopping."

She laughed. "Almost!" She looked up at the darkening sky. "You better go home now. I'm so sorry. You're going to get caught in the rain."

They looked at each other with regret.

He stood up. "I'll walk you the rest of the way."

"Bobby, you'll get soaked."

"I don't care." He placed one arm around her shoulders, and with his other arm he steered the bike over the bumpy road. They passed through the rest of the orchard and came to the edge of the field just as the rain began to fall. They sheltered under the branches of a crabapple tree and watched the storm in silence, glad they'd taken the risk. It was worth it just to feel Bobby's arm warm across her shoulders, to hear the rhythm of his breathing and smell the coarse soap he'd used that morning to wash the printer's ink from his skin after the midnight shift. She lifted her hand to his chest, felt his heart beat, strong and slowing after the long ride. Then lightning flashed, illuminating the entire field.

"We should get away from the trees," he said.

"I know." They looked at each other. They both saw Siobhán's house on the far side of the field. But they couldn't go there. Her father was home. If he found out she'd been out alone with Bobby, there would be hell to pay. That's how Frank had phrased it himself: hell to pay.

Lightning flashed again. A crack of thunder.

"The greenhouse!" cried Siobhán. She pointed across the field, and Bobby nodded.

They made a run for it, sliding on the wet grass, hard raindrops pelting their backs. He pulled off his sodden shirt and held it above them like a sail. She fell, and he pulled her to her feet. She leaned on him, and they stood still a moment. Then the sky turned white and they tore through thick, silver sheets of falling rain, the sky dark and light at rapid intervals, the thunder continuous. Rain in their mouths and their ears and in their eyes so they could not see.

They reached the greenhouse, laughing. Her wet hands slipped on the door handle as they spilled inside, panting, their hair plastered to their heads, their clothing drenched. He closed the door and then they were surrounded by the hollow sound of rain rattling hard on the glass roof. The west wall so white with water they couldn't see the house. They were alone, enveloped in the rich, sweet smell of roses and peat moss. He touched her face. He wiped her forehead and her cheeks with his wet fingers and then he kissed her and his lips tasted like rain.

———

Inside the greenhouse, with their soaked clothes sticking to their bodies, Siobhán and Bobby began to shiver. The rain beat so hard on the glass roof they couldn't hear each other talk, so they communicated with gestures. Reaching under the table, Von pulled out the blanket she kept there for her secret reading sessions. She pointed to the extra pair of overalls Manuel kept hanging on a nail. Turning their backs to each other, they stripped off their wet clothes. She wrapped the blanket around her, thick, scratchy wool on her damp skin, and he put on the overalls. Together, they laid kindling in the stove and lit a fire, hanging their clothes above it to dry. Then they sat close, sharing a crate of tulip bulbs for a chair, and watched the sky, a light show more spectacular than any they'd witnessed before, though they'd both grown up on the electric prairie. The panes rattled. The frame of the greenhouse seemed to shake.

Siobhán wanted to stretch her cold fingers out toward the stove, but she knew if she let go of the blanket it would slip from her shoulders.

As if he knew this, Bobby stood up and moved behind her, placed his hands on her shoulders. Even through the heavy blanket, she felt the warmth of him. He stroked her arms, all the way down to her fingertips and then back up to her shoulders. She arched back, leaning her head against his chest. He bent and embraced her. The sound of the rain slowed, then ceased. He buried his face in her neck and then began to kiss her. She opened her eyes. The glass panes were clear now. The rain had stopped. She could see the sky, still dark with clouds. She could see the house. She saw the figure of her father standing at her bedroom window, both arms raised above his head, touching the upper window frame. A thrill of fear radiated from her heart throughout her body.

"Warmer now?" asked Bobby.

"Yes."

He kissed her neck again, lowered his hands to her waist, and began to move them over her ribcage. Her father's fingers traced the rectangle of the window, as if sealing its seams.

Then a crack! Bobby jumped backwards. Siobhán jumped to her feet. The greenhouse was under attack. Hail. Danger — ruin, collapse, an avalanche of broken glass. She ran for the door and he followed.

Outside, hailstones pelted down on their heads with great force, as if hurled from the clouds. They were small, but hard. One hit Bobby just above his eye. Instinctively, Siobhán opened her blanket and let him in, drawing it over their heads. They stood together in the woollen tent, her bare skin pressed against the rough denim of the overalls. He held her close until the hail abated. It lasted less than a minute. Then the sun came out.

Wrapped in her blanket, Siobhán walked around the greenhouse, relieved to see no broken glass. Tomorrow, she'd get on a ladder and check for any hidden damage. For now, she should go inside, reassure her father.

Bobby had to go home and cook dinner for his grandfather. She hated to part with him, yet at the same time she was so filled with joy she couldn't help smiling. He was smiling, too, as he kissed her. Both of them were smiling too much to kiss properly, and this made them laugh. He tied his boot laces together and hung the boots across the back of his neck and bundled his sodden clothes together and tucked them under his arm. She stood in the doorway of the greenhouse as he splashed across the field. Hailstones glistened among the grass blades. At the edge of the woods, he picked up his bicycle and turned to wave at her, and though he was too far away for her to see his face, she knew he was still smiling, could not stop smiling, and neither could she. She inhaled and felt as though she held the whole shining field and the orchard and the forest and Bobby inside her, so that he would never be apart from her, no matter how far he went.

As soon as she entered the house, her father heard her and called her name.

"We had hail," he said.

"I know. Don't worry. I checked and there's no glass broken."

"Good." He stood, waiting, and she let him wait. "Where were you?"

"I was at the library," she said. Every lie she told widened the gap between them.

"Did you get wet?" He reached out, but she darted away, before he could feel the blanket.

"Not too bad!" She turned and ran up the stairs. "I just need to wash and change."

Upstairs, she turned on the taps of the shower and let the blanket drop to the floor. She looked at herself in the bathroom mirror and thought about the moment when Bobby had touched her, just before the hail began. While she waited for the water to heat up, she stood on the tile floor, rubbing her arms and shoulders. Her skin was cool and clammy, but inside, her body still glowed like the embers she'd left to smoulder in the warm grey ash at the bottom of the stove. She remembered what her mother had said about men and respecting yourself, and she knew that if it hadn't been for the hail, she would not have stopped, neither of them would have wanted to stop, and she was glad the storm had come.

6.12

NOBODY SAW ROSHEEN UP IN THE ATTIC THE DAY OF THE HAIL storm. She had taped a long piece of paper to the attic wall, and she was painting, in watercolours, the scene below — field and orchard and highway and treetops and distant water tower. Dark, gathering clouds, pale, sea-green sky. The attic was muggy and hot, but she was avoiding her father, who was brooding downstairs over the state of the house, worrying over roof shingles and window frames. Her mother was in Morden, and Siobhán was at a concert with her friends. Rosheen had made plans to go swimming at the gravel pits with Raymond Ross and his parents today, but they had cancelled because of the weather. So she was stuck at home with her father. It was silly, now that she was twelve and a half, but she was still afraid of him. Even today, when he seemed to be in a good mood, she was keeping a heavy chair near the attic door, in case she needed to jam it shut.

She put down her paintbrush and fished another pill out of her pocket. She had used up the first bottle of pills she'd taken from Bobby's medicine cabinet, but since then she'd taken another. The pills in this second batch weren't quite as good, and when she felt anxious and achey, she often needed to take two. She wanted to try a different prescription. Bobby's grandfather had moved up to the lake and left them all behind — so many bottles she was sure Bobby wouldn't notice a few missing. And now that Siobhán and Bobby needed Rosheen with them all the time — or almost all the time — Rosheen had plenty of opportunities to experiment.

Something shiny caught her eye in the trees below. A silver streak, wobbling like spilled mercury among the trees. Handlebars. Someone was riding a bicycle through the orchard. Rosheen waited for the bike to enter the field. With her smallest brush, she tried to reproduce the silver squiggle weaving among the trees in her painting. But her squiggle only looked grey. How to make it shine? More white? Suddenly, the entire sky flashed white. A second later, thunder cracked the clouds open and rain poured down. A fresh, electric breeze blew through the screen, dispersing the humid air of the attic. Rain drummed hard on the roof.

Out of the orchard, two people came running, holding hands. Siobhán and Bobby. He ripped off his shirt and held it over her, but it was hopeless. They were getting soaked. They were slipping on the wet grass, laughing. They were together. Just the two of them.

The betrayal took her breath away.

Siobhán had said she was going out with friends. She had lied right to Rosheen's face and then left Rosheen at home. Alone with Dad. And now here she was, laughing and not even seeming to care. Another flash of lightning ripped across the field and suddenly Rosheen was afraid for them. Didn't they know an open field was the worst place to —

Oh no. They were heading right for the house. Had they gone insane?

But they didn't enter the house. They entered the greenhouse from the far door. Would he hear them? She hoped the sound of the thunder and rain would serve as cover.

Rosheen watched, transfixed and frightened, through the glass roof of the greenhouse, as her sister and Bobby dashed inside and stripped off their wet clothes. If her father walked in on them now, he'd kill them both. Bobby leaned over Siobhán. She let him touch her all over. Let him kiss her. A long kiss. Longer than any kiss Rosheen had seen before, even in the movies. Hot shivers rushed through her body. Then the hail came crashing down, splitting Siobhán and Bobby apart, sending them running into the storm for shelter.

Rosheen felt light-headed, all shaky inside, or itchy, or — she didn't know what she was feeling, but she didn't like it.

6.13

BOBBY SULLIVAN WAS SWEET, EILEEN ADMITTED WHEN FRANK was not around, but seventeen was too young to be serious about a boy. A girl could ruin her life by falling in love too soon. Siobhán must be careful. But Siobhán knew it was too late to be careful. She was already in love. She'd known it since the afternoon of the hail storm. She was going to spend the rest of her life with Bobby. He said it was their destiny to be together, and though he said it with a smile she knew he believed it. They both believed it. So when she wasn't given time with Bobby, Siobhán stole it. When Bobby went to the lake to visit his grandfather, she went with him, telling her mum she was camping with girlfriends. And now that school had begun again, she'd skip whole days, if they were his days off, to be with him. But most of the time, they had to take Rosheen along. Siobhán didn't need Rosheen to watch her all the time. Bobby never tried to take her to bed, though she knew he wanted to. He cared about her. And she cared about herself. She wanted to tell her mother that. She wanted to tell the truth. But she feared the scene that Frank might make if she defied him. The punishment he would deal out, not just to her, but to her mother and her sister. So whenever she sneaked away to be alone with Bobby, she lied. Someday she'd be old enough, brave enough, and smart enough, to reason with her father. But for now she waited, and she lied.

"I'm going for a walk," Siobhán told her mother. It was a sunny Saturday afternoon, early in October. Nobody seemed to need her. Mr Ross had come by to help her father change the tires on the truck, and her mother was on the couch, reading a Margaret Laurence novel. As for Rosheen, she was engrossed in her painting, a new hobby, which had gained Siobhán many hours of freedom.

Was Rosheen becoming obsessive? Making pictures used to be a sheer, simple joy for her. When she was seven and Bobby brought her the first long paper roll, she had fun making a crayon street as long as the attic, with a pet store and a fire hall and fourteen houses, all different sizes and colours, shaped like broccoli and mushrooms, with zany windows and people dancing on the roofs, and exuberant star-shaped rain and planets falling from the sky, and by the time she was done there was nothing left of the crayons but a few stumps of coloured wax. These days, Rosheen performed careful paintings, or drawings contained in spiral-bound books. She hunched over her sketches, tight, as if closing in on herself, and worked — it was work to her now, not play — for hours, trying to make whatever effect she wanted to make exactly perfect.

"Where are you going?" asked Eileen.

"Just down through the woods and maybe to visit Sara," said Siobhán. Sara was a girl at school she barely knew. She went out through the porch and circled the house and snuck into the greenhouse from outside. An old trick. She didn't intend to stay there long. She only wanted to read for an hour or two. It seemed weeks since she'd been alone. Her family and school and Bobby took up all of her time. Falling in love, exciting as it was, cut severely into reading time. She lay on an old quilt, which she still kept stashed at the far end of the greenhouse for this purpose, and opened *Tess of the d'Urbervilles* and forgot about the rest of the world.

At the astonishing end of the novel, Siobhán lay on her back, staring through the glass at the sky, imagining the sunrise over Stonehenge. She sat up. Where was the sun? It was beyond the roof of the house. What time was it? She leaped to her feet.

Hurrying past the porch window, she heard the murmur of her own voice. One of Frank's tapes. W. B. Yeats. "The Wild Swans at Coole." She liked the poem, but hated the sound of her own voice, gravelly and too earnest.

He heard her come in, and by the time she entered the hall, he was there, arms crossed over his chest. Head held high and chin thrust upwards. Trouble. "Where have you been?"

"Dad, I—"

"Your mother is not well, and you *know* she's not well and yet you *insist* on disappearing."

Siobhán said nothing. Even her taped voice paused, between poems, as the whispering reels continued to turn.

"You were out with that Sullivan kid again."

"No." She wanted to say, *Yes! Yes, I was.*

"You go out with him a lot. You get in his car and ride around with him where everyone can see you." Frank's voice, cold and controlled, rose in volume with every sentence. "The school principal saw you yesterday. He phoned this afternoon to let us know he'd seen you. How do you think your mother feels, with him implying she lets you run loose?"

While he was talking, Eileen came downstairs. "Frank, please."

"Keep out of this, Eileen." Frank stepped forward, his out-thrust chest inches from Siobhán's nose. She had grown very tall very fast this summer, but he was still much taller. She was looking straight into his collar bone and saw above it an oozing sore where a piece of shrapnel was pushing through. The strained tendons of his neck, a muscle twitching in his clenched jaw. She stepped away. Immediately, his arm snapped out. "Stay where you are."

She did not move except to tighten her shoulder against his grip. With his other hand he grabbed her arm, the arm that held the book. She pulled away sharply, desperate for privacy, not wanting him to know she was reading or to know anything about her. He clicked his tongue against his teeth, a tsk of disgust at her pathetic attempt at self-defence.

"If you can't obey the rules, you don't belong here. Remember me telling you that?"

"Yes."

"Then you get in that kitchen and you take that pickerel out of the fridge and fry it up for dinner. Do you hear me?"

"Yes." She walked away. Out on the porch, her voice was reading "Easter, 1916."

The kitchen was quiet and cool. She took the cast-iron pan from the hook on the wall. Eileen came in for a minute and patted her on the shoulder gently, saying, "It's all right," as if it were all right. Siobhán opened the refrigerator and stared in. The fish was wrapped in waxed paper and tied with white string. There was a bowl of shelled peas and some lettuce and a half-pound of butter in a dish and a lemon. She took all these things out of the fridge and set them on the counter. She thought of calling Rosheen to set the table, but she didn't want to have to talk. She put water in a pot and oil in a pan and turned on the gas under two burners.

On the front porch, Frank had rewound the tape. He was listening now to the parts of the poem he'd missed when she came into the house. Otherwise, the only noises were small. In the living room Eileen turned the pages of a newspaper. The oil sizzled and spit.

Siobhán untied the string and unwrapped the fish. She dredged the fillets in flour and salt and pepper and laid them in the pan, giving the knob a quick twist to raise the heat. Then she laid a clean dishcloth on the counter and turned her back to wash the lettuce at the sink. From the porch, Yeats's contemplative rhythms, Siobhán's husky voice, and then, behind her, a crackling.

She spun around and saw flames consuming the wax paper she'd left too close to the stove. That one last twist of the knob and surge of gas was all it took to set the paper on fire and now the dishcloth was on fire too. Pinching a corner of the paper, she lifted it from the counter, threw it in the sink and turned on the tap. She tried to grasp the burning cloth, but the flames licked at her fingers and she let it fall, leaving a long scorch mark on the countertop. She whipped the box of baking soda off the shelf and doused the flaming cloth. What a mess, and by now the fish was turning black and starting to smoke. Siobhán snatched the pan from the stove and the hot handle seared her right palm. "Damn!" She dropped the pan back onto the stove. Hot grease splashed her shirt. She pulled the cloth away from her breasts and belly. "God damn it."

"Why, Siobhán!" said her mother, from the living room, as if she had never heard such wicked language. As if she had been sitting quietly in church in her Sunday best.

Siobhán heard the armchair creak as her father stood up. With her left hand she snatched up a tea towel to pull the pan from the flames. The pan lurched off the element, spattering grease and sending the flame high. She heard her father's deliberate footsteps coming for her. She turned off the gas. She shook her right hand hard, trying to cool it off.

He entered the kitchen. "What did I just hear?" he asked.

"That was me. I said, *God damn it.*"

A grimace — no, it was a smile — crossed her father's face.

"God damn it all to *hell*," Siobhán said.

He raised his arm and swung with the back of his hand, belting her across the face so hard she went down flat on her back on the floor.

"Frank, no!" cried her mother, who had appeared, too late, at the kitchen doorway.

He stood there, uncertain where his daughter was. According to the rules, she had to make a noise, to reassure him. But she lay still, tasting the blood on her lip. The spilled grease soaked through her shirt in two hot sticky patches.

"Where are you?" he demanded. "Siobhán?"

She lay still.

"You come when I call you, you hear?"

"I hear," she said. She stood up, facing him. On the heel of her hand, a red blister was rising. "I hear you just fine."

"So you are *choosing* to disobey?" His tone was deliberately measured and mild, calculated to enrage her.

She stepped sideways, silently, out of his range.

Eileen came skittering across the floor and reached out for her, but Siobhán pushed her gently away, without even looking at her. She kept her focus on her father.

"Is that what you choose, Siobhán?" he asked. "Because if it is, then you do not belong in this house. Do you understand? We do not need you here."

She understood then that she could kill him, that she would kill him. She would aim the hot iron skillet at his head and let it fly, swift and sure into his temple, crack his skull in two.

"Answer me," said Frank. He moved forward, sweeping the air with one arm. His tongue between his teeth, determined.

"Frank," said Eileen. "Don't."

"Mum!" called Rosheen. She came flying into the kitchen, and Eileen embraced her. Eileen clung to her. How a woman could let a little girl, *this* little girl, witness such a scene was beyond Siobhán's understanding.

She stepped forward and peeled Rosheen off her mother. She pulled the girl by one arm through the swinging door and commanded her to go to her room, and she obeyed.

Siobhán was alone. She bent over, placed her hands on her thighs, and tried to breathe. She wanted not to be inside her body anymore, this Garrison body, this burnt and burning thing.

The kitchen door swung open and her father appeared. "Siobhán, if you are not prepared to cooperate, we do not need you in this house."

His tone tore a hole in her chest, that disdain, that pretence. She knew it was pretence — he needed her and he knew it — and then suddenly she felt her anger so pure and clean within her it burned away her desire to kill him. Instead of killing him, she inhaled. She exhaled, and the pain in her chest eased a little. She pressed her palms against her thighs and pushed herself upright. All right then. She'd let him see if he needed her. Let everyone see. She straightened up and turned her back on him and mounted the stairs.

Rosheen had collapsed in a heap on the floor of the second-storey hallway. Siobhán stepped right over her and entered the bathroom, locked herself in and took a long shower. Afterwards she towelled off and bandaged her hand and dressed in a clean T-shirt and blue jeans.

In her dresser mirror she could see into the hallway behind her. Rosheen was sitting up now, cross-legged on the floor, rocking, with her face in her hands. Her sobs were hushed, slowing, winding down. She was watching Siobhán through her fingers, waiting for her big sister to take her in her arms and tell her everything was going to be all right, but Siobhán could not do that. From the kitchen below, she heard the rhythm of her mother's quiet pleading and the screen door creaking on its hinges as little gasps of wind swung it back and forth, and loudest of all she heard her father's silence. The day was still. The house teetered, waiting for that door to slam or for an object to fly into a wall or window — a radio, a jar of peaches — in this house anything at any moment could become airborne, and then everyone would start up all over again, as if they were alarm clocks set to go off.

A late beam of sunlight illuminated the hall behind her. She looked at the reflection of the glowing path of light across the wooden floorboards, like a scene in a film, motes of dust drifting upward, the nimbus of Rosheen's red curls above her bowed head. It struck her that this was all a repetition, or more accurately a re-enactment, like those imitation battles at Gettysburg or the Easter crucifixions in the Philippines, where people acted out the motions of past events, rehearsing again and again what's already happened and can't be changed.

She retrieved her empty school bag from the closet, tossed in socks and underwear, a sweater, and a thick novel — *Anna Karenina*.

It was hard to walk past Rosheen's huddled body. Siobhán wanted to offer reassurance, a promise of some kind, but she didn't want to lie to her. As Siobhán started down the stairs, Rosheen ran to her own room, where she could eavesdrop safely on the coming confrontation. But there wasn't one. When she reached the bottom of the stairs, Siobhán said nothing. She walked straight out through the front door and closed it quietly behind her, thinking that would hurt him more, later, when he remembered it. She marched down the driveway and across the field into the old orchard without turning to see if anyone was watching. The apples were ripe, and she picked four to take with her. When she reached the highway she stood on the gravel shoulder and stuck out her thumb. She knew there were dangerous men in the cars that sped across the country on the highway, but she felt that nothing bad could happen to her now. The girl she used to be had been annihilated. Nothing could touch Siobhán because Siobhán no longer existed.

Bobby was still at work when Von arrived at his house, so she waited on the steps. She ate an apple and read Tolstoy's opening pages. Every once in a while she stopped reading and looked up at the cloudless sky and knew she'd escaped something harder and more terrible than her own death. When she was a girl, she'd been afraid of Frank. But now she was a woman and understood that she was the dangerous one. It wasn't something to admit to others, to discuss with Bobby, for instance. No. She would keep it to herself, examine it only in darkness.

Bobby was surprised and happy to find her waiting for him. As he listened to her story of the stolen hours with *Tess* and the burnt dinner and her father throwing her out of her own home, he made sympathetic sounds. But his eyes were bright with victory. She was his now.

She liked being his. She wanted to start a whole new household of her own. Bobby's grandfather had moved up to the cabin for good, so she and Bobby were alone. She put his things in order, covered his kitchen shelves with shelf paper, mended his curtains, and he thanked her. If ever she neglected her homework to learn a new recipe and cook a special dinner, it was only because she wanted to make him smile. If the next evening they went to the movies and ate popcorn for dinner, that was all right, too. Home was a place of freedom, where a person could read a book whenever she wanted, a place where a person could leave a cupboard door open once in a blue moon without risking a major trauma to the psyche.

Von phoned home to speak to her mother, letting her know where she was. Eileen packed a suitcase with the clothes and books Von asked for and delivered it to Bobby's house. He was at work when she came, and Von invited her in for a cup of tea. Eileen looked cautiously around the house, as if expecting to discover some awful secret. Von asked her to take a seat while she made tea. She saw her mother lift a corner of the carpet with her shoe, as if checking for dirt, before she sat down. Had her mother grown smaller? Her arms and legs seemed thinner, and the sturdy shoes she wore looked like heavy weights tied to her stick ankles. The wiry white hairs that had begun to appear on her head two years ago were now taking over, and if Von squinted a bit she could see her mother as an old, old woman, perched, uncertain and adrift, on the overstuffed couch. Lost. Quickly she fixed a tray and carried it to the coffee table.

At first they kept to everyday topics, the weather, the greenhouse plants. Rosheen was having trouble with French verbs. Frank was taking a long time to recover from the anaesthetic after his last operation. He had a worse reaction to it than ever before, and could not sleep. When Rosheen had woken him from a nap one evening he had been "very annoyed." Von could tell the two of them were wearing Eileen thin, using her up. She tried to steer the subject to books. She was asking an elaborate question about *Emma* when her mother interrupted.

"How long do you plan to…stay away?"

"Mum," said Von. "He threw me out."

"You know he doesn't mean that."

"The tea must be steeped by now," Von said. She served her mother first, pouring from the blue and white willow-patterned teapot. She had scrubbed half an hour last night to rid it of its old brown stains. The house was silent. The street was dead-ended because of the Seine river, so there was rarely any traffic. Eileen's spoon clinked against the side of the cup. The clock ticked. Von felt a light breeze pass through the house. It was a house without ghosts, without memories, where nobody lurked in his own darkness, ready to explode at any second. It was — how could she describe it? Open. Peaceful. She wondered if her mother could feel it too.

"He's sorry," Eileen said.

Von let that pass.

"You know how he gets."

"He said he didn't need me," said Von.

She took the tea tray back to the counter. The woman across the street passed by the window and waved. She was walking her two children and their cocker spaniel to the playground. Von waved back. She wasn't isolated here, as she'd been at home. She was part of the neighbourhood.

"You'll be careful, won't you?" asked Eileen.

"Yes, Mum," said Von. She did not say she was on the pill, because she knew her mother didn't want to hear that. Living with Bobby was sin enough.

———

Von kept track of her spending in a Hilroy scribbler, listing groceries purchased and bills paid. They weren't poor, and she wanted to keep it that way. Bobby's job at the newspaper paid well, very well. The pressman's union was strong. In January, he became a journeyman, and his wages went up. In June, when Von finished high school and started to look for a job, he asked, "Why don't you go to university, like you always wanted to?" He could pay the tuition, he said, and he was right.

He screwed hooks into the wall of the basement stairwell for hanging up coats. Then he cleared out the coat closet and took the closet door off. He built a small desk and bookshelves inside the closet space and bought Von a typewriter. She sat in a kitchen chair while he adjusted the height of the desktop and fastened it to the wall where it would be most comfortable for her to type. When he was finished he went down the street for beer while she picked spinach and tomatoes in the garden and made spaghetti sauce. Rosheen was coming for supper.

Rosheen often came for supper and a game of cards, and it was always good to see her. Sometimes she complained about life at home, but usually, within minutes of her arrival at the Edgewood house, she began to relax. Von could see her shoulders loosening up. Von was sorry for leaving Rosheen behind in that tense household, but she reminded herself it was her mother's job to look after Rosheen, to protect her from Frank. Von had a life to live.

Von could feel a new space expanding inside her own body. It was the space where she used to store her worries, the part of her mind that was always buzzing, *where is he, is he in a good mood, what time is it, did I do what I was supposed to do, what's going to go wrong?* Sometimes, when the weather was good and she was dozing out in the backyard swing or lost inside a book, her body, suddenly startled, jerked her to her feet. Her heart pounded. What had she neglected? Was her father all right? Was he hungry? Angry? Had she left something undone? Then, when she realized everything was fine, she felt relieved. Yet somehow empty.

6.14

ROSHEEN SAT ON THE BROKEN, OFF-LIMITS PLAY STRUCTURE IN the corner of the schoolyard, away from the other kids. It was picture day. Girls were obsessing over their hair. Those with pimples applied cover stick. Those with freckles powdered until they looked like ghosts.

She gazed through the chain-link fence at the little park across the street, where she used to eat lunch with Von. Two years ago, Rosheen had finally started junior high, and for the first time since grade one, she got to attend the same school as her sister. So even though Von had walked out of the house and gone to live with Bobby, Rosheen had still been able to see her every school day, until Von graduated. It had been heaven to have someone to eat lunch with, someone to talk to in the halls, someone who scared the mean kids away. Von didn't have to say anything to them. They just knew not to bother Rosheen when Von was around.

But Von was starting her second year at university now. Although she was glad for Von, and loved to visit her, and adored Bobby, Rosheen didn't think she'd ever truly forgive her older sister for deserting her.

Von had been gone two years now, and home had been a misery since she left. These days her father was angrier than ever and her mother was always on the couch with a cloth on her forehead, eyes red, claiming to have a headache. Her father was always stepping on things and shouting at Rosheen to pick them up. Von wasn't there to fix the dripping tap or mow the lawn or shine his shoes or make macaroni and cheese the way he liked. Rosheen, in his opinion, couldn't do anything right.

"I'm only fourteen!" she had yelled at him yesterday. He chased her all the way upstairs and when she tried to keep him out of her room, he pushed the door open. So she hid in the closet. Long ago, Vonnie had fitted Rosheen's closet with a hook on the inside, so she could lock herself in.

He had said, "Stay in there, then. You'd *better* stay in there, if you know what's good for you." He slammed out, and she sat down and cried. He used to love her. Now, she disgusted him.

A commotion outside the school caught her attention, a gang of ninth-grade boys, whistling and hooting as her classmate Suzie came out. Suzie gave them the finger, and they began to clap and cheer. They considered every movement of her body a performance staged for their amusement. They seemed to think she'd grown her breasts on purpose to attract their attention, and the more attention they paid her, the more derision the girls heaped on her head. Suzie had become a rebel, smoking cigarettes and wearing eyeliner that made her narrow eyes look smaller and closer together. Today she was wearing a tight, hot-pink dress and matching lipstick and high-heeled shoes, which were against the school dress code. Recently, she'd scrawled an obscene word on the door to the boys' locker room and gotten herself suspended for a week. Suzie was no doubt proud of herself for that. A whole week off from punishment.

To avoid the boys, Suzie chose the only route possible, which brought her into Rosheen's corner. She sat down and began to cry, as if Rosheen weren't even there. As if she didn't count.

"Don't let them get to you," said Rosheen.

"That's easy for you to say," Suzie spat out. "You've got nothing to lose."

A wave of laughter arose from the yard, and both girls turned to look. The popular girls were clustered around their leader, Em Lowler, who was prancing in a circle, her chest stuck out in a bad, but obvious, imitation of Suzie.

Suzie looked away. She took out a pack of cigarettes and ripped it open. "You want one?"

"Sure," said Rosheen. What did she have to lose?

They moved down the lane, so they wouldn't get caught. Suzie sucked in her cheeks and took a long drag. She blew smoke rings and said, "That's what I've been needing all morning."

Rosheen smoked too. She had practised smoking before, with cigarettes she stole from Bobby and Von's house — she'd found them hidden behind all the cancer meds.

"Now if I only had a drink," said Suzie.

Rosheen laughed. "Where would you get a drink from?"

"My cousin can get beer any time he wants."

"How old is he?"

"Sixteen. But his mother works in a bar. You know the Nicolette? His mum's the manager. He can get into the bar any time and get a dozen beers."

"Cool."

"Him and me are gonna get an apartment together," Suzie said. "And throw big parties, and I'm telling you I'm not inviting any of *them*." She gestured back toward the schoolyard.

"Your parents would let you do that? Get an apartment?"

Suzie shrugged. "My mum doesn't care what I do. And my dad's dead." She looked defiantly at Rosheen. "Someone stabbed him to death with a butcher knife."

"That's awful," said Rosheen. "I'm so sorry."

"What are you sorry for? You didn't do it."

"That's just something people say," Rosheen told her. "To be nice."

"Really?"

"Yes. It means *I feel bad for you*, and I do. That's terrible, to lose your father."

"Yeah. Now me and my mum live in a crummy bachelor apartment, with her boyfriends always coming over and eating the groceries she pays for. You're lucky. I've seen where you live, in that big house with all those flowers. I remember your sister. She was the prettiest girl in the school. Isn't she living with Bobby Sullivan now?"

"Yeah. I miss her."

They finished their cigarettes and crushed them under the heels of their shoes.

"Anyway," said Suzie. "Maybe I'd invite *you* to our parties."

The school bell buzzed, calling everyone back in for class.

"Oh, joy," said Rosheen. "Time for picture day."

"Let's ditch," said Suzie. So they ditched.

———

Suzie's cousin, Jean-Claude Allard, looked old enough to drink. He worked for his mother, cleaning and doing repairs in the hotel, and had keys to every room. When he wasn't working, he hung out in an empty room, drinking and watching TV or doing whatever he wanted to do.

He took Suzie and Rosheen up to a room and gave them each a beer. Rosheen didn't like the way it tasted. It filled her mouth with malty froth. But she liked the way it made her feel. Suzie and Jean-Claude sat on the bed and talked about the jobs they were going to get to pay their rent. Suzie wanted to be a hairdresser and Jean-Claude wanted to be in a band. Rosheen wanted to laugh, not because she thought these were dumb ideas, but because she was so happy they were talking to her. The second beer was even better, lifted her spirits higher. She told her new friends about her old friend, Raymond Ross, who was studying music in Montreal. She showed them the postcard he'd sent, a view of the city from the mountaintop.

"Now that's a real city," said Jean-Claude. "Not like this lousy hick town."

At five, he offered her a ride home, and she accepted. But when they were halfway there, she changed her mind. "Take me to my sister's house, on Edgewood. Will you?" She was slightly tipsy, but Jean-Claude gave her some gum to chew, to hide the smell.

She walked up the front path, swaying, and Bobby let her in.

"Hey, look who's here!" he said. "Come on in. Can you stay for dinner?"

Von was cooking a meatloaf. "Did you tell Dad and Mum you were coming here?"

Rosheen didn't want to phone home. Her father had said she shouldn't come here. It was a corrupt environment. Von was a bad influence. Vonnie. Her own sister. The straightest arrow she knew. "They know where I am," she said.

"Stay for the evening," Bobby said. "Do you know what we've got now? Scrabble! And I need you to help me beat your sister."

Rosheen watched Von moving around the kitchen as if it were her own kitchen. It was her own kitchen. This was her own house and Bobby her own husband, almost. Rosheen wondered when they'd get married. Maybe when Mum got better. Maybe when Dad changed his mind about Bobby. Rosheen would be the maid of honour and take care of all the decorations. Something creative and different. She'd lately been experimenting with folded paper, designing abstract shapes. Like origami, only with cut-outs. She imagined the church hall hung with hundreds of these paper sculptures, all in different shades of white, for Vonnie's wedding.

For her own wedding, Rosheen wanted to elope. As soon as she was old enough to have her surgery, she wanted to marry and get out of the house. Out of the city. She wanted a husband who liked painting and music. Someone who liked to travel. But most importantly, she wanted someone happy. She watched as Bobby chased Von around the table, trying to tickle her, and Von was killing herself laughing even though he hadn't caught her yet. Nothing like that ever happened at home. Or if it did, it didn't last ten seconds. Yes, the most important thing was a husband who knew how to have fun. Someone who'd move with her to New York City or Montreal, where they could have a real life.

She went to wash her hands before dinner, and there was her face again, in the mirror on the cabinet. She yanked the door open. The inside of the cabinet looked different since Von had moved in. Tidy and clean, covered in blue shelf paper. Toothbrushes and combs and a razor upright in a clean jam jar. They had taken all the old pill bottles out and stashed them in an empty shortbread tin, with a guy in a kilt and bagpipes on the lid, and shoved it to the back of the bathroom closet, behind the cleaning supplies, and forgotten all about it. Rosheen knew they'd forgotten, because she'd been dipping into it for a couple of years now, and neither of them had said a word. She turned the taps on full to mask the noise she made while rifling through the plastic tubes, skimming the labels rapidly, looking for those magic words: *when needed, for pain.*

6.15

DURING VON'S THIRD YEAR AT UNIVERSITY, THE WINTER WAS brutal. Like everyone else, she rarely went outside unless she needed to. She read books. She was in an honours program in English Lit, planning to continue into grad school. She read all day long if she felt like it. She was *supposed* to read. That was what her program required her to do: read good books and write about them. University was the best invention on the planet.

Sometimes, when her heart was full of new poems she'd discovered, she imagined reciting them to her father, how he would love them. But that was not possible. Instead she read the poems to Bobby. He didn't fully understand them, she knew that. The poems didn't move him the way they moved Von, the way they would have moved her father. But Bobby listened, because he liked her voice and because he knew she wanted him to listen. He would say "wow," and that was good enough for her. Then they'd cook dinner and go skating at the arena, and when they got home they'd bathe together and climb into bed and make love.

She spoke to her mother on the phone and was worried by the weariness in her voice. But Eileen was stoically cheerful, always wanting to hear Von's news about recipes she'd tried or the books she was reading. She related stories of her own university days, the dances she'd organized and the essays she'd written about Shakespeare. But when the conversation turned to Eileen's present life, Von heard the sighs. Eileen never said she was angry at Frank, or at Rosheen. Always her reports of their behaviour were couched in loving terms. Eileen could see both sides to every conflict. It was true Frank was too hard on Rosheen. He grounded her for the slightest infraction, and he yelled too loud. My goodness! Did Von remember how loud he sometimes yelled? Von did. But it was also true that Rosheen was getting wild. She skipped school and stayed out past her curfew, even past her bedtime, and Eileen had found a marijuana cigarette in the pocket of Rosheen's blue jeans. She didn't know what to say to her. Could Von perhaps talk to Rosheen about drugs? Remind her that marijuana was against the law?

Von did talk to Rosheen about it, though smoking a little pot hardly seemed very serious. Didn't everyone try it in high school? She and Bobby had tried it a few times, and enjoyed the giggles. So she only warned Rosheen that Mum had found the joint, and she should be more careful. Try not to upset Mum, she said, for the hundredth time.

Once or twice a week, Von or Bobby picked up Rosheen after school and brought her over for dinner, and afterwards the three of them played board games or cards or watched television on their scratchy black-and-white set. Rosheen loved those evenings. She wanted Von and Bobby to visit her at her home, too, to see the paper art projects she was making. But Von preferred to stay in the car when she drove Rosheen home. If ever she had to come in, to pick something up or drop something off, Von exchanged only brief, cold words with Frank.

"It's like a game of chicken with you two," Rosheen complained. "You're both so stubborn. Why don't you just come home for dinner?"

"He hasn't invited me," said Von.

"*I'm* inviting you!"

"Sorry," Von said.

They all had surgery that year. Eileen had her appendix out, Frank had his eardrum reconstructed again, and Rosheen underwent a procedure designed to "reduce the appearance" of her scar. Once in a while, but not often enough, Von visited her mother and her sister in the hospitals where they were confined. She drove to Las Roses, bearing casseroles and loaves of homemade bread. She said hello to her father and he said hello to her, and that was all. She never stayed more than twenty minutes. She thought of them daily, though. She thought of their post-op bleeding and bruises, the intravenous holes in their arms, their skin grafts.

On cold nights, she lay in bed while Bobby traced the curve of her cheek with his fingers, caressed her shoulders and breasts with his strong hands. She watched his smile widen as he drew the sheet down and gazed at her hips and legs with a happy hunger. At those moments, she forgot her family completely. But after Bobby fell asleep, she remembered them again — mother, father, little sister. Exaggerated versions of them visited the dark bedroom on Edgewood Street.

Their stitched-up bodies loomed in the shadows like creatures escaped from Frankenstein's lab. But as she lay there in her smooth, unblemished skin, the warmth of Bobby's love still humming through her veins, she knew she was the one who was a monster.

At Christmas, Eileen's heart began to fail. It was surprising, the doctor told Von, that her mother had lived so long. In January, he moved her to a cardiac ward at Victoria General, all the way across the city from Las Roses, and Rosheen had no driver's licence yet. So Von left Bobby's house and moved back in with her family, temporarily, so she could ferry her father and sister back and forth to see Eileen. So she could cook and clean and help Rosheen with her homework and iron her father's shirts and type his notes and keep up with the winter chores in the greenhouse. So she could take care of them both and, most importantly, take her mother's place between them. To try to keep the peace between them, as Eileen had done.

The temperature was thirty-two below when she arrived back home, with her clothes piled, still on their hangers, in the back seat of the Mustang. Bobby helped her haul them out, but she carried them herself up to the door. She'd asked him not to follow her into the house. It was easier for her that way, she said.

"Come in, come in," Frank said, though she was already in. She saw him stand in the cold open threshold and raise one arm, waving to his unseen enemy, before closing the door against the frigid air. A strange gesture. Offering Bobby a truce? Or declaring victory? Then he reached out to touch her for the first time since she'd left home three years before. When he first grasped her arm, a jolt of the old fear zipped through her body, even though she knew he wouldn't hurt her. He couldn't hurt her now. Could he? She'd been standing on one leg, removing a winter boot, and he set her off balance. She toppled into his arms and for a second he held her close.

"It's good you came," he said. He patted her back.

"Of course, Dad," she said.

"Take as much time as you have to," said Bobby, when she phoned him that night. "I understand. They need you right now. Can't I help? Are you sure there isn't anything I can do?"

Every night after dinner, Von drove Frank or Rosheen down the winter roads to the hospital to see Eileen. It was too tiring for Eileen to have all three of them at once.

When Frank stayed home, the two girls visited an hour or two with their mother, chatting quietly. These hours reminded Von of afternoons when they were small and Frank was at work, and Eileen devoted her time to her girls, showing them how to bake bread or can preserves or gather rose hips for their seeds. So long ago it seemed another life.

When Rosheen stayed home, she sent cards for Eileen, with drawings of ordinary things around the house, the roses or the icicles hanging off the roof or a cake that Von had baked. On those nights, Frank sent Von home early. He didn't trust Rosheen to be left alone in the house. Von didn't protest. She delivered Rosheen's cards, checked to see if her mother needed anything, and kissed her good-bye. Then she drove home, where she applied herself to her studies while Rosheen usually sketched or cut and pasted her paper collages, and the evenings were serene. The hard stars glittered over the roof of the house and the snow fell and the joists creaked in the wind. Then at ten or eleven he'd call and ask Von to pick him up and drive him home. Sometimes he'd fall asleep in the hospital room and stay all night and call Von in the morning to come and collect him. The house was peaceful in those days, all three of them on their best behaviour for Eileen's sake, all quelled by their fear of losing her.

One night when Von dropped off Frank, her mother asked to speak to Von in private before she went home. As soon as Frank left the room, she reached for Von's hand. "You *will* look after Rosheen, won't you?"

"Of course, Mum." Von pulled away and stood, reaching for her parka. "Always."

"No, Siobhán. I mean you'll be her mother, once I'm gone."

Von stopped, one arm halfway into a sleeve. "Don't talk like that."

Her mother reached again for her hand and held on weakly. "You know she's going to need you. Frank doesn't understand how hard life is going to be for her. I mean, how hard it is, for a girl, to be like — to be the way she is."

This angered Von. "Frank doesn't understand how hard it is," she hissed, "because *you* didn't want to tell him."

Two tears slid from under Eileen's closed eyelids.

"I'm so sorry. I didn't mean it, Mum. I'm sorry."

"She'll never be married."

"Maybe she will."

"Men marry beautiful girls, Siobhán. Or at least pretty ones. You know that. Even the bad sort of men marry normal-looking girls. Rosheen is going to be alone. She'll need your help."

"Yes, Mum, but things are different now. Women get jobs. They support themselves."

Eileen shook her head, putting little effort into the gesture. "The world hasn't changed as much as you think it has."

Outside in the parking lot, Von leaned on the hood of the car and watched the sky a while before she went home. The air was cold, but she was grateful for the silence and the solitude. The sky was clear, the bare moon drifting high and small above the frozen river. She wondered who she was going to be without her mother.

At home she sorted invoices and bills, unable to tell which ones had been paid or when. Eileen had let the record-keeping lapse. A recent notice proclaimed in bold red letters that the mortgage payment was overdue. Von hadn't even known the mortgage existed, and when she saw the date it was taken out, three years ago, she winced. It was right after she'd left home, when the Garrisons had to hire a man to do the work she used to do. Immediately, Von paid the mortgage up to date. This left the bank balance frighteningly low. But if they lost the property, they'd lose the whole business. And where would they live? Her father's income, even with the army pension, was barely enough to rent an apartment in town.

Two weeks later, Frank stayed late at the hospital, leaving Von and Rosheen alone in the house. It was Rosheen's turn to plan menus for the week, and she was in the kitchen studying recipes. Von was in bed, reading *Mrs Dalloway*, drifting off now and then until the book fell onto her chest and woke her. Finally she turned off the lamp and lay in the darkness.

When the first ring of the telephone sounded in the hallway below, she sat up and looked at the clock. There was only one reason the phone would ring at four in the morning. In the bottomless silence between the first and second ring, she understood that her mother was gone. Her father was calling from the hospital. Von could picture him there at the nurses' station, dialling, the receiver pressed to his good ear. He would need her to help him through the hospital corridors, to fill out paperwork, to drive him home. He would need her so he wouldn't be alone.

In her slippered feet she descended the stairs to the kitchen, where Rosheen was still leafing through cookbooks. Their eyes met and neither of them spoke. Von sat across from her and pulled one of the cookbooks from the pile. *American Traditions*. Lots of illustrations. Rosheen took a marijuana cigarette out of her bathrobe pocket and when Von did not react, she lit it up. The phone rang and neither of them moved to answer it. It rang and rang as Rosheen took a deep toke and handed the joint to Von. They smoked together. Once in a while the ringing stopped for a while. As night deepened toward morning, the sisters smoked and turned the pages of their mother's cookbooks, looking at casseroles and pots of baked beans, corn bread and stuffed tomatoes. Von kept coming back to an illustration of a picnic table covered with a blue and white checked cloth all laid out for lunch with sliced watermelon and those little pinwheel sandwiches, each one with a slice of green olive in the centre, and a pitcher of lemonade, and all the while the telephone rang and outside the snow swirled in the darkness surrounding the house and collected like white dust in the corners of the windowpanes.

6.16

FRANK WOKE WITH HIS HEART BULGING IN HIS CHEST, BEATING erratically, too fast. His throat was dry. He groped for the water jug, trying, out of habit, not to wake Eileen, and then remembered she was gone. She had been gone three months. He drank, three long gulps. Pain burned through his lungs and travelled down his left arm. Don't panic. He managed two breaths. It was all about control. His heart lurched, seemed to stop entirely, then began again. He counted. Counting was the best way he knew, now, to block out thought. One two three. Four five six. Seven —

Out of nowhere. Rush of wind. Tangle of night trees, that schoolyard in France. Cold scatter of raindrops shaken from the branches above, and inside his own ear the liquid, rasping breath of the boy he was strangling. The sound of wire grating through the slick mess of the boy's throat. The squirming torso horribly solid. Dense human muscle and gristle and fat. Frank lay on his side, sweating, nauseated.

He wasn't afraid. Something worse than fear was barrelling toward him: sorrow. The sheer sadness of killing the boy. Since he lost Eileen he could no longer battle grief. It hit him this morning with all the force he'd spent in burying it for over forty years. He clenched his fists. He must not start. Must not. But already tears were dripping down his face. A sob swelled, threatened to break like a wave and drown him. The boy was dead. All these years, and he was still dead. All the boys he'd killed, sneaking up on them with his garrotte, pumping them full of bullets, lobbing grenades at their heads.

And the boys he'd known. Loved. Connor and Roger and the others whose names he knew, twenty, thirty, forty names, and the ones whose names he did not know, the boy with no hands and the naked boy he'd found in the mud one morning, freshly blown apart, not a dog tag or a shred of uniform left to say which side he'd fought on.

The boy named Frank Garrison had been lost, too. The one who believed in a better future, whose faith in God was so much like part of his body, his lungs or the blood in his veins, that he could never have imagined it leaving him. Gone. Supplanted by this crying man, this *little* man who clung to his bed, afraid to get up in the morning.

Everything he had accomplished, the university degrees, the clients he helped, the furniture he built. The wife he couldn't save, the children he couldn't protect, even from himself. All nothing more than show. False front to hide what he was. A brute who didn't deserve to live. He grasped the blanket with his fingers, gathering a fistful of cotton. If he knotted the sheet — no. Do not give in.

Do not give in.

He keened, silently, with every muscle in his body, aware of his daughters sleeping in the rooms below. Then he pushed the sobs down. He eased himself to the edge of the bed and sat up, placed his hands on his knees and exhaled. Heartbeat still wild, but the pain easing.

"It's all right," he said to himself, because there was no one left to say it to him. "It's all right." He could not allow himself to fall apart. He had two girls who needed him. Clients. Storm windows to take down. Screens to put up.

The alarm rang. Six o'clock. He wanted sleep. Only sleep. He shut the alarm off and placed his feet on the floor, stood upright, and ventured into the day.

When he came near the top of the staircase, he reached for the railing but could not find it. He knew he must simply have miscalculated his reach, counted his footsteps incorrectly, made a mistake of some kind. He slid one foot forward. How close was the stairwell? Again and again he groped for the railing. The railing existed. He knew it was there. Perhaps in this life after light he had retained some form of faith after all.

————

Downstairs, showered, shaven, dressed for work, he ate cold cereal. Smelled spring through the open window. Heard birdsong and a light breeze in the branches. The kitchen was quiet. Only the sound of his own chewing and swallowing, and across the table the sound he associated most with his older daughter: the turning of a page. She had made his tea and set it before him with a sigh and then begun to read — a novel, by the sound of its size — shutting him out. She had softened slightly toward him when she came back home, and softened yet again after her mother's funeral. She rarely raised her voice in anger. Yet he did not like this change in her. Her rebellious nature was defeated, not by his will, as he had once desired, but by some greater force. Her grief, perhaps. How long would she stay here with him?

They had argued, bitterly but briefly, before the funeral, because she wanted Bobby to drive them all to the service. But Frank had refused.

"You broke your mother's heart," he reminded her. "Living with that boy. I will not walk into the church with him. Manuel will drive us."

So Manuel had driven them. Siobhán at first declared that she would go with Bobby and join her father and sister at the church. But at the last minute she relented and climbed into Manuel's truck with them. Later, Frank learned that Bobby had arrived with his grandfather, and they had sat in the pew behind the Garrisons.

At first, Siobhán never mentioned Bobby. She spoke to Frank about everything else, repairs to the furnace and the truck, the bills. When she spoke to Bobby on the hallway phone, she stretched the cord into the closet, so Frank could not hear what she said, but when her harsh whispers rose in volume, he knew she must be arguing with him. Then she started announcing, "I'm going to see Bobby," when she went out, as if daring him to object. But Frank did not object in words. He preferred to make his disapproval clear by his silence. Perhaps that had been a mistake. By spring, she was letting Bobby into the house when he came to pick her up. In their brief exchanges, Bobby and Frank remained polite, but it was no secret to anyone they hated each other.

When Rosheen asked her if she was going to live at home now, Siobhán had promised to stay for the summer. "I'll see the season out," she'd said, to Frank's relief.

She kept up with the laundry and put meals on the table and helped Rosheen with her homework. She was working long hours in the greenhouse, because she'd had to let all the staff go, except Manuel and Yvette. She wanted to pull the business out of debt. But come September, he expected her to move back into Bobby's house and return to her classes. The only good thing Frank could say for Bobby was that he paid for her education. Yet it was also the thing he hated most about him. Living free and easy, in a paid-for house, with a union salary, doing for Frank's daughter what Frank could not do.

By June, Siobhán was letting Bobby hang around Las Roses. Many times Frank was surprised to come home from work and find Bobby there. It galled him to hear the kid call out, "Hello, Mr Garrison," comfortable as you please on Frank's sofa in Frank's living room. Did she not hear the edge of rancour in the kid's voice? The disrespect? Frank wasn't sure. He kept his temper and made himself say, "Hello, Robert." Reminding the kid that he should grow up.

Across the table, Siobhán turned another page. Was it possible that she could read so fast? So many books?

He could hear Rosheen upstairs, getting out of bed and walking into the bathroom, turning on the shower. She was late. She was always late. He didn't know what to do with her. Eileen had protected her too much. Never making her carry her share of the work. Allowing her to miss school or stay out past her curfew, without consequences. He had several times discovered, after the fact, that she'd broken rules, and her mother had not punished her. He'd warned them both that she was growing up with no direction, no sense of discipline. And he'd been right. Now here she was at sixteen, turning to drink to ease her pain. A weakness he scorned in others, but absolutely feared in his own daughter. At the breakfast table, Sunday, he had smelled beer on her, just a wisp, but foul and skunky as the breath of a soldier coming back to camp from leave. It shook him. How many beers did it take to make a person smell like that the following day? He could not imagine.

But he'd said nothing. This latest problem seemed too big, too difficult to face, without Eileen. He admitted to himself he didn't want to broach the subject with Rosheen. He only hoped it was a phase of mourning she could pass through with no lasting harm.

He sipped the last of his tea, and set his cup down. His wife would have noticed his cup was empty. Siobhán needed to be asked. Or wanted to be asked. Was she deliberately pretending not to notice? Her hatred, these days, seemed so passive he sometimes dared to hope that it was dissipating.

"May I have some more tea?"

"Sure, Dad." The page turned. She read for a minute before rising and filling the kettle.

"Thank you, sweetheart."

She placed the kettle on the stove, turned on the gas, and said, "Oh no!"

"What is it?"

"Eight o'clock," she said. She hurried to the hall and called up, "Rosh! You'll miss the bus!" No response. "Rosheen!"

By the time Rosheen came down, the school bus had departed. Since Manuel had taken the day off, there was no way to get her to her class on time unless Siobhán agreed to drive her.

"Make yourself some breakfast," said Siobhán. "I'll get dressed and take you in."

"It doesn't matter," said Rosheen. "I can miss first class. It's only English."

"What did you say?" Frank rose from his chair. "It's *only* English? For crying out loud, Rosheen! You will get ready and go to school and that is all there is to it. And then you'll come home and you'll *stay* at home and study. You will go nowhere — nowhere at all, do you hear me? Until final exams!"

"That's not fair!"

"I'll show you what's fair," said Frank. He moved toward her, reaching out —

A sudden cool hand on his wrist brought him to a standstill. Siobhán. Von, she called herself now. A man's name.

She said, "Dad. No."

Two words only, but her tone silenced him. Quiet authority. A warning. The message that it does no good to scold Rosheen. All this he read in the tone of her voice — and one thing more. She was tired of him. He was irrelevant. A nuisance. He stepped back.

"Just let me go!" cried Rosheen, as though they were holding her prisoner. She stormed out of the house without any breakfast.

Siobhán, or rather Von, returned to the kitchen table. Frank thought she should get dressed and go after her sister, make sure she got to school on time. But he felt somehow unqualified to say so. For the next fifteen minutes he sat across the table from her, sipping his tea, checking his watch and wondering what to say, while Von drank her own tea and turned her pages. Something had shifted in his house, something he dared not put into words.

In good weather, Frank often walked all the way from the house to the highway and along the highway, on the gravel shoulder, to the bus stop. He enjoyed the walk. Today, glad to get out of the house and away from Von's unsettling mood, he declined her offer of a ride and set out on his own. Like all people on the prairie, he felt the exhilaration of freedom after the long winter. Freedom from parkas and heavy fur hats and boots. Freedom from the snow so difficult to wade through, the treacherous ice. When the snow was deep and the path unploughed, Frank could not make it by himself without the danger of becoming hopelessly lost, possibly freezing to death before anyone found him. Years ago, when Eileen had been trapped in the house with small children, he had relied on Manuel, or taxi drivers, to take him back and forth. When Siobhán grew old enough, she would come out through the snow to meet him at the bus stop and then walk home with him. He missed those walks. She was companionable, then, late afternoons, age eight or ten, talking of books or poems, describing to him the snow on the trees or high-flying crows or the Christmas lights he'd strung along the eaves of the house, how they shone on the hanging icicles and turned them red and green. But today it was spring. May. His mother's birthday. He'd have to phone her later this afternoon. She had not come for the funeral. She was getting old. If he needed her now, to help with Rosheen and the housework, she would not be able to come. He was alone. He had to rely on Von. Was that what she had sensed, when she placed her hand on his this morning, and told him *no?* That he could not afford to anger her? Could not risk driving her away again?

Yet all children leave their parents. Some day she would, too. She'd return to that kid—he wasn't a kid any longer, but he still behaved like one—and leave Frank to handle Rosheen by himself. And when Rosheen grew up?

Hearing the traffic, he turned his thoughts to the highway. He concentrated on keeping his cane between the gravel and the grass, and counted his footsteps while he listened hard to the passing cars, making sure he was far enough away from them, yet still visible. This part of the walk always made him tense. The sound of a bulldozer or cement truck sometimes gave him chest pains, but he persevered. At last, on the two-hundred-and-fortieth step, he heard the voices of teenage boys and knew he'd reached the stop.

"Hi, Mr Garrison," one of them called, and he said, "Good morning," though he wasn't sure who they were. It was mostly teenagers and the occasional housewife who caught the bus out here. Everyone else drove into town. When the bus arrived, the boy helped Frank to board and showed him to a seat. Frank didn't need the help, but over the years he'd learned to accept it. He realized now that he was doing people a favour, giving them a story to tell.

Within minutes, they had turned off the highway, and the bus wove through the nearby residential streets, picking up passengers. At the stop after the railway crossing, a large woman squeezed herself in beside him. She wore a strong perfume that smelled like a chemistry experiment gone wrong. His nose began to itch.

He went over his schedule for the day. His first appointment was with Maisie Brown, a young woman who'd suffered from polio as a child. Maisie's doctor thought she could walk without a cane, now, as long as she wore a brace on her bad leg. But Maisie was too fearful. Too attached to the cane. Frank had been working with her for months, trying to coax her to give it up. Today, he planned to take her out for a cup of coffee — just at the restaurant one block from the Agency. They would take the elevator down, of course, but he would make her leave her cane in his office and walk along the sidewalk without it. He'd be holding on to her arm, just in case she lost her balance. How could he convince her she'd be safe? He ran through her case history in his mind, seeking the key.

Sharply, he forced his thoughts back to the present. He had to focus while he was on the bus, or he'd end up across the river. He straightened his back and paid attention to the sounds around him and the movement of the bus. He waited for the smell of the meat-packing plant, but it didn't come. Had he missed it? They were moving fast, straight, on a busy street. But which one? He turned to the perfumed woman beside him.

"Excuse me," he said.

"Yes, dear?"

"Could you tell me, please," he asked. "Where are we?"

She patted his hand. "It's all right, dear," she said. "You're on the bus."

The Orchard

7.1

PARKER PEARS, MANTET APPLES, CHERRY PLUMS. THESE ARE THE fruit trees in the paintings Kyle has found in the Amsterdam studio. They are water colours on loose pages torn from a sketchbook and kept together in a folder. Von is becoming an expert on dating the fine art of Rosheen Garrison. She takes into account the skill level, the medium, the subject matter, the style, and whether it's based on extant photographs. These orchard pictures were painted when Rosheen was about seventeen, Von thinks. She remembers her taking an easel into the orchard that summer. Fruit hangs on the trees, greenish in some pictures, lush and reddening in others. Whatever Rosheen was planning to do with these paintings, why she brought them to Amsterdam, Von can't guess. Doesn't want to guess.

"That's the orchard on our property," she tells Kyle.

"There's an orchard too?"

"It's an old one. No one's taken proper care of it for years," she says. "It's a matter of luck these days, if you manage to snag any fruit."

"You should restore it," Kyle says. "Replant. I could help. I worked on orchards in B.C. when I was sixteen, picking cherries and peaches. I learned about pruning, too."

Von remembers he worked on prairie farms, too, when he was only sixteen.

"Why did you quit school so early?" she asks. "The Penners let you do that?"

He turns away, hides his face. When he looks at her again, he's blushing. "I didn't do too good in school back then. Stupid."

"Don't say that. You know what? Your mother didn't do so well in school, and neither did your grandfather, and they're — they were two of the smartest people I've ever known. School just didn't suit them."

"Really?" He leans forward. "What about you?"

"Oh, well, me... I liked it. I wish I could have... Anyway, the point is, school's no measure of talent. Some people have other gifts. You must be like that. I can tell, just by talking to you, that you're smart. Curious. You want to know things. You care. That's a kind of intelligence they can't teach in school. You must have inherited that from your mum."

He grins openly, and his face seems to light up.

"You have your mother's eyes, too," she says. "That little fleck of green. That's how I knew who you were, when you came back." She reaches across the table and briefly touches his hand. "Thank you for coming back."

Von was in Bobby's house, lying on his couch with her head on his thigh, watching *The Stepford Wives* on his television. When did this house become Bobby's house again? Little by little, she had emptied it of her own possessions as she needed them, articles of clothing, books, her typewriter. Gradually all traces of her disappeared, while Bobby's things accumulated on the desk he'd made for her, a wrench he forgot to put away, his baseball cap. His checkered flannel shirt draped over the chair. Her tiny study, like an abandoned house reclaimed by the forest, was vanishing. The sight depressed her. This was the first autumn she could remember when she wasn't going back to school. She had to devote herself to the greenhouse this year, get the family business back on track. But she missed having classes to look forward to. Boredom was seeping daily into her bones, making her heavy and slow.

Bobby stroked her hair with his fingers, and began to play with her ear. She remembered, as if it were years ago, how his touch once worked on her like a magician's wand, causing her to levitate. Now she felt only weariness. Even her irritation was worn thin. He slipped his hand up the back of her shirt and with two fingers unhooked the clasp of her bra. Could he think of nothing else?

At first, Von's grief had been so wild she'd struggled to restrain herself. The night after the funeral, she'd thrown herself into Bobby's arms, howling like an animal, and they'd made ferocious love, as if by vigorous effort they could force the pain from their bodies, rinse themselves clean of it. And perhaps, for Bobby, that had worked some healing. But then Von went home to Las Roses, waking morning after morning to a house — a world — without Eileen. She had thought death was an end, but it was only a beginning, the dull days piling up, mounting evidence that Eileen was never coming home. Her father and sister, bewildered, did not know how to function. So Von ironed shirts, set alarm clocks, made oatmeal, washed floors, paid Manuel and Yvette, and kept the plants alive. She clenched her muscles and kept her mouth shut so long her body began to go numb. Now, six months after the funeral, she was thoroughly anaesthetized. Bobby's desire seemed merely one more chore she had to manage.

"Babe?"

"I'm tired, Bobby. Can't we rest a while?"

He patted her shoulder. "Sure. Sure. Want a beer?"

"Okay." But she fell asleep before he returned from the fridge.

She woke alone, on the couch, covered by a blanket. He had finished both bottles of beer and the bowl of popcorn, turned off the TV, and gone to bed, hoping she'd follow him when she woke. She sat up and looked at her watch. Almost midnight. She jumped up. Then she remembered Rosheen was safe in the hands of Mrs Ross, who had taken her out to the movies and would be sure to get her home well-fed and sober.

Von's coat was still on the kitchen chair where she was sitting when she took it off before dinner yesterday. She hadn't bothered to hang it up. She'd been late, and when she arrived, Bobby was keeping a take-out pizza hot in the oven. He was usually patient about things like that, but last night he'd been hurt. She could tell. Ever since she'd decided to stay at Las Roses for the winter, he had become sensitive about everything.

She gathered her purse and coat. Since she'd already slept a couple of hours, she'd be able to stay up late and get some work done. Stepping into her boots, she quietly let herself out.

She'd have to be careful slipping back into Las Roses, too. Lately, Frank's sleepwalking habits had returned. Over the summer she had twice found him at five in the morning, performing odd rituals. Once, he was scribbling with an unsharpened pencil on the living-room wall. Eerie. And once — much worse — he was stalking back and forth on the lawn outside the porch, holding the baseball bat he kept in the front closet, in case of intruders, as if it were a rifle. Both times she had watched, wary, until he settled himself on the living-room chair and seemed to fall back to sleep.

It had taken months of poring over the greenhouse accounts to understand what had happened, and when the picture came clear, it wasn't good. The greenhouse suppliers had all respected Eileen, and many had adored her. When she fell ill, they'd sympathized and continued delivering supplies without insisting on payment. When she passed away, they sent condolence cards and then, after a decent interval, the overdue notices. By the time Von figured out the full amount owed by Garrison's Greenhouse, it was too high to settle. She decided to give everyone a percentage of what they were owed, hoping to restore their faith. She planned a payment out of the Christmas sales, and perhaps another after Valentine's. But in order to climb completely out of debt, she had to find some way to increase the sales in spring.

One of Von's schemes was to get Rosheen to help out more in the greenhouse. She had given her the reponsibility of taking care of six flats of roses, miniature white Cinderellas that would have sold very well in pots. If Rosheen had remembered to keep them in full sun. And remembered to bring them inside before the temperature dropped. The Cinderellas didn't die, but sent out shoots that never bloomed. Another time she asked Rosheen to dispose of plants with tomato blight by burning them in a firepit in the garden. But Rosheen had tossed them in the compost, and by the time Yvette discovered this, the entire compost heap had been contaminated. But Von hadn't given up hope yet.

On a Friday afternoon, mid-September, she sat at her mother's desk, jotting down numbers until there wasn't an inch left on the paper to squeeze in another calculation. She ripped the page off the pad and began again. If she could swing a bank loan, and put up another greenhouse dome before the snow began to fly, she could start hundreds of new plants — upscale bedding plants, the most popular ones. Maybe in spring she could set up a temporary stand, right in the suburbs, and sell the new plants at retail prices. She'd look into the cost of renting space, maybe in a vacant lot, near a big grocery store or gas station. Frank and Manuel could build a stand, nothing big, just enough shelter for a cash drawer, some shelves for wrapping paper and a receipt book. Maybe she'd even stoop a bit, buy flower seeds wholesale and sell them. Yvette and Von could haul the plants out early every morning and bring them back at night. If Rosheen would run the stand during the day... She rested her forehead on her hands and groaned. Where was Rosheen?

When the phone rang, she almost tripped over her own feet in her rush to answer it. But it wasn't Rosheen, or anyone who knew where Rosheen might be found. It was Bobby.

"Finished your work yet?" he asked. "The concert starts in an hour."

"I don't think I can go," she said. "Rosheen's not home yet."

"Oh, come on, he can get his own dinner."

Bobby was right. And anyway, Von had already made a lasagne, which would be ready in ten minutes. But she was worried what would happen if Rosheen came home late. If she'd been drinking. "He's not feeling very well," she said. "And neither am I. I think I'm coming down with something."

Bobby greeted this news with silence.

"Bobby?"

"I'll give the tickets to the girls next door," he said. "They're jazz fans. Let me know when you're feeling better." He hung up. A small part of her was relieved he wasn't going to the concert without her, and another small part felt guilty.

Frank came into the house. "Isn't Rosheen home yet?"

Von hung up. "Oh," she said. "That was her on the phone. She's staying for supper at Suzie's tonight."

"She's out of the house too often," he said. "What's going to come of all this running around? What about her homework?"

"She has all weekend for that. Say, I can serve dinner now, if you're ready."

They ate in the kitchen, their conversation more lively than usual. Von unfolded her plans for the greenhouse, and Frank approved, adding suggestions of his own. Soon they were collaborating, sitting late after the meal, sharing ideas and looking forward, together, to setting their plans in motion.

Rosheen did not come home at all that night.

Von was washing the breakfast dishes when she heard a rustle in the lilac branches, and then her sister's whisper, like a light breeze through the screen. "Vonnie?"

Von walked through the greenhouse and unlocked the door. "Where have you been?"

"Is he mad?" Her blouse and cotton pants were wrinkled, as if she'd slept in them. A rivulet of mascara had dripped down her cheek and run sideways along the ridge of her scar.

"He hasn't noticed yet," Von said. She reached up and blotted her sister's cheek with her shirt sleeve.

"Is he in a good mood?"

Von shrugged. "Not bad. He thinks you're sleeping late this morning." She walked across the lawn and peered in through the living-room window. He was in his chair, elbows on his knees, resting his head in his hands. She came back to the greenhouse. "He's listening to the news. If you get upstairs right now and into bed, he'll never know."

Rosheen nodded. "Thanks, Vonnie." A quick hug and she fled light-footed through the kitchen and up the stairs. Right past him. Like an invisible girl.

Von returned to the dishes. She was thinking about her friends in the Shakespeare seminar she was missing. All summer, still believing she'd return to school in fall, she had prepared for it by reading the tragedies. Now she had no one to discuss them with. She missed her mother so badly a chill ran through her. A wind blew yellow leaves against the screen, and all at once the warmth leached out of her body, out of the kitchen, out of the house, and she stood with her hands in the cold dishwater, shivering.

By spring, Von's plans were coming to fruition. The new greenhouse dome was now full of healthy hostas and day lilies and a glorious crop of young peony plants. Frank and Manuel had assembled the new retail stand, and the Garrisons had reserved a rental space at the edge of a shopping mall parking lot, surrounded by miles of residential homes with gardens. If all went as planned, these projects would pay off this summer and for many summers to come. She reported all of this progress to Bobby over the phone.

"Is this going to be your job for life?" Bobby asked. "I thought you wanted to write or teach or something."

"I can't think that far ahead," she said. "Right now I need to get this business out of debt and turning a profit again. Maybe expand. Hire more people."

"I miss you." His voice dropped low. "I mean, I really miss you." Even over the phone, the way his voice dropped when he said it gave her pleasure. It was over a year now since her mother's death, and the early spring air seemed to be waking her again.

"I miss you, too." She wanted him, wanted to feel his arms around her.

"You should come home."

"I can come on the weekend. Can you get the weekend off?"

"If you'll come over, I'll *take* the weekend off," he said. "You know I will. But I mean home for good, Von. It's been too long."

"Oh, Bobby, not yet. You know they could lose the whole business. They could lose the house. They'd have nowhere to go."

"Do they need you twenty-four hours a day? Can't you go in to work there every morning and come home at night?"

Von imagined Rosheen staggering drunkenly into the house at night. Angering her father. Or merely startling him. And him descending on her like a mad commando with a baseball bat, a hammer, whatever he might lay his hands on in the dark.

"Haven't you done enough for them?" Bobby asked.

In her memory, she heard again that soft slam, the feathered bird, like a winter glove thrown at the window. Then the rustling, the sweep of her sister's bed sheet on the floor. Why didn't she turn around?

———

Rosheen was seventeen the spring her old friend Raymond Ross returned from Montreal, where he'd been studying music.

The first thing he did, after spending a day with his parents, was drive up to Las Roses to see Rosheen. Von remembered him as a skinny kid with a runny nose and mitten strings and a home-knit woollen hat with ear flaps. He had always seemed harmless. But now he was nineteen. He came home tall and broad-shouldered, and talking in a deep, serious voice about jazz music and politics. He drove up the Garrisons' long driveway in his dad's gold Chevrolet convertible while Von was in the side lot, mulching rosebushes. Rosheen must have been watching for him, for she came flying out the front door, down the steps and across the lawn to fling herself into his arms. He wrapped her in a hug and pulled her off her feet, swinging her around in a circle, and Von could hear them laughing. All day she heard their excited voices as she went about her work. Rosheen showed him her papier mâché masks, and they spent a good two hours trying them on and making up skits and engaging in a long discussion about theatre.

Rosheen never had time to help with the new retail stand Von was setting up. She never had time to vacuum or finish her math homework or study for a history test. But somehow she always found time for her art projects. Her favourite teacher, Mr Tate, taught his class a new technique every month. In April, it had been papier mâché, and Rosheen had become a papier mâché fanatic, slopping pails of water upstairs and making a mess of the attic. For the first time ever, she used up a roll of newsprint before Bobby could bring another. Von had to admit the masks were beautiful — charming, frightening, and mysterious animals, their faces reflecting the myriad moods of human beings. It was hard to believe they were made by a teenage girl. But a person couldn't spend her life at play, no matter how good she was at playing. She had to grow up, eventually, and support herself somehow. She had to grow up *soon*, and pass her year and enter grade twelve in the fall. Von had invested too much time and effort to allow her to fail now. She had given up too much. Rosheen must graduate on time and the greenhouse must become a success again, so that in a year from now — two at the most — Von would be free to resume her life.

Soon after that, she'd start trying to convince Frank to retire. Maybe she could even — a burst of high-pitched laughter interrupted her thoughts. Rosheen. That was a sound she hadn't heard in this house for over a year. A long trill of a laugh. Almost flirtatious. Distracted, Von picked up the bouquet she was about to wrap and pricked her finger on a thorn.

Upstairs, Rosheen laughed again. Definitely flirtatious. Eager. She was full of expectation, and suddenly Von was afraid for her. Rosheen was expecting too much. She was falling in love. Von could hear it in her voice. She felt a surge of compassion for her sister. Lately she'd been so annoyed with Rosheen, she was forgetting how vulnerable she was.

When Frank invited Ray to stay for dinner, Von made a point of reminding him they were very busy. It was wedding season, and they had a full crop of grandiflora to harvest and dozens of arrangements to wrap.

Frank dismissed this concern. Ray's presence seemed to rouse him from the stupor of his grief, and he was in a rare, sociable mood.

Over dinner, Frank inquired after Raymond's parents, who had always been kind to the Garrisons. They were a gentle couple, who had taken the time to teach their children that there's nothing wrong with people who are different. And since Eileen had died, they had been wonderful, delivering homemade cookies and meatloaf, taking Rosheen on outings and driving Frank to work on cold or rainy days.

Ray said his parents were fine. He spoke of his life in Montreal, where he was studying composition now and playing saxophone in the university band. He told of travelling to Halifax to play in a nightclub and getting paid for it. He hoped to travel more with the band after he graduated next spring. When he talked about his music he lowered his eyelids and looked at the table, as if savouring a memory he could not impart to others. His lashes were dark and thick against his skin, and when he sensed Von watching him, they flickered open, and he looked at her, the way a man looks at a woman.

Frank asked about the location of the nightclub and the other concert halls and theatres in Halifax. He described an old building on the harbourfront, and Ray said he knew the place. "Big brick building with pillars out front," he said. "Facing the ocean. It's a movie house now."

"That's it," said Frank. He smiled. He didn't smile often, but he smiled at Ray. Or at something he was remembering. "I saw my first live play there," he said. "About 1940."

"Cool," said Ray. "What did you see?"

"I was a kid," said Frank. "I was just a dumb kid."

Ray stayed late. While she washed the dishes, Von could hear him and Rosheen out on the double swing, talking in low quick voices and laughing, but the creak of the swing and the splash of the dishwater kept her from hearing their words. Frank sat in the living room, listening to the radio. Von thought he'd get up and tell Ray it was time to go home, but after a while she heard him snoring and knew he was out for the night.

Von finished the pots and pans and wiped the stove and made coffee and stepped out onto the porch. The night was warm. The scent of lilacs lingered on the still air. Rosheen was sitting sideways on the swing, with her bare feet in Ray's lap. When Von came out, she bent her knees and lowered her feet to the floor. Ray stopped the swing. They waited to see what she wanted.

"Would you guys like some dessert?" she asked. "We've got sponge cake."

"I don't know," said Rosheen.

"The coffee's fresh. Come on in."

"In a minute," she said.

Von went back to the kitchen and set cups and plates on the table and waited an hour and then she went upstairs to her room.

She sat on her bed and brushed her hair, wondering if she should say something. Rosheen was so excited she couldn't see that Ray wasn't the same kid she remembered. He was becoming a man, sophisticated and dangerous. She remembered the way he had looked at her across the table. She remembered her mother's words, *Men marry beautiful girls.* Raymond could hurt Rosheen. He could hurt her badly. He was going to become an important person, maybe even a famous person, who would draw many people to him, many women. Beautiful women. He wouldn't stay here on the prairies, and he wouldn't marry a girl like Rosheen.

———

The morning after Ray's visit, Von woke early and lay listening to the stillness of the house. The sky was not yet light, but already the air was heavy and hot. The birds were beginning to sing. Quietly, so as not to wake Frank or Rosheen, Von went up to the attic, where the summer clothes were stored, to find a sunhat.

From the attic window she saw the whole field, and beyond the field, the tops of the fruit trees in the orchard. It was early Sunday morning, and the apple blossoms were newly open, like a white net thrown over the branches.

She rummaged through the trunk and came up with two sunhats and a pair of sandals.

Before she turned to go, she glanced out the window once more. Through the fine lacework of the blossoms she saw the metallic flash of a car coming up the road. She lowered herself and knelt before the windowsill to get a better look. It was Mr Ross's convertible. But too early for a visit. Just past sunrise. Then the car entered the clearing and she saw that the top was down and Rosheen was sitting in the passenger seat. Ray was driving and Rosheen was close beside him. She must have been with him all night. Her head rested on his shoulder. Her bright hair streamed out behind her, tangling in the wind.

———

There was only a week left in Ray's visit when he invited Rosheen to opening night at the Red River Ex. Rosheen loved the roller coaster and the noise and the funhouse. Ray and Rosheen had often gone to the Ex together as kids. But now there was a dash of adult romance in the mix. They were going in the evening and taking in a country music concert on the fair grounds. Rosheen had bought a new summer dress and asked to borrow Von's high heels. She was in such a state of happy anticipation that she forgot about partying with Suzie. Instead, she stayed home, reviewing notes for her exams, so she'd be there when Ray called, as he always did, to say good night.

But when she came home from school that Friday, Von told her Ray had called to cancel.

"What? Why?"

"He got invited to the lake," said Von. "Some friends from high school have a place on Lake of the Woods, and it's his only chance to see them. His last weekend here. He said he couldn't pass it up."

"He didn't ask if I could go?"

"He didn't mention it."

Rosheen ran to the telephone. "Oh, he's gone already," said Von. "He said they had to leave by three to beat the weekend traffic."

Rosheen was puzzled. She wasn't hurt, not then. Not yet. She was confused. Something had happened that she didn't understand, but she was sure there was an explanation.

Von had already called Bobby and asked him to take Rosheen with him when he went to his grandfather's cabin this weekend. Von couldn't get away herself, too many chores, but it would do Rosheen good. Bobby said sure. He'd like the company on the long drive.

When Bobby came by an hour later, Von had already packed a beach bag for Rosheen and a picnic of fried chicken and fruit salad. Rosheen, having nothing else to do, agreed to go. She threw a sketchbook and her camera into the bag and jumped in the front seat, grinning.

"You get the front seat at last!" Von teased. She waved as they drove away.

Von watched for Ray's car from the window, and when it arrived she ran outside so he wouldn't come up to the house, where her father might hear his voice.

"Rosheen's gone to the lake for the weekend," she told him.

When he looked up at her, the sun hit his eyes and he squinted. He shaded his forehead with his hand and smiled, as if she had told a joke. "We're going to the Ex tonight," he said.

"She's gone up to the lake," Von repeated. She told herself it was the truth. "A friend came by this afternoon and invited her out to his cabin."

"And she went?" Ray stared hard at the door to the house, as if trying to see through it.

"He's a dear friend," Von said. "His parents have a gorgeous cottage. With a heated pool." She wasn't sure why she added that last bit. Had she gone too far? He looked skeptical.

"Didn't she mention we're going to the Ex?"

"Not to me."

Ray sent a letter from Montreal, postmarked the day after he left. Von took it out of the mailbox before Rosheen got home. She didn't read it. She just fed it into the wood stove in the greenhouse. Leaving no trace.

7.2

ROSHEEN SWAM UNDERWATER, HER EYES OPEN, MARVELLING AT the shafts of green and blue light, and the particles drifting through them — sediment, fish scales, algae. The light clarified the colours of the stones and pebbles on the lake bottom and everything resting on the sand, clam shells, a half-buried golf ball, Bobby's bare white feet and his grandfather's feet in wrinkled blue canvas shoes, because the sharp rocks hurt his soles. They both said the water was too cold for swimming, but Rosheen loved it. She wished she had an underwater camera. She swam farther from shore, out deeper, where the sunlight didn't penetrate to the bottom. She could see it hit the lake and then sink in until the water swallowed it. She came up for air and turned in a circle, treading water, looking out across the surface. At its deepest depths, too far away for her to swim, the lake must be completely dark. In the ocean, there must be miles of darkness.

She swam back to the shallows, where she scooped up some small stones. A round white one with a brown ring around it. A grey one with brown stripes. And a solid black one. She carried them onto the beach and laid them on her towel.

"Finding treasure?" Bobby asked.

"For my drawing project," Rosheen told him. "Mr Tate says I should draw every day. Use the things around me."

After lunch, Bobby and his grandpa took the boat out on the lake to fish, but Rosheen stayed on shore to draw. She dragged a wooden crate onto the beach and covered it with a towel. She laid upon the towel all the objects she'd collected: the lake stones and the golf ball, a crow's feather, a pine cone, a hunk of moss, the curled rind of an orange Bobby had eaten, and a broken bottle, its sharp edges worn smooth by the water. She sat in a lawn chair, with her sketchbook balanced on her knees, and began to copy what she saw.

When she was a kid, she'd copied the comic books, because the other kids, having no idea how absolutely easy that was to do, were so impressed by it. Then she went through a stage where she wanted to make everything pretty. She made things she knew the other girls would like, fairy princesses and rainbows and dancing girls with flowers in their hair.

She had left behind her ambition to make pretty things when she discovered beauty. Pretty things were cute and colourful. Pretty things were sparkly and childish. You could see a pretty thing all at once. But a beautiful thing revealed itself slowly. A beautiful thing had depth. Maybe even mystery. She read about the golden mean and the rules of composition. She even read some nonsense in a men's magazine about the difference between a pretty girl and a beautiful girl, and at the time she'd considered this to be of genuine importance. But now she thought it was a matter of taste. What a person liked or didn't like. Categories. Peacocks but not chickens. Orchids but not onions.

Anyway, she was leaving all that behind, too. She was concentrating, now, not on beauty but on skill. Mr Tate had said to the class, straight out, that they were too young to be artists. If they wanted to make art, they should spend their youth learning its methods. So that is what they did. They mixed watercolour washes and constructed colour wheels, took photographs, moulded clay, carved wood, and made papier mâché. And they studied draughtsmanship, first with pen and ink and now with Rosheen's nemesis: the pencil. She laboured every day over shape and form and lighting and perspective. Sharpening and smudging and erasing.

"That looks so real," Bobby said, when he returned from fishing. "You're amazing, Rosh."

Rosheen knew it didn't look real. The feather looked too heavy, the stones were flat, and the shading of the whole thing was wrong in a way she couldn't identify. Still, it was nice to hear Bobby say she was amazing. Someday maybe her drawings would be amazing for real. If she kept practising. When she compared this year's work to the work she did last year, before she met Mr Tate, she could see the difference practice made.

Right now, Bobby was admiring the stones. The real ones, not the drawing. "Wow. Nice colours. You have a good eye, Rosh."

"Hold them," said Rosheen. She pulled out her camera and took a few pictures of the lake stones in the palm of Bobby's hand.

The next day, when the two men waded in again, Rosheen studied their legs and feet more closely, watching the wavery, muted colours, the play of light on the water. She memorized details, a blue bruise under Bobby's knee and the blond hairs on his leg, moving in the current of the lake water.

She raised her head above the surface, to drink the air. In the world above, the men's bodies were solid, their dry skin absorbing the light. Light had an entirely different texture under water. She'd like to paint both worlds in the same scene, to show the contrast.

Could you see both worlds at the same time? She waded in until the water was up to her chin and then bent her knees until it was up to her eyes. She tried to stand still with her eyes half in and half out of the water. A blur of bobbing light and water up her nose and sputtering.

You couldn't really see the line between the air and the water. You couldn't photograph it, either. Could you draw it?

That evening, she opened her sketchbook and drew, high on a blank page, a horizontal line: this was the familiar, often-drawn horizon between the far shore and the sky. Closer to the bottom of the page, she drew a second horizontal line: the surface of the lake, threshold to the underwater world. She held the page as far from her eyes as she could. The composition was too rigid. The space too tight. Turning the page on its side, she experimented with a wider view.

She got out her box of paints and began to sketch the underwater details she remembered. Bobby's leg, the light freckles on the calf, the delicate, indigo bruise — on Bobby's real knee, the bruise was turning brown now, fading into history — the ankle bone, the high arch of the foot, a broken toenail. Ordinary details, yet now she had lavished so much time and attention on them, they were beautiful to her.

She remembered a phrase she'd overheard her mother say one day: serious beauty. That was what Rosheen was after. Not ordinary beauty. Not a category. But what was hard earned, what was loved. What was truly seen. The best artists drew your attention to these things. Things most people didn't notice. The dark blue of blood blooming privately under the skin. The exit wound on her father's arm, its silvery radiating lines, like a burst star. Even her own scar. The graceful angle of its curve as it descended. And the delicate bundle of scar tissue on her lower lip, pebbly, the colour of a Jocelyn rose. She wondered if anyone would ever look at her and really see that.

As the light began to fade, she put her paints away and joined the men, who were building a fire on the beach. Bobby's grandfather was finishing some tale about his youth.

"Put it this way," he said. "None of the pretty girls I knew then are pretty now."

He and Bobby laughed.

Bobby lit a match and the kindling caught. Pale flames, barely visible because the sky was not yet dark.

Yes, thought Rosheen, as her life clicked into place for her. Serious beauty. That would be her work.

Bobby's grandfather welcomed her to come and sit beside him by the fire. He was seasoning the pan of fresh pickerel he was going to cook. "So, what about you? Any boyfriends yet?"

Rosheen shrugged.

"What about Raymond?" Bobby asked. "You like Raymond, don't you?"

"Raymond stood me up!" said Rosheen. "We were supposed to go to the Ex last night, but he went out to Lake of the Woods with somebody else."

Bobby frowned. "Not another girl?"

"I don't know," said Rosheen, realizing she didn't. Another girl? She hadn't considered that possibility. It made her uneasy.

On the ride home, Rosheen's thoughts returned to Raymond. He'd be on his way to Montreal by now. He had missed seeing her before he left.

"I didn't even get a chance to say goodbye to him," she said to Bobby.

"He left already? I thought he was here for the summer. I thought he'd take you to the school dance, end of June."

"No. He has a bunch of concerts dates in Montreal. I won't be going to any dance."

Bobby parked the car in front of her house. "You can go to the dance with someone else," he said.

"Oh, come on, Bobby. Who's going to ask me out?"

"Lots of guys. You'll see."

"No one is gonna want me."

"Sure they will," he said. "Cheer up." He tapped her nose with his fingertip. "There's no one in the world like you, Rosh. No one."

"Are you coming in?"

"I can't today. Gotta work. Tell Vonnie I'll see her tomorrow."

Rosheen ran into the house with her beach bag, calling Von's name. But nobody answered. She took out her sketchbook, wanting to look again at her drawings and to show them to her sister. She smelled something cooking, so she went into the kitchen. "Guess what, Vonnie?"

But it was Frank at the stove, stirring a pot of chili. "Von is working at the plant stand in town today," he said. "I'm just heating up the dinner she made for us. Are you hungry?"

"Not yet."

He ladled some chili into a bowl for himself. "Well, it's here for you when you want it. Tell me, what did you do out there all weekend, at the lake?"

Rosheen hugged her sketchbook, full of everything she'd seen. "Nothing," she said.

She went into the livingroom and sat on the rug in a window-shaped patch of light. On the coffee table, the fruit bowl held one half-ripe pear, green and golden in the sunlight. Just by looking at it she could feel how round it was, and its shadow was orange and heavy against the curve of the bowl. She could see. Anything she wanted to see. All day, sunlight streamed into her brain through two holes in her head, blue and transparent, like two beams of sky. All the colours of the world. For the taking.

The orchard, in fall, smelled of overripe apples and plums. Wasps burrowed into the rotting fruit that lay on the grass, and Rosheen, wearing open-toed sandals, stepped carefully around them as she made her way to Jean-Claude's truck.

He had parked in the clearing, off the road, to wait for her. Led Zeppelin on his tape deck cranked so high she couldn't hear what he said as she climbed in. His eyes were closed, his leathery face screwed up in concentration as he bobbed his head in time to the beat, drumming his fingers on the steering wheel. His new T-shirt said *Led Zeppelin North American Tour, 1977*, though Rosheen knew he'd never been anywhere near their tour. When the song ended, he placed his hand on her thigh and said, "So?"

"So I couldn't get any."

"What the hell? Why not?"

"It's all gone. Cleaned out."

"Shit, Rosheen. You said it was a sure thing."

"Sorry." She wasn't sorry, though. She was lying. She had gone to Bobby's house and cleaned out the last of the pills herself, stuffing the empty bottles with vitamins and headache tablets, in case anyone ever looked in the shortbread tin. For Jean-Claude and Suzie, the pills were fun, a way to get a quick high. They didn't need them like Rosheen did. She should never have told them about that tin. She blabbed too much when she was drinking, made all kinds of mistakes. Last week she'd let Jean-Claude kiss her, and when she sobered up, the vague, disjointed memories of the kiss disturbed her. She wasn't sure exactly what had happened. Jean-Claude wasn't the sort of person she'd imagined as her true love. But even if Jean-Claude was going to be her boyfriend, she couldn't afford to share her stash with him. She'd run out of the scrip from her surgery last winter, and Dr Chan refused to renew it again.

"You'll have to pay for the weed, then, if you got nothing to trade."

"Sure." She pulled out the cash she'd earned at the grade-twelve car wash. The money was supposed to go toward the big prom at the end of the year, but she'd kept every dollar she earned, and only pretended to put her cash in the basket when they passed it around at the end of the day. She wasn't like the other kids. For one thing, she sure as hell wasn't going to the prom. Who would take her? Even Raymond didn't care about her anymore. He hadn't written to her once all summer. For another, she had no job. Most of the girls worked part-time in restaurants, but no one would hire Rosheen. Can't have the customers losing their appetites. She couldn't get a job in a drugstore or a clothing store, either, not even the one Katy-Ann's father owned. And Von refused to give her a job, saying she should work in the greenhouse for free, because it was a family chore, like housework, which by the way Rosheen should be doing, too. Rosheen should do her part. Contribute to the family. Blah, blah.

Jean-Claude gave her a plastic bread-bag with a couple of inches of weed rolled up in the bottom, and she stuffed it into her purse.

"You ever had sex?" he asked. He pulled her hand toward his crotch, while sliding his other hand farther up her thigh.

"Hey, stop it."

He leaned forward, exhaling stale-beer breath into her nostrils, but luckily the sound of another car interrupted him.

"Someone's coming," she said. It was Bobby, approaching from the highway. Rosheen took the opportunity to slide away from Jean-Claude and get out of his truck. "I'd better get going. See you."

Rosheen got a ride with Bobby back to the house.

"Who was that?" he asked. "Was that Jean-Claude Allard?"

"He's Suzie's cousin."

"Why were you sitting out here in the orchard with him?"

Rosheen shrugged. "Vonnie doesn't like him."

"Maybe she has a good reason," Bobby said. "I've seen him in the Nicolette and in the bars downtown. Selling drugs."

"He just gave me a ride home from Suzie's place, that's all."

"Believe me, he is not a person you should be hanging around with."

"I got my photos back from the drugstore yesterday. Nice shots from the lake." She had gone with Bobby to Clear Lake several times this summer, though Von never went with them. Von always claimed she had too much work to do. "Come in and see them."

"Is your dad home?"

"When are you going to get over that?" asked Rosheen.

"Hey, don't blame me. That's your dad's thing, not mine."

"It's Von's thing," Rosheen said. "She thinks if you and my dad enter the same room at the same time, her world will explode."

He laughed. "She *is* a little dramatic about it."

"She's crazy," said Rosheen. "Don't tell her Jean-Claude was here, okay? She'll ground me or something."

They pulled into the driveway, and Bobby parked the car. "She actually *grounds* you now?"

"She's worse than my dad."

"I doubt that," said Bobby. "She just wants you to have more wholesome friends. To do more wholesome things. Like skating. Or swimming. That's why she encourages you to come up to the lake. She cares about you."

"She just wants to get rid of me," said Rosheen.

A robin flew down from the eaves of the house and Bobby followed its flight with his eyes. He said, "Maybe it's me she wants to get rid of."

"What?"

Bobby shook his head. He waved a hand as if erasing what he'd said. "Oh, you know, she has other things to do these days. She's busy."

"She's boring."

"Come on, Rosh."

"Sorry, but she is, and you know it. When was the last time you had any fun with her?"

Bobby rested his hands on the steering wheel and dropped his head. He said, "1975."

Rosheen had never heard him talk this way before. It made her sad.

Just then Von came out of the house. "Are you two going to sit in the car all afternoon?" There was a sharp edge to her voice.

Rosheen glanced at Bobby. When their eyes met, both of them quickly looked away. She got out of the car, feeling she had somehow wronged her sister. But what was wrong with a bit of gossip among family members? After all, she and Vonnie often talked about their father. This was the same thing.

But deep down — or, rather, not very deep — she knew it wasn't the same at all.

7.3

NIGHT, IN THE MIDDLE OF THE WINTER, ON THE PRAIRIES, IS NOT dark. After the sun goes down, an eerie afterlight radiates from the colourless sky. Even when no moon is visible, the snow clouds reflect the lights of the city for miles around, and the snowdrifts reflect that light back into the sky, so at two o'clock in the morning, in January, Von could clearly see the field outside her bedroom window. Bobby's Mustang came sliding slowly down the road, and in the beam of his headlights she could see the snow had once again begun to fall.

He parked on the road, so as not to wake her father. Von saw him get out of the car and walk toward the house, boots squeaking on the hard-packed snow. She lay back down under the covers. Bobby threw a loose snowball against her window. Then another. She would not get out of bed. She was furious with him. She had told him earlier this evening not to call her or come by. They had spent the afternoon together at the skating rink, but they hadn't been in synch. His motions seemed mechanical to her. Later, over dinner at the Blue Café, their conversation had dissolved into a meaningless argument over why they had nothing to say to each other and whose fault it was, and finally she'd walked out and called a taxi. He had a colossal nerve to show up now, in the middle of the night.

Von could hear Frank snoring above her in his third-floor bedroom. His hearing wasn't good enough to detect the sound of snow against the glass. So they were all safe for the time being. Von rolled onto her side and pulled a pillow over her ear. Sharp pains shot up her neck. She realized she was clenching her shoulder muscles so tightly she was hurting herself. She tried to relax. Nothing bad is going to happen. Frank is fast asleep. For a few minutes, everything was quiet, except Frank's snoring. Then Bobby flung a harder snowball at the window. Thud! Immediately, she heard Rosheen next door get out of bed and pad quickly down the stairs. Good. Let Rosheen deal with him.

She heard the front door open. Bobby and Rosheen whispering. Then Rosheen turned on the radio, low, to mask the sounds they were making. Maybe Rosheen could talk some sense into Bobby. They were alike, Von thought, two needy people, tugging at her from opposite directions.

No more noises came from below, but Von's anger kept her awake. How dare he try to cause disruption in this house where she was trying to foster peace? He didn't seem to understand the consequences. Or he didn't care.

He cared only for his own needs, she thought. When she compared him to her father, he seemed weak. She was often angry with her father — even right this minute, when he was sound asleep, she was still angry with him — but at least he had integrity. He would never whine. She didn't like boys who whined. Maybe she didn't like boys at all, maybe she liked grown men. Maybe she wanted a man for a husband, instead of a sulky kid.

In the morning, when she crept down before sunrise, Bobby was asleep on the couch.

"What am I going to do with you?" she asked.

"Come home with me."

"I can't," she said, "and you know it. I can't leave Rosheen alone with him, and I can't leave him alone. Now that my mother's gone, I'm all they've got."

"You're all *I've* got," said Bobby. He threw off the blankets Rosheen had given him and sat up. "Can't we work something out? Isn't there some way we could all live together?"

"You and my dad? In the same house?" She buried her face in her hands, shaking her head. Sometimes she thought the tension would torque her bones so hard she'd come apart.

"I could talk to him."

"Not now," said Von.

"Then when?"

"Let me get the business back on track. Let me get Rosheen through high school. And my dad, I don't know. Right now he needs support to get to work, to keep his job. Maybe if he retires, we could sell the place? He could live in town?" But she knew, even as she said it, that she could never sell this property. It was all they had, their one sure source of work and income.

"You need to make up your mind," Bobby said. "Him or me." He stood up. "No. Him or *us*. Which do you want?"

"I can't think about what I want right now, Bobby. I can't think about us, or what *we* want. We don't get to have what we want. Don't you understand that? You used to understand."

Bobby shoved himself into his coat and boots and stomped out the door. Von could see him banging the dashboard in frustration as he tried to start the frozen motor of his car.

In January, Rosheen turned eighteen, and Bobby seemed to view this milestone as some sort of release date for Von. He started talking again about her moving back home. A celebration. He got down on one knee and offered her a diamond ring, an act he would have considered cheesy even just a year ago. He was getting desperate. Von didn't have the heart to refuse the ring, which she wore without telling her father about it. But she wouldn't agree to set a date. "Not yet," she said, so many times that Bobby asked her if that was her middle name. He was becoming just as difficult to handle as the other two.

Her sister and her father both worried her that winter.

She was afraid Rosheen was on some dangerous drugs. She knew Rosheen had been drinking and smoking weed for quite some time, but now her behaviour was stranger than ever. Her pupils widened and narrowed in unnatural ways, and her energy levels were out of control. Sometimes she stayed up all night, in a frenzy of painting or paper creation, and was still wide awake and alert at eight in the morning, dressed for school, usually with a sheaf of paintings to show to her favourite teacher, Mr Tate. Other days she could barely summon the strength to pull on her shoes.

As for Frank, he seemed frail, somehow. Von wanted to be glad he was more co-operative, more willing to compromise, to seek her opinion. But these small transformations made her uneasy. To tell the truth, he was easier to handle when he was angry and unjust. It was easier to hate him than to love him. That was an awful, unworthy thought, which she tried to unthink. He had been terrifying to her when she was a child. Unpredictable and violent as the weather. Dangerous. Yet it frightened her, now, to see him as an ordinary man. To feel that source of strength, at the centre of the family, diminished.

All these thoughts ran through her mind while she was getting dressed in Bobby's bedroom. It was the middle of the afternoon, the only time she could ever get away from home. As soon as she'd come in the door, he had taken her to bed, and they'd spent a good, wordless couple of hours together. But now that they were talking again, things were taking a familiar turn. Bobby was sitting on the edge of the bed, pulling on his socks.

"Don't you think so?" he asked.

"Think what?" She hadn't been listening.

"Rosheen could come too," he was saying.

"What do you mean?"

"She could come live with us. We could put her up on the living room couch."

Von must have frowned because he said, "If you want, we could get another place, with an extra bedroom. She could live with us and go to school. I could drive her in, if she doesn't want to change schools. And you could pick her up after four. She only has a few months left."

"But my father —"

"Jesus Christ," said Bobby. He flung himself backwards onto the bed and lay with his arms above his head, wrists crossed, staring at the ceiling.

———

The following weekend, when Rosheen said she was staying overnight at Suzie's house, Von went to see Bobby again, to apologize, to try to ease his anger. To beg him to be patient.

The house was dimly lit, but through the window she saw the fridge open and its light come on. So she knew he was home. She knocked once, softly, and then entered. On the counter and the kitchen table, candles burned in empty wine bottles. Bobby, leaning over the record player, had his back to her. He set the needle down and Gordon Lightfoot started singing "Sundown." Von smelled incense and marijuana.

"Bobby?"

He turned, surprised. Then he broke into a grin. "Von! I was just going to call you!" He crossed the room and embraced her. She smelled the beer he'd been drinking and something else. "Are you smoking pot?"

He pulled back to see her face, but continued to hold her. "Just a couple of hoots."

In the darkness behind him, the bathroom door opened. Who was here? One of his fishing buddies? No. It was a woman. Smoking a cigarette. She entered the room and walked in front of the row of candles. A shapely woman. In a sleeveless blouse and short, short skirt. Sheer net stockings. No shoes. In this cold house?

The woman put one hand on her hip and said, "Hello, Vonnie."

"Oh, my God. Rosheen? What are you doing? Let me look at you." Von flicked a switch, flooding the scene with light.

"Whoa!" said Rosheen. "Is that necessary?"

She and Bobby both covered their eyes with their hands.

It was a harsh light, revealing grimy linoleum, an overfilled ashtray, dripping wax and empty bottles. Rosheen's face had a brittle sheen to it. She had plastered herself with makeup of some kind, and where did she get that outfit? It was cut too low and made her look like, like… Von didn't know what to think. What would their mother have said?

Rosheen swayed over to the light switch, glaring at Von through narrowed eyes. "Oh, these inferior people," she said, "who require light." She snapped the switch off.

"You're drunk," said Von. "How much have you had to drink?"

Rosheen laughed. "Not nearly enough."

Von turned on Bobby, flailing with both arms. "You're giving *alcohol* to my *sister?*"

"She's eighteen," Bobby said. "She can drink if she wants — Ow!"

Von quit beating on him. What was the use? She turned on a table lamp, a gentler light, and faced her sister.

Rosheen was pulling on a white turtleneck sweater, and her head was caught inside it. Her face was a blank woollen mask. Then her head popped out of the collar, her make-up smudged, her red hair bristling with static electricity. She said something angry, but inaudible.

"Oh, Rosh," said Von.

"Just leave me alone," said Rosheen. "I don't need you protecting me! From Bobby? Jesus!" Her eyes had that glazed look Von remembered from the days when she was a kid in the hospital. When she mumbled on like a crazy person about floating in space.

"Rosh," said Bobby. "Don't go. Let's —"

"Both of you, leave me alone!" Rosheen slipped her feet into her winter boots. She scooped her purse from a chair and skittered toward the door.

Von followed, reaching out to stop her, but Rosheen pulled away. "Don't *touch* me."

Von shrank back. "All right. Here. Wait in the truck for me." She held out her keys, and Rosheen stared at them as if she'd never seen a key before. Then she snatched them up. She slammed the door behind her.

Bobby was sitting at the kitchen table, a newly opened bottle of beer cupped in his hands, his head bowed low on his chest, as if beleaguered. Von wanted to slap him.

When he finally lifted his head, she saw he was sober. "I'm sorry, Von," he said. "I didn't realize she was drinking so much. She came over with a six-pack and a pie." He gestured toward the counter. "And we were just talking."

Von saw the blackberry pie on the counter. The one Von had made herself last night. In one of her best tin plates. One slice was cut out of it.

"She brought you a pie," Von said.

He nodded.

"She came all the way over here to bring you a pie because she felt sorry for you, and you start giving her booze and pot? Can't you *think?*" She recognized that phrase as her father's, but she was too angry to stop herself.

No. She was more than angry. She was scared, scared, scared. Rosheen was out of control. That look in her eyes. That wasn't from beer. Or pot. That was something else. Something bad.

"When are you coming back home?" Bobby asked her.

"This isn't my home."

"Vonnie —"

She took the ring off her finger.

"Don't do that," he said. Warning her.

She set the ring on the table. He was still talking, but she couldn't listen anymore. She wanted an end to this terrible indecision. She opened the door and stepped out into the winter.

Snow was falling. The roof and hood of the truck were already covered with a thin skein of white flakes. The door was unlocked and the keys were on the dashboard. Rosheen lay crumpled in the back seat, sleeping. Thin, stockinged legs askew. If she were alone, she would have frozen to death out here. Von took her home.

On Valentine's Day, the first Valentine's Day in five years they had spent apart, Bobby sent a dozen red Gypsy roses to the house. Von opened the box out on the cold porch and when she read the card she chucked the flowers off the side of the steps into a snowdrift before the delivery van had even cleared the yard. They lay out in the cold, day and night, freezing and crumbling until the blizzards of late February buried them completely.

When Bobby phoned, Von hung up immediately. She couldn't speak to him. She had made the necessary choice, the only choice, and she didn't want to spend time weeping over it.

"Why are you so mean to him?" cried Rosheen.

"Girls! Girls, settle down," said Frank.

"You can't blame Bobby," Rosheen said. "After all, *you* left *him*."

"I left him *because* of you," Von hissed. "So shut up. Both of you just shut up."

And they did. They disappeared upstairs and stayed in their own rooms most of the day while Von cleaned house. They finally came out when they got hungry. They didn't seem angry. They seemed contrite. Maybe even content. Maybe they knew, in their hearts, that they had won.

In spring, Raymond Ross returned. He drove up to Las Roses in the family car with his mother, who wanted to deliver a cake and some jam she had made.

"It's been too long," said Mrs Ross to Frank.

Frank embraced her so fully that Von was startled. But Mrs Ross just hugged him warmly, saying, "Far too long."

Ray and Rosheen greeted each other politely, Ray apprehensive and Rosheen pretending to be bored. In the living room, Frank and Mrs Ross kept up a lively conversation while Von served tea. Mrs Ross, excited to have her son back home, touched him often as she spoke. Ray wore a cotton shirt with a bright African pattern and wide sleeves that reached just halfway down his forearms. No watch, only a braided leather band around his wrist. Blue jeans and short leather boots, which he took off at the door. He had shaved carefully at some recent point, but black stubble was growing in along his jawline. He wore his dark hair longer and, if possible, his dark eyes seemed deeper, as if they'd captured and contained a wealth of memory in the past year. He was a man. He answered Frank's questions about his music. He had graduated and now played sax in a band that was booked into a series of summer festivals. Rosheen was apparently too absorbed by the pattern on her cup and saucer to comment. But Frank congratulated Ray with great enthusiasm and said he would love to hear him play. He invited them to stay for dinner, and Mrs Ross said they would be happy to, if it wasn't too much trouble.

"No trouble at all," said Frank. "Is it, Siobhán?"

Not for you, thought Von. But automatically she said, "Of course not." Then, when she saw Frank's genuine smile, she relented. "We'd be delighted," she said. She had almost forgotten Frank's smile, slightly warped because part of his upper lip was missing. He used to smile when Eileen read funny things to him out of the newspaper, or teased him or kissed him or exclaimed, "Oh, Frank, how marvellous!" over some new piece of woodworking he'd done or some story of how he'd helped a client. He was lonely now, she realized. He needed friends.

During the meal, Ray tried to engage Rosheen. "Are you making any more papier mâché?" he asked

"Not really." She sipped her water.

"Painting?"

She shrugged.

"Rosheen had a painting in the art gallery," Frank said. "Young Artists' Exhibit."

"I'm surprised you remember that," Rosheen said.

"Von, this is a lovely casserole," said Mrs Ross. "It's some kind of Mexican cooking, isn't it?"

"It's curry, Mum," said Ray.

Von said little, afraid any reference to the last time Ray had been here might expose her lies. She hoped that Ray and his mother would leave early, without that topic being raised. But after dinner, while Von was washing dishes, and Frank and Mrs Ross were listening to records, Ray and Rosheen left the house together. Von saw them sitting out in the car, talking.

7.4

BEING IN RAYMOND'S PRESENCE HAD ALWAYS MADE ROSHEEN FEEL peaceful. Even now, with all her doubts about his feelings, and after six days — no, it was almost a whole week — without using, her body relaxed into the seat beside him.

He pressed the radio button, and they heard a news story about the pope, who was too ill to perform the Easter service. Raymond lowered the volume and tuned instead to a jazz program. Oscar Peterson on piano. Ray shifted his body sideways and turned toward her, stretching his right arm along the top of the seat. It was a chilly evening, and both of them wore jackets.

"So?" he asked. "How are things, really?" He touched her shoulder and squeezed lightly. Instantly she scooted over to him, and he held her close. "Ah, Rosheen. It's good to be back home. I've missed you."

"I missed you so much," Rosheen said. They sat quietly. The sun had set, and no one had turned on the outdoor lights yet. The living room and kitchen windows shed the only light. Rosheen could see Frank and Mrs Ross very clearly, their heads bent together as they talked, and she could see Vonnie at the sink, washing the dinner dishes. Vonnie was leaning too far forward, as if trying to peer out the window at the car.

Rosheen closed her eyes, taking pleasure in the warmth of Ray's safe, familiar body next to hers, his arm across her back, around her shoulder. She wasn't in love with him, but she needed this, to be held, to be held still. Grounded. She knew they would be interrupted any moment. They would both return to their own families very soon.

But for now she was savouring his presence. She wished she could fall asleep surrounded by his arms.

Ray was silent a long time, just stroking her hair. Then he said, "Why didn't you ever write to me?"

"I'm sorry," she said. "I should have. I guess I just didn't know — if you wanted me to."

"But I wrote to you," said Ray.

"You did?" Rosheen let her head drop back, against his shoulder. Inside the house, Vonnie was closing the blinds. Horizontal strips of light were visible across the pane. Then they narrowed and the window went dark.

"I wrote to you right away," he said. "I wrote you a letter on the plane. I felt bad we didn't get a chance to say good-bye. But you were at the lake, so —"

"It must have got lost in the mail," Rosheen said. In the kitchen window, a small pinch of light appeared, and she knew that Vonnie had lifted one of the slats with her fingers so she could watch them in the car. "Let's get out of here," she said. "Let's go for a ride."

Raymond laughed. "I don't think my mum would appreciate that!"

"Oh, of course. Of course not. Maybe —"

"Some day soon, we'll go for a ride," Ray said. "I'll be here all summer. We'll have time for lots of rides."

Rosheen knew that she was failing grade twelve. She felt as if she had dropped something over the edge of a cliff and there was nothing she could do about it now but watch it fall. At first, she'd been the only one who knew. But now the school knew, too. Her teachers, in French, Biology, Math, and English, had all told her it was hopeless. With only four weeks left of school, she couldn't possibly pass now — even if she aced her exams. "Which you obviously won't," her English teacher said. "Have you even *read* the play?" The play was *Hamlet*. Rosheen had read the Classic comic and then made a collage out of three Ophelias — innocent, mad, and dead — cut from different pages of the comic book and glued onto a mirror. Even the guidance counsellor, who once had tried so hard, taking Rosheen to the beauty parlour, giving her fashion magazines and tapes about self-confidence, seemed to have given up on her. Only the art teacher, Mr Tate, the old reprobate, was pleased with her. Just this morning, while she was smoking a joint with him in the parking lot, he'd been encouraging her to study fine arts. At the university! He had no clue she was never going to finish high school.

So far, Vonnie and Frank had no clue, either. Rosheen had intercepted a note of warning sent to her father months ago, and forged his signature on it. Every morning she left the house as if she were going to school. But she wasn't. Most days she met up with Suzie at a fast food restaurant, and they drank coffee until their hands shook and then went over to the Nicolette Hotel to drink beer.

Rosheen wasn't using. She was keeping herself in check with beer and weed and 222s. A spoonful of cough syrup, sometimes, just to help her sleep. But she was putting the morphine behind her. She had only a small stash of pills, left over from the last time she forged a renewal of Dr Chan's prescription — more powerful than anything she'd ever scored downtown. She was going to toss them very soon. She was only keeping them for those times when she grew anxious. Then she soothed herself by thinking about them, twelve blue pills in their cracked and cloudy plastic bottle, tucked inside a sock in the back of her dresser drawer. Just in case.

It was going to be bad when Vonnie and Frank found out she wasn't going to graduate. But Rosheen tried not to think about that. Winter was finally over, and she deserved a good time after the long, horrible deep freeze. The best thing about the warm weather was taking rides in the convertible with Ray. One day they drove out early to Grand Beach and stayed until sunset, building elaborate sandcastles. Playing. Life with Ray was like being a kid again. She told him so when he dropped her off at home that night.

"It's fun, isn't it?" he said. Then he asked, "Who did you go to the lake with last year?"

"Just Bobby," said Rosheen. "And Bobby's grandfather. I got some good photographs. I've been thinking I'll make some paintings from them."

"No, I mean the night we were supposed to go to the Ex. Remember? I came to get you and you'd gone up to the lake with some rich guy. Some place with a heated pool?"

"A pool?" Rosheen laughed. "Bobby's grandfather isn't that rich. But wait a minute. You came to get me?"

"Sure. Of course. But you were already gone."

Rosheen looked out across the field. Then toward the house. There was a light on in the kitchen, but she couldn't see anyone. She remembered coming home from school last year, Von telling her that Raymond had gone to the lake with his friends. Being disappointed. Then being sent off to Clear Lake with Bobby. Was it possible? Finally she said, "She lied to you."

"Von? No way. I'm sure it was some kind of mix-up."

But Rosheen knew it was no mix-up. She remembered Von's words. *Some friends from high school, Lake of the Woods, weekend traffic.*

Later, she had a hard time remembering the rest of that night. Her memory was like a story with big holes torn out of it. A series of gaps with scenes as short as sparks.

She remembered standing over Von, who was working on the account books, and wanting to confront her. Von raising her eyes and saying, all irritated, "What *is* it, Rosheen?"

She remembered chickening out. Phoning Suzie to come get her.

Then, on her way out of the house, grabbing the pills from her sock drawer. She had been right to save them. She'd have to remember that in future, when she got in one of her idiotic self-improvement moods and wanted to destroy her drugs. It was always best to hold something back, in case of an emergency. There was always an emergency ahead.

There was a moment at Suzie and Jean-Claude's apartment, when she was drinking rye and ginger, and Jean-Claude was trying to kiss her. Then she was in Suzie's car and Suzie was driving, they were going to a bar downtown. Bright lights and people from *Saturday Night Fever* dancing badly under a disco ball, and then they were parked on Edgewood Street.

"Doesn't your sister live here?"

"Not anymore."

They took the bottle of rye inside and shared it with Bobby.

"Vonnie's gone up to the lake," Rosheen told him. "With some guy she likes. Yeah. Nice place on Lake of the Woods." She remembers offering him a lit joint, and him taking it. "They have a heated pool."

Memory of waking in the easy chair, wrapped in a blanket, Suzie passed out on the couch. Rosheen stood up and the room whirled. She staggered and hit her knee on a coffee table.

And then she was standing outside Bobby's bedroom door, which was not a door at all, but only a threadbare cotton curtain.

7.5

ALMOST EVERY WEEKEND THAT SUMMER, ROSHEEN PACKED A BAG and went to the lake with friends. Sometimes her friend Suzie was driving. Von didn't trust Suzie on the highway, but there was nothing she could do about it. Sometimes Raymond took Rosheen to Grand Beach. At least Ray was a safe driver, though Von still worried that Rosheen was too attached to him. Von would prefer Rosheen to be going up to Clear Lake with Bobby. But Bobby never invited Rosheen anywhere these days, and Von couldn't blame him. Now that she'd broken up with him, she could hardly expect him to take care of her little sister.

Since winter ended, Von had relented a little toward Bobby. She understood, now, that it wasn't his fault Rosheen was drinking and getting high. If Von couldn't control Rosheen, she couldn't expect Bobby to do it. She knew she had blamed him unfairly, using her anger as a way to break free of him. But she had needed to break free, because he would not stop asking her for something she could not give him.

But he had stopped now. He had turned reticent with her. If she ever ran into him, he was polite, but did not meet her eyes the way he used to. She found this new attitude hard to take. He had once been so bold. That was how he had won her over in the first place. Now he seemed defeated. She wanted to ask him if he had really given up on her. But of course she could not. She didn't want to open up any possibilities with him, not yet. She would make it up to him later, she promised herself. Some day, when her family didn't need her any longer, she would go back to him. They were meant to be together. It was fate. Bobby always said so himself.

It was Labour Day, and Von had registered Rosheen at a new high school, where she could repeat grade twelve with a new set of teachers and, Von hoped, a whole new set of friends. Younger, more innocent classmates. School was to start the day after tomorrow, so when she came into Rosheen's room and saw her packing a suitcase, Von was surprised.

"Where do you think you're going? I told you, no more weekend trips now that school is starting. You have to be disciplined this year."

"I'm moving out," Rosheen said.

"Don't be ridiculous. You're too young."

"I'm eighteen."

"You're not finished high school!" Von was desperate for her sister to finish high school. With everything Rosheen had against her, she couldn't be a drop-out, too. Even if she didn't want to go to college, she needed the diploma to find a decent job. And maybe she'd change her mind in the future, as Von had argued many times this summer. Maybe she'd want to go to secretarial school someday, or study design or something artistic like that at the University of Manitoba. She'd need a high school diploma to do that. But Rosheen didn't listen. All she wanted to do was draw and paint. And play her music at top volume and drive out to the lake and party.

"Vonnie," Rosheen said now, "don't freak, all right? But I have to move out. Sit down."

Von sat down on the bed.

"I'm pregnant."

Von blinked. Poor Rosheen. So young.

"I can't stay here. Dad won't allow it."

Von thought about that. Dad most certainly would not allow it. No daughter of his, etc. For a lapsed Catholic, Von had often thought, he was horribly Catholic. Maybe she could throw that at him. Times were changing, after all. "I'll talk to him," she said. "I'll —"

"I talked to him already," said Rosheen. "He wants me out."

"But where will you go?"

"I'll share an apartment with Suzie for a while. I'll get a job. When the baby comes, I guess I'll apply for welfare."

"Welfare!" Von jumped to her feet. "That's not a plan! Welfare! Christ!"

Rosheen continued shoving clothes into the suitcase.

"Can't you stay at Raymond's house? With his parents?"

The suitcase was stuffed full. Rosheen closed the lid and looked at Von.

"They have to take some responsibility," said Von. "They're good people. I know they are."

"I have to go," said Rosheen. She took the suitcase, leaving a mess behind, and ran down the stairs. Her friend Suzie was waiting in her car.

Von ran out to the driveway. But Suzie peeled away before she could stop her.

Yvette and her little daughter, Jeanne, were finishing their lunch at the kitchen table. "Let her go," Yvette said. "It's for the best."

"You know about this?"

"She told me, yes." To Jeanne, she said, "Honey, why don't you go take a cookie to Dad? Here you go." Jeanne ran out the door, cookie in hand.

"I'm going to speak to Raymond's parents," Von said. "We have to come up with a plan. Her education. The baby's future. Rosheen can't do this all on her own. I will not let that happen." She stepped into the hall to use the phone.

But as she was dialling, Yvette came into the hall behind her.

"Vonnie, no," said Yvette. She depressed the two buttons on the phone cradle with her fingers, breaking the connection. "Don't call them."

Von was still holding the receiver to her ear. "What are you telling me? Don't they know?"

"Come and sit down," said Yvette. She took the receiver and replaced it in its cradle and tugged on Von's sleeve until Von followed her into the kitchen. They sat at the table and Yvette poured two cups of tea.

"It's not Raymond's baby," Yvette said. She flinched and then said it. "Bobby's the father."

For a minute, nothing made sense. And then it did. In her memory, the whole year shifted, took on a different cast, every event weighted with a new interpretation. Rosheen's eagerness to jump in Bobby's car and go to the lake last summer, the way they had driven off together, leaving Von behind. Taking the picnic she'd made for them. Bobby and Rosheen partying at his house, smoking dope. And then Von appearing. Ruining their fun. *These inferior people, who require light.*

It occurred to her, all at once, that her sister hated her.

———

Von stuffed two suitcases full of Rosheen's belongings and set them out on the porch. For a long, long time she did not speak to Rosheen. When Bobby phoned, she hung up quietly and quickly. When he sent letters, she threw them away, unopened. When he drove into the yard and pounded on the door, she would not answer.

"I never trusted that Bobby Sullivan," her father reminded her.

When Raymond's parents came to visit, Frank stood in the doorway after they left and said, "Poor Raymond."

Poor *Raymond?* Von would have been angry at her father, but she had spent all her anger, she had overspent it. She was depleted.

———

Von watches Kyle, as she remembers his inauspicious beginnings. They are in Bergen-op-Zoom at last, and Kyle is talking to the young woman at the front desk of their small hotel. His mother would have been glad to see him here, in this place she regarded with such reverence.

Rosheen had tried hard to make Von bring their father to this town before he died. According to Rosheen, Canadians were regarded as heroes here. Frank would finally get some recognition for what he'd done, instead of being ignored as he was in Canada. In Canada, he was viewed as a nuisance, or a freak, she said. "A prop hauled out once a year for Remembrance Day." She could be very bitter.

Kyle thanks the hotel clerk and joins Von and Meredith on the hotel patio. "She doesn't know where it is," he says.

"Maybe the waitress knows," Meredith says. When another young woman serves their coffee, she asks, "Can you tell us how to get to the war cemetery?"

"The memorial?"

"The cemetery. Where the Canadian soldiers are buried?"

"Canadians?" The woman shakes her head. "Sorry. I'm not certain."

Later, at the tourist centre, they look at posters and pamphlets while they wait. The staff is busy. It's a sunny day, one of the few sunny days since they've been in Holland, and the small centre is full of families looking for something to do. Meredith is interested in the origins of the town. "Look at this, the town square is hundreds of years old." She hands Kyle a book of photographs. "Look at all these medieval buildings."

"Can I help?" asks one of the young employees.

Kyle asks about the war cemetery.

"Ah," he says. "An actual cemetery? Canadian? I do not think so."

He confers with the other staff. Only one, a man about forty, has heard of it. "Ja. A mile or two east of town. Here." He points to a vague, greenish splotch on the tourist map.

"There are many more things to see," the younger man tells them. "Restaurants, shopping. The flower market. You can rent bicycles, too." He gives Kyle a tourist map.

Afterwards, Meredith says, "The war was over fifty years ago. Most of the people running things here today, the people working in the stores and restaurants, wouldn't remember."

"I guess not," says Von. But in Canada, the grateful Dutch are legendary. Rosheen had believed in them.

They visit the Drake Hotel, because there's a photo in Rosheen's scrapbook showing a Nazi tank parked right in front of it. The hotel was built in the fourteenth century, according to the tourist information. It faces a large town square, and today it's the site of a wedding reception. Musicians assembled on the cobblestones play polka music while wedding guests flock around them, drinking from champagne flutes, and the groom escorts his bride, in her frothy white gown, out of a horse-drawn carriage. Von turns in a slow circle as she films the celebration and the magnificent church and all the buildings that surround the square.

Later, they tour the neighbourhood where Marijke once lived with her family. The whole block was rebuilt after the war, and of course they can't see Marijke's destroyed house or the ruins where she hid or the café or the butcher shop she described. But they walk the length of the street, knowing they're walking the ground Frank walked, the place where he lost his sight, where he survived. At the end of the block, they rest in a small park, looking out to the countryside beyond. Meredith takes photographs and Kyle sits by himself at a table with his pencil, writing in his travel journal. Von isn't sure what Kyle is feeling. He says "wow" a lot. But to him, this expedition must be like a movie he's watching, and to Meredith it's twice removed, a pilgrimage to the site of a battle involving the father of her boyfriend's estranged mother. But how does it feel to Von? *Shut up, shut up*, she tells herself. *I'm here. What more do you want?* She trains the camera on the horizon, visible across a long, flat field of tall grass, very like a Manitoba landscape. The quality of the light, too, is like Manitoba light, a rich expanse of illuminated sky, nowhere to hide from it.

———

During the final days of their father's life, Rosheen flew from New York to Winnipeg to be near him. Von didn't invite her to stay at Las Roses, not at first. But she did make an effort to connect. She spoke to Rosheen daily. She stood in the hospital corridor beside the pay phone, holding the receiver to her ear, while Rosheen sat on the edge of the bed in her hotel room, holding the receiver to her ear. Mostly they listened to each other breathe.

After Frank died, Von had to communicate certain practical details to her sister, to ask her consent. For instance, Frank wanted to donate his body to science. To let medical students dismember and dissect it. He had written it into the will his lawyer had drawn up.

"Like he hasn't given enough?" Rosheen asked.

Von was silent. She didn't like the idea either. But it was Frank's request.

Rosheen later said she had come to the veterans' hospital seven times. The whole week it took him to die she'd taken the bus there every single day. Von saw her twice from the window of his fifth-floor hospital room. The first time, Rosheen was at the edge of the hospital gardens, smoking a cigarette in the falling snow. She wasn't dressed warmly enough. She never dressed warmly enough. Von watched her smoke for a while, then turned to check on Frank, and when she looked out the window again, Rosheen was gone. Von assumed she was on her way up, but she never arrived. A few days later she appeared again on the hospital grounds, closer this time, smoking and pacing in the snow-covered flower beds. The snow was melting, and her boot prints when she walked away were starkly visible behind her, full of mud. Von put on her coat and went outside to look for her. She followed the footprints she'd seen from above. Rosheen's muddy boots had marked a path all the way around the corner of the building, where they began to overlap themselves, circling the building twice, three times, before returning to the entrance. Then, after tramping round a pile of cigarette butts, they snaked on out through the flower gardens past the parking lot to the front street and the transit stop where Rosheen must have caught the bus that took her back to her hotel downtown. Not once did she enter the hospital.

———

The following morning, Von and Kyle and Meredith plan their visit to the war cemetery.

"Should we bring something?" asks Kyle. "Flowers?"

"No one brings flowers to a funeral anymore," says Meredith.

"This isn't a funeral," Kyle reminds her.

"The flower market is too far away," Meredith says. "We don't have time."

They are heading off to photograph the statues around town, while Von is going in the opposite direction, to record some scenes featuring the town's historic churches. They have agreed to meet at the bus stop at two. There is only one bus that goes out past the cemetery. It runs only once a day and returns in the evening.

But when Von shows up at two, Kyle and Meredith aren't there yet.

"I'm going to the war cemetery," she tells the bus driver. "Do you know it?"

"Cemetery, ja," he says.

"The Canadian war cemetery?"

"Ja, get on," he says. "We are late."

She asks the driver to wait, but he won't wait long, and when the bus pulls away at four minutes after, there is still no sign of Kyle and Meredith. As the bus turns right at the top of the street, Von looks back and thinks she sees them arriving at the stop. They must have gotten lost along the way. Or didn't realize the schedule was so strict. But Von feels abandoned, making this journey alone. Annoyed, she remembers it was Kyle's idea in the first place. She settles back in her seat and gazes out the window. Actually, it was Rosheen's idea. Rosheen was pretty moralistic about visiting this place, seeing as she didn't even visit Frank when he was still alive.

———

Von wasn't present when he died. She had left him in the evening, saying, "See you," wondering if those would be her final words to him. He had not spoken a word or eaten a bite of food for seven days. A kindly nurse had warned her that he wasn't likely to recover. It was she who phoned the next day to say he had passed. Manuel answered the phone and handed it to Von, shaking his head, so she knew.

After Von hung up the phone, Manuel said, "He was a good man, your father. The best. You know, when I came here to work, I was a stupid kid. I didn't know anything. Your father taught me how to make things. How to do carpentry. You know what he said to me? He said, *There are no stupid kids, only kids who haven't yet learned what they need to know.* If it weren't for your dad, I'd have been out in the streets, getting in trouble. Who knows where I'd be now? Jail, maybe." He smiled. "I'll go and get Rosheen from the hotel."

"No, Manuel. We're not — I'm sure she doesn't want to come here."

"She does," he said. He threw a raincoat on. "I'll bring her and her luggage."

So Rosheen sat on the porch at Las Roses with Von that night, as they watched a heavy rain come down. Rosheen excused herself and came back with a bottle of gin and two cold cans of tonic water. She brought two glasses, even though Von said she didn't want a drink. They sat in silence while Rosheen polished off two drinks and the rain came down until the yard was drenched.

"We should at least have flowers," Rosheen said.

"What are you talking about?"

"Flowers. For Frank. Remember what Mum always said about 'in lieu of flowers'?"

Von laughed, remembering how their mother had railed against that custom. Not just because flowers were her business, but because she felt that any practicality, if taken too far, was an affront to gracious living. Almost mean. Like furniture covered in plastic, or artificial Christmas trees. It was better, she believed, to be extravagant than to be ugly. In Eileen's obituary, at her request, her daughters had ended with the line, "Support your local florist."

Rosheen jumped up and went down the hall toward the kitchen. A few minutes later, Von could see her in the greenhouse, walking through the roses, clipping. Then the door to the greenhouse opened into the yard and Rosheen came out, running across the slippery wet lawn with a pair of shears, a typically Rosheen thing to do, and began to clip branches from the wild rose bushes outside. The rain was still falling, though it had slowed to a light spatter.

Von went into the kitchen and began to fill Eileen's vases with water.

Rosheen returned, her arms laden with long-stemmed roses, lots of the snow-whites with the apricot edging, and some of the most luscious lemony yellows, which Von had been saving for a customer — no matter — and elegant bright carmines, mixed in with the scrubby branches of pink blossoms from the prickly rose and the Morden Centennial. Von and Rosheen filled five vases, the wild and the hothouse flowers together, and carried them out to the porch where they arranged them on the window ledges. It wasn't dark yet, but Rosheen lit candles. The porch was warm with colour and light.

Rosheen kneeled backwards on the chair by the window, clutching the chair back, looking out on the lawn and the bushes and the garden. She'd been away from home for sixteen years. Her dress was wet and the bare soles of her feet were dirty from walking through the greenhouse.

"Warm enough?" Von asked.

"He never wanted me to go out," said Rosheen. "Remember? He wanted me home for every meal. And I always had to help in the workshop. Holding the damn wood while he sawed. I was terrified. You were way better at that kind of stuff than I was. But he made me do it."

"That's because you were his favourite," Von said softly.

"You were the one he liked," said Rosheen. "You were the one who read to him."

Von didn't answer. She picked up the *Collected Poems of W.B. Yeats*. The gold letters on the red cover had faded, the gold crest rubbed off. "Remember this?"

Rosheen was silent, still gazing out the window. With her finger she traced a raindrop sliding down the pane. She pulled the tab on the second can and poured tonic water into her glass. She added a few fingers of gin and took a sip. Then she said, *"The trees are in their autumn beauty."*

Von laughed.

"*The woodland paths are dry,*" Rosheen continued.

"Mm hmm." Von decided to pour herself a drink after all.

"*Under the October twilight the water…*"

"*Mirrors a still sky,*" said Von.

They were both quiet, watching the rain.

"How many swans?" Rosheen asked.

"Nine and fifty."

Rosheen nodded. She reached into the pocket of her cardigan and took out a pack of cigarettes. "And they flew away."

"They hadn't flown away yet," Von said. "But he knew they would."

"Right," said Rosheen. She struck a match, and for the six or seven seconds it took her to light the cigarette, her scar glowed an eerie orange.

Von thought of her conversation with Manuel, his surprising gratitude. "You know," she said. "Since Dad's been gone, I've been remembering more of the good times."

Rosheen snorted. "Oh yeah," she said. "Why yesterday *both* of them came rushing back to me at once."

And neither of them could help it. They began to laugh. They laughed until their bellies ached and they could barely breathe and tears were spilling down their cheeks and dripping onto their necks and clothing, so many tears they couldn't catch them all with their bare hands and had to wipe their faces with handkerchiefs until the handkerchiefs were soaked.

The bus weaves through the streets of Bergen-op-Zoom, picking up passengers and dropping them off every couple of blocks, and then turns onto the highway. About two miles out, the driver pulls onto a narrow parallel road and stops. He motions Von to the front of the bus.

"Here you are."

There is nothing to see except a steady stream of traffic, bordered by grass and dense clumps of trees.

"I don't think this is it," she says. "On the map it was on the other side of the highway."

"The cemetery is there," he says. He points off to the right, behind the bus. "That way."

It's another sunny day. The sun is beating down. She is afraid to get off here and be stranded in the middle of nowhere. But the only alternative is to stay on and spend the next five hours on a tour of every small town in the region.

"Are you sure?"

"Sure, ja," says the driver. "The cemetery is there."

"All right." She steps off the bus and he pulls away. Traffic whizzes by so fast and close she jumps off the shoulder into the trees. She is sure she's on the wrong side of the highway, but she can't see any way to get across. She begins to trudge back the way he pointed, and in ten minutes she sees a sign: *Begraafplaats*. She follows a winding path leading through the trees, and finds a cemetery. But there's no hint of a military or Canadian connection. The driver had no idea what Von was talking about. Like the staff at the tourist centre, and the staff in the hotel, he's never heard of the place she's looking for. There is nothing to do but head back to town on foot.

But five minutes later she spots an overpass. She makes her way there and crosses the highway, using her umbrella as a sun shield, walks back as far as the spot where she got off the bus and keeps walking until she sees the sign.

The Bergen-op-Zoom Canadian war cemetery is planted with sage and flowers and maple trees. Von reads the plaque. There are 1,115 Allied soldiers and air force men buried here, 968 of them Canadian. The white headstones fan out across the yard in beautiful, geometric designs, and she walks among them, reading. Carved into each white stone is a white maple leaf, a cross or Star of David, the soldier's first initial and last name, his regiment, his age, and date of death. Some were eighteen or nineteen, but most were in their early twenties. Hundreds of them were killed here in late October, 1944, within days of Frank's blinding. Under their names, their regiments are listed: The Black Watch, The Royal Hamilton Light Infantry, The Queen's Own Cameron Highlanders, The Royal Fusiliers. A few rare headstones add a line from Scripture, and one lists the names of a dead soldier's three young sons. But most stones bear only the necessaries, and some don't even bear a name, just three words: Known Unto God.

Von searches for Connor Flynn and finds him, finally, or finds his headstone. Connor himself has disintegrated, merged with the soil of the lowlands, river clay and peat.

"Go with God, Uncle Connor," she says, thinking that is what he would like her to say. But she's not really speaking to Connor, who is lost. She is speaking to her mother and father, who loved him and lost him. The person Connor really was seems somehow irrelevant, and she apologizes to his mute headstone for this fact. For the things she doesn't know.

7.6

"WE CAN'T GET MARRIED," BOBBY SAID TO ROSHEEN. HE WAS standing in his living room, beside the front door. The conversation had begun in the kitchen, with the two of them sitting down over two cups of coffee like calm adults, but as they talked and disagreed and began to argue, he kept moving farther away from her and closer to the exit. It was almost as if he were afraid of her.

"The baby has to have a father," Rosheen pointed out.

"The baby does have a father," Bobby said. "I never said I wouldn't be the baby's father."

He cared about the unborn baby. She could see that, feel that. It was in his eyes and even in his hands, the way he was holding them open, palms up and slightly curved, as though to cradle the child. His whole body was bent forward in a giving gesture that was not for her. Not for Rosheen. Even that night, that one night, when she slid into his bed, he did not look at her like that. He had barely looked at her at all. His heart, she knew now, had been broken. But not over her. Not over Rosheen.

"You don't love me," she said.

"I love you the same as I've always loved you, Rosheen." His voice was low, intense. "But not like a wife."

He crossed his arms in front of his chest. His head was bowed. Rosheen could not see his face. She remembered a long-ago summer evening, when Bobby took her to the marshes so she could pick bulrushes and pussy willows for her mother. The red-winged blackbirds. The love between them then so simple it was nameless, invisible. The best kind of love is the kind you don't feel at all, she thought. The kind you're not even aware of, because you don't have to be.

"I'll pay for everything," he said. "The clothes, whatever you need."

"I need a place to live."

"I'll pay your rent," he said. "It'll be like… I'll pay your rent for you."

Rosheen sat down on the couch and folded her hands in her lap. She had never in her life known how to make other people do what she wanted them to do. She heard the edge in Bobby's voice. He was afraid to say what he was saying. He didn't want to hurt her. But he was standing his ground. Rosheen would not be coming to this house to live.

"It's Von," said Rosheen. "It's Siobhán, isn't it?"

"Yes," he said.

"She'll never come around, you know," said Rosheen.

"I believe she will," said Bobby.

There was no moving him.

Rosheen had the feeling that she and Bobby were trading places. That Bobby was a Garrison and she was not. He belonged and she was excluded. A trick had been played on her. She felt the flutter of the baby turning over, floating free and happy in its ignorance.

Strange. After the baby was born, she missed him. She could see him now and hold him. Tickle him and sing to him. But he was no longer part of her.

"Who are you, little creature?" she asked him. "Where did you come from?"

She found an apartment near the Nicolette, a cheap one-bedroom, and Bobby came by every couple of days, looking miserable, and spent an awkward hour, asking her what she needed. At first, she recited long lists, to punish him. A crib, a stroller, a bassinet, a high chair, a playpen. A special kind of bottles and a special kind of formula. Mobiles, sleepers, receiving blankets, towels. But as he bought everything she asked for, and the bright parcels began to pile up, conspicuously unopened, she gave up the game.

Sometimes she confused her own body with the body of the baby. Holding a spoon to Kyle's mouth, she felt her own lips part, as if waiting to be fed. Laying an outfit on the bed and preparing to place Kyle's arm in the sleeve, she felt her own arm rise, her own hand prepare to enter the sleeve.

She couldn't breastfeed. Not enough milk.

"Just as well," Suzie said. Because if she was breastfeeding she'd have to stay away from alcohol and medications. That's what she read in the pamphlet from the health nurse. It didn't say anything, specifically, about morphine, but Rosheen assumed it was included.

Sometimes she was so tired she wept. She looked around the apartment, barely able to see through her tears, and couldn't believe she was alone. Couldn't believe Vonnie wasn't there to help her. Here she was, nineteen, stuck here with no husband, let alone a fun, artistic husband. No New York. No Montreal. No family. Just diapers.

Once the baby started sleeping through the night, Rosheen wanted to sleep, too. But she was so uptight about everything, she couldn't. Suzie brought her a few sleeping pills, and they worked. The next day she felt fresher, more alert. She was a better mother entirely, and took Kyle for a long walk in his carriage and sang him to sleep in the afternoon, and while he was napping she made a batch of strained carrots and peas and stocked up the fridge. But the pills ran out. She stayed awake for two nights straight, and when Bobby came by she told him she was being watched by the police. She told him not to tell anyone where she was in case they came to get her.

Bobby took her to the hospital, where the blessed doctors gave her something excellent that let her sleep for fourteen hours. When she woke, he was sitting on the couch, feeding Kyle from a bottle, looking haggard.

"See what it's like?" she asked him. Then instantly regretted it. The point was to make him like her, to make him want to come over.

The quivering in her belly returned. The crawling feeling in her arms and legs. The tension that ratcheted up bit by bit during the morning until she was stomping her feet and flailing her arms by noon, just for a little relief.

Finally she asked Jean-Claude for help, and he fronted her some high-quality tranquillizers that helped. But they were expensive. She told Bobby she needed money for vitamins. Or orange juice. Or milk. Whatever she could think of that sounded necessary and consumable. And for a while she had a steady supply. The only thing she had to worry about was nodding off, which she did once or twice — luckily Kyle was napping at the time.

Then one day Jean-Claude came over and found her passed out on the floor while Kyle was howling, naked in his crib.

That was when Jean-Claude dumped her on Vonnie. He said he was taking her home so she could retrieve some clothes she'd left behind, and instead he drove her to Las Roses and left her there. Von didn't want to let her in. Rosheen knew that. But Von had no choice, since the baby was there, too. Now that Rosheen was the mother of a little baby, Von had to help her.

Von loved the baby, even though she didn't know him. For some reason she just took to him right away. So she let Rosheen stay, and for a while Rosheen believed that Von was going to forgive her at last.

7.7

ON HER SECOND-LAST DAY IN AMSTERDAM, VON VISITS THE SHOPS near her hotel. She's running out of time to find a souvenir for Leif. What would he like? She wanders through antique stores, cheese shops, and garden markets offering everything from tulip bulbs to marijuana seeds. In a gift shop along the canal, she buys a calendar for Jeanne with photographs of Amsterdam, and boxes of Dutch chocolate for Alex and Carol. She meets a woman on the bridge selling beautiful hand-made scarves, and she picks one out for Ingrid. But so far nothing makes her think of Leif.

Finally, Rosheen's studio in Amsterdam is cleared out. Kyle and Meredith raid the janitor's closet for cleaning supplies. They sweep and mop the floor. They wash the windows. Von is waiting for them, watching sunlight spill across the floorboards, when Durgan comes in to say goodbye. He walks to the middle of the room, taking in the emptiness, and sighs. He looks at Von, and she can see he's desolate. Now that Rosheen's studio is empty, her art packed up, her son about to leave, he's losing his last connection to her. Durgan is not so bad, she thinks. He loved Rosheen, too. In his own way. And Von can't claim her way was any better. She can't claim to know anything about how to love.

The crates have been delivered to the shipping company, and their flight to New York doesn't leave until tomorrow night. Durgan recommends they spend their last day at the Van Gogh Museum. He has some day passes they can use. He can't go, but they should.

Not just because it was Rosheen's favourite place in Amsterdam, but because it is beautiful. Everyone should see it.

"Did she go there a lot?" Kyle asks.

"Sometimes she'd spend the whole day there," says Durgan. "Just looking."

"Will we have enough time?" Von asks. "We don't want to miss our flight."

"It'll be fine," Kyle reassures her. The thought of the museum excites him. He can't suppress a grin. He looks so much like Bobby right now that Von turns away. She has grown to like Kyle on this trip. She has come to respect him. But she'll be relieved when she's finally back in her greenhouse, alone. This constant dredging up of memories exhausts her.

———

After Jean-Claude brought Rosheen home — "dumped" her, as Rosheen put it — she stayed, apparently humbled and contrite, for about six weeks. By fall, she was back in her own apartment, making good progress, and for a year she saw a counsellor regularly and controlled her drinking, stayed away from drugs. Bobby paid her airfare to New York so she could visit Deirdre for three months, and when she returned, she brought Kyle to Las Roses every few weeks. Kyle was a sort of buffer between the sisters, keeping them civil with each other.

During this time, Kyle turned one, and Rosheen hosted a small celebration. Von took Frank to the party, nervous because Bobby would be there. Worried there might be an angry scene.

She wasn't worried about her father. The stroke he suffered, shortly before Kyle was born, had made him agreeable, almost docile, a side of him his daughters had never seen. The things that used to trigger his temper seemed to have lost their power, as if some deep layer of history had been washed from his brain, leaving him gentle. She liked to think this was his true self, earnest and friendly, even affectionate at times, especially when she read to him. But he would never work in his office again. His ability to concentrate was limited. He lived on the surface of consciousness now, his thoughts unmoored, free-floating objects that collided in odd ways. He surprised her with small, irrational remarks, claiming his soup spoon was stolen or his car wouldn't start. But most of the time he was fine. He could perform small tasks in the greenhouse, as long as Von helped him. The greenhouse was turning a profit at last, since Von devoted all her energy — all her loneliness and rage and jealousy — into making it thrive. So it wasn't Frank's temper she was worried about at the birthday party. It was her own.

Rosheen had bought a chocolate cake, which she served on paper plates, along with paper cups of cheap red wine. Rosheen seated Frank in an easy chair and gave him a huge chunk of cake to keep him busy. Von walked around the apartment, avoiding Bobby. She chatted with Suzie and Yvette. She collected dirty plates and carried them into the galley kitchen.

But Bobby was already in there, pouring himself a cup of wine. He offered her one, but she refused it. He stepped in front of her, cornering her against the stove.

"Your father seems happy," he said.

"It's his stroke. It's made him…it's knocked the stuffing out of him, somehow." She felt the ironic twist of her lip, and saw Bobby seeing it. Here we all are, at the end of the play, and it turns out the monster wasn't real.

But Bobby didn't smile. He nodded solemnly. Possibly wishing the stroke had arrived a year or two sooner. A wish that had crossed her own mind more than once.

"Von," he said. "Did you read my letters?"

She shook her head and tried to step around him, but he wouldn't move.

His words came out in a rush. "She told me you were with another man," he said. "And I believed her. I wish I hadn't believed her but I did. I'm sorry."

Von was speechless.

"She was drunk," he said. "We were both drunk. It was only the one time."

Von reached out and took his cup of wine from him and downed it.

"Von?"

She shook her head. She couldn't listen to him right now. She squeezed by him into the living room, among family and friends, where he could not speak of these things to her.

She perched on the arm of her father's chair and watched everyone. Kyle trying to walk, while Rosheen held both his hands. Her father eating a second piece of cake. Bobby coming out of the kitchen and stretching his arms out to Kyle. Walk to Daddy!

Bobby, no matter what he'd done, was family. Not in the way Von had once wanted him to be, but he was family. When her father warned her, long ago, that Bobby was trouble, she had not believed him. She had believed her mother, who always said Bobby was sweet. Well, they were both half right. Maybe she could forgive him if they were living in some future in which Kyle had never been born. But she could not wish Kyle hadn't been born. Kyle was beautiful. She loved them all, damn it — Kyle and Bobby and her father and even Rosheen. She could never un-love Rosheen, even though she hated her. It was all impossible.

In the weeks that followed the birthday party, Rosheen began to drink more heavily again, though Von didn't notice at first. Rosheen would drive to Las Roses for an evening visit, and after dinner, when Kyle got sleepy, she'd ask if he could stay the night. He was too big to sleep in a drawer now, so Von bought a playpen for him and put it in her room. She bought a baby monitor and a baby gate for the head of the stairs, and a lot of toys.

At first, this arrangement worked. Von washed and dressed him in the morning and gave him breakfast, and Rosheen picked him up before Von started work. But gradually, and she should have seen this coming, Rosheen came later and later. Nine o'clock. Ten o'clock. Noon.

"I can't watch him for you in the daytime," Von told her. "I have work to do."

But Rosheen always had a good excuse. Her alarm clock or her car broke down. Weather, traffic, neighbours, flu. Everything conspired to keep her from her son.

One morning in autumn, she didn't come at all. Instead, Bobby appeared at the door to pick up Kyle.

"Where's Rosheen?" Von asked.

"I stopped by her apartment, and she's still in bed," he told her. "She's hungover. She's a mess. You shouldn't help her with Kyle so much."

"What do you mean? Of course I should."

He shook his head. "As long as one of us is looking after Kyle, she's down at the Nicolette, getting high with Jean-Claude Allard and his buddies."

"At least Kyle's not around while she's doing it."

"But the next day she's no good, Von. She makes mistakes. She forgets things. She's in a vicious temper this morning, threw a coffee cup at me."

"I'll talk to her," Von promised.

But when Von talked to her, Rosheen said Bobby was exaggerating. He had a new girlfriend, she said, and the two of them wanted to take Kyle away from her. "He's trying to say I'm unfit, so he can get custody. He wants to marry this girl and have a family with her, starting with my Kyle."

"I can't believe that," Von said. "Bobby getting married?"

"She's already living in his house," said Rosheen. "Sleeping in his bed."

Von had no reply. It was another one of Rosheen's lies. She was sure of it. Pretty sure.

"Bobby says he's in love with her and he wants to start a *real* family. So whatever you do, don't let him take Kyle. I don't want Kyle getting attached to her."

"If you don't want me to give him to Bobby, you'd better pick him up earlier."

"Vonnie, I couldn't help it today. I've got the flu."

Von hung up and buried her face in her arms. Rosheen had been doing so well. But it was time to face the truth. She'd worn her sunglasses inside the house the last time she came over. Long sleeves. She'd borrowed fifty dollars. And Bobby had seen her with Jean-Claude Allard. She was likely using. Von called the counsellor Rosheen had seen last year and tried to make her an appointment, but the receptionist said Rosheen had to make the call herself.

"The client has to want the help," she said. "That's how it works."

———

Van Gogh's heavy-headed sunflowers bow low. The blooms on his peach trees flare like pink and white candle flames. Von loves his twisted olive trees and his oil-thick skies, like blue butter. She loves the four beached fishing boats, their masts leaning out to sea toward the four curved sails upon the water.

It is possible, easy in fact, to spend an entire day here. Kyle and Meredith and Von spent the morning walking through an exhibition

of Van Gogh's contemporaries, his influences, and his letters. They
lunched outside in the square together, and then Kyle and Meredith
went for a walk through the grounds while Von has come in to visit the
Van Gogh paintings on her own.

She's falling in love with *The Sower*, a peasant farmer trudging
through a field, one casual, magnanimous arm flung out, the hand
open wide, the large thumb parting from the palm in a generous curve,
dispensing seeds from a bag he wears across his shoulder. It's evening,
his work of regeneration almost done. Behind him the sun is whole
and low on the horizon. The right side of the painting reveals the layers
of the world — long pink strata of clouds, a lemon-green sky, blue river
of polder, a dark crooked tree, its trunk reaching deep into the earth.

Meredith and Kyle enter the gallery just as Von decides to go
outside. She waves at them from across the wide room, and they wave
back. Casual. No matter where they go, or where she wanders, Kyle
always seems to find her. She knows he'll gravitate toward her again
before the gallery closes. Then they will have dinner together, collect
their luggage, and go to the airport. Somehow, at least during this
sojourn in a foreign country, they've become family. She isn't sure how
long they can sustain it, but right now it feels good.

Outside, the wide lawns stretch in all directions. The square is full
of tourists, but they're all at a distance. The only person nearby is a young
woman with a Canadian flag on her backpack, who sits demurely on the
grass, running through scales on a silver flute. Von sits down on a bench
in a secluded spot that seems designed for contemplation. She writes in
her journal, describing what she's seen today. Blossoms and boats and
so many skies, created from copious eddies of paint laid down over a
hundred years ago. She's not sure who she's describing these images for.
She just feels the urge to translate them into words. She writes page after
page until she feels her fingers begin to cramp. That old sensation, trying
to get everything down on paper before it flits away. Wanting to get it
right. She hasn't felt this urgency for a long time, but since she embarked
on Rosheen's project it's been coming back to her.

Across the lawn, the young woman begins a low and playful
melody on the flute. Watching her, Von thinks of herself at the same
age. About twenty-one. The young woman even looks like Von,
perhaps is very like Von. Except for the travelling through Europe and
playing a flute part. A sudden trill of high notes seems to suggest the

melody could go anywhere, at any time. Von looks at her watch and feels something shift within her. She no longer wants to return to her former life.

Back in the gallery, she spots Meredith flopped down on a bench in a corner with their bags and umbrellas and sweaters. Kyle is standing before *The Sower*. It takes him a moment to turn from the painting and face her.

"How are you doing?" she asks him. "Tired?"

"A bit." He looks at Meredith. "Her feet are sore."

"Of course. Do you want to go back to the hotel?"

"No," he says. "Please, not yet."

"Why don't you two go and get some coffee?" Von suggests. "I'll stay here and watch your things."

They invite her to come with them, but she declines. She wants to let them have one more private hour together on their last day here. Kyle has left his journal on the bench, a pencil between the pages, marking his place. Von sits down beside it, drops her bag at her feet and stretches her arms above her head.

What is he writing? Casually, she slips her right hand in beside the pencil, lifts her finger, and the pages flip open. She glances right and left. Kyle and Meredith are nowhere near. She has a sudden memory of just such surreptitious reading as a girl, in assembly, at church or home, stealing a few minutes with a book, without anyone knowing. She turns her head slightly, casts her eyes down, and sees on the page no writing — no words at all.

Only the globe of the setting sun, the curve of the tree trunk, and the shape of the sower in the painting, a pencil line, accurate and loose, tracing the peasant beret, the sleeve of the smock, the sack of seeds, the open hand.

The sky was still dark when Bobby came to Las Roses for the last time. Von saw his headlights from the window of the living room, where she was kindling a fire before dawn. She was listening to the radio, turned low so she wouldn't wake anyone. Linda Ronstadt was singing "Heart Like a Wheel." When she saw the car coming, she stepped out onto the cold floorboards of the porch in her sock feet. It was early December. A recent warm spell had melted the top layers of snow, and they'd frozen again last night, coating the field in a hard white crust that glittered in the headlights. She flicked the switch to turn on the coloured lanterns strung above the driveway. Last night's storm had coated everything in ice. Icicles hung from the glazed roof of the greenhouse, and the brittle branches of the lilac clattered, every twig encased in ice.

Bobby's Mustang moved slowly across the field, its tires barely gripping the polished surface of the road. Rounding the curve of the driveway, it slid sideways, veering toward the greenhouse wall. Von cringed, but Bobby, always competent, pulled hard on the wheel, pumped the brakes, and got the car back onto the driveway. He came to a stop in front of the porch.

Von stepped back inside where it was warm. Upstairs in his makeshift bed, Kyle began to cry. He and Rosheen had both stayed overnight, because of the storm. Von let Bobby in and ran upstairs for Kyle, before his crying woke her father. As she passed her sister's room, she peeked in and was angry but not surprised to see the bed had not been slept in. Rosheen must have sneaked out in the night.

Von dressed Kyle and carried him downstairs. He was sleepy. He buried his face in the soft flannel shoulder of her housecoat.

"Bon," he said, which she interpreted as her own name.

"Yes," she told him. "Von is taking Kyle downstairs."

"Kai."

"Yes. Kyle is going downstairs."

Bobby was in the kitchen, making coffee.

"Make yourself at home," she said.

He let his mouth twist into an angry smile. To Kyle, he said, "Hey, Buster."

Kyle turned around. "Dada!" He waved his arms in excitement and reached toward Bobby. Von held him tightly against her.

"Black?" asked Bobby.

"Black."

He poured two cups of black coffee and sat at the kitchen table, placing Von's cup across the table from himself. "She's still sleeping?"

"It's early," said Von. She placed Kyle in his high chair and he waved his arms in the air.

Bobby's eyes narrowed. He could tell something was up. "She better get up soon, or I'll have to pack his things myself. I'm taking him to see my grandpa. He's not feeling so good."

Rosheen had not mentioned this plan to Von. Rosheen had only warned that Von was not, under any circumstances, to let Bobby take Kyle anywhere, especially not home to his house in St Boniface, where he was living, according to Rosheen, with a new girlfriend.

"Your grandpa is in town?"

"No. He's up at Clear Lake. I promised I'd bring Kyle to visit him for the week. I got the whole week off."

"Rosheen didn't say anything about this to me."

"Rosheen's memory is not very good these days," said Bobby. "Why don't you wake her up and ask her, if you don't believe me?"

Von went out to the hall and turned the volume up on the radio. She dialled Rosheen's home number and pulled the long cord taut to take the receiver into the closet. This was how she used to talk to Bobby on the phone, so her father couldn't hear. But Rosheen didn't answer. Von hung up and opened the phonebook and looked up the number of the Nicolette Hotel.

Aline Allard answered. "Front Desk."

Von stepped back into the closet and spoke in a low voice. "Aline? It's Von Garrison. Listen, I need to know, was Rosheen there yesterday?"

"All night," said Aline. "With my boys Denis and Jean-Claude and their friends. We had a country band. It was jam-crowded, I tell you. She didn't come home?"

"Did you notice who she left with?"

"Not with my son, I hope," Aline said. "Those two together are like a match and a stick of dynamite."

"Was he driving?"

"Jean-Claude? He had the red pickup. But they were all pissed. I told him to stay in the hotel. Let me look." She put down the receiver, and when she returned she said, "It's in the lot. He's still here, thank God."

"Can I talk to him?"

"I'll connect you."

The phone rang six times before Jean-Claude heaved it across the room. The receiver must have come flying off in midair because the clang of the telephone hitting the wall came through so loudly it hurt Von's ear.

She could hear Jean-Claude and Rosheen arguing and finally Rosheen's voice asking, "Who is this?"

"It's me," said Von. "Bobby's here."

"Vonnie, I'm sleeping, for Christ's sake."

"He wants to take Kyle. Can he take Kyle?"

"Not if he's with that woman."

"He's by himself. He says he's taking Kyle up to his grandfather's cabin."

"Don't trust him," Rosheen mumbled.

"Well then, you better get back here," Von said.

"Jean-Claude's asleep," she said. "I got no ride. It'll take me a while, Vonnie. Can't you just tell him no?"

"No, I cannot tell him no. Kyle is his son. For Christ's sake, Rosheen, can't you think? He's either taking Kyle away for a week or he's taking him for good. If you give a damn about your son you'll get here as fast as you can."

"I guess I could borrow Jean-Claude's truck," she said reluctantly. "I could get there in a half hour."

"Get here *now*, Rosh. He's not going to wait."

Von hung up quietly and crept up the stairs to her bedroom, buying time. Would Bobby take up with another woman? He'd once asked her, angrily, if she thought he was going to wait forever, and she realized now that the answer was yes. She'd thought he would wait forever. But now she saw clearly that this was unreasonable. It was crazy. If she didn't change her mind — and change it soon — Bobby might marry someone else. He *should* marry someone else. It would be the only sane thing for him to do. God! The swiftness of the insight nearly brought her to her knees. *She* was the crazy one. *She* was the one asking the impossible.

Still, she was certain he'd never take Kyle from his mother. Rosheen was wrong about that part. She hoped. She packed a tote bag with Kyle's clothes and toys, thinking uneasily of Bobby's concerns about her sister's drinking.

As she came downstairs again, she saw he had taken Kyle's snowsuit from the closet and was zipping him into it. "That's my boy," he said. He sat Kyle on the bottom stair and kneeled down to push Kyle's feet into his little boots. He wasn't going to wait for Rosheen.

Von decided to ask him point blank. "Who is this girl you're living with?"

He looked up at her. Not quickly. "Where did you hear that story?"

"Around," she said.

"Your sister."

"I just heard you've fallen in love." She couldn't help it. She hated the sound of her own voice. The nasty tone that was coming out of her body without her permission.

Bobby stood up. He took the tote from her hand. "I'm already in love," he said. Steady. "I fell in love long ago and you know it."

"Really?" She crossed her arms in front of her chest. "Then why don't you —"

"I know I did a terrible thing," he said. "I know I hurt you. Hurt you both. I went against…what's right. I did it because I was angry at you, because I needed someone, because I didn't realize Rosheen was so —"

"Human?"

"Von, please. It was wrong. I was wrong. But I can't change that now. We all have to live with it and Kyle has to live with it, so can't we just try to? And to tell the truth —"

"The truth? If you're telling the truth, then tell me who it is you're living with."

"I'm not living with anyone," Bobby said. "I'm alone." He put Kyle's mittens on.

She looked into his eyes. "So who is it you're in love with, then?" she asked.

"It's you, Von," he said. "You know it's you. It will always be you." He carried Kyle out to the car.

She believed him. No. She wanted to believe him.

The sun was coming up as she watched him fastening Kyle into the car seat, tightening the straps. Checking the buckles. Then he got in front and started the motor. He raised his hand, waving to her. But she didn't wave back. He started down the driveway toward the road.

Von turned from the door and ran up the stairs. On the second floor, she stopped and looked out the window. Bobby's black Mustang was entering the orchard. It disappeared among the iced, leafless branches of the fruit trees. She ran up past the third floor, not caring if she woke her father, to the attic. She kneeled before the gable window, her elbows resting on the low sill, and waited for his car to emerge into the clearing. She wanted to see which direction he'd turn when he reached the highway. If he went north, she'd know he was telling the truth, driving up to the lake to see his grandfather. If he turned south, he'd be going home, to whoever she was. Taking Kyle to play house with some outsider, someone who had no right —

She saw the bright red pickup truck come racing down the highway. Jean-Claude Allard's truck. It accelerated to pass a line of cars and then swerved in front of a semi-trailer to make a hard right onto the gravel road. As it entered the orchard, it picked up speed again and for a long moment appeared as a blurred red streak, moving too fast beneath the glassy canopy of branches.

The truck collided with the Mustang on the hairpin turn at the edge of the clearing. Its grille ploughed into the driver's door and pinned the car against the broad trunk of an ancient crabapple tree. Von, on her knees, thirty feet above and a quarter mile away, pressed her palms to the window. Her breath clouded the pane. The sun was rising, clearing the treetops, illuminating everything, the sudden white slash of the splintered tree trunk, the white steam rising from the wreck and Bobby inside with the baby, the baby, and Von was the one who had told Rosheen to hurry, it was Von who said *if you give a damn about your son you'll get here as fast as you can,* she said *get here now.*

8

The Opening

8.1

TO TRAVEL THROUGH THE DARKNESS REQUIRES EQUILIBRIUM. YOU must balance the force of the outer atmosphere against the force inside your body, match the invisible density of the world with a density of your own, or be crushed. You stretch out your arms and — only if you're certain you feel nothing — step forward into emptiness. At times, you believe you've pierced the core of darkness, that infinite starless night of the interior, and then you discover there still remains a way to travel deeper.

In the long months after Bobby's death, Von sometimes believed she understood what it meant to be blind. At first, there was nothing. Winter. Short days that passed unseen and unremembered. She was in shock.

Later, it came back to her in flashes. Phoning for help. Ignoring her father's questions. Pulling on her boots. The awful trembling. Trying to start the truck. Her hands shaking so hard she couldn't get the key in the ignition. Then somehow standing in the orchard beside the vehicles. Seeing Rosheen open the door of Jean-Claude's truck and fall out onto the road. Hearing Kyle's crying. Weeping in relief to hear him cry. Reaching through the broken glass to touch Bobby's forehead. His eyes were closed, his face peaceful, as if he were sleeping, though she knew, by the angle of his neck, he must be dead. And then the sirens. A police officer pulling Kyle out of her arms. Rosheen on a stretcher, sobbing. The emergency waiting room. A doctor, his mouth moving as if he were explaining something. Manuel arriving with her father to take her home — not to Las Roses, not past the ugly wreck — but to Manuel's house.

When the shock wore off, she was sedated by the doctor. All responsibility was lifted from her. Manuel and Yvette moved into Las Roses and looked after everything. The state took custody of Rosheen, and Kyle, and Bobby's body. In the greenhouse, all living things bent toward the sun, stems bowing in a shallow arc from east to west. But Von moved through the house with no awareness of the sun.

Nights, she lay in her childhood bed, where she would sleep forever now, alone. As if she were a child again, flinching at the night sounds. Or the silence. Waiting for ruin, catastrophe. She was on the other side, now, of catastrophe, and yet the fear did not subside. It was diffuse, emanating from the depths inside her body, staining all existence.

8.2

SOME UNBEARABLE WEIGHT HAD DESCENDED ON THE HOUSE. Frank lay as still as he could, willing himself to recall the nature of the trouble. He wanted to go downstairs and make a pot of oatmeal, put the kettle on for tea. But he dared not leave his bed until he knew exactly where he was and what was wrong. He touched the nightstand. Ah, the cedar stand with the tongue-and-groove joints. He had made it himself in the workshop. So the war was over, then. He must be at Las Roses already. He found the radio, tuned to CBC, and listened for the details. 6:28 a.m., 23 below. Jets 5, Rangers 1. Overcrowded hospital wards. Water-main breaks. Whatever tragedy had befallen his house, it was not on the news. Not yet. Or not any longer. He sat up slowly. The very air in the room seemed to resist him, as if the force of gravity had gained strength in the night.

Why so strange? Even his headache, familiar old enemy, felt different: colder. Maybe if he started moving, it would all come back to him. He swung his feet to the floor and pushed them into his slippers. The slippers helped. They recognized his feet. His mother had knitted them — no, that wasn't right. His mother made clothes for other people. He wondered that they let her bring her sewing machine into the hospital, when it was so crowded. He turned off the radio and sat on the edge of the bed, listening in vain for clues. Were the girls not up for school yet? Perhaps they had already gone to school. No. It was too early. Six-something, the radio said.

He put his eyes in and wrapped himself in a robe. In the bathroom, he washed his face and hands. He went downstairs slowly, careful not to wake the girls. He would make breakfast before he dressed for work. He stopped abruptly, halfway down. Was he going to the office today? It seemed a long time since he'd been to the office. So difficult to keep track of the days with part-time work. When he got on full-time it would be easier. He realized he was gripping the side rail of the bed too hard, or no, it was the railing on the staircase, the thin wrought iron banister at Las Roses. It must have been grafted on, or welded, or dislocated in the accident. That was it. An accident. One of the girls had been hurt. He hurried the rest of the way down the stairs to the kitchen, pushed through the swinging door.

"Eileen?"

He heard nothing. His wife was not at home. The girls were sleeping. Surprising that the baby had not woken. He didn't think the hospital was a good place for the baby. He didn't want the baby to hear about the hand grenades. The hole in Tomas's head. Germs had gotten in. His hand grazed the frying pan, and he remembered about breakfast. He could fry an egg.

It was important to be careful with the carton of eggs. He wanted to use two hands to take it out of the fridge, but he could only find one. He set the carton on the counter and opened it and ran his hand across the eggshells, rough with tiny bumps. He chose an egg.

"Dad? Dad, what are you doing?"

He held the egg above the pan, its cool curves light in his palm. "Rosheen?"

And he remembered suddenly. Rosheen had gone off with that boy, the boy Siobhán had loved, and crashed a car. He should have kept her home. She was too small. How could he tell Eileen? Suddenly, someone lifted the egg from his hand. A trick. He tried to grasp it back, but frost gathered where his hand had been, thick and rough, like the frost on the inside of the window panes. One whole side of him was gone. It was amazing the things they could do these days. The cold crept into his skull. Blades of ice pricked his brain.

He felt he was falling. Then a woman's hand reached out for him. Always, all his life, a woman's hand was reaching toward him. Touching him. Inviting him to let his guard down. To let go.

"Dad?"

One of his daughters. He didn't know which one. Even mad King Lear could tell Cordelia from her sisters. He dragged one foot forward, heavy. How could a person move in here? The atmosphere was too thick. All mud and mist. A woman's hand. Women's voices.

She said, *It's all right. A boy can be hungry.* She said, *Will you go to university? After the war?* She said, *It's a world of mist and fog. I can't see a foot in front of me.*

He heard the ice crackle as it moved through his veins, stopping his blood.

"There is an end to everything," he said. "Even Frank Garrison." But he heard his own voice speaking without words. Sounds a baby makes. A man with no tongue.

And then she was guiding him, cool fingers on the back of his hand, and it was like walking through rainclouds. Into her open arms.

8.3

FRANK'S SECOND STROKE PARALYZED HIS RIGHT SIDE, LEAVING him nearly helpless, so Von was forced out of her bed to care for him. Rosheen was three months in hospital and then six months in the Women's Correctional Centre. They took away her driver's licence and took away her son. Kyle was sent to live in a foster home run by a Mennonite couple, out in a small town. Rosheen did not protest. In a letter she wrote to her grandmother from jail, she said she would not fight the court's decision. She did not trust herself to care for the baby, she said. It would be good for him to be with peaceful, reliable people. Rosheen was going to change her life, become a good mother. First she needed help, needed time to rest, get herself off drugs, quit drinking. Once she recovered she would take good care of Kyle. She would start a new life. But she had nowhere to go. Her dad was sick, and her sister wouldn't let her in the house, wouldn't even take her phone calls. Could she please come to New York?

When she was released, Rosheen sent word to Von that she was moving to New York to stay with Deirdre. She did not say that she was leaving Kyle with the foster parents. But then, Von did not ask.

———

"You have to see this," Alex says. He comes out of his storage room into the gallery, where Von and Ingrid are measuring walls to see where *The Winter Garden* will fit best. Kyle and Meredith have gone to pick up coffee for everyone. They have been back in New York for a week, now, and they're a week away from the opening of *The Afterlight*. Ingrid's students have been helping, and today even Carol has come in, taking a day off from the law to help out.

Von follows Alex into the back and sees that Carol has opened the one plywood crate that Rosheen packed and sealed herself before she left Amsterdam. Carol is arranging the contents, a series of framed collages, on a long table.

"Look at this," says Alex. "I've never had such a chill up my spine. I thought she hadn't seen Kyle since he was five or six." He points to a watercolour painting of a teenaged Kyle, riding no hands on his bicycle. "It's eerie. Did she sneak up to that little town and spy on him, or what?"

Von catches her breath. Here he is. Bobby Sullivan on his bicycle. The painting is based on a photograph she took herself, on Memorial Boulevard, the day of the concert, before the storm began. He's sixteen. In the next image, one year later, he's in the backyard at Edgewood Street, on a ladder, cleaning the eavestrough. Seventeen. That's how old he was when she moved in with him. She'd thought he was a man. Because he had a job. Because he built a desk for her, sent her to school. Cleaned the eavestroughs. But he was just a kid, an orphaned kid.

She realizes she's standing here with both hands clamped over her mouth. Tears streaming down her face.

"This isn't Kyle," she tells Alex and Carol. "It's Bobby."

A little boy's name, her father had said. A name for a boy who would never be a man.

There are pictures of him a few years older. At the cabin, sleeping. Wading in the lake. His leg, in knee-deep water. Even after all this time, she recognizes his leg, its shape and colour, the bruise he got playing football at St Vital Park. His foot, on the rippled sand of the lake bottom. Three stones in the palm of his hand. She'd know that hand anywhere.

"You can really see the process here," says Alex, pointing. Rosheen has created collages by layering the old black-and-white photos, the fading coloured photos, the amateur pencil sketches, and the later, skillful watercolours, and coating the layers with shiny, tinted gel. Translucent memory. What must it have felt like for Rosheen to work with these images so carefully, mere months ago? Images of the person she killed.

"It's like a kind of punishment," says Carol, the lawyer, who must be thinking along the same lines.

Alex looks sick. Maybe finally he's encountered something he deems too personal to hang on the gallery walls.

"Atonement, maybe," Von says. "She took him away. She's preserving his memory."

"For Kyle," says Alex. He points at a series that shows Bobby holding Kyle.

And for me, Von thinks.

"Kyle is going to be so glad to see these," Carol says.

"Um, Carol? Alex?" They look up. "Kyle still doesn't know."

They stare at her, not comprehending.

"He doesn't know, exactly, how his father died."

———

Back at the apartment, Von sits down with Kyle and Meredith and pours cups of tea. Offers them cookies and cake, as if sugar might help. Kyle has shown her his journal, shyly, and there's no writing in it at all, except a few dates. It's completely full of drawings. Scenes from his travels and copies of the art he's seen, including his mother's art.

"You have your mother's talent," she tells him. "And your mother's eyes. Otherwise, you're very like your father." She touches his hair. "You said the Penners told you quite a bit about him. But do you understand what happened to him? How he died?"

"He was killed in a car accident," Kyle says. He looks up. "I always thought my mother must have got her scar in that same accident. That's what the Penners thought. But now...you told me she got the scar when she was eight. Was she even *in* the accident?"

"Kyle." Von reaches over and covers his hand with her own. "Your mum was driving."

Meredith, stricken, takes his other hand in hers.

At first, his expression does not change. "Driving where?"

"The car," says Meredith gently. "She was driving the car."

"She was in another car," says Von. "A truck. But yes, she caused the accident."

"Was she...?"

"She was drunk, yes."

He crumples then. As she knew he would. This is the moment she's been dreading ever since she saw his name in Rosheen's will. This is exactly why she didn't want to see him. She knew she'd only lie to him or hurt him. And she chose to hurt him. She hates herself for it, right now. But she's finished with lying.

Meredith hugs him while he cries, and Von goes into the kitchen, to make more tea. To find more sugar. *Your mother killed your father, kid. Have a cookie.* She wishes she'd bought a bottle of wine. A quart of whisky. A little goddamned heroin.

"She was arrested," Von tells him later. "She went to court, and the judge sent her to jail. He ordered you into foster care. Later, when she got out, she tried to get you back, but the social workers wouldn't support her case. The court would not allow it."

He raises his head. "So she really *didn't* give me away?"

"No, she didn't," says Von. "She had no choice."

"She really *was* sick, like Mrs Penner said?"

"Yes."

He nods. From his blue-green eyes, Von imagines Rosheen looking out at her. She thinks she sees a glimmer there, of understanding.

Von arrives at the Northside Gallery early in the morning, the day of the opening, and lets herself in with the key Alex gave her. She walks through the exhibition, contemplating the arrangement. Alex has put it together like one big collage of collages.

Rosheen must have been working on these pieces since Kyle was a little boy. Yes. The craft she'd learned, the methods she practised, the works she created, and the way she arranged them fit together like a pattern or a story, and suddenly — no, not suddenly, but finally, at long last — Von realizes that this whole show is a story that Rosheen is telling Kyle. A story she's been composing for him almost all his life. The story of where he came from.

Von doesn't know what inspired Rosheen to begin this monumental task. It must have been when Kyle was five or six, shortly after she'd lost custody for good. How had she ever found the strength? Von had retreated from the world, confined herself to house and greenhouse, to her father and the roses, given up on friends, on school, on writing, while Rosheen had woken up, begun to study and to work. To make something beautiful again, after she had destroyed so much.

And she understands now why Rosheen insisted she participate. Because it's Von's job to provide the words. *I want you to explain what happened.* She thinks of all the words in all the notebooks she filled this summer, and never let Kyle read.

On opening night, the Northside Gallery is noisy, full of artists and students and people from the neighbourhood. The excited voices carry all the way down the street, and people are leaking out the front door and the side door, which opens onto the parking lot. It's a good thing Kyle and Meredith got the idea to close the lot for the evening and string lights among the skinny trees and set up chairs, so the lot has become a patio. Ingrid's students are serving wine and cheese.

There are even some international guests. Jeanne Lajoie has left the greenhouse in the care of her parents and come all the way from St Boniface to see the show. Durgan came from Amsterdam, saying he couldn't resist the opportunity to see it all set up. He plans to mount it in Amsterdam next year and then maybe in Galway. And Mr Lassiter, son of Dickie Lassiter, has come from London. It turns out he's an artist himself. A photographer. He documents the opening with his camera.

When Leif arrives, he's friendly, but cool. Von never did phone him, never did bring him a souvenir. She's not ready yet to bond with anyone, and she isn't sure she ever will be. But he seems to have accepted this in her absence. He congratulates her, gives her a quick, firm hug and brings her a glass of wine from the bar. Then he disappears into the crowd.

Even Kyle's foster parents have flown in for the occasion. The Penners are small people, timid but friendly enough, though they're clearly not used to crowds and noise. They resisted the invitation at first, but as Von knows, Kyle can be pretty convincing when he wants to be. So they came. It's obvious they find the war material distasteful. But they're interested in the parts about Kyle's parents. And they've never seen his baby pictures before. Von watches them as they walk back and forth, speaking quietly to each other, glimpsing a part of Kyle's life they never shared.

Sean O'Neill, the son of Patrick O'Neill, who helped with the Cobh research, is in New York on business and happy to attend. The next day, Von invites him and his wife to dinner. His wife is charmed with the apartment, says it's a shame Von has to sell.

"I'm not selling it, actually."

Kyle's head whips up. "You're not?"

"We can rent it out to tourists, I discovered," says Von. She winks at Kyle. "You never know when we might want to come to New York."

"Wow!" Kyle shouts. "Fantastic!"

When she shows Sean the driftwood harbour seal on Deirdre's dresser, he verifies that his Uncle Daniel must have carved it. He has seen herds of Daniel's carved seals and knows his style. Kyle says the seal should be in the show, that Rosheen would have included it if she'd known. So Alex makes a label for it: Daniel Mac Michael. Untitled. Driftwood. Ireland. c. 1916.

Kyle has made a contribution, too. From the photographs of Marijke's family, he has made a collage. He also photocopied Marijke's spidery letters spelling out the names: *Hans, Saskia, Akmed, Antje, Assia*…all forty-six of them, criss-crossed and repeating, to form the background onto which he's mounted the images.

Alex has spliced together Von's photographs from Ireland with the interviews from Galway and Cobh, and set them running on a loop on a screen near the entrance.

The most popular part of the exhibit is the large wall devoted to Rosheen's work with Frank's old sketchbooks from the 1930s. This is what draws in the neighbours, because it features so many of the streets and buildings surrounding the gallery. Rosheen has deepened the lines of Frank's sketches with coloured pencils and painted lightly over his Brooklyn streets with their clapboard houses, dirt yards and broken wooden sidewalks, adding new buildings, cars, outdoor cafés and throngs of contemporary people in pale, transparent colours, the future haunting the past.

Von's favourite in this series is a sketch that looks as though Frank made it while lying on his back on a Manhattan street corner. It's a skewed, modernist perspective. The tops of many tall, windowed buildings, leaning crookedly toward each other. They slant in from all four sides and corners of the picture, framing an irregular expanse of sky, onto which Rosheen has painted a dark and brilliant Van Gogh night, stars that whirl and burst with such intelligence you know the light's alive.

8.4

DEIRDRE COULD SEE, RIGHT AWAY, THAT RÓISÍN WASN'T THE SAME after the car accident. When she came to Brooklyn to live with Deirdre, the light in her blue-green eyes was dim. She didn't speak. She sat in the kitchen in a bathrobe, as Lucy used to do, and smoked too many cigarettes. She received regular reports about her son from the foster parents, and on his third birthday she flew back to Manitoba to visit him. Deirdre paid the fare and paid for a motel room in the small town where he lived. She told Róisín to take a lot of photographs.

Róisín was only away for a weekend, but the trip did her good. It changed her. She applied for a green card, and in the meantime she worked cleaning houses for cash. She joined a support group for alcoholics, though Deirdre didn't think the girl was an alcoholic. She had never seen Róisín take more than one or two drinks, not during the day, anyway.

The photographs were sad. The boy looked puzzled and shy.

"I don't think he recognized me," Róisín said. "He doesn't talk much. The Penners said he's a quiet kid. When I hugged him he ran back to Mrs Penner."

"A child knows his mother," Deirdre said. "It will take some time for him to get used to you again, that's all."

"Yes," said Róisín. "If I can get a job, I can start saving. I'll need a solid bank account when I go back home. I'll need to prove I'm sober and financially stable." She took a small notebook from her purse and started a list. She made a lot of lists that year.

Eventually, Róisín got a job. Not in one of the nice Manhattan hotels where she applied when she first started looking. And not as a server in the lounge or restaurant, as she'd hoped. But cleaning empty rooms, where nobody would see her face, in a rundown motel on Staten Island. Still, it was work. She got up early and took the subway and the ferry, and after work she went to support group meetings or watched television programs with Deirdre. Sometimes she got out the coloured pencils and sketched pictures, or played a game of solitaire or made lists of all the things she planned to do.

Deirdre phoned Siobhán in Canada to ask after Frank's health. The news was no better than before. The recent stroke had left him bedridden and unable to speak. They talked for half an hour, about treatment plans and hired nurses and finances and all the low, despairing details of serious illness. Then they said good-bye, and Deirdre was about to hang up when she heard her granddaughter say, "Wait."

"Yes?"

"How is she?"

"Better. She's better. Working at a motel. She'll be getting her boy back soon, I think." Deirdre paused. "You know —"

"I cannot have them here. It's all I can do to look after Dad and run the business."

"She needs —"

"If she needs money, I'll send money. But I cannot have her in this house."

"Róisín would help you," Deirdre said.

"No."

One thing you could say about Siobhán, she knew her mind.

8.5

ROSHEEN FELT SHE WAS READY. SHE'D BEEN IN TREATMENT FOR three years, with very few lapses, and she'd held down a job for two. She consulted a counsellor and got up her courage to call the Children's Aid in Manitoba and tell them she wanted to come and see her son. She was ready now to come home and look after him. She would soon have enough money saved to rent an apartment in Winnipeg, and enough experience in housekeeping to land a job. She wanted to start visiting him now, so that he could get used to her.

Over the phone, the social worker seemed rushed and distracted. He asked Rosheen to call him again once she got to Winnipeg, and he'd arrange a meeting with the foster parents. "It's best to ease into something like this," he warned. "The boy has been with the Penners since..."

"Since he was twenty months," Rosheen reminded him.

"Yes, and he's now..."

"Almost six."

"I see."

Rosheen didn't like his tone of voice. When she related the conversation to Deirdre, she said he seemed cold.

Deirdre shrugged. "Social workers. What do they know?"

Rosheen was worried. She arranged to take a week off work and got a haircut and new clothes for the visit with the social workers and the foster parents. She bought a picture book for Kyle, about Coney Island. "I don't know what else to buy him," she told Deirdre. "I'll have to wait and see what kind of things he likes. I don't really know him anymore."

"Don't be nervous," counselled Deirdre. "You'll be fine. You're his mother."

But Rosheen was beyond nervous. It seemed as if she'd just now woken up and realized she'd left her baby with strangers for well over three years. She was in a panic.

At the meeting in Winnipeg, the social workers were armed with thick files, which they ranged around them like ammunition. The first worker explained in a gentle voice the concept of bonding. Kyle had come to the Penners when he was a sad and frightened toddler, and the Penners had comforted him. He associated them with security, now. The second worker was more stern. He spoke about trust and responsibility. He said children need someone they can rely upon. Kyle had been abandoned once. To remove him from the Penners would feel, to the boy, like a second abandonment. It was possible he'd never be able to form a trusting relationship in later life. The third social worker had the police report of the accident and the medical reports of Rosheen's blood alcohol level. He read from them without mercy. If the baby had not been strapped into a car seat, he said, he would have died along with his father. He showed Rosheen some photographs the foster parents had sent along. Kyle was a big boy now. There he was with his kindergarten class, and he'd be going into grade one soon. The photographs were cruel, revealing all the conventions events of happy family life that Rosheen had not provided. Sunday school concerts and Christmas stockings. Even a puppy. For an absurd moment Rosheen suspected the photos were not real.

By the time the foster parents arrived, Rosheen was in shock. The truth was closing in on her and she was suffocating. She knew she could not take Kyle out of his home.

"Can I see him?" she asked. "Couldn't I meet him, just as if I weren't his mother?"

"We don't recommend that," they said.

Mr and Mrs Penner came in then, and gave their report. Kyle was a happy boy, they said, as you can see. Well-adjusted. Healthy. A little hyperactive, but learning how to settle down.

Rosheen was utterly defeated.

"What will you tell him?" she asked Mrs Penner before she left.

"I'll tell him you loved him very, very much," she said.

Rosheen nodded. The two women stood looking into each other's eyes for a long time.

"I'll tell him you weren't well enough to look after him," Mrs Penner said.

Rosheen wanted to penetrate Mrs Penner's life somehow, to place a magic charm around her neck, to see she came to no harm.

But she had to leave. She gave the Coney Island picture book to the Penners and shook hands with them and managed to leave the building and get out onto Portage Avenue without collapsing. She walked like an automaton, barely seeing where she was going, down Notre Dame to the St Charles Hotel, where she ordered a good stiff drink. It was an easy place to score, and within the hour she was nodding in a corner, her veins full of warmth and comfort.

When Rosheen's mother died, the ladies at the church had tried to be kind. Mrs Ross had said that Eileen was an angel now, looking down on her daughters from heaven and protecting them. Eileen would want the girls to go on with their lives and succeed in school. She would want Rosheen to study catechism and be confirmed and to play hostess with Mrs Ross at the annual church fair, and Rosheen had known, even then, that this was nothing but a fairy tale.

When the priest at the funeral said that Rosheen's mother was dancing with the angels, Rosheen wept to think she lived in a world with such poor stories. The valley of the shadow of death, she understood. She had been down in that deep vale of ash when she was a patient in the children's hospital, in those hours when everyone else was still asleep, when the medicine wore off and the truth descended and she knew who she was — a girl someone had cancelled out — and all she wanted was to fall back into that grey sleep. That was the valley of the shadow. That was real.

She raised her head and saw a window. Smokestacks on the skyline. She was in her grandmother's kitchen in Brooklyn. Sitting at the kitchen table. Yes. She had come back here. Nowhere else to go. She closed her eyes again. Strange she could remember small details of her childhood, but the recent days had blurred and run together like spilled paint. She wasn't sure how long she'd been here.

"Róisín," said Grandma Deirdre. "Why don't you go for a walk? It's a lovely day."

She still called her granddaughter Róisín. She pronounced it in Irish, with its long *o*, and spelled it the Irish way, as if Rosheen had never told her she had changed it. As if that were a phase Rosheen would outgrow. Maybe it was. When Deirdre pronounced her name, Rosheen felt it might be possible to be restored, washed clean. To be again a girl with a pretty face. Back when Von protected her and Bobby brought her presents. She remembered watching Bobby push the roll of newsprint, letting it roll out all the way across the whole long attic floor, and shrieking with delight to think that she could draw *forever* now.

"Róisín," said Deirdre. "Why don't you have a cup of tea? Drink some tea."

A cup of steaming tea appeared on the table. Rosheen tried to lift her hands, to feel the warmth of it, but they were too heavy. She raised them a few inches and let them fall back in her lap. She noticed she was wearing her pyjamas. What day was it? It didn't matter. Vaguely she recalled that a policeman had taken her off the airplane and locked her in a cell. How did she get here to her grandmother's apartment? Carol. Her lawyer, Carol Hart, had come to get her. Carol had signed some kind of bond and brought Rosheen back here, where she would die. She wished she would die.

She was aware of her grandmother walking back and forth — slowly now, for she was old — rummaging through the contents of a kitchen drawer, as if she were looking for something. She shuffled to the table and sat beside Rosheen. She placed her wrinkled hand on Rosheen's hands.

"I once wanted something very badly," Deirdre said. But Rosheen could not, would not listen. She rose from the table and went to the window, leaned her forehead on the cool glass.

"Why don't you make a painting?" Deirdre asked her. "Just try. You'll remember you liked it."

"There's no point, Grandma," she said.

"It's not right to waste the talent God gave you," said Deirdre. She wandered back into her bedroom and Rosheen could hear her opening her dresser drawers, one by one, searching, always searching for something.

Across the rooftops of Williamsburg, the sun was setting. The sky glowed a deep blue and the low clouds were flushed with gold.

Rosheen lowered her eyelids. She could not bear any beauty, could not let it in. She stayed that way for a long time, her eyes closed, pressing her palm so hard against the window pane she suddenly realized she might break the glass. She relaxed a little, and as soon as she did, a wave of pain rose up and broke across her body. She remembered the small brown robin that would not stop trying to enter the greenhouse, the bird that couldn't imagine itself closed off from the lush green foliage it could see right there, close enough to touch. Flying again and again into the glass.

8.6

DEIRDRE STOOD IN FRONT OF THE CLOSET AND TRIED TO remember. Where had she tucked it, over, oh, almost fifty years ago? She ran her hands between the stacks of linens. Then she felt it, yes. She tugged, but it would not budge. She removed the heavy layers of fabric, the tablecloths and bedspreads, piling them onto the bed, and there it was, underneath. The book Frank used to draw in when he was a boy. There were some good pictures in there, if Deirdre remembered right. She had taken the book away, years ago, when he was becoming too attached to it. He had wanted to take his pictures into Manhattan, to throw his future away on some fool art lessons. But she had hidden them. There was a folder of some kind as well, wasn't there? With coloured pictures, in paint? She pulled a chair over to the closet and stepped up onto it. She ran her hand along the top shelf. A heavy shower of dust cascaded onto her head and made her sneeze. But she felt the cardboard edge and pulled it toward her. Yes, here it was. He spent so many hours on these pictures. Trying and trying to match the colour of that kitchen kettle. A plain, ordinary kettle, patched and battered. Junior had bought her a new electric one long ago.

She carried the awkward package back into the kitchen, where Róisín had been sitting for an hour without speaking. She dropped the book and folder onto the table. A small cloud of dust rose into the air.

"What's this?" Róisín asked the table.

"Your father's pictures." Deirdre opened the sketchbook to the first page. "Here's our street, back when we didn't have trees. See? This is the old church on the corner, before they renovated. He even put in the owl. See? That owl is still there, at the edge of the church roof, to this day."

Róisín sat with her hands clasped tightly in her lap. She did not seem to be listening.

Deirdre turned a page. "That's the coal wagon. See how skinny that old horse was. The kids used to run after that cart, picking up any coal that fell off the back. And the coal man let them do it. Kevin, his name was. Kevin Higgins. A good man when all's said and done."

Róisín unfolded her fingers and laid her hands flat on the table, one on either side of the sketchbook. Deirdre continued to turn the pages for a while, providing narration, telling stories of events that she herself had forgotten until she saw the drawings. There was Tomas, dear God, in his overalls, and there was Tomas in his Sunday suit, smiling at Frank. He never smiled at anyone else that way.

Then she opened the folder of paintings and there was the kettle.

"Look at that beat-up thing," she said. "Why, I don't remember it ever being new. See how he put in every dent and scratch?" She pointed out the portraits, naming everyone: Mr Edison, who used to live across the hall, Mrs Heintz and her daughter, Deirdre's nephews, Junior and Davey and Paul, though the picture of Paul was not finished because he never could sit still.

Róisín didn't say a word.

Finally, Deirdre said good night. She placed a hand on Róisín's shoulder and kissed the top of her head, but Róisín did not respond.

At midnight, Deirdre woke and lay a long time in the dim room. From beyond the closet, at intervals, she heard a faint rustle. The wretched mice were back. Each time she thought they were eradicated they returned, or their children returned, or their great-great-grandchildren — how many generations of rodents had harboured here, in this apartment, eating the wallpaper paste and chewing the wires? By the light of the streetlamp that seeped in under the curtains, she could see the outline of the plaster Virgin Mary on top of her dresser and beside it, thumbtacked to the wall, the calendar from the butcher shop, and though it was too dark to see, she knew it had a picture on it of two boys on two red sleds, racing each other down a hill in the countryside, bright clean snow flying all around them. She had to go to the bathroom. She sat up with her legs dangling over the edge of the bed and felt with her toes for her slippers and put them on. Not wanting to wake Róisín, she navigated through the apartment in the dark, feeling for the turns in the hallway with her hands. She was on her way back to bed when she saw the thin band of light under the door of the bedroom where Róisín slept. Had she fallen asleep with the lamp on? Deirdre moved toward the door and heard the rustle again. A dry crackling, like old sheets of paper, and then Deirdre knew. Of course. She knocked softly and pushed Róisín's door open and there she was, cross-legged on the bed, with her father's sketchbook on her lap, turning the pages.

Róisín looked up, and for the first time since she'd arrived, she met Deirdre's eyes. She didn't smile. Deirdre wasn't sure if she would ever smile again. But her eyes were open. She was looking.

8·7

"WE HAVE SOME NEWS," KYLE SAYS, WHEN HE PHONES VON IN MID-December. His voice vibrates with joy.

It can only be one thing. "You're getting married?"

"We got married. We are married. We're going to have a baby. I mean, Meredith's having my baby. I mean — "

"Congratulations," Von says. They're too young, she thinks. Then she thinks again. Kyle is young, but he's responsible, and loving, and terribly loyal. And Meredith's a model of maturity.

"I hope you're not mad that we didn't invite you to the wedding," he says. "We were in a hurry. As soon as we got the test results, we wanted to do it right away. We just had two friends for witnesses and a minister Meredith knows. There wasn't any reception or — "

"It's all right, Kyle. I'm happy for you."

"I still want to see the place," he says.

"I know. But we're very busy right now." She looks out across the field of snow. Nothing moves. It is the season of waiting. When she returned home in October, she'd been struck by the sameness of everything. Slight variations in the plants, of course, for they were living things and varied with the seasons. But this October could have been any October, the outdoor beds ready for winter, the shrubs wrapped in their burlap. Rows of poinsettia seedlings sprouting in the domes. Even Jeanne was the same. No. Jeanne seemed happier, more confident. Jeanne had handled everything beautifully while Von was away. Now it is December, half the poinsettias already sold. The usual cut flowers ready for winter bouquets. Valentine's Day will follow, then spring.

"I want to see you," he says.

When she first saw Kyle, in Brooklyn, back in July, when he was rifling through her sister's desk, she'd thought he was a burglar. When he reappeared, and she saw who he was, she'd felt a tightening in her chest, the premonition of a change too drastic to endure.

"We both want to see you," he says.

Is it possible that breaking and entering could be an act of love? She thinks of Rosheen leaving that triple ring of footprints in the snow outside the hospital. Maybe that too was a kind of love, or trying to love, circling the building, wanting in.

"Come for Christmas dinner," she says.

He says, "Thank you."

––––––––––––––

For Christmas dinner, Von roasts a turkey and makes two pies: apple and pumpkin. She arranges in Eileen's glass vases two dozen pale and scarlet roses, the very best of the Lady Creams and the Morden Fireglow. She puts fresh sheets and blankets on the new bed in the third-floor bedroom, so Kyle and Meredith can stay the night. In the morning, she'll invite them to stay longer. She'll invite them to stay for good. They can't raise a child in a rooming house.

She gathers the notebooks into a pile — Rosheen's bulging green notebook with its elastic bands, the red cardboard journal Von took to Ireland, and the thick black one she bought when the red one was full, the blue hardcover journal she started in New York, the soft orange one she bought in Amsterdam, and the thick white journal she's filled with writing during these past two months since she returned. Her memories. Her reflections. Her plans for the future.

It's rather a new concept, the future. She's been discussing it with Jeanne, who is convinced that Kyle will make a great greenhouse worker. As for Meredith, Jeanne's hoping to train her as assistant manager. The three of them apparently had a good long talk about all of this when they met in New York. A year or two from now, says Jeanne, Von will be free to take a long vacation, as long as she pleases.

Von cuts a length of white ribbon and ties the notebooks together, topping the stack with a bow. Kyle's Christmas present. *These notebooks will tell you about your family*, she writes on the card. *It's a hard story to read, but it's your story, the story your mother wanted me to tell you.*

For Meredith, she has bought a pair of soft moccasins for the cold winter floors. For the baby, nothing yet. But she and Jeanne have already talked about making over Rosheen's room for the baby.

She walks into the greenhouse and stands among the roses, breathing the heavy, earthy air. Looks up at the weight of all that glass. Her nephew and his wife will be here soon, but for a few more minutes her sanctuary is quiet. The sanctuary that imprisoned her, the privacy that was nothing but another name for loneliness.

She looks out at the snow. Yes, she should take a vacation. Imagine going south for a winter. Or she could go west, north, east. She could go to Dublin or Reykjavik or St Petersburg or New York. Or somewhere wholly new.

She can't imagine it yet, this future. It is still too dark. But what is darkness? Only what you don't know. What you don't know yet. Everyone else walks into it, every morning. So can she.

———

Near the end of that lonesome day in the Netherlands, at the Bergen-op-Zoom cemetery, Von fell asleep in the gazebo, weary after her walk along the highway. By the time she woke, the clouds had moved in and a light drizzle was falling, glazing the scene before her eyes. She yawned and stretched, and as she stood up, she thought she saw a movement in the graveyard. A shadow wandering among the headstones. She blinked, and it was gone. She tightened the laces on her shoes and opened her umbrella. She was about to leave the shelter when she saw it again, the blurred silhouette of a human figure under the dripping branches of a willow. The spirit of some young soldier, searching for his lost friends. It vanished behind the tree and then, as she watched, it materialized again. Closer now. Walking toward her, beckoning. And she saw that it wasn't a ghost. It was Kyle. He had found her again.

"Kyle," she said, though he wasn't yet close enough to hear her. She thought, *we are the only ones left*, and then she saw Meredith coming through the gates of the cemetery to stand beside him.

Meredith was wheeling a bicycle. She walked beside it, with her beautiful hands on the handlebars, steering. She must have changed her mind and agreed to go to the flower market after all, for the wicker basket was overflowing with tulips and daffodils and gladioli.

———

Acknowledgements

Many thanks to the University of Winnipeg for research leave and travel assistance, and to my colleagues in the English department for moral support. Thanks to *Prairie Fire* for publishing an early chapter in progress, and to Theatre by the River and Joff Schmidt for his reading of a passage at Wine and Words. Thanks to research assistants Jessica Jacobson-Konefall, Nyala Ali, Cynara Geissler, Kelly McGonigle, and Sarah Cozzi; and astute readers Melody Morrissette, Anne Marie Resta, Rebecca Widdicombe, Chandra Mayor, Barbara Schott, Méira Cook, and Marnie Woodrow. Special thanks to Margaret Sweatman and Pat Sanders for sharing their literary insights, criticisms, encouragement, and time: your generosity, patience, and brilliance astonish me. Remaining errors and other flaws are, of course, all my own.

This book would not have been possible without the following resources: the Irish Studies Program, National University of Ireland, Galway; the Cobh Heritage Centre in Cobh; the Dutch Resistance Museum in Amsterdam; The Brooklyn Historical Society Museum in Brooklyn, New York; the Ellis Island Immigration Museum in New York; the Canadian War Museum in Ottawa; and Library and Archives Canada in Ottawa.

The lines alluded to on page 54 and the line quoted on page 69 are from the poem "Easter, 1916," c. 1916, by William Butler Yeats. The line quoted on page 322 and the lines quoted on pages 405-406 are from the poem "The Wild Swans at Coole," c. 1917, also by William Butler Yeats. Both poems may be found in *The Collected Poems of W. B. Yeats*. London: MacMillan, 1961. Used with permission.

I am indebted to Berenice Abbott's photographs of New York City and Brooklyn in 1935 in her project "Changing New York" (Abbott's photos may be viewed online).

This is a work of fiction, but some of it is inspired by stories told to me by my family: my brother Kevin Hunter, my Aunt Winnie O'Donnell, my cousin Maureen Young, my mother, Doreen Hunter, and most especially my father, Thomas James (Jimmy) Hunter, who served with the Canadian Black Watch in World War II, was wounded at Dieppe, and later lost both his eyes at Bergen-op-Zoom, Holland, on October 26th, 1944.

Although many history books were important to this project, the following personal accounts were invaluable for insights into the experience of individual Canadian soldiers: *Canada en Noord-Brabant: Een band voor altijd* by Jan A.F.M. Luijten, *Because We Are Canadians* by Charles D. Kipp, *The Guns of Normandy* by George Blackburn, and *Veterans with a Vision: Canada's War Blinded in Peace and War* by Serge Marc Durflinger.

The fictional Frank Garrison's experience in the candy factory battle is based on the strategy of real Canadian heroes Major Herbert Owen Lambert and Sergeant Charles D. Kipp. Kipp tells the harrowing true story of a much-outnumbered Canadian company in a pitch-dark gin factory in Bergen-op-Zoom, when "Lambert ordered the men to run all over the factory, shouting and yelling to make the Germans think we had a regiment" (201).

The fictional events that occur on Frank's landing craft at Dieppe are based loosely on events recorded in interviews with 18 soldiers of the Canadian Black Watch, mere days after their participation in the raid. These interviews are appended to the Black Watch War Unit Diary for August 1942. If not for Library and Archives Canada, these stories would be lost forever.

About the Author

Poet and novelist Catherine Hunter has published three collections of poetry, *Necessary Crimes*, *Lunar Wake*, and *Latent Heat* (which won the Manitoba Book of the Year Award); three thrillers, *Where Shadows Burn*, *The Dead of Midnight*, and *Queen of Diamonds* (Ravenstone Press); the novella *In the First Early Days of My Death*; and the spoken word CD *Rush Hour* (Cyclops Press), which includes a bonus track featuring The Weakerthans. Two of her novels have been translated into German. Her essays, reviews, and poems appear in many journals and anthologies, including *Essays on Canadian Writing*, *The Malahat Review*, *West Coast Line*, *Prairie Fire*, *CV2*, *The Echoing Years: Contemporary Poetry from Canada and Ireland*, and *Best Canadian Poems 2013* and *2015*. She edited *Before the First Word: The Poetry of Lorna Crozier*, and for ten years she was the editor of The Muses' Company press. She teaches English and creative writing at the University of Winnipeg.